MW01400581

MAYHEM AT THE HAPPY VALLEY MOTOR INN AND RESORT

May all your mayhem be merry!
Leslie Noyes

MAYHEM AT THE HAPPY VALLEY MOTOR INN AND RESORT

by

Leslie Noyes

Published by Scout's Honor, Havana, FL, USA

Copyright 2020, Leslie Noyes

All rights reserved. No part of this book may be reproduced or transmitted in any form or by any means, electronic or mechanical, including photocopying, recording or by any information storage and retrieval system, without written permission from the publisher, except for the inclusion of brief quotations in a review.

This book is for Mom and Dad. They'd get a huge kick out of this.

And my brother, Kelly Hall, for teaching me how to drink and appreciate bourbon. That has nothing to do with the story except I now have that talent to fall back on.

Rachel Carrera, editor, cover designer, sounding board, idea generator, and all-around great person, without whom this book likely would've stayed on my computer for all time.

My friends and first readers: Luri Owen, Shirley Blamey, and Lila Moore. Thanks for your support and suggestions. Thanks also to author, Michael Steeden, for providing advice and support, and to Flora Diehl, friend extraordinaire, who cheered me on.

Author and great advocate and inspiration for fellow authors, Sheehan Moore. Thanks for giving me a push every time I needed one.

Rebecca Jordan who provided information on different quilt patterns. If I could write as beautifully as she quilts, I'd be a happy woman.

And finally, to my sweet kitty, Scout, who helped co-write *Mayhem at the Happy Valley Motor Inn and Resort* but died before we saw it published. She was the best listener and provided lots of hugs and kisses when I needed them.

CHAPTER ONE

Paula Jean Arnett wiped a trickle of perspiration from her forehead as she turned away from the small knot of friends gathered beside the freshly prepared gravesite. Alone, she began the slow trek to the black limousine reserved for her use on this day.

Paula's dearest friend, Cassie Campbell, broke from the group and rushed to Paula's side. Taking Paula's hand in hers, she said, "Hey, sweetie, why don't you come to my house for a few days? There's no need for you to be brooding in that big old house by yourself."

The women's heels made crunching noises on the gravel path as Paula considered her answer. "Oh, I appreciate the offer, but I think I need to have some brooding time. Really, I'll be okay."

"Well, if you're sure, but you know I'm just a phone call away, and I can always come over. You just let me know."

Cassie's concern was evident in her big brown eyes as she opened her arms to Paula.

Paula fell into her friend's embrace and allowed a few tears to fall. "How am I going to do this without Cal?"

Cassie remained silent as she hugged Paula until the blistering July sun bore down on them. As she took a step back, she said, "Sheesh, Paula, you've gone and sweated all over both of us."

In other circumstances, Paula might've gotten a case of the giggles, but after having just buried her husband of fifteen years, all she could manage was a forced smile. "Love you, Cassie."

"Love you more."

Melvin Atkins, the owner of Atkins Brothers' Funeral Home and Crematorium in Dempsey, Texas, and one of Paula's oldest friends approached the women, his boots scuffing the burned brown grass of the cemetery. He nodded at Cassie who stepped back, allowing them some privacy. He took Paula's hands in his and said, "Paula, I hope everything was just right for you."

"Cal would've loved this. Nothing fancy, you know. It was a beautiful tribute." She sensed Melvin was struggling to get through this almost as much as she was. Paula touched his arm, "We're going to be okay, Mel."

"You know Sue Ann and I would love to have--" Mel started, but Paula stopped him with a shake of her head.

"I know. Thanks. Cassie offered, too, but I really just need some time for myself right now. Since the accident, I haven't been alone for even two minutes. I'm so glad we decided to have the meal before the service. This way I can go home and sleep and cry and then maybe cry some more. Do I need to handle anything else this afternoon?"

"No, hon, you just let Daryl take you home and we'll finish up here... unless you want a few minutes alone at the graveside."

Paula managed a smile, "Oh, Mel, I'm not much for visiting graves. I think I'd like that ride home now." She hugged him to her side as they headed to the waiting car where a gangly teenager opened the back door of the limo.

Mel held the door wide and said, "Daryl, take good care of Ms. Arnett. Walk her up to her door when you get there now, you hear, son?"

Daryl climbed in the driver's seat and started the engine. "Of course, Uncle Mel." He pulled into the slow stream of traffic and lifted his eyes to the rearview mirror. "Ms. Arnett, I'm sure sorry about Cal."

"Thank you, sweetie. I appreciate it."

Paula leaned back against the leather seat of the car's cool interior and closed her eyes for the duration of the ride. Her heavy eyelids fluttered open when Daryl slowed to turn into her long semi-circular driveway, and the car rested in front of the ornate oak front door. As he opened her car door, she said, "Daryl, it's okay. You don't need to walk me to the house."

Daryl shook his head and offered her his elbow. "Uncle Mel will skin my hide if he finds out I didn't see you all the way in."

Paula forced a grateful smile. "Thanks. I'll make sure he knows what a wonderful job you've done."

"Ms. Arnett, I just wanted you to know that I always liked Cal. He helped me learn to tie a Carolina Rig fishing line when I was still a kid, and every time I saw him, he taught me something new. He was a real special guy."

Tears burned behind her eyelids. "He was special, wasn't he? Thanks for sharing that with me."

As they reached the door, Paula fished through her purse for her house key then fumbled as she attempted to get it into the lock. She blushed. "Oh! Sorry. My hands are so shaky today." She held her breath as the keys tumbled to the ground.

Daryl stooped to pick up the key ring. "Here, let me get that for you." On his first and only attempt, he fit the key into the lock and opened her door. "See, Uncle Mel knew what he was talking about. You take care, okay?"

"I will. Thanks again." Once inside, Paula closed and leaned against the door, welcoming the solitude and air-conditioned coolness of her comfortable ranch style home. For the first time since she and Cal moved in, just months after they were married, the house felt big and empty. She supposed that if she tried, she could pretend that Cal was just gone on one of his business trips or even on one of his treasured fishing expeditions, but she feared that if she allowed herself to pretend, she might not ever make it back to the real world.

She kicked off her heels in the foyer, and made her way to the oversized, yet underused kitchen. She grabbed a can of diet cola out of the fridge and relished just how remarkable it felt to do something so normal as popping the lid and taking a sip. She sat at the table and sifted through the stack of mail that Cassie had brought in for her over the past few days. She brushed a tear from her cheek as a thought occurred to her: *You'd think time would stop after a tragedy, but no, here I am dealing with bills and junk mail. Don't they know my Cal's gone?* The thought that the world could be so uncaring undid her, and she laid her head on the table indulging in her grief. Paula thought she'd already cried all the tears in the world. She was wrong.

She replayed the events in her mind: *The phone rang. Car accident. Cal. Critically injured. Lubbock.* She'd hopped in her car and started the engine before she realized that she'd neglected to put on her shoes. Her heart pounded like thunder as she raced back into the house, grabbed her sandals, flipped off the lights and hurried back out to the car. Tears streamed down her cheeks as she dialed Cassie and told her everything she knew as she navigated the highway to Lubbock.

The cars ahead of her were no more than blurry prisms as her eyes filled with tears and fear and grief that threatened to smother her. A few minutes after she said goodbye to Cassie, she jumped when her cellphone rang, and she held her breath as she answered, whispering a silent prayer that it wasn't the hospital calling to say it was too late. It wasn't.

Cassie's voice was rushed as she said, "I just wanted you to know I'm on my way to meet you at the hospital in Lubbock. I called Mel and Delbert for you. Mel and Sue Ann are heading up right away, and Delbert's coming just as soon as Sherry gets home."

Paula sniffled. "Thanks. I don't know what I'd do without you. I need to pay attention to the road right now, though. I'm a mess."

"Of course. You be safe. I'll see you at the hospital."

When Paula reached the hospital, nearly two hours away, she rushed to the emergency department where she accosted the first nurse she saw. "Cal Arnett's room!" She managed to choke out her words through her sobs.

The nurse led her to the room and touched Paula's shoulder before pushing open the door. "Here you go, honey."

As Paula rushed to the bed, a different nurse pulled a sheet over Cal's face and turned off a flatlined machine. She shook her head and said, "You must be Mrs. Arnett. I'm so sorry. He's gone." Taking Paula's hand, the nurse guided her to a chair beside Cal's body. "Here, honey, sit with him for as long as you need to. I'll go get you a glass of water."

Paula felt the air leave her lungs, as her knees buckled and she dropped into the armchair. "No, Cal! I didn't even get to tell you goodbye or hold your hand one last time or feel your warmth." She sobbed until her tears were dry then, her mind in a fog, she planted a kiss on her fingertips and touched Cal's forehead, leaving his side for the last time. There were decisions to be made and she was the one who had to make them. No Cal to lean on now.

As she wandered down the corridor, she heard a familiar voice calling her. Fresh tears spilled down her cheeks when she saw Cassie approaching. Mel and his wife, Sue Ann, as well as her friend and lawyer, Delbert Derryberry, and his wife, Sherry, were watching from where they were seated in a waiting area. Yet, despite so many of her friends there to support her in her hour of need, Paula felt like a butterfly in a glass jar, isolated and insulated. Alone.

Now, back in her kitchen, Paula recalled a time when she and Cal were barely out of their newlywed stage when her mom lost her battle with pancreatic cancer. Less than six months later, despite being in relatively good health, her dad died of a broken heart. At the time, Paula couldn't understand how her big, strong daddy had lost the will to "be."

No matter how she and Cal had attempted to coax him out of his decline, her dad just faded away. Now that Cal was gone, Paula considered that "ceasing to be" just might happen to her, too. She could just be until being wasn't an option anymore. And, then, in her mind's ear, she heard Cal say, "Don't be so melodramatic Goldilocks-- you're not going to die anytime soon. Damn it all to hell, woman, stop moping around."

The voice was so real, the words so "him" that for a second Paula looked up hoping to see his almost handsome, beloved, mischievous face--the one he told everyone resembled Harrison Ford. Paula always asked if he didn't mean Henry Ford or even Edsel, to which Cal would say, "Either way, I'm one good looking guy, right?"

Knowing Cal wasn't there but that his words could still give her a kick in the butt was just the motivation that got Paula up and moving.

Dabbing her eyes on a paper towel, she sipped on her soda and considered her immediate needs.

Thanks to Cassie and other friends, the house was spotless. Cassie had organized a group from their church to come and stock the refrigerator with all sorts of casseroles and snack foods. Paula took a mental survey and estimated that she had enough food to last for at least two months. She thumbed through the mail again; it could wait.

Right now, she just wanted out of her funeral garb. *What a perfect phrase for such dreary clothes--funeral garb.* Heading down the hallway toward her bedroom, Paula stopped to trace her finger across the photo of Cal and herself on their wedding day. She'd looked so young and happy, and Cal, so confident.

She recalled how her parents hadn't been that enthusiastic about the marriage when she and Cal first announced their engagement. Part of her parents' concern was due to Cal's being thirty-five to Paula's twenty. Once her parents really got to know him, though, they came to love Cal as much as she did. He'd been a rock during her mother's illness and made sure that Paula's dad had everything he needed right up until he passed away.

Once in the room she'd shared with Cal, Paula carefully hung the summer-weight navy suit on a hanger, then she pulled on her favorite soft, faded green t-shirt. Catching her own reflection in the mirror she saw a stranger with red rimmed green eyes, dull now, where they usually were bright and filled with laughter. Her hair, always unruly, looked even more so after time in the heat. Although Cal always loved her ash blonde hair, it had a mind of its own and after the hot Texas sun had done its damage, what wasn't clinging in damp clumps to her forehead was hanging in heavy strands on the back of her neck. She lifted the weight with her hands and pulled it up in a ponytail. Her face, always too pale for her liking looked even more so today. Crying had done an effective job of removing what little make up she'd applied before the funeral and little blotches of red dotted her complexion.

Again, Cal's voice startled her. "Hey, Goldilocks, quit admiring yourself in the mirror. That's my job."

"Oh Cal!" Paula said in a tone pitched just above a sigh. She hugged herself as she collapsed on top of the cool blue coverlet and closed her eyes before another crying jag could claim her.

CHAPTER TWO

The tantalizing aroma of bacon sizzling pulled Paula out of a deep sleep. Groggy and puzzled, she raised up on one elbow. *Why is Cal cooking now? He never did this before.* A pang of anguish stabbed her in the heart as she realized it couldn't possibly be Cal. She buried her face in her pillow and stifled a sob. Moments later, she sat up and wiped her eyes with her fingertips as she hung her feet over the side of the bed. *What time is it?* She glanced at the alarm clock beside her bed. *It's almost ten.* The sunlight beating through the window assured her it was ten a.m. and not ten the night before.

She grabbed a pair of shorts and pulled them on then slipped her feet into her flip flops. Bleary-eyed, she wandered into the kitchen and found Cassie cooking.

Cassie flipped a few strips of bacon in the pan and turned. "Morning. How are you today?"

Paula sat at the bar and breathed a heavy sigh. "I've been better." She gestured to the stove. "You know, this is totally unnecessary. Between you and the church women, I've got enough food for a small army."

"I know, but I wanted to come check on you and you know I can't just sit. I was getting all fidgety. Didn't want to wake you, so...." Cassie transferred the bacon to a paper towel-lined plate. "Eggs over easy?"

"Thanks, but the bacon will be plenty. I'm not even a little bit hungry."

"Well, you're going to eat a couple of pieces of bacon and then you're going to go shower while I finish cooking. If you won't eat eggs, I'll find something you will eat. But right now, you stink to high heaven and you look like hell."

"Thanks so much, friend." Paula snatched a piece of bacon and bit into it as she pouted.

Her heart warmed as she recalled the day she and Cassie had met. They'd been five years old when Cassie took Paula's hand and announced to their kindergarten class that "Me and Paula Purdy is bestest friends forever." *I'm so glad Cassie's put up with me for so long. She's the closest thing to family I've got now.*

She stood and snatched another slice of bacon, realizing just how ravenous she actually was. "This is delicious. Thanks. I'm gonna go shower now."

As she stood under the water, she allowed her tears to fall freely and watched as her grief spiraled down the drain. *If only it were that easy*, she thought.

After a few minutes, she pulled herself together, stepped out and dried herself off, then dressed in a soft, yellow t-shirt and khaki capris. She combed her hair and splashed cool water on her face then returned to the kitchen where a virtual feast was waiting for her. She raised an eyebrow. "What's all this?"

Cassie carried two plates to the breakfast nook. "Come on. I made your favorite: grilled cheese and bacon sandwiches and my signature gazpacho."

Paula forced a smile and slid into the cushioned booth. "You are so not the boss of me."

She eyed the food recalling how Cassie's efficiency in the kitchen always made Paula slightly envious.

"Am so," Cassie said with a grin, and to prove it added, "Now, eat!" She took her place across from Paula and took a swig from her Dr. Pepper.

Paula picked up a spoon and slurped a spoonful of the cold soup. "Don't you have some function to oversee? Some catering magic to perform?"

"As a matter of fact, for the time being, Campbell's Catering is officially closed for vacation. The June wedding season is over and I don't have anything big looming on the horizon until the Foster-Fleming rehearsal dinner in September, so I have two months of clear schedule in front of me."

Paula furrowed her brow. "You better not have done that on my account."

"Well, partly," admitted Cassie. "Mostly, though, I needed a break. I've been working crazy hours since the Sweethearts' Ball in February." She covered Paula's hand with her own as tears welled in her eyes. "And, honey, Cal wasn't just your husband, you know. He was a dear friend--and the husband of my sister in everything but blood. In some ways, I think he knew me even better than you did."

Paula stifled a sniffle as tears burned behind her eyes. "I know you loved him, too," she said with a lump in her throat. "And he returned that love." She sniffled then straightened her shoulders and put on a playful grin. "Although, he always did think you were just a terrible influence on me."

Cassie lips turned up at the corners in an almost smile. "He only thought that because it was true. Remember that night when he called you to come and get him because he'd had too much to drink down at the Unruly Longhorn and—"

Paula snorted and pulled her sandwich out of her mouth before she choked. "We drove off and left him standing on the side of the road out in the middle of the country! Well, he should've gone to the bathroom before he left the bar."

"I know! That's what you said at the time when you talked me into driving away from him down that dirt road as soon as he stepped behind the tree to do his business."

"I really thought he was going to throttle us when we finally went back to pick him up. I'd never seen him so pissed off or so cold," Paula said with a chuckle. "As I recall, it was midwinter and below freezing that night." Her smile grew pensive. "He got his revenge though, many times over. Like the time he hired those two men to play the part of detectives, and they raided our counterfeit purse party! I was so sure we were going to jail." She shook her head as she took a spoonful of soup.

Cassie giggled and tore a crust off her sandwich. "Yeah, you kept saying, 'Officers, please! I'm sorry, please don't arrest me.' And when Cal walked in and told the detectives they could just hand you over to him, you weren't sure whether to bash him in the head with your fake designer bag or to faint with relief. As far as I know, that purse party was the one and only time you crossed a line."

When the phone rang, Cassie grabbed it, "Arnett's residence, Cassie Campbell speaking. Just a minute, Delbert, I'll see if she's able to take your call."

"Paula," Cassie said, "It's Delbert Derryberry."

Paula wiped the corners of her mouth with a napkin and took the phone. "Hi Delbert. What's up?"

"Hello, Paula, I'm sorry to bother you today, but we need to go over Cal's will pretty soon. I can come over to the house if you'd like."

"Um, sure, Delbert, but what's the hurry? I know the details of the will that we set up last year when Cal turned fifty...."

Delbert cleared his throat. "Paula, Cal left something else that needs to be taken care of pretty quickly."

"Well, what is it?"

"I, uh... I'd rather discuss it in person."

Frown lines creased her forehead. "Okay. I guess in that case, you'd better come on over."

"Um, you might want Cassie to be there when we go over this."

"Okay. I'll make sure she stays. See you soon."

"Fine. I'll be there within the hour. Goodbye"

"Bye." Paula frowned as she put away the receiver.

"What was that about?" asked Cassie.

"I'm not sure. Delbert wants to come over and he wants you to be with us when we go over a part of Cal's will. I can't imagine what it could be."

Cassie waved her hand and picked up her sandwich. "I'm sure it's nothing to worry about. Cal was all about taking care of you while he was alive. I'm positive he'll continue to do so now that he's gone."

CHAPTER THREE

As Paula's doorbell rang, Cassie emerged from the bedroom with an armload of dirty sheets. She headed toward the laundry room, pausing in the kitchen just long enough to wipe a lingering crumb from the counter as Paula answered the door.

Paula pulled the door open to a tall, lean man who was as weathered as an old fencepost and looked more like a rancher than an attorney. He held his Stetson hat in one hand and his battered cowhide briefcase in the other as he tipped his head. "Afternoon, Paula."

"Hey, Delbert. C'mon in." Paula stood back as he set his hat on the entry table then stepped into the warmth of his embrace.

He stepped back and patted her shoulder. "I'm sorry I didn't get to speak with you after the services yesterday. Sherry's parents were in town from Dumas, and we had to get back to the house. Oh, and Sherry said that you *are* coming to dinner at our house tonight. No excuses."

"Thanks, Delbert. Thank her for me. I might take you up on that."

He craned his neck and looked past her. "Where's Cassie?"

"Right here, you old coot," Cassie said, coming in to the room. Normally, Cassie would have cast a few salty aspersions regarding everything from Delbert's lineage to his college alma mater. On this day, however, she just gave her friendly adversary a hug.

Paula led them to the kitchen table where Delbert pulled out chairs for both ladies. Delbert and Cassie sat, but Paula hesitated, twisting her fingers. "Y'all want something to drink? I'm going to get some tea." Without waiting for a response, Paula got down three glasses, filled them with ice, and topped them off with sweet tea. Delbert opened his briefcase and pulled a thick file from its depths as she placed the glasses on coasters in front of her friends then perched on the edge of her chair between them.

Delbert held up a stack of papers clipped together. "Paula, this is the will you and Cal set up back in January." He flipped to the middle and paraphrased the section that expressed Cal's wish that in the event of his death, all of his worldly goods would go to his wife, and she would be the beneficiary of all life insurance policies in his name.

Paula nodded, "Yes, without children, our wills were pretty simple. Plus, with Cal's mother being gone and his father, well, not in the picture, there really wasn't anyone else to consider. If I had died first, Cal would have been my only beneficiary, as well." Her eyes narrowed. "What's wrong? What are you afraid of telling me?"

He cleared his throat then took a long drink of tea. "I... I wanted to make sure everything was in perfect order for you, so you didn't have to worry about anything. So, the day after Cal passed on, I went in to the office and looked through the paperwork. Everything looked pretty simple, so I called to check on the accounts he'd set up to see what you'd need to do, if anything, to put everything in your name." He held his breath and looked back and forth between the women. "Paula, there's nothing left other than this house, a life insurance policy, and another property. Oh, and of course CalNet Enterprises."

Her face blanched. "Well, there must be some mistake, right?"

Shaking his head, Delbert said, "No mistake, Paula. I overstepped my bounds and did some investigative work. Sometimes my connections come in handy, but Lord, I wish I hadn't discovered this."

Paula's hands clutched for something to anchor her. She felt as if she'd just been punched in the gut.

Cassie jumped to her feet and went to the sink, then returned with a damp cloth. She handed it to Paula and said, "Here, hon. Put this on your neck. You look like you're about to faint." Her eyes narrowed as her hands clenched at her hips, and she glared at the attorney. "Delbert, you sick Aggie son of a bitch, this is no time for one of your jokes! Everyone knows how careful Cal was with his money. And, if he'd lost everything, don't you think he'd have told Paula?"

Delbert tugged at his shirt collar, "Ladies, I don't think he exactly lost everything. It seems that he paid off the house, so Paula, this house is yours free and clear."

"What about this other property you mentioned," Cassie asked. "Paula did you know about that."

Paula's voice quavered. "Yeah, that's our little bit of ranch land out near the XIT, right?"

Delbert shook his head. "It seems he sold that off to buy this other piece of property back in January."

Paula felt the color wash out of her face. "He never said anything to me about either buying or selling anything."

Delbert bowed his head. "Last November, Cal asked me if I could move my cattle off your acreage before the end of the year, but I didn't think anything of it then. Now, I realize he must've been planning to liquidate."

Paula grabbed a paper napkin and began twisting it to shreds. "But why wouldn't he have discussed this with me? We talked over even the littlest decisions. I mean, he knew I really didn't care about the business end of our marriage; he was so practical that I never had to worry and now—" She flung the napkin remnants to the side and buried her face in her hands, willing all of this to be just a really bad joke. She hoped she could eventually forgive Delbert for being so cruel as to shake her faith in Cal.

Cassie flopped into her own chair keeping her eyes on the attorney. "So, what property is it?"

Delbert gulped another swig of tea as tiny beads of perspiration formed on his brow. "Um, it seems as though Cal went and bought a motel."

Cassie threw back her head and laughed, "Why that's just the most insane thing I ever heard. Where is this alleged motel?"

Delbert bit his lip as he grabbed a napkin and patted his brow. "It's out in east Texas. Near a little town called Happy Vale."

Cassie pursed her lips and eyed him like he'd brought in a bunch of dead fish and plopped them on the table.

Paula raised her head from her hands. "At least that makes some sense. Cal went fishing out there a couple of times a year. But I don't get it. If Cal owns it, who's operating it?"

"I'm not sure," Delbert said, not meeting Paula's or Cassie's eyes, "But I know who he bought it from." Both women looked at him expectantly as he slid a piece of paper across the table.

Cassie grabbed the document and her face turned scarlet. "For Pete's sake, Delbert! It says here he purchased it from a Mrs. Calvin Arnett!"

Paula looked back and forth between them, feeling as if she was suspended in time and space, her friends' eyes burning a hole through her to her very core. After a quizzical moment of silence, she said, "But that's me. I just don't get this at all. What—" The lump in her throat grew and threatened to suffocate her as her voice cracked. Tears burned behind her eyes and she hung her head again.

Cassie rested her hand on Paula's arm and glowered at Delbert. "Do you have contact information on this Mrs. Arnett? A phone number? Anything?"

He winced. "No. I just have the name of the motel. It's the Happy Valley Motor Inn and Resort at—"

Paula's head snapped up and she held one hand in front of her face as if she pushing back against all the things Delbert had revealed, "No. I don't want to hear this. Not right now. You two need to go on home so I can think."

Cassie grabbed Paula's hand. "Look, if we—"

"I mean it. Y'all go on. I have to digest this then I'll be ready to talk. Delbert, give Sherry my apologies, but I won't be coming to dinner tonight."

Cassie and Delbert stood in silence before starting toward the door. Cassie paused in the foyer and spun around. "Paula, this could be nothing—"

"Go. Now." Paula didn't raise her voice, but she didn't have to, there was steel in each word. "I promise I'll call when I'm ready.'

CHAPTER FOUR

Paula locked the door behind her friends then spun on her heel and headed to Cal's study, her knees threatening to buckle with each step she took. The smell of leather and a faint odor of cigar smoke permeated the room, nearly causing her to swoon. Cal's presence was so strong in there, his inner sanctum, that with just a little imagination she could hear him breathing and see his lopsided smile. She was grateful at that moment that the cleaning ladies hadn't eradicated his signature scents from the room.

Paula took her time looking around the office as if she were seeing it for the very first time. She stared at each of the pictures, hung in no particular order, of Cal and his buddies on their fishing trips all over the country. The first was of Cal and Delbert with a huge bass one of them had caught on Lake Tenkiller out in eastern Oklahoma the summer before last. Next to it hung a picture of Mel Atkins holding a fishing trophy, and another one of Cal and Delbert and a couple of other local anglers posing with their tackle before embarking on an expedition.

On the wall facing his desk hung a mounted swordfish Cal had caught on a deep-sea fishing trip off the coast of Florida. Paula had hated the trophy, but didn't mind it being in the house as long as it never ventured out of the study. She always claimed it watched her, which Cal had thought was amusing. Before she sat, she spotted a map on the table where Cal always left his set of keys to her car and his spare sunglasses. She unfolded the map and draped it over the fish's head, removing some of her apprehension. "There. Take that, you ugly old thing!" she said to the fish, half expecting it to reply as she sat at the desk.

Paula looked over the items on top first. A stack of invoices sat beside a baseball signed by several members of the 2005 Chicago White Sox championship team. Two photos adorned the corners of the desk. The left one was of Cal's mother, Eunice, in a blue dress, all dolled up for a special occasion. Paula had never met her, but her eyes looked kind behind her wire framed glasses. Paula always imagined the talks she and her mother-in-law might have had if Eunice had still been living when she and Cal married.

The right corner was home to a snapshot of Paula that Cal took on one of their vacations. She was seated in a reclining folding chair, under a striped umbrella on the beach. Her hair was pulled back in a ponytail, and her pink painted toes peeked out of the sand. She picked up the frame and examined it. In the photo, she was smiling at something in the distance, but she couldn't recall what. Maybe it had been a school of dolphins or an annoying seagull. A tear rolled down her face as she recalled how Cal always said it was his favorite picture of her.

She wiped her cheek with her knuckle and replaced the picture, then blew a frustrated puff of air as she said in a whisper, "I'm sorry about this, Cal. I never snooped on you before, but I deserve to know." Holding her breath, she opened the center drawer of the simple old walnut desk. As it squeaked, she recalled how, as soon as they'd moved into the spacious house after they'd married, Cal had a small moving truck deliver the desk and a few cartons from his bachelor pad. The desk was one of the few material items, other than fishing gear, photos, and clothes, that he'd brought into their marriage. She'd never even opened the desk before today. She rolled the chair back to see what was in the drawer, all the while assuring herself that Cal wasn't the kind of man who had kept secrets. At least she never thought he had.

The center drawer held pens, stamps, and a small stack of cartoons clipped from the *Lubbock Avalanche-Journal*. Cal always loved to incorporate quips from the funny pages when he spoke to groups at seminars throughout the country.

Thumbing through the stack, she came across one of a turtle, and her breath caught in her throat. She set the others aside and held the turtle closer to inspect. The room seemed to spin as the funny little turtle turned back the clock and transported her back nearly sixteen years.

She'd barely been nineteen at the time, an introverted sophomore at Texas Tech University in Lubbock, unsure of where life was taking her. She recalled how pressured she'd felt to declare a major, so she'd signed up to take a series of assessments geared to help her narrow her choices. The seminar, at which Cal had spoken, was a culminating event, meant to tie all of the data together for the attendees once they'd been given the results of their assessments.

She'd originally balked at the idea of attending a seminar that her advisor had recommended, but once she'd gotten there, she'd felt an instant attraction to the tall man at the podium. He was plain spoken with a dry sense of humor that kept her entertained. And, while no one could call him handsome in any conventional sense of the word – his hazel eyes were a little too big for his narrow face and were hidden behind horn-rimmed glasses, his jaw line wasn't quite square, his smile a bit lopsided, and his coffee-colored hair was on the shaggy side and too long for her taste, there was an appealing sincerity about him that grabbed her from the beginning of the lecture and wouldn't let her go.

When she was almost the only student to laugh out loud after he showed a clipping of a bandana-clad turtle heading the wrong way on a busy one-way street, she caught the way he looked at her in gratitude. That's what had given her the courage, after the seminar, to linger near a table that displayed cassette tapes of his talk until she'd caught his eye. She wasn't surprised when he approached her and started a conversation. After everyone else cleared out, he'd invited her to coffee which led to dinner. Usually awkward in one-on-one social situations, Paula found herself chatting with Cal like an old friend, one she found charming and witty and sincere.

Soon she was telling him things she couldn't tell her parents--things like not being cut out for university life and sororities and dating. She'd even confessed that all she'd learned from the series of assessments and his seminar was that she was wasting her parents' money.

Rather than chastising her or trying to talk her into giving college another year, he'd hung on her every word and suggested that she consider taking some time off so she could make an informed decision.

From anyone else, his advice might have sounded trite, but coming from Cal, it was a comforting balm to her soul. After the waiter had cleared the last of the dessert dishes, Cal checked his watch. He'd said he had to leave soon in order to catch a flight to Miami for a speaking engagement the following afternoon. They'd exchanged contact information, but Paula doubted that she'd ever encounter Cal Arnett again. After all, he was much older and sophisticated, and his life was so exciting.

That was why, when the phone rang at her dorm the next evening, Paula was shocked and flattered to hear Cal's voice. He'd said he wanted to get to know her better and wondered if he could come calling on her at semester's end. He'd actually used the words "come calling" which made her giggle before jumping at the chance to see him again. For the two remaining months of the spring term, he'd phoned her at least once a day just to pass on a tidbit of conversation he'd overheard or to ask how she was faring in her classes.

Having never been romantically pursued by anyone before, Paula had been swept off her feet. She'd regularly called Cassie, who was miserably involved at the time in her own academic endeavors at The University of Texas in Austin, and the two of them had endlessly discussed Cal as well as their own decisions to forgo another semester at their respective universities.

True to his word, Cal paid his first visit to Paula's house the week after she returned to Dempsey from Lubbock. Seeing him in the flesh again after only talking to him on the phone for months caused her breath to catch in her throat, and she was aware that she already had true and intense feelings for this man. Of course, her parents were taken aback at first. Paula had rarely dated any of the Dempsey boys, saying they were all too much like brothers, so when this older, much worldlier man appeared at their door asking to court their daughter, they weren't sure what to think.

All that summer, Cal made regular visits to Dempsey, not an easy feat since it was well over an hour from the nearest airport. He seemed just as content to sit and play dominoes with Paula's dad or to shell black-eyed peas with her mom as he was to spend time alone with Paula at the movies or on drives around Dempsey to visit her old haunts. It wasn't long before her parents both loved him as much as she did, so when she finally got up the courage to tell her folks that she wasn't going back to school, they assumed that Cal had already proposed. Truth was, he waited until after she made up her mind about school to pop the question, not wanting to influence her decisions.

But when he did propose, oh, Paula still got goosebumps thinking about the way Cal had picked her up after her shift at her summer job and driven the two of them out to the wide-open prairie just as the sun started to set. Not being a native of Texas, Cal was entranced by the vast flatness of the area and especially by the spectacular sunsets peculiar to this part of the country. With the brilliant hues of yellow and orange settling over the sage brushed vista providing his backdrop,

Cal had asked Paula to become his wife. As she'd nodded and then whispered an enthusiastic yes, the colors swirled into pinks and purples, more beautiful than any sunset she'd ever experienced. She'd always thought that sunset had been a sign that she'd met the right man and made the right decision. Now, she wondered if it had been just a sunset, and nothing more.

The turtle cartoon fell from her fingertips to the floor, and the smile melted from her face. She shook her head, dismissing her reverie, and slammed the drawer shut. She turned her chair to go through the drawers on the left side of the desk, but found nothing out of the ordinary.

She scratched her head and twisted her chair to inspect the right-side drawers. As she pulled the top drawer open, goosebumps rose on her arms when she spotted an envelope wedged between two boxes of cancelled checks. It was postmarked Happy Vale and dated November of last year.

As if in slow motion, she lifted the flap and withdrew the letter, written on soft green stationery. She knew she should put it back, certain that this was private and that no matter what, she should trust the man who had never given her any reason to doubt his love or his honesty. But with trembling hands, she unfolded it, and her heart threatened to pound out of her chest. The words, flowing in unmistakably feminine handwriting, simply said, *"Calvin, I need you."* It was signed with a single initial: **M.**

CHAPTER FIVE

For the remainder of the afternoon, Paula alternated between sobbing and pacing around the house, in an effort to vent her rage. She ignored her cellphone's frequent rings, figuring it was either Cassie, Delbert, or some other well-meaning, but clueless acquaintance. At 5 p.m. on the dot, she opened a bottle of Cabernet Sauvignon and poured a hefty serving. By 6:30, she'd finished the bottle and was rip roaring drunk.

She re-read the note. *Calvin, I need you.* The knots in her stomach twisted tighter and tighter each time she speculated what the note could have meant. The page crumpled in her clutched hand, and she felt like throwing up. "Funny, I thought it was my heart that was supposed to break, not my stomach…. And who the hell is M?"

One minute she would sob Cal's name in longing, and the next, she'd curse the day he'd been born. In the middle of one such curse her stomach growled reminding her that she hadn't eaten since breakfast that morning. She looked through the casseroles in the fridge and settled on a serving of lasagna, courtesy of Sherry Derryberry, Delbert's wife. Opening a new bottle of wine, she poured yet another glass. Paula raised a toast to the microwave as her meal went around and around on its little carousel.

"Here's to friends who feed the widows of lying, cheating, heartless bastards!" Hearing the unfamiliar rage in her own voice, she winced and wished she could swallow her words. She took a deep breath and said, "No. Here's to friends. Until I know the whole story, I refuse to think the worst of Cal."

When the microwave dinged, she dumped the lasagna onto a heavy paper plate, carried it into the family room, and plopped in a chair. "Take that, Cal! You were always old-fashioned enough to believe that dinner was to be served in the dining room, on real plates. No exceptions. Ha. Well, things are gonna change around here, starting now. I'll eat dinner anywhere I damned well please on any surface I damned well please."

The lasagna was good. After taking the first bite, she ate without pausing, she still felt like she'd been run over by a semi-truck, but at least she wasn't hungry anymore. And she hoped the lasagna had soaked up a little of the wine.

She swayed as she stood. "Whoa! Who the hell is M, anyway? What kind of help did M need? How would I kill Cal right now if he wasn't already dead? Her hand flew to cover her eyes then slid down over her mouth. "Oops. Stop. I promised not to go there again." She picked up her plate and her empty glass then headed toward the kitchen.

"So, there was no return address on the envelope, just the Happy Vale postmark. Huh. What was it Delbert had said? The Happy Valley something or other?"

She tossed her plate in the trash, then plunked her fork in the sink, and refilled her wine glass. She headed back to Cal's study, pulled M's desperate missive from her pocket, and smoothed it on the desk. *I need you. M.* "Who the hell is M?" She scowled and pounded her fist on the note.

"Well I needed him, too! And right now, I need some answers. And where does one go to find answers in this day and age? Google, of course." She stood and rushed to her bedroom then returned with her laptop. She plopped it onto Cal's desk and typed in her password, "CalsGal4Ever." A tear welled in her eye as she considered the irony. "Could some other woman have had the same feelings for Cal?"

She Googled *Happy Vale, Texas*. "Wow. Population almost 2,000. That's even smaller than Dempsey. Not much help though." She Googled *Hotels in Happy Vale* then perused the results. "Hmm…two bed and breakfasts, but neither has anything to do with a happy valley. Dang." She typed in "Happy Valley, Happy Vale" then shook her head at the lack of any hits. She deleted "Happy Vale" then hit *enter*. An entire page of results popped up.

She scrolled down the list and gasped. "Pay dirt! The Happy Valley Motor Inn and Resort. "Bingo!" She clicked the link.

A pastoral tree-lined lake at sunset filled her screen. *"Come for the Fishing; Stay for the Fun! Happy Valley Motor Inn and Resort"* scrolled across the top of the page in bright green script. She snorted. "Ha! Fishing and fun, indeed. Not for me."

She clicked on the menu bar, and a list of options popped up, including area information, local weather, room descriptions, and photos. Summer prices were $80 a night for a double in the motor inn. She scrutinized each page then clapped her hands, startling herself. "Oh! I've got it!" She grabbed the house phone and dialed Cassie's number.

"Paula, thank goodness! I've been calling you and—"

"I need your American Express card."

"You need my what?" Cassie asked.

"Or any credit card."

"Hold on! I'm on my way over. Don't do anything stupid until I get there."

CHAPTER SIX

As soon as the doorbell rang, Paula pulled Cassie into Cal's office and directed her to the still-open website on her laptop. "Look. We need to go there." Paula said, scrolling to the room rates.

Cassie raised an eyebrow and snorted. "Are you kidding me? Wait, is this what I think it is?" She scanned the monitor. "Oh, wow! Is this the property Delbert was talking about?"

"Yeah, I'm pretty sure it is. And look at this." Paula pulled the crumpled note out from under the computer. "I found this in Cal's desk. This M person has to be the one he bought the motel from, right?"

Cassie chewed her lips as she scrutinized the stationery. After a deep sigh, she said, "That's a bit of a stretch, don't you think? I mean, a single initial doesn't exactly tell us if the last name is Arnett. There could be any number of reasons that this M contacted him. But, if Cal *was* cheating on you and he wasn't already dead, I'd kill him."

"Yeah, I went through that kind of thinking at first, too, but this is Cal we're talking about. Straight-shooting, straight-talking Cal. I've *got* to believe there's something besides an affair here. Regardless of how it might look."

Cassie pulled her hair back into a messy pony tail and flopped into the chair across from the desk. "Girl, I hope you're right. I really do. So, why do you need my credit cards? Did he also clean out your bank accounts before he died?

Paula rolled her eyes. "No, of course not. If I call and book a room with my credit card, they'll know I'm Mrs. Calvin Arnett. I want us to be stealthy. We're going on a clandestine investigation, so Ms. Cassie Campbell needs to book the room. Get it?"

Cassie's eyes lit up like sparklers. "Oh, of course! We're going to go ambush this hussy."

"No! We're going to go do some reconnaissance work. And, if it happens that we find out Cal had a second wife or for some reason was dealing with a woman who was borrowing my name, *then* we're going to ambush the hell out of that hussy."

Cassie chuckled. "Okay, I'm game. I'm just still in shock over all of this."

"I know. I don't want to believe the worst. But I won't be left in the dark, either. And I need to go inspect this piece of property. Apparently, I own it."

"Oh, yeah. I hadn't thought of that. You're absolutely right. We have a duty to look after this investment of Cal's. In fact, it'd be foolhardy to neglect your business responsibilities by not going."

Paula stood tall and saluted Cassie. "Damned straight. Can we be there tomorrow night if we leave first thing in the morning? On second thought, can you even be ready to leave first thing in the morning?"

"Hell, I can be ready in half an hour."

Paula melted into the desk chair. "No, I'm too drunk to drive tonight. Let's Google the driving distance and make reservations." She turned the computer to face Cassie.

Cassie typed in *driving distance from Dempsey, Texas, to Happy Vale, Texas* then read the screen. "Okay, it looks like if we leave by 8 a.m., we can be there by supper time tomorrow evening. Of course, that's going to take us right through Dallas."

Paula rolled her eyes. "Ugh."

"It'll be fine. Remember, Court lives there. I go see him all the time."

"Oh, I forgot. He transferred there when he started flying for Southwest, right?"

"Yeah, last March."

"Your folks oughta be happy he's closer now. So, if you don't mind, you can drive us through Forth Worth and Dallas. You know I hate that damned big city traffic."

"You sure are cursing a lot," said Cassie.

Paula pounded her fist toward the desktop but missed. "It's the new me," she said. "Until I figure out what's going on, I'm going to say whatever the hell I please."

Cassie unlocked her cellphone and dialed the hotel. "Good. Let's figure out what the hell is going on." As the phone rang, she put it on speaker.

After the second ring, a feminine voice answered. "Happy Valley Motor Inn and Resort. How may I help you?"

Paula's eyes grew wide, and invisible pins pricked her skin.

Cassie cleared her throat. "Yes, I'd like to reserve a double room starting tomorrow night through next Friday. Do you have anything available."

"Let me check. How many adults will be staying with us?"

"Two. No children."

"Hmm. Yes, we have a room available with two queen beds. It's $80 per night."

Cassie raised an eyebrow and covered the speaker with her hand.

Paula nodded and whispered, "Of course."

Cassie pulled her hand away from the speaker and said, "That'll be just fine." She read off her credit card information and took down a confirmation number. "Thanks so much. We'll see you tomorrow evening." She disconnected the call. "Looks like we're committed now. Or maybe we *need* to be committed now."

Paula took in a deep breath and closed her eyes as she blew through pursed lips. "Maybe, but I think this is something I have to do for my own peace of mind."

"I understand. Really, I get it. Hey, I need to get home and get packed if this road trip is going to include me."

"I wouldn't think of doing it without you."

They walked to the front door and exchanged a hug. "Call me if you change your mind," Cassie said. "This isn't exactly *your* normal, straightforward way of doing things, you know.

Paula nodded, "I know. But this might just be my new normal. At least until I figure out what's going on...."

With Cassie gone, Paula watered her lone house plant, Mabel, then packed a week's worth of t-shirts, shorts, a skirt, and jeans, underwear, pajamas, tennis shoes, and flip flops into a suitcase. On a whim, she grabbed one of Cal's old Columbia fishing shirts, and two battered fishing hats and stuffed them in a tote bag. She pulled her favorite summer dress, a demure scoop-necked navy sheath, from the closet and slid her best pair of strappy heels over the hanger, then laid it across her bag. As she eyed the shoes, she nodded and said, "Just in case I need to exert some authority over this M person." At five feet, five inches, Paula knew she'd never look formidable, but two-inch heels would help level any playing field. "I hope."

As it hit her how much wine she'd consumed, she used the restroom then examined herself in the mirror. She wasn't ugly. Not gorgeous, like Cassie, but not ugly by a long shot. She ran her fingers through her hair then changed into her comfiest pajamas. As she lay in bed, she stared into the darkness and said, "Cal, did I do something wrong? Were you tired of me? I thought these last fifteen years were good. Really good. You know I don't *want* to hate you, right? I don't want to doubt what we had."

Silence.

Tears burned behind her eyes. "Damn it, Cal!" She squeezed her eyes shut and cried herself to sleep.

CHAPTER SEVEN

Early the next morning, Paula took her suitcase and other bags outside and waited for Cassie. She smoothed her capris and t-shirt. "Where is that girl?" She kicked a stone with her flip flop then tightened her ponytail, brushing a blonde strand from her eyes. She pushed up the bridge of her sunglasses camouflaging her swollen eyes. *I hope they look better before we get to Happy Vale.*

She checked her watch again and shook her head. "Where is she?" She loaded her bags in the trunk of her car and backed out of the garage, then rushed inside and topped off her stainless-steel coffee mug.

"Hey, girl, you got any extra?"

Paula spun on her heel to find Cassie in the doorway, sipping from a Texas Longhorns travel cup. Paula topped off Cassie's cup then rinsed the coffeepot.

As they headed out, Cassie asked, "Do you want to take my van?"

Paula eyed Cassie's catering van then said, "You know what? This is my journey. Let's take my car." She opened the trunk.

Cassie stowed her duffle bag next to Paula's gear and said, "Good. If we have to dispose of the hussy's body, I don't want anyone knowing that Campbell's Catering committed the crime."

Paula choked on her coffee then laughed. "Leave it to you to make me forget I'm in mourning. Pull it into the garage and let's get this show on the road before I lose my nerve."

Cassie moved her vehicle then tossed her keys into her duffel bag and shut Paula's open trunk. "I wasn't sure what to pack. I see you brought a dress. Do you think we should swing by my house and get one, too?"

"Nah. That's totally in case I need to pull rank on this M chick. I thought I might need to look like an authority figure."

Cassie snorted. "You? An authority figure?"

Paula blinked back a tear. "Thanks so much for your confidence"

Cassie touched Paula's arm. "Hey, I'm sorry. It's just that you're such a sweetheart. So by the book. You never step on anyone's toes. Never pull rank. I've never seen you do anything even the least bit intimidating. I meant it all as a compliment. Really."

Paula forced a smile. "It's okay. You're right. But I have to find some way to get to the bottom of this. And if that means I have to be a little badass, then so be it."

"Yes. Yes. Okay. I'm with you, regardless, you badass."

They climbed into Paula's silver luxury sedan and started driving. After a minute of silence, Paula said, "I'm sorry I acted like a big baby. I'm so confused. So hurt. I promise I'm not going to let every little thing get to me."

Cassie turned in her seat to face Paula. "Girl, you just buried the love of your life. You discovered that his finances might be a little hinky. You don't have to apologize to me. You're my best friend. If you can't be honest with me, then what am I here for?

A lump formed in Paula's throat. "I love you, Cassie Campbell. Thank you. You know, before Cal and I started on any road trip we had this little ritual. Would you mind saying it with me?"

"Not at all. Is it a prayer or a blessing or something?"

"Well, not exactly. It's... Repeat after me. Off again, on again, gone again, Flanagan."

"Huh?"

"It's something Cal's granddad used to say. Just humor me."

"Okay. I'll repeat after you."

"Off again, on again..." Paula said.

"...gone again, Flanagan," they said in unison.

A huge grin stretched across Paula's face. "Thanks. Oh, I almost forgot; we need to run by the post office and put our mail on hold."

Cassie raised an eyebrow. "We won't have to say that crap again, will we?"

Paula giggled. "I'm not making any promises."

After a quick stop at the post office, they pulled in near the gas pumps at the convenience store on the east end of Main Street. Paula got out and said, "I'm just going to top off the tank."

Cassie stood and stretched her arms over her head. "I'm gonna go in and grab us a couple of breakfast burritos. I was going to make us some this morning, but I was out of eggs. Do you want any more coffee or a Dr. Pepper?"

Paula unlocked her gas tank. "I don't need anything to drink. Just a bacon and egg burrito would be great. I haven't had one from here in ages."

As Paula waited for Cassie, her thoughts turned to Cal. After replacing the nozzle in the gas pump, she slid behind the steering wheel and allowed her regrets to encompass her. Tears soon streamed down her cheeks.

Cassie climbed in the passenger's side, and her smile melted. "Hey! What's— Oh, girl! Are you sure you want to go on this trip? We can cancel our reservations right now and just go on home."

Paula shook her head. "It's not that. I just realized that I didn't do anything for Cal all these years. I was an awful wife. I didn't cook. Didn't clean. Couldn't have babies."

Cassie handed Paula a napkin from the food bag. "Hush now. Cal certainly didn't see things that way. He wanted you to have a carefree life. And you helped with his business. You know you did. No telling how much money you saved him and helped him make. He always said you had the very best ideas."

"But maybe if I'd been a better wife, he—"

"No buts. Not a one. You were exactly the wife Cal wanted and needed. So, stop. And about those babies, Cal didn't care one bit. He was only disappointed because he knew how much it meant to you."

Paula blew her nose then managed a small smile. "You're right. I know that. I swear I'm going to get these tears under control. Any minute now."

"Well, cut yourself a little slack," Cassie said, opening the food sack. "And look here. An honest to goodness bacon and egg burrito, two packets of salsa, and a side of jalapenos. If this doesn't cheer you up, nothing will."

Paula reached into the sack and grabbed a burrito fairly burgeoning with bacon and eggs. She took a bite and her taste buds exploded with pleasure. "Oh, my goodness! This is almost as good as the ones you make. Why don't I stop by here more often?"

Cassie snorted and said, "Because you know better. C'mon girl, let's go if we're going. Off and on and all that Flanagan jazz."

Paula balanced the burrito on her lap and pulled onto Main Street. "Remind me to call Delbert when we get to Dallas."

"Why?"

"'Cause we'll be too far down the road for him to chase after us."

Cassie took a bite of burrito and said, "You know, you are a grown up. Delbert's just going to have to appreciate that. And, hey, I'm with you. What could go wrong?"

CHAPTER EIGHT

Cassie tuned the radio to an oldies station, and for miles, she sang along to their old favorites. Paula tapped her foot and occasionally sang a phrase or two.

As a commercial came on, Paula said, "You know, you really have a beautiful singing voice. I always thought it was such a shame that the Dempsey schools didn't have much of a music program."

Cassie shrugged her shoulders. "I can sing and I can cook. That's about the extent of my abilities."

"Oh, I don't know about that. You're a heck of a softball player, too. I can't do any of that."

"Do you ever wonder what we might've done if we'd stayed in college?" Cassie asked, turning down the volume on the radio. "I mean, I know we were both miserable, but we were too young to know what we wanted to do back then."

"I probably would've been a teacher. Maybe. Especially when I didn't have kids of my own. How about you?"

"Culinary school would've suited me fine. And maybe some business courses. I still think I'd like to have my own restaurant."

"You totally should. Your catering business is so successful. Everyone raves about it. Maybe I should go back to school, too. I'm only thirty-five. It's not too late to get a degree and start teaching."

"Wow. I can just picture you in front of a classroom of unruly kids." Cassie mimicked Paula's soft-spoken voice as she said, "Please children. Please sit down now."

Paula narrowed her eyes and smiled. "Well, maybe not. But I need to find something to do. I have my whole life ahead of me, right? I certainly can't take over Cal's business. No one's going to listen to a college dropout talk about choosing a life path. And, I'd die of stage fright before opening my mouth in front of a crowd. I'd literally hit the stage face first."

"Hey, that reminds me. What do you need to do about CalNet Enterprises?"

"Honestly, I haven't thought all that through yet. Damn."

"Could Delbert go by the house and get the schedule for this fall?"

"If I need him to, but we'll be home in a week. Surely I can have this week without thinking about it."

The Temptations started singing "My Girl," and Cassie turned up the radio and joined them.

As miles of flat Texas prairie disappeared beneath her car, Paula's thoughts drifted to worrying about the logistics of CalNet. *How will I know who to book for university lectures or whose talk is worthy of marketing video and audio discs of?*

Cal's counselling and consulting business had been lucrative, but he always insisted that finding Paula had been his biggest payoff of all. "Goldilocks," he'd say, "I never knew I was looking for you until I found you sitting in that auditorium in Lubbock, Texas, of all places."

Paula turned off the radio mid-song. "Tell me the story of why Cal called me Goldilocks."

Cassie's eyes twinkled. "You know darned good and well why."

"I know. I just need to hear it today."

Cassie shifted in her seat. "The fishing guys came up with it. Cal, Delbert, Mel, and someone else, I can't remember who, went fishing right after you two got married. Cal couldn't stop talking about you. Everything you did was *just right.* Finally, Delbert or Mel, one of the two, said, 'Sounds like you found yourself a Goldilocks. Everything is always just right." Cal thought that was hilarious and started calling you that. The name stuck."

Paula shook her head. "I still can't imagine what it was he thought I was doing right."

Cassie rolled her eyes. "C'mon now, Goldilocks, even *you* can't be *that* innocent."

A rosy blush covered Paula's cheeks. "Oh my gosh! Surely Cal didn't talk to the guys about—you know—sex!"

"Probably not, but then again, men will be men. I'm sure they ribbed him about it. And he really thought you could do no wrong. That never changed as far as I could tell."

Paula hung her head. "I always thought that about him, too. Until yesterday. Yesterday kind of changed everything, even if I'm willing it to be otherwise."

"It's all going to be okay. It really is. Hey, could you pull over at the next rest stop? I need a potty break."

A few minutes later, they came to the town of Gallo and Paula pointed to a Dairy Queen sign. "How about there? It's a little early for an ice cream, but we could get a little snack."

"Suits me, but who says it's too early for ice cream?"

Paula parked and raised an eyebrow. "First burritos, now ice cream, and all before noon. None of my pants are going to fit."

Cassie opened the door. "It wouldn't hurt you to put on a few pounds, Goldilocks. I'll bet you've lost five just since... Well, since Cal's—Um, speaking of that, have you heard from the highway patrol?"

Paula pulled the Dairy Queen door open. "They're still investigating, but the preliminary report is that he just went to sleep and drove off the road. Apparently, the way his car landed in that ditch, his airbag didn't deploy."

They remained silent as they took their place in line. Paula gestured to a narrow corridor down the side of the dining area. "You go on to the ladies' room. I'll order your usual: Hot fudge sundae, extra fudge, a smidge of whipped cream, and a cherry on top. No nuts. Right?"

Cassie smiled. "You know it."

As Cassie headed to the restroom, Paula watched a table of coffee drinking men turn their heads in admiration. There was no doubt her friend was eye-catching. She was a couple of inches taller than Paula and curvier. Her gorgeous raven hair hung to her shoulders in soft waves, and the headband she wore added a touch of innocent sexiness. Paula always joked that if she was Goldilocks, Cassie must be

Snow White. She always thought it was such a shame that Cassie had never married. She'd never even had a long-term boyfriend after high school, as far as Paula knew, and she knew Cassie better than anyone. As the line moved along, she became caught up in her daydream...*There probably is a right man out there for her, but he'd have to be one perfect Prince Charming to match Cassie's Snow White.*

Paula was seated with their food by the time Cassie returned. She nodded at the ogling men at the back and said, "Don't look now but those men are checking you out."

Cassie rolled her eyes. "Yeah, I noticed, too. Tried not to. Obnoxious asshats."

Paula stifled a grin as she pushed Cassie's sundae across the table, and they ate in silence until George Strait started singing about all of his exes living in Texas as the juke box lit up in neon colors.

Cassie pushed away her empty ice cream cup and wiped the corners of her mouth with a napkin. "You want me to drive awhile?"

"I'm good, but let's plan on switching just before we get into too much Dallas traffic. I sure don't want to deal with that mess."

"No problem. We'll need to stop again anyway for gas pretty soon. Maybe have a light lunch then you can nap while I navigate the jungle."

"We're eating hot fudge sundaes at 11 a.m. and you're already planning lunch? I like the way you think."

They turned their heads when a man from the coffee drinkers' table approached them.

The man tipped his head and held his hat in his hand. "Mornin', Ladies. My name's Derek Tuttle. I'd like to welcome you to the fine town of Gallo, and invite you to attend services at the First Baptist Church on Sunday morning. I'm the minister there."

Cassie pursed her lips. "Thank you very much, Derek, but we're just passing through. And we're heathens."

Paula's hand covered her unexpected giggle.

Derek's jaw dropped open and he steadied himself on the back of the both. "Well, we welcome heathens. Everyone is welcome."

Cassie collected her trash as she said, "Oh, we're also communists. Heathen commies. And Wiccans to boot."

Paula's eyes grew large and she blushed. "Uh, I think it's time to go. You know, before they bring out the pitchforks."

Cassie stood and batted her eyes at Derek then sashayed out the door.

Paula, unable to make her feet move, or even find her voice, looked back and forth between Derek's look of shock and Cassie's confident strut out the door. "Um, I'd better go chase after my heathen commie friend." She jingled her keys. "It's my car."

She rushed outside and hurried to get seated behind the wheel. "What was that all about?" she asked as Cassie buckled her seat belt.

"I don't know. I just snapped. Don't you ever get tired of men thinking you want to talk to them. Just because they happen to be male and you're female, and they think that they should be in your life just because of that dynamic?"

"Well, just to make sure you understand this... he was just being nice. And I never have men come up to me."

"You will, though. If you ever take that ring off your finger, you'll be inundated."

Paula backed out of the space. "Yeah, right. I doubt that's ever going to happen. Listen, let's stop this. We need to drive if we're going to be in Happy Vale by supper time. Just try to keep from going all feminazi on me."

"Hey! Where'd you learn a term like feminazi?"

"I do know how to use Google, you know."

Cassie rolled her eyes. "There's a talent!" She found a soft jazz station and kicked her shoes off then reclined her seat as far as it would go. "Do you care if I take a little nap?"

"Go for it."

Cassie grabbed a pillow from the backseat. Within minutes, she was quietly snoring as Paula negotiated through traffic. She shook her head at the memory of Cassie's outburst. *That Derek guy'll sure have a tale to tell for quite a while. I wonder if he'll make it into an upcoming sermon. Hmm... Ministering to Communist Heathens with Wiccan Tendencies.* Paula chuckled to herself. *I'd love to be a fly on the wall at his church Sunday morning.*

CHAPTER NINE

After filling her car at a gas station outside of Dallas, Paula leaned in the car window and tapped Cassie's shoulder. Paula's palms were moist at the mere thought of navigating the Dallas interstate system. "Hey, wake up, sleepyhead. It's almost half past one. Your turn at the wheel."

Cassie yawned and rubbed her eyes. "Huh? Oh, right. I totally thought I was in my own bed. Such sweet dreams."

Paula tossed the keys in Cassie's lap. "Well, wipe the drool off your face and let's find something healthy for lunch. Maybe a salad."

Cassie flipped down the vanity mirror and examined her face. "Yikes. Good thing I didn't waste time on makeup this morning."

Paula opened the passenger door. "You always look gorgeous, makeup or no makeup. But I have to say, the red sleep marks aren't all that flattering."

Cassie stood. "No? I think they're an improvement. They'll keep the would-be suitors away." She headed to the driver's side and drove down the block to a mom and pop café where they enjoyed an incident-free lunch. A half hour later, they were encroaching on Dallas traffic.

Cassie ran her hands over the steering wheel. "I just love your car. Seriously, I'd marry it if I could."

Paula patted the armrest between them. "Yeah, it is nice. And, it's paid for. If I have to scrape some money together, though, it'll have to go."

"Oh, I'll kick in to help you keep it. As long as I get to drive it every now and then.

Paula chuckled. "Deal. This hangover headache is starting to get to me. I'm going to close my eyes now. You're okay with the GPS thingy?"

"Oh yeah. I was born to use GPS."

Paula flipped the pillow over, but sleep wouldn't come. She tried counting breaths, counting sheep, counting everything she could think of, but her mind raced with apprehension.

She eventually dozed off, but woke with a start when Cassie slammed on the brakes and laid on the horn. "Sonofabitch! Stop texting and stay in your freaking lane!"

"Alrighty then," Paula said. "I think my nap time is over."

Cassie grimaced. "Oh, honey, I'm so sorry. I'm just trying to avoid hitting stupid drivers who won't put their freaking phones down!"

"So I gathered. I couldn't sleep anyway. And maybe you need another pair of eyes on this job."

"Nah, we're through the worst of it."

"Really? How long has it been? It feels like I was only asleep a few minutes."

"A few minutes? Try more like two hours. You were sawing logs."

Paula rubbed her eyes. "Wow. Are you okay to keep driving?"

"Sure, I'm good. You going to try and nap again?"

"No, I was just thinking we need a game plan. We're less than three hours out now. What are we going to do when we get to the motel?"

"I've been thinking about that, too. Since the room's in my name, maybe I should go in by myself and check out the people in the office. Who knows, Cal's needy M might even be behind the desk."

Paula pondered the suggestion. "That's better than anything I've thought of so far. You know, if this M is a... you know, mistress, she may have seen photos of me. I'd like to stay anonymous for a little while, anyway, until we can figure things out."

"Good idea. I'll go in all sweet and innocent and case the joint, then report back to you."

"Case the joint? We're not robbing the place."

"I know! But I'll look for evidence that Cal was a frequent guest. They might have pictures on the wall or something."

"And then what?"

"Then we'll plan. Tonight. It'll be like one of our old sleepovers from when we were kids. We ruled the world back then. We'll solve this."

Paula slapped the dashboard. "Damned straight!"

Cassie eyed her friend and bit her own lip. "Uh, Paula, no matter what we find out, you know Cal loved you. I can't imagine he had some woman on the side, but even if he did, he always, *always* loved you."

Paula sighed. "I know that. Part of me understands that anyway, but the other part of me won't be sorry he's dead if he had a mistress."

"Don't say that!"

"I know it sounds horrible, but it's true. I think it'll be some kind of divine karma. Maybe that makes me a bad person, but I hate to think Cal might have deceived me all these years. It's the worst feeling you can imagine to put your trust in someone then have it just poof! Disappear."

Cassie took a deep breath and turned the radio back to the 60s channel. After they passed the next exit, she said, "You know, people can't always be as honest as you are. You've always had that Goldilocks thing going for you, but not everything is black and white. Just don't forget all the love you two shared. Regardless of what we discover this week."

Paula hung her head and picked her fingernail. "No promises. I can't imagine being able to forgive him, but I'll try to remember what you said. We did have fifteen really great years."

"Yes, you did."

Paula leaned back against the pillow and watched the world flicker by as Cassie's sweet voice lulled her back to sleep.

CHAPTER TEN

Paula woke to the sound of the driver's side door opening, and the sudden urgency for a restroom had her scrambling for the door handle. She gathered her bearings and got out of the car then scanned the rest stop parking lot. Cassie was already a blur in the distance. Paula slammed her door shut and started jogging. "Hold up, Cassie! I'm coming, too!"

After using the facilities, Paula stopped at a rack of tourist brochures. Colorful flyers for fishing guides and campgrounds blended together in a kaleidoscope of color until a simple tri-fold brochure for the Happy Valley Motor Inn and Resort drew her in and almost grabbed her hand as she reached for it.

As Cassie joined her, Paula held up the tiny trophy in triumph and said, "Look! Just look!"

The brochure showed a pleasant looking old-fashioned L-shaped motor-hotel with covered car ports between every other room. A rustic log cabin with a wrap-around porch looked to be the office, and behind that a pastoral expanse of lake was ringed by motor homes and campers.

Cassie grabbed a small handful of the pamphlets. "Let's take a couple of these. We're just a few miles from the Kilgore exit, then we'll be headed south for about two hours. I tried to hold out and take a potty break in Kilgore since we need gas, too, but my bladder couldn't wait."

Paula's mouth formed a silent O. "From your bladder to my ears."

Cassie wrinkled her nose. "Eww!"

"Yeah, that didn't come out like I planned. Sorry. I think my hangover's finally gone, at least. I can drive the rest of the way." She stretched her arms over her head and yawned. "Wow, I feel a lot better. I didn't even realize I'd gone to sleep."

Cassie chuckled and gave Paula the keys. "Hangover, huh? Is that why you snored like an old man?"

"Had to keep you awake. I'm selfless like that."

The highway narrowed to a two-lane country road not far outside of Kilgore where they'd stopped to gas up the car. Paula's fingers tightened around the steering wheel. "I'm not crazy about driving on curvy roads, but this sure is pretty country."

"I know what you mean. Give me a long straight road so I can see where I'm going and what's coming at me. I like the trees, though. I've already seen more trees in two miles than exist in the entire town of Dempsey."

After a moment of silence, Paula said, "Thank you for coming with me. And don't worry, I'll reimburse the cost of the room."

"What? No way! I needed an adventure. You pay for meals and gas. I'll get the room. Deal?"

"Deal."

Cassie rested her arm on the passenger door and stared out the window in silence.

Concerned about traveling the unfamiliar route, Paula watched the road, but her thoughts soon turned to Cal and who the *other* Mrs. Arnett could be. She pulled into the first fast-food stop she saw once they got to Nacogdoches.

As they stepped out to stretch their legs again, Cassie said, "I might've had too many Dr. Peppers today. I'm going to visit the ladies' room." Cassie pursed her lips as she shuffle-ran to the restroom.

Paula clicked her key fob. "I'm right behind you."

When they were back on the road, Paula said, "Unless we need to stop again, we should make it all the way to the motel now."

Cassie opened one of the motel brochures and read aloud. "Happy Valley Motor Inn and Resort: A home away from home for avid fishermen. Whether you're an expert or a novice you'll enjoy endless hours of relaxation in beautiful Toledo Bend Lake Country. Rated the number one bass fishing lake in the nation by *Bassmaster Magazine* two years in a row, Toledo Bend Reservoir is the place to test your fishing mettle. And there's no better place to stay than the Happy Valley Motor Inn and Resort."

"Keep going," said Paula when Cassie paused.

Cassie flipped over the pamphlet. "Well, there's not much more. It just lists the types of facilities. Let's see, it says, double rooms in the motor inn are $80 a night in-season, but we already knew that; $75 off-season. And the trailer hook ups are $45 a night. Looks like they even have some rustic fishing cabins for guys who really want to rough it. Those are only $25 a night."

"I see. Something for everyone."

"Yes! Get this, they even have a honeymoon package. Can you imagine spending your honeymoon at the Happy Valley Motor Inn?"

"Heavens no. Although, I'm sure Cal would've loved that. Fish a little, romance a little, fish a lot more...."

Cassie winked. "Well, they do use the tag line, 'Come for the fishing; stay for the fun.'"

The GPS indicated that in two miles they'd reach their destination. The color drained from Paula's face. "Oh, mercy. I don't know if this was such a good idea after all."

"It's going to be fine. Just get us there."

CHAPTER ELEVEN

Paula's hands trembled as she turned off the main road onto a graveled driveway. She drove under a faded green sign with a picture of a smiling fisherman showing off a huge bass while a woman stood beaming behind him. Even the fish looked happy.

Cassie pointed to a large log cabin. "Look. Over there's the office."

Paula parked and bit her lip. "You sure you want to go in?"

Cassie opened her door. "Yep. Give me a few minutes. If I don't come out before nightfall, call the S.W.A.T. team."

"Very funny."

"I wasn't joking. This place doesn't look all that welcoming to me."

Paula's palms began to sweat as she took in her surroundings. The trees lining the drive were overgrown and in need of some aggressive trimming. Long, sturdy oak branches dragged the ground, and the pines crowded in so close, it made the lot feel claustrophobic. But despite the rocking chairs on the wrap-around porch needing a coat of paint, they still looked inviting. Paula frowned. "I don't know. It just looks like it needs some T.L.C."

"More like TBN. Turn Back Now."

"Let's be positive. Go in and get our room key and see if you get a sighting of M."

Cassie stood and leaned back in the car door. "Okey doke. But remember, call S.W.A.T. Save yourself."

Cassie gave Paula a wide-eyed look of horror as she crossed in front of the car to the office door.

Paula giggled as Cassie squared her shoulders and straightened her spine as if she were going into battle. *Now that is a formidable woman.* Paula rolled down the windows and switched the car ignition off. A languid, sauna-like heat rolled in along with the heavy scent of pine. These pine trees looked different from any she'd seen before, and she was fairly sure the massive tree draped with Spanish moss in front of the office was an oak. She felt as if she'd entered a different world, one where normal rules didn't apply. It was a heady and terrifying thought.

"C'mon out, Cassie," she mumbled under her breath. She thought maybe she should start the car, just in case they needed to make a fast getaway. Her hand hovered over the start engine button, as Cassie came bouncing out of the office holding up a pair of green tags with keys attached.

"Get in! Tell me everything," Paula said in an urgent whisper.

"Let's get into our 'newly renovated and modernly appointed' room," Cassie said, mimicking perhaps the voice of the desk clerk. "And I'll tell you everything."

Paula followed Cassie's directions to the unit furthest from the office and pulled into the covered space reserved for Room 23. "At least we won't be bothered by noisy or nosy neighbors," she said, noting that the room nearest theirs was two parking slots away.

Cassie gave Paula a smug smile. "That's because I specifically asked for something with a little privacy. C'mon. Let's get our stuff inside."

As soon as they'd unloaded the car and were safely inside, Paula said, "Okay. Tell me everything. Did you see M?"

"Yes, I certainly did."

CHAPTER TWELVE

Paula held up her index finger. "Hold that thought for a second. Bathroom first. Then info."

Cassie opened one of the drawers of the pine dresser. "Sure."

Paula's fingers fumbled to unbutton her capris. *I can't believe Cal may have stayed in this very room and I never even knew it.* She fought to suppress her pending tears.

"Do you care which bed you sleep in?" Cassie asked through the door.

"No."

Then I'll take the one by the window."

Paula fanned her eyes. Her legs trembled as she fastened her pants. She exited to the exterior vanity sink and Cassie took her place in the restroom. Paula washed her hands then splashed water on her face. "Why, Cal? Why couldn't you tell me about all this?" she said under her breath with a sniffle. She stacked a few water bottles and half a Dr. Pepper in the small refrigerator then started unpacking her clothes. She folded the blue and green bedspread down on her bed and caught herself smiling at the coverlet where pictures of smiling fish frolicked in a clear blue lake, adding a touch of whimsy to the room. "If I'm stuck owning this place, at least it's clean," she said as she headed to the vanity.

Paula hung her dress on the rod adjacent to the bathroom and made the mistake of looking in the mirror. "Whoa!"

"Whoa what?" Cassie asked, as she came to wash her hands.

"Whoa that!" Paula said, pointing at her own reflection in the mirror.

"We have looked better," Cassie admitted. "Let's talk, then we'll clean up and go find something for supper."

A lump grew in Paula's throat, and she sat on the edge of her bed. "Tell me."

Cassie drew the curtains closed before sitting next to Paula, tucking her foot under her bottom as she sat. "Alright. So, a cute, twentyish aged girl checked me in. Tall, slender, long dark hair, brown eyes. Very friendly. Her name tag said, 'McKenzie.'"

Paula's lungs deflated. "Damn."

"Just wait. Then another woman came out from a back room. I figured maybe she's McKenzie's mom. Nice lady, tall like McKenzie, maybe 5'8", super short dark, curly hair. Looked to be mid-to-late-forties, maybe? Anyway, her name tag said Melinda."

"Hell," said Paula.

"Wait. There's more. Another woman came up from the back. Maybe there's an M replicator back there or something, because this woman, who might've been an aunt or a mom to the second woman. Her name was Martha."

"Sonofabitch! Are you kidding me?"

"Girl, you've known me for thirty years. Would I make up something as serious as this?"

Paula's heart sank into her stomach. "I know. But now I've got more questions than ever."

CHAPTER THIRTEEN

Paula and Cassie freshened up then drove into Happy Vale in search of food. As they cruised the ten-mile stretch of scenic two-lane road, Paula's head spun. "So, about those 3M's, how old do you think the last one was?"

"Three M's?"

"Yeah, you know – the 3M's at the motel."

Cassie rolled her eyes. "The oldest one was probably seventy."

"Did you happen to notice any photos on the walls? Anything that might indicate that Cal was a frequent visitor?"

"I walked in, and the youngest M, McKenzie, helped me straight away, so I didn't get to look around much. I did see a few photos of folks posing with oversized fish but didn't see them up close and personal. Maybe after supper I can go in and ask for something and look around a little."

Paula chewed her lower lip. "I'm dying to get in there myself. Maybe I could put on a baseball cap or something and wear my sunglasses. Would that be enough of a disguise?"

"Probably. We'll look for a hat while we're in Happy Vale."

"I brought a couple of Cal's fishing hats for us."

"Eww! And those probably stink. Surely we can find something better." Cassie's stomach growled. "I don't know about you, but I'm starved. Let me look on my phone and see if I can find us a restaurant…What the—I've got no signal. Let me see yours."

Paula fished in her purse as she drove and tossed her phone to Cassie. Her voice cracked as she said, "The pass code's 0724. That was Cal's birthday."

Cassie's brow wrinkled as she attempted a Google search on Paula's phone. "Nope. Yours doesn't work either. Guess we'll just have to wing it."

Paula turned down the town's Main Street, and both women looked down their respective side of the road until they reached the end. Paula turned the car around and said, "I guess that's it in the way of choices. A Mexican restaurant, a Tex-Mex, an Authentic Mexican Fiesta, and the Oaks on Main Café."

Cassie pointed at the café sign. "Look, the sign says their food is better than grandma's. I don't know about theirs, but my grandma was a pretty good cook. Let's see if this Oaks on Main lives up to the hype."

Paula parked on the street in front of the Big Lake County Court House. As they walked across the street to the café, the delicious aromas wafting on the air enticed Paula's stomach into an anticipatory growl. She blushed. "I think my salad wore off a couple of hours ago."

Cassie closed her eyes and inhaled. "Mine, too. If the food's as good as it smells I'm going to have to hang up my apron, 'cause I can't compete."

Business was brisk at Oaks on Main, and a friendly waitress instructed them to sit wherever they wanted. Cassie led the way through a maze of occupied tables to a booth near the kitchen. "How about here? I want to watch the staff in action." Every eye in the place watched as the two strangers passed them by.

Cassie perused the dining area as they sat then she nodded. "This is exactly the set up I'd want for my café. Simple décor. Not fussy, but not too modern. Artwork by locals on the walls. It really says welcome!"

"Well, if a town this size could support a café like this, surely Dempsey could."

Cassie's gaze left Paula's. "Uh, I'm… I'm not sure I'd open a cafe in Dempsey. In fact, I'm not sure I even want to be there much longer."

Paula's mouth dropped open. "What? Why would you move? Dempsey's your home. It's *our* home."

The waitress returned with two menus and Cassie waved her hand. "Oh, it'll probably never happen, anyway. Let's see what looks good here… Oh, good, you have Dr. Pepper. I'll have a large."

Paula considered her choices. "And I'll have an iced tea, please."

The waitress smiled. "My name's April. Tonight's special is chicken fried steak with gravy and mashed potatoes, green beans and a salad. Trust me, it's the best chicken fry you've ever tasted, but then I think everything on the menu is the best. Let me know if you have any questions, and I'll be back in a sec."

Cassie nodded and Paula said, "Actually, I think we both want the special. That'll save you some time."

April's cheeks dimpled. "Good choice. I'll go get this order in, then I'll be right back with your drinks. Waters, too."

Paula waited until April was out of earshot. "She's like a little ray of sunshine, isn't she?"

Cassie grinned. "Yeah, she reminds me of someone, too. Hmmm. Could it be Paula Jean Purdy Arnett?"

Paula laughed. "No way was I ever like that!"

"Are you kidding me? You're going through a low point right now, but normally, you are a big ol' dollop of sunshine."

"Oh, I don't know about that."

"Well, I do. I knew the day we met that you were someone I wanted to have as a friend."

"I remember that day you claimed me for your best friend. It always puzzled me, but I'm so glad you did. My life would've been oh so boring without Cassie Campbell in it."

April returned, carrying a tray of drinks, a basket of fresh, hot rolls, salads, and a trio of salad dressings in a stainless-steel caddy. "Y'all's orders will be right up," she said. "Does everything look okay so far?"

Cassie's eye grew large. "Better than okay."

Paula popped a bite of buttered roll in her mouth. "Mmm-hmm,"

April tucked her tray under her arm. "Good. I'll be back soon."

As the waitress left, Cassie plucked a roll from the basket and buttered it. "Folks like her are what make places like this successful. I'm sure the bread is divine, and the salad probably tastes like the vegetables came fresh from the garden, but people are what make small cafés work."

Paula dressed her salad. "Oh, I don't know about that. The cook gets my vote."

"Yes, but April is the face of the place. And in a small town, the face is everything."

"Well, she's got a cute face, so I guess that does help. Okay, what else did you notice about the 3M's? Anything that might help us get a handle on what Cal did with our money?"

Cassie took a bite of her salad. "The middle one, Melinda, was really thin. Like she'd been sick. She was pretty, but compared to the other two, she didn't look like she'd been getting enough sun or enough rest. Dark circles under her eyes.

"You think she needed Cal to help with medical bills? But why would she turn to my husband? Oh, my gosh! What if Cal had a whole second family? I've read about guys who've done that. Two wives living blocks apart and never knowing about one another. Kids going to school with half-siblings." Paula's face blanched and she felt as if she'd been punched in the stomach.

"Hon, you look like you're going to be sick. You've simply *got* to calm down. To tell you the truth, that idea did cross my mind. But we just got here. Let's do a little more investigative work before we follow that path."

They broke off their conversation when April returned with two plates of hand-breaded chicken fried steaks covered in thick white gravy with a hefty portion of creamy mashed potatoes on the side. "Here ya' go!" April sang out. "Can I get you anything? More bread?"

Paula closed her eyes as she inhaled the delicious aromas swirling around her plate. "No, April. This looks amazing. Thank you."

"Good. I'll run grab the pitcher of iced tea to refill your glass. Y'all just holler now if you need anything else. Oh, we've got pecan pie for dessert, so you might think about leaving a little bit of room for that."

As April hurried off, Cassie cut off a piece of meat and sighed as she placed it in her mouth. "Oh, this is so good. The real deal, none of that pre-battered stuff some places try to pass off as chicken fried steak."

Paula smothered a bite in gravy then popped it in her mouth. "Wow! I could eat this for every meal and never get tired."

"If we could only eat it every meal and never get fat. That's the trick."

"We'd be happy, though."

Cassie sampled the potatoes. "Oh, and these are real. Little bits of the skin mashed in. Holy cow, this is good!"

A few minutes later, April refilled Paula's iced tea glass, and asked if Cassie would like another Dr. Pepper. Cassie declined a refill, but said, "This was heavenly. Who should we thank for cooking such an excellent meal?"

April's smile broadened. "Oh, that would be Delilah Oaks. She's the owner and the main cook, but her son, Jeffries is helping out tonight. He does that when he's home. He's going to culinary school in Dallas to learn the ropes. Although, I don't think he could have a better teacher than his mom, but that's just my opinion."

Paula scraped the last drop of gravy off her plate with a scrap of roll. "Well, please pass along our thanks to Delilah and Jeffries."

Cassie pushed her empty plate to the table's edge. "And please bring out a piece of that pecan pie, with two forks."

April collected the empty plates and giggled. "You got it. Be right back. Y'all want ice cream with that, too, right?"

Paula shrugged her shoulders. "Why not?"

April left and Cassie said, "So, what's our next move? We go find you a hat?"

"Yes. We'll get me a hat. Maybe that grocery store we passed will have one. What can we ask for at the front desk?"

"I could take the batteries out of the remote for the television. Or maybe we can just go ask about fishing gear. We're staying at a lake, after all."

"Good idea. I brought along one of Cal's fishing shirts, along with those fishing hats I told you about, but maybe I do need a different kind of hat for meeting the 3M's. Do you know how to fish?"

"A little. But surely you listened to Cal and the boys over the years."

Paula grimaced. "Only when I couldn't find a reason to excuse myself. I can't bear to think about touching one."

"Well, we probably won't have to worry about that. I doubt we'll catch anything."

"Ladies, you two driving through our little town?" The voice, like honey, came from a tall, generously proportioned woman with autumn-red shoulder length hair.

Cassie looked up to see who was speaking. "Um, we're staying out at the Happy Valley Motor Inn for a few days. Girl trip."

"Uh huh. I'm glad you stopped in at our little restaurant. I'm Delilah Oaks, by the way. April passed along your compliments."

"Oh! It was incredible," Paula said, gesturing at her now empty plate. "I almost inhaled mine."

Delilah's eyes twinkled. "Well, I'm glad you enjoyed it. Ah! Here's April with your pie..." Delilah stepped aside until the pie was served and Cassie and Paula had taken a bite. "So, have you already checked in out at the Happy Valley?"

April, who'd taken a couple of steps toward the kitchen, did an about face. "You're staying out there? But isn't that place—"

Delilah frowned and shook her head. "Hush, child. Run on back and give Jeffries a hand."

"Yes ma'am,"

Cassie and Paula exchanged wide eyed looks.

As soon as April was out of audible range, Cassie said, "Yes, we checked in before we came here. Is there something about Happy Valley we should know?"

Delilah tapped her fingernails on the table's edge and lowered her voice. "Do you ladies mind if I have a seat?"

"Not at all," Paula said, scooting down the bench. She admired Delilah's high cheekbones and sapphire eyes. *I wonder if Cal had ever tasted this woman's cooking. Surely, he'd have mentioned something this good.*

Her thoughts were interrupted by Delilah. "Could I ask why you chose Happy Valley? You two look more like bed and breakfast types to me, if you don't mind me saying."

Paula took a deep breath. "Actually, my husband passed away recently, and he used to come out here to stay. My friend and I are retracing some of his steps. Just trying to feel close to him, you know."

"Oh, I'm sorry for your loss. Are you sure he stayed at Happy Valley, though?

Paula grabbed a napkin and dabbed her mouth. "Well, we think so. At least I found some correspondence that hinted at that. And, we found their brochure at a rest stop. It looked like a nice place."

Delilah nodded. "It used to be. Once. Fishermen came from all over to stay out there. Then the man who owned it lost his wife and kind of went cuckoo. Next thing we knew, he died, and those women took over the place and it just went to seed. I don't think they knew the first thing about running a motel, but they don't mix with the townspeople, so no one really knows what goes on out there."

"I hear they practice devil worship," April said as she wiped a nearby table.

Delilah cut her eyes at the girl. "That's nonsense!" She cleared her throat. "But they have had some odd goings-on out there."

Cassie raised an eyebrow. "Such as?"

"Well, they had a psychics' weekend one time, and the townsfolk got all up in arms about that. And I hear they hosted a group of folks who like to dress up like forest animals and, um, cavort in the woods. I think one of the local churches protested out there."

"Whoa!" said Paula.

April shook her head and started wiping down a bench. "It's certainly not your run of the mill fishing resort, that's for sure."

"Do you know the women at all," Paula asked, as she cut a bite of pie with her fork. "Are any of them married?"

Delilah shrugged her shoulders. "I know them to give them a nod at the grocery store but can't say I've ever had a real conversation with any of them. How about you, April?

"That youngest one is about my age. When they first came out here, what was it, a year ago? I invited them to church and told them about the restaurant here, but nothing. And I haven't ever seen a ring on any of their fingers."

Delilah pursed her lips. "I did hear that they just got an infusion of cash. Or maybe somebody bought the place but left it to the ladies to manage. Big waste of money, if you ask me, unless the new owners are going to oversee the business for a while. Help get it back on its feet."

Cassie wiped the corners of her mouth with a napkin. "Do you think we'll be all right staying out there? We've already paid for our rooms for a week, but if it isn't safe maybe we should just move out tonight."

Delilah waved her hand. "I don't think there's a safety issue. There's just something that's not quite right. This is a pretty close-knit community, and when small business owners give you the cold shoulder, that just sends out the wrong message, you know. She checked her watch then stood. "Listen, I'd better get back to the kitchen and help with the clean-up. Looks like you two just about closed the place down. Y'all come on back in the morning and we'll cook you a breakfast you won't soon forget,"

"Thanks, we might just do that," Paula said. "Although, I may not need to eat for a week."

After Delilah and April walked back to the kitchen Paula gave Cassie a meaningful look. "Let's pay our check and go buy me a hat. I need to get up close and personal. Right now."

CHAPTER FOURTEEN

At the store, Paula found a black and gold New Orleans Saints baseball cap and asked the cashier to cut the tags off. Cassie bought a case of bottled water, some breakfast bars, a Styrofoam cooler to take fishing, and a bag of ice.

As they headed across the parking lot, Paula gave the keys to Cassie. "Would you mind driving?"

"Of course not. I wanted to buy some wine to take back to the room, but would you believe this is a dry county?"

Paula nodded. "I asked about that, too. There's a liquor store out on the highway east of town. Let's run out there first. I might need a little liquid courage before I meet the 3M's."

Paula reeled off the directions, and soon, they were armed with a box of red blend and a case of Shiner Bock beer. Before they left the liquor store, Paula spied a poster warning against fishing without a license. "Look," she said pointing. "Can we apply for fishing licenses here?" she asked the clerk.

"Of course," the ruddy-faced young man said, passing two applications across the counter. You two doing some fishing on the lake?"

Cassie started writing on one of the forms. "Yes. We're staying out by Toledo Bend Reservoir."

The clerk stamped Cassie's completed application. "Cool. I just need to see your driver's license, and that'll be thirty bucks a piece…"

On their way back to the motel, Paula stuffed her hair underneath her cap. "How's that look?"

"You look like a twelve-year-old boy. With boobs.

"Hmm. But do I look like someone who'd be nicknamed 'Goldilocks'?"

Cassie gave Paula a sidelong look and raised an eyebrow. "No. Your locks are well hidden. You'd never pass for a real boy, but you don't look too frilly, either."

"Good enough. Let's go do some reconnaissance."

Paula squinted as Cassie navigated the motel's dark gravel road. When they hit a bump, Paula winced. "It's so dark here. If this were my place, I'd install some security lighting."

"Honey, it *is* your place."

"Oh, yeah. I guess it is. Well, if I had the money, I'd install some security lighting."

Cassie parked beside their room. "Let's take our stuff inside and have a glass of wine."

"Yes. And we'll have to rearrange the stuff in the fridge to make room for everything.

Cassie's eyes twinkled and she suppressed a grin. "Are we stalling?"

"Maybe, but only because I need a glass of wine. Or two."

After the fridge was stocked, Paula fiddled with the spigot on the wine box, then grabbed a couple of glasses from the counter beside the sink. She rinsed and dried them before dispensing two generous servings of wine. Handing one to Cassie, she raised her own glass and said, "To the discovery of truth!"

Cassie clinked her glass against Paula's. "To truth."

Three glasses later, Cassie said, "Well, ol' pal o' mine. Shall we away to the office?"

"Certainly," Paula said, a goofy grin plastered across her face.

"Gosh, you're a cheap drunk," Cassie said in a woozy voice.

"Look who's talkin'."

Cassie stood, leaning on the wall beside the door and gestured. "Lead the way."

"After you."

Arm in arm, they marched to the office where a red neon VACANCY sign blinked on and off in the otherwise dark night.

Paula's face grew grim. "It's July, and a fishing resort has vacancies. That's not good."

"Nope. You need to get to the bottle of this," Cassie said with a hiccup.

"You mean bottom."

"Yes, bottle."

The bell over the office door tinkled when they opened it. Cassie approached the desk while Paula walked around the room, inspecting snapshots of dead fish and triumphant fishermen. If what Delilah had told them was accurate, most of these photos had been taken before the 3M's took possession of Happy Valley.

Photo after photo showed one or more grinning man with a huge dead bass or a string of crappie in hand. Only a couple of pictures featured a female, but Paula reasoned that women probably were in the minority in the sport of fishing.

A young woman entered from a back room and said, "Hey, there. What can I do for you?"

Paula's heart stopped between beats. *That must be McKenzie. Surely, she's far too young to have been tangled up with Cal.*

Cassie cleared her throat. "Hi. We're staying in Room 23. You checked us in earlier."

"Sure! Is there a problem?"

"Oh, no, the room is fine. We were just wondering about fishing gear. Do you rent poles and stuff? And how about bait?"

"Well, we have a few things, but we don't keep bait out here. You can get that at the Big Lake County Bait store a couple of miles from here. Hold on a sec. Mom!"

Paula turned as a slender, attractive woman appeared from the back. *What did Cassie say her name was? Melinda? Is she the other Mrs. Arnett?*

McKenzie moved closer to Melinda. "Mom, these ladies are staying in twenty-three, and they were wondering if we have any fishing gear."

The woman smiled at Paula and Cassie and said, "I think we can rustle up some gear if you two are interested in fishing. I recommend you go out early. It gets awfully hot here after 11 a.m. or so. By the way, I'm Melinda Arnett, manager of the—"

Paula felt the blood rush out of her face and her legs turned to jelly. She managed to squeak out, "Help!" before her head hit the floor and the room went black.

CHAPTER FIFTEEN

As Paula came to, she found herself being observed by a quartet of women. Cassie's face and those of three unfamiliar females, swam above her. *Wait, I know who they are. McKenzie. Melinda. The third must be Martha.* When she recalled Melinda's introduction, her head spun again.

"Sweetie, just lie still," Cassie said. "You must've had one too many glasses of wine. You got all pasty and then, bam! You hit the floor."

Martha pulled her glasses to the end of her nose and furrowed her brow. "I still think we should call an ambulance."

Melinda's hand rested on her heart. "Or at least call a doctor out to look at her. Mark will be out here soon."

Paula bumped her elbow on the floor as she attempted to sit up. "No! No, I'm okay. Cassie's right. I must've had too much wine. I'm not much of a drinker and we drove all day, you know. I'm pretty tired, too." Paula heard herself babbling but was powerless to stop.

Cassie helped Paula to her feet and said, "Let me get her back to our room. I'm sure she'll be just fine after a good night's sleep."

Paula nodded, and wished she hadn't. "Yes, yes, I'll be good tomorrow. I just need some rest. It's been a long day. Just help me to our room, and thank you all for your concern, I'm fine, just fine. No need for alarm, honest." Cassie's grip tightened around Paula's arm, and Paula blushed. *Crap! Why can't I shut up?*

Cassie dug her fingernails into Paula's arm. "Hush now, Pa...*tricia*. You're wearing yourself out."

Paula raised an eyebrow. "Who's Patr—Oh." She bit the insides of her cheeks to keep from talking and patted her head, relieved that her cap was still in place.

Melinda nudged McKenzie. "Honey, why don't you walk these ladies back to their room."

Paula waved her hands in front of her. "No. No, that won't be necessary. I feel so foolish. Never fainted a day in my life. I guess that'll teach me to indulge in more than one glass of wine after a long day of driving. Too much excitement, I guess."

Cassie's stare bored a hole into Paula, and Paula shut up. Through clenched teeth Cassie said, "Let's get you back to the room. Thank you, ladies. So sorry for the fuss."

Melinda raised an eyebrow at Paula and stepped closer to her. "Do I know you? You look so familiar."

Paula's voice rose an octave. "I doubt that, highly, really doubt that. I, uh, have one of those faces, though, and you know, I get around. Like right now, I'm getting around to go to my room."

Cassie pushed Paula out the door and made a crazy face behind her back. "Thanks, ladies. I'm just going to get Miss Patricia to her room. Come on Pat. Let's go."

Like a docile child, Paula let Cassie lead her across the courtyard to their room. "Are they watching us?" Paula whispered.

Cassie turned to look and waved. Through a plastered smile, she said, "Yes, yes they are. Keep walking. Almost there."

Once in their room, Paula flopped on her bed. "Damn, damn, damn! Well, I guess that's our proof."

Cassie paced the room. "No, not necessarily. Arnett isn't an uncommon name. And, there are all sorts of explanations."

"Tell me one. One explanation that covers why Cal bought this, this, place from someone who isn't me but calls herself Mrs. Calvin Arnett?"

Cassie stopped walking and grabbed Paula's shoulders. "She did not call herself that. She said her name is Melinda Arnett. There's a big difference."

Paula laid back, pressing one of her pillows over her face. "I'm just going to smother myself."

"I don't think it works that way. I'm going to get ready for bed. Do you want in the bathroom first?"

"No. You go first. I'm going to just let this pillow do its job."

While Cassie cleaned her face and changed into pajamas, Paula closed her eyes beneath the cool cotton pillow and pictured Cal. *Had he been different over the past few months? I don't think so. I teased him mercilessly when he turned fifty in January. He'd been working so hard, on the road a lot, but none of that was different from normal. What was it?* Paula's breathing slowed and she drifted into sleep and dreams of Cal.

"Hey, Goldilocks," Cal said, entering the kitchen from the garage. "What's for dinner?"

Paula grabbed him and hugged him with all her might. "Cal! You're here. Oh my Cal. It's been so hard these past few days. Thank God you're all right."

"Oh, sweetheart! Dry those tears. I'm right here. I never left you."

"But you were injured. But look at you now! You look fine. I knew there must've been a mistake. Oh Cal!" She held him close, smelled his spicy cologne mixed with the scent of cigar, and felt his arms tighten around her.

"Goldilocks, I can't stay long, but we need to talk."

"But why can't you stay? You just said you never left me."

"Well, Goldilocks, there's leaving and then there's leaving. I'll always be with you, but not like I was before the accident."

Paula sat on a chair in her kitchen. She knew now this was a dream, but she really felt Cal's arms. She felt this chair. "Can you help me understand why you spent our money on this place in Happy Vale? Who are these women? Did you cheat on me, Cal?"

"It's complicated. But you have to believe that I loved you more than anyone or anything. Don't lose sight of that. I'm glad you came down here. I think you'll like it. Just keep an open mind, Goldilocks."

Paula realized they were now back in the motel room and Cal was slowly fading away. "Cal don't go. I need you.

"And I need you. *They* need you. I love you Goldilocks."

"Cal! *Ca-a-a-a-al!*"

Paula awoke to Cassie shaking her wrist. "Sweetie wake up. You were dreaming."

Tears streamed down Paula's face, as she buried it in Cassie's shoulder. "It was Cal. He was *right* here! I mean, first he was in Dempsey. He'd just walked in our kitchen. He was as real as you. Then he was here. With me. I could smell his cigar! He said he'd always loved me. And something else. Oh, I wish I hadn't woken up." She covered her face with her hands and sobbed.

Cassie patted Paula's back then stood and brought her a box of tissues. Here, hon, let me get you a wet washcloth. Through clenched teeth and in a low, purposeful tone, she said, "Cal Arnett, if you're still here, if you're still listening, there'd better be a damned good explanation for this mess, or I swear I will follow you to hell and make the devil crank up the furnace!"

CHAPTER SIXTEEN

Early the next morning, Paula sneaked out of the room while Cassie slept. When she returned, Cassie's bed was empty, and the shower was running. "Cassie?"

The water stopped and Cassie said, "In here. Where'd you go?"

"I ran into town and got us some breakfast and some bait. Figured if we were going to go fishing, we'd best do it early."

"Seriously? After you fainted last night?" Cassie walked out with her towel wrapped around her, took one look at Paula and guffawed. "Oh, my. Look at you!"

Cal's faded green fishing shirt was at least two sizes too large for Paula, and even with the mesh belt she'd added, it hung well below her khaki shorts. "What?" she asked as she spun in a slow circle. "Don't I look like a fisherman?"

Cassie snickered. "You look like *something,* all right! I don't have anything even close to that outfit, thank goodness."

"Well, hurry and throw something on. The fish are biting."

Cassie began combing her hair. "You sure are chipper this morning. I was afraid that after last night, you'd be ready to head home."

"You know, I thought about it after we got back to the room. Thought about putting this place on the market and selling it. Those women would never even know that I was the owner. But then I got to thinking. Cal came to me for a reason last night."

Cassie's face grew grim. "Hon, that was a dream. You *do* know that, right?"

"It was the damnedest dream I ever had then. Cal was here just as real as you are. I saw him. I *touched* him. And I remembered the rest of what he told me." Paula sat on the bed and selected a chocolate covered donut from a box as Cassie dressed in khaki shorts and a burnt orange t-shirt.

Cassie pulled her hair into a ponytail. "What's that?"

"He told me he loved me. He said that he needed me. And, he said *they* need me. *They.* He has to mean the 3M's."

"But don't you think maybe that's just wishful thinking? You always want to help people. Why would these women need you?"

"I don't know. But I think we need to stay and get to the bottom of this thing. If Cal had something going on with this Melinda, then I'll deal with the emotions and all that pain. But there's something here. Something that I need to fix."

Cassie let out a deep sigh. "Okay... Then let's go fishing. Want me to go get the gear from the office?"

"Nope. *We'll* go get the gear. If I'm going to figure this out, I have to be willing to get to know the 3M's. No more hiding."

"Don't forget your hat," Cassie said, throwing Paula the Saints cap.

Paula stuffed her hair under the cap and pulled it down when a corner of the visor snapped up. "Oh, no!" she said pulling it off her head. Look, the stitching is ripped. Cheap cap!

Cassie inspected the hat then tossed it toward the garbage can. "Twenty-two bucks wasn't cheap for something you only got to wear once. Now what are we gonna do?"

"Well, we still have Cal's hats." Paula pulled the battered caps from her tote bag.

Cassie took a hat and wrinkled her nose. "Ugh. Did Cal ever wash these?"

"I doubt it. This one was his lucky hat," Paula said, looking in the mirror to position the green hat just right, her blonde ponytail swishing through the hole in the back.

Cassie held the other cap at arm's length. "So, this one was his backup?"

"Oh, I think that's Delbert's. See the little Texas Aggie tag inside?"

Cassie tossed the cap to the bed. "No way am I wearing an Aggie hat. I'll go bareheaded before I put that on."

"Oh, you big ninny. Here, you wear Cal's hat and I'll wear Delbert's."

Cassie nodded. "Okay, deal." They exchanged hats and Cassie helped herself to a maple chocolate donut.

Paula headed toward the door. "You ready to go? I packed us a cooler. I figure we'll probably be ready to come in by lunchtime, but in case we don't there are sandwiches in there."

"Sounds good. Let's get this party started."

They retraced their steps from last night and found Martha manning the office desk.

"Good morning," Martha said. "I was worried about you, young lady."

Paula felt herself blush. "I appreciate that, but honestly, I just needed to sleep off my wine. I feel really awful about fainting in your reception area."

Martha rolled her eyes and waved her hand. "Honey, trust me, we've had all sorts of interesting things happen here. Your fainting spell was pretty innocent."

Cassie jabbed Paula in the ribs and Paula said, "Oh?"

Martha chuckled. "My granddaughter, McKenzie, accidentally booked a convention of people who like to dress up like animals and frolic in the great outdoors."

Cassie cut her eyes to Paula. "Accidentally?"

"Well, she read a letter from the group's president and thought it was The American Funnies Association. She thought she was booking a clown convention. Turns out, it was the American Furries Association."

Cassie snorted as she giggled. "Oh my!"

"Yes, that was an interesting group. Nice people, but they wore beaver and rabbit and bear outfits while running around all over the place. I think they might have had a bit of an orgy, but that's not for me to judge."

Paula shuddered, "Thank goodness all I did was faint!"

"See! Perfectly harmless! So, what can I do for you ladies?"

"Last night we asked about renting some fishing gear. Your granddaughter thought you had some laying around," Cassie said.

"We do, but you don't have to rent it. Let me get the key and I'll take you all out to the shed. Hold on. Melinda," she called through the door behind the counter. "Can you come watch the front? I'm going to take these ladies to get some gear."

Paula steeled herself to see Melinda again, and managed a smile when the woman appeared from the back.

Melinda smiled when she saw Paula and Cassie. "I was worried about you! Patricia, right? And, is it Cassie? But look here, you're already up and dressed for fishing!"

Cassie snorted, "We aren't exactly experienced in the art of dressing to catch fish. We scavenged this gear from our um, menfolk's rejects."

"Well, the fish don't seem to mind how you dress. And we do have a fine lake here. It's been named the top bass fishing lake, two years running."

"We couldn't help but notice that you don't have many fishermen staying here," Paula said.

"Well, we've had a rough go of it. It seems folks around here haven't been crazy about a fishing lodge run by three Yankee women. We've had to get really creative to attract groups that might not have considered staying in such an out of the way place, but this weekend we have a convention of jugglers coming in."

"Honest? I always wanted to learn to juggle," Cassie said. "Do you think they'll mind if we hang around and watch?"

"I couldn't say, but who knows? McKenzie said that in her text messages from the group's president they seem like a nice bunch of folks. They should start arriving soon, so when you ladies get back from fishing maybe you'll get to meet some of them."

"That should be a hoot and a half," Cassie said with a grin.

Martha dangled a set of keys in front of Melinda and said, "I'll be right back. Let's go get you two set up."

When they'd left the office, Paula asked, "So you're Melinda's mom?"

"Yes, I am. I'm very proud of that girl. She's raised McKenzie all on her own. Didn't have to, but that's all in the past."

"So, it's just the three of you ladies?"

"If you're asking where the menfolk are, there aren't any. My husband died a couple of years ago. We were blessed to have another daughter, Marie, Melinda's twin sister, but she passed away when McKenzie was a baby."

Paula felt a pang in her heart. "Oh, I'm so sorry. I've never had children, but I can't imagine losing a child."

"It was definitely hard. It's something you never really get over."

Cassie cleared her throat. "Did I hear you say last night that your last name's Arnett?"

"Me? Oh, no. My last name's Murray. Melinda married a man named Arnett. Well, here we are."

Paula felt her face go white and Cassie laid a calming hand on her arm. They exchanged glances as Martha fumbled with her key ring until she found the key she was looking for.

"Here it is," Martha said. "As you can see here, we have everything you might need from water skis and life preservers to rods and reels. You two going to fish from the shore, or do you want to borrow a boat?"

Cassie stepped forward. "I think we'll stay on shore. We get into enough trouble on dry land. There's no need to venture out into the water."

"Well, the best fishing is done out on the lake, so if you change your mind, we'll hook you up with our little dinghy."

Paula nodded and her voice caught in her throat as she said, "Thank you."

After Martha left for the office, Paula smacked Cassie's arm with the back of her hand. "So, Melinda *was* married to an Arnett! The question is *when* was she married to him, and is it *my* Arnett?"

"That's two questions, and the answer to both is we don't know."

Paula hoisted the cooler up on her shoulder. "Which way do we go?"

Cassie bundled the gear and pointed at an arrow-shaped sign. "This says *Lake*. Um, looks like it's that way."

The gravel path led them on a winding trek through the resort part of the property, with ample hookups for modern campers as well as spaces for rustic campsites. Each space contained its own picnic table and barbecue grill, and a communal space in the middle featured a large concrete slab.

Paula's eyes took in every detail. "This is lovely back here. And it's an older part of the place, but it's well maintained. Maybe the bulk of the guests use this part of the facility. The restrooms look brand new."

Cassie cracked open a door. "They do, at that. Let's peek inside." They ventured into the women's restroom and Cassie said, "Wow, these are really nice. Someone put some thought into the shower design. There are even lockers and hair dryers."

"Maybe the 3M's ran out of money before they got around to trimming trees and modernizing the motor inn part." Paula held the door open for Cassie then they started back down the path.

"Yeah, maybe. Or maybe it just got away from them. Things grow faster in this part of the state than they do in the panhandle, you know."

As they neared the clearing, Paula said, "I don't know why but I really like them. The 3M's, I mean."

"I know. I do, too. I don't want to, but I do. There's certainly nothing sinister about them. Of course, we don't know much. Even serial killers can come off as charming."

Paula raised an eyebrow. "Serial killers? Really?"

"Hey, I watch 'Criminal Minds.'"

The clearing opened up to reveal a number of picnic tables scattered at varying distances from the water.

Paula set the cooler on the closest table. "Is this spot okay? I've got the bait here in the cooler."

"With our drinks and sandwiches? Eww!"

"Oh, it's fine. The bait's in one sealed bag and the sandwiches are in another."

"Just don't get them mixed up! I'd hate to munch on worms instead of ham and cheese.

Paula chuckled. "Surely you'd notice the smell before you took a bite."

"Maybe, but I'm not willing to take that chance."

They spent some time figuring out the workings of the fishing rods. Cassie said, "I've fished a couple of times before. I think we can do it. I just hope the poor little worms didn't die of frostbite in there."

"They weren't in there that long, but if they're a little lethargic, it might cut down on the chance I actually catch anything.

"Why go fishing if you don't want to catch any fish?"

"It's just part of our cover. Plus, if we catch a fish, we have to clean it. I always made Cal clean his own fish. Nasty things."

Cassie laughed, "You're a mess. We'll just throw them back. Catch and release."

"Oh, well, I still don't want to touch one."

"Chances are we won't have to after you've put the worms in cryogenic storage."

Paula hesitated to reach in the bag and touch a worm. "I... I can't do it. Will you please bait mine?" She watched Cassie handle the worm with ease then cast her line and examined the rod assembly. "Are we supposed to reel these in?"

"No, we aren't fly fishing. Just wait until you feel a nibble, or something."

Paula wiggled her pole back and forth. "Okay, so, back to the 3M's..."

Cassie cast her line. "Yeah. So, Melinda raised McKenzie by herself. She got pregnant young. Somehow, I don't think Cal, if Cal was her husband, is McKenzie's dad. I mean, if he recently came back into their lives don't you think Martha would've said that differently?"

"Maybe. Unless Melinda didn't tell her mother that Cal was involved. So, what's the connection? Maybe Cal met Melinda when he was a student at the University of Illinois."

"Maybe. She's about the right age. Or maybe they met after he graduated, but before he started giving seminars..."

They fished in silence for a while before Paula said, "This is so beautiful out here. Birds singing. I saw a flash of a cardinal over there, and the little minnows sparkling in the sun. I believe this is the most peace I've felt since Cal's accident. I feel close to him here. Fishing was something he loved so much. I don't exactly get that part of it, but for some reason, I love being right here."

"It is a little like I imagine heaven might be. Only with mosquitos. You did pack repellant, right?" Cassie slapped her thigh.

"Yep, in that bag strapped to the cooler.

Cassie sprayed Paula down then spritzed herself. "There!"

Paula's line jumped and she flinched. "Eeeeeeeee! I think I've got something!"

"Bring it in. Slowly, I think. Or you'll lose him."

"Oh, OH! It's trying to get away! Maybe I want to lose him."

"Well, of course it's trying to get away. It doesn't want to have a hook stuck in its mouth. He's going to fight."

Paula pulled the fish out of the water then felt a pang of guilt as it struggled at the end of her rod. She grimaced. "Help! He's heavy. How do I get him over here?"

"Maybe one of us has to go out in the water and get him."

Paula bit her lip. "Maybe that should be you."

Cassie shook her head. "Your trip, your fish."

"I'm just going to swing the whole thing around. Watch out."

Cassie ducked as Paula's fish went flying over her head. "Be careful where you aim that thing! Let's go get it off the hook and throw it back fast."

"Eww! I don't want to touch him."

"Me either, but one of us has to. And again, he's your fish."

"Damn. Okay." Paula crouched down to where the fish was flopping. "Poor little guy."

"Did you bring Cal's tackle box? Maybe there's something in there we can use."

"Crap. Yes, but it's in the car. Would you run and get it?"

"On my way. Give me your keys."

Paula tossed Cassie the keys while holding the fishing line at arm's length. "Maybe I should put you back into the water while we wait." Paula grabbed the line well above the fish's mouth and maneuvered him back to the lake. *At least he can stay hydrated until Cassie gets back.*

Moments later, Cassie returned. "Look, I found someone to help."

A tall, fit looking man followed behind Cassie with an armful of fishing gear. "What do we have here?" he asked.

Paula looked at her trophy and winced. "I've hooked this poor fish, and I have no idea how to unhook him."

Taking a pair of pliers from his tackle box, the man plucked the fish from the water, and in a couple of deft moves, freed him.

Paula smiled into the man's sparkling hazel eyes. "Thank you, so much."

"No problem. I'm glad to have helped. First time?"

"What? Oh, yes. I've never really fished before, but my husband was a fisherman."

"Was?"

"He, uh… he passed away recently. I guess I'm trying to understand why he enjoyed it so much."

"Oh. I'm so sorry for your loss." He extended his hand to both ladies in turn. "My name's Mark Fields. I'm a doctor in Nacogdoches. The ladies at Happy Valley let me fish here any time I have a free spot in my schedule."

A blush rose to Paula's cheeks. "Oh, that's nice of them."

"Really nice," Cassie said.

"It's kind of a business arrangement. But there's no better spot on the lake."

Cassie cleared her throat, "So, what kind of doctor are you?"

"I work in oncology."

Paula bit her lip. "Oh, that must be hard. I lost my mom to pancreatic cancer."

"I hate pancreatic cancer. Just hate it. My job is sometimes difficult, but it's often rewarding, too. We're getting better at the fight, even winning a lot of battles that we would've lost a few years back."

"Paula," Cassie interrupted. "Have we finished fishing today?"

"Oh, yeah. Definitely. I'm finished forever. Thank you, Dr. Fields, for your help. We'll clear out and let you get to your fishing."

"Oh, call me Mark, and no problem. I seldom see any fishermen out here, and never any as pretty as you two ladies."

Paula blushed and Cassie harrumphed as they gathered their cooler and rods. "Hey, um, Mark, we have a whole bunch of bait left. I'll leave that for you," Paula said.

Cassie smirked. "Of course, they're half dead from being in the cooler."

Mark laughed. "Thanks. You two be careful."

After they'd wound their way back along the path from the campground, Paula said, "Where'd you find the hunk?"

"Hunk? Him?"

"You know how to pick 'em, is all I'm saying."

Cassie shrugged her shoulders. "If you say so. He was convenient, and that's all that mattered to me."

CHAPTER SEVENTEEN

Paula and Cassie made it back to their room and leaned their fishing equipment against the outer wall before unlocking the door. A welcome blast of cool air greeted them. Cassie made a beeline to the fridge and grabbed two bottles of water, tossing one to Paula as she sat. "For no longer than we were out there, I sure am exhausted!" she said before taking a long swig.

Paula opened her bottle and giggled. "Well, fishing is hard work. At least it is the way we do it."

Cassie lay across her bed and propped herself on one elbow. "So, did you catch that Dr. Fields is an oncologist?"

Paula plumped up her pillows and leaned against them. "Yes, and, he has a business arrangement with the 3M's."

"Melinda does look like she's been ill. Maybe he's her doctor."

"Could be. That short, short hair is a tell-tale sign. And, she is awfully thin, poor thing."

"Is that another way of saying 'Bless her heart?'" Cassie laughed. "Come on. Let's clean up a bit and go into Happy Vale for some lunch. Look around town a little."

"Sure, then when we get back maybe the jugglers will be here. Oh, let's not forget to take our fishing gear back to the shed."

A few minutes later, the girls headed to the office, fishing gear in hand. Martha met them at the desk. "Hello again, ladies. You two are back early. Any luck?"

"I might not be cut out for fishing," Paula admitted. "Too tender hearted."

Martha chuckled. "If I'm being honest, I don't care much for it either."

Cassie's jaw dropped open. "But you run a fishing resort! That seems like an odd choice."

"My husband was a fisherman, and his brother was from down here. When he died last year, he left this place to us. Well, actually to Melinda. We were going through some rough times back in Indiana, and this seemed like the perfect place to start over."

"And has it been?" Paula asked, leaning against the counter.

"It's certainly been an adventure. Like I told you this morning, the townsfolk haven't exactly been welcoming. And my brother-in-law must've burned a lot of bridges. He was kind of radical in his politics. He even tried to declare this resort a sovereign state so he wouldn't have to pay his taxes."

Paula gulped. "Oh no! So, you were stuck with big tax penalties."

"The I.R.S. has been pretty understanding so far, anyway. I think we found an agent who was more interested in helping us bring things up to date than in penalizing us for what James – that was his name, James Murray – screwed up. But it's a beautiful place, and my daughter has felt so much better here. She's been really sick, you know."

Paula frowned. "Oh? I had no idea. I'm so sorry."

Cassie nodded. "So am I."

Paula stepped toward the door. "If you'd like we can put the fishing equipment back in the shed."

"No, just leave it outside the office, and I'll have McKenzie put it away when she gets back from town. She's out buying ice to supplement what's in our machines and getting provisions for us for the weekend. Once the group of jugglers checks in, we'll be busier than a trio of one-armed paper hangers.'

Paula laughed. "If I can be of help let me know. Speaking just for myself, I'm not doing any more fishing, and we're here for several more days. So, feel free to put me to work if you need some extra help."

Cassie narrowed her eyes at Paula. "Right. We could at least run into town for you if there's something you need."

"That's so kind. We might just take you up on that. I'll let you know. Well, if you'll excuse me, ladies, I've got a living room to straighten up."

The women left the office and Cassie said, "Are you sure you want to help these women? One of whom might have been Cal's secret wife?"

Paula stopped in her tracks. "I... Yes. I'm sure. For one thing, as we both keep forgetting, this is *my* property. I want it to succeed. And, look how much we've already learned. Melinda's been sick. That could be why she wrote Cal the note. Maybe they needed money and she didn't have anyone else she could turn to."

"But why wouldn't he have told you unless there's something unseemly or illegal going on?" Cassie kicked a couple of rocks and watched them clatter down the lane.

"Cal said they need me. And that's what I'm going to focus on.'

"Dream Cal said that. Real Cal never said such a thing."

Paula pursed her lips and shoved her hands in her pockets. "Are you with me or not? You can head home right now if you're not willing to help, and I promise I won't be angry. But this is just something I feel like I need to do..."

"I just don't want you to get hurt. I'm not leaving you. And if you say that was Cal, then I'll try to believe it really was."

"Thanks. I know it's hard to believe, but I swear it was him."

Cassie blew air out of her puffed cheeks. "Hey, look. A camper's pulling in. Maybe they're with the juggling group." They watched as a red Dodge pickup with Oklahoma plates towing a fifth wheel trailer made its way up the path toward the office.

Paula squinted. "What's that driver's door say? N.J.O.A. Talent on Display."

"Mmm hmm. I wonder what N.J.O.A. stands for."

"Yeah, I have no idea."

"About lunch...maybe we should just stay here and eat the sandwiches you packed for our fishing trip."

Paula nodded. "Ooh, good idea. We can keep an eye on the action that way. I'll go get the sandwiches and we can have lunch on one of the picnic tables. You want water?"

"Hey, we're on vacation, make it a Shiner Bock."

"Right. Two Shiner Bocks coming right up."

Paula ran to the room and returned to find Cassie brushing dirt off a picnic table under a sprawling oak tree near the office. It wasn't yet noon, but it was hot, even in the shade. The humid air was almost a visible entity between the table and her view of the resort. Paula set the food, a roll of paper towels, the beer, and a couple of water bottles on the table. "I brought water, too. We need to stay hydrated."

Cassie opened a Shiner Bock bottle. "I plan on hydrating with beer."

"Any more cars yet?"

"Nope, but I waved at the man from the red Dodge before he went into the office."

Moments later, a small teardrop shaped camper pulled by a four-wheel drive pickup truck rolled up to the office. A magnetic sign featuring a picture of a juggling court jester wearing a red and white striped hat with bells dangling at intervals around the bottom hung on the side of the door. Paula raised an eyebrow. "Huh. There's something off about that picture of the jester." She wiped off the table with a paper towel then passed a sandwich to Cassie. "Here, let's spread some of these paper towels out. It's not a tablecloth, but it'll keep our food from interacting with whatever germs have accumulated here."

"Everyone knows germs don't live on picnic tables," Cassie said with a wink. She twisted the top off Paula's beer and raised her own in salute to her friend. "To dreams and jugglers, hotels and fish."

Paula chuckled and touched her bottle to Cassie's. "Indeed."

"Oh, that beer is good. Do we have any chips?"

"Drat! I left them in the room."

"I'll get them," Cassie said as she stood. Without waiting for a reply, she jogged to the room.

Paula watched as Melinda came out of the office, deep in conversation with the driver of the Dodge pickup. *She sure is a personable lady. As much as I want to paint her as a hussy, I just don't see her in that light.* She took a swig of beer. "Cal is that what you wanted me to know?" she said under her breath. She kept her eyes on Melinda and the juggler. *He's got to at least be in his late sixties, and he's not bad looking, but Melinda isn't the least bit flirtatious. I wonder if that's because she's still hung up on Cal?*

Melinda laughed at something the man said and gestured toward the campground. As she headed back to the office, she spotted Paula and made her way out to the picnic table. "Hey. I heard you decided fishing isn't your thing," she said with a grin.

A blush crept up Paula's neck. "Yeah, I made the mistake of catching one. And I was afraid it was going to breathe its last breath before we could get it back in the water."

"But you did it, right?"

"With a little help from Dr. Fields. Cassie snagged him on his way to the lake." Paula watched for a hint of reaction.

"Who? Mark? He's just the best. May I sit?"

"Certainly. You want a beer or some water?" Paula asked, scooting down the bench.

"I'd love a beer; although, I'd better have the water. I am working, but I might need that beer later."

"We'll save you one, then."

Cassie returned with chips and another couple of beers. "Hey, girls, what'd I miss?" She sat beside Melinda.

"I was just telling Melinda how Dr. Fields saved the day," Paula said.

Cassie laughed. "Yes, he knew just how to rescue our poor little floppy friend"

"I could teach you two how to do all that, if you'd like," Melinda said. "You'd be fishing like pros in no time."

Paula and Cassie exchanged glances. "So, how'd you learn to fish?" Cassie asked. "Martha said she doesn't enjoy it. I guess I figured you didn't either."

Melinda brushed an ant from the tabletop. "Mom never came down here much, but Daddy did when he had a rare vacation. In the summers they'd ship me and my sister, Marie, down to stay for a month with my Uncle James and Aunt Chloe. That was before he declared it The Sovereign State of Happy Valley Motor Inn and Resort. He went off the deep end when Aunt Chloe, died. Blamed everyone and everything. He decided the government, or as he said, *guv'mint,* was hiding a cure for her disease so they could make money off the suffering of people like her."

Paula's eyes grew large. "Oh, that's just awful."

"It was, and his reaction drove everyone away." Melinda looked out over the property, and a tender smile played on her lips. "But I remember the good times when we'd come visit. He taught me everything he knew about fishing this lake. I remember him being a normal, fun uncle, and Aunt Chloe was the best."

Cassie asked, "How did your aunt die?"

"Cancer. And Uncle James wouldn't let anyone come help." She took a deep breath and smiled, "Gosh, I didn't mean to bring us all down. There's something about you ladies that makes me want to talk. I don't have many friends here. If it weren't for Mom and McKenzie and Mark, I'd be totally friendless. I'm really glad you two are here."

"Us, too," Paula said, surprised to realize she genuinely meant it. "We needed a change of scenery, and even if we stink at fishing, I'm glad we came."

"Me, too," Cassie said, opening a second beer.

Another car drove through the gate, and Melinda stood. "Okay, I guess my respite is over. I've got a feeling it's going to get really busy for the next few hours. Mom told me you two might be willing to help out. Still interested?"

"Sure!" Paula said. "I mean, I am."

Cassie eyed Paula then said, "Sure, why not?"

"Well, I have something fun for you to do. The guy I was just talking to, Zeke Fitzgerald, is the president of the N.J.O.A., and he needs some impartial judges for the juggling contest they've got scheduled tonight. I suggested they hold it back in the campground area at seven. What do you say?"

Cassie raised an eyebrow. "Um, sure, but we don't know anything about juggling."

Melinda smiled. "I don't think it's a big deal. He said he's got a sheet of criteria to watch for. There's no prize money involved. It's more of a bragging rights sort of competition according to Zeke—a way for the newer jugglers to show off what they've learned this year. What do you say?"

Cassie looked at Paula. "I'm game. Pau...tricia?"

Paula choked on her beer. "Excuse me. Oh, yes, count me in. What fun. And, Cassie, here's your opportunity to ask if they'll teach you to juggle."

Melinda's eyes sparkled. "Good. Zeke said they'll feed you, too. They're bringing stuff to barbecue back there, hamburgers, hot dogs, plenty of beer."

"Well, then that seals the deal," Paula said.

"Great. Well, I really better get back in to help Mom. I don't know what's taking McKenzie so long, I'll see you ladies at the campfire tonight."

As soon as Melinda was out of hearing range, Paula said, "That's quite a story. You notice she didn't mention that Cal had taught her to fish. That was my biggest fear. I'd probably have fainted again."

"That doesn't rule out her having fished with Cal, though. That might've been what lured him to her."

"Lured? Really? This is my deceased husband we're talking about, and you're making fishing puns?"

"Sorry. It's just... So, where did they meet? How long was Cal married to her? Was your marriage to him even legal?

The color drained from Paula's face. "Oh, Lord! I didn't even think about that! If he was already married to her when I married him, then *I'm* the illegitimate wife! That makes *me* the hussy!"

"I think you have to do it knowingly to be a hussy," Cassie said, patting Paula's hand. "You don't have a hussified bone in your body. You're the anti-hussy. You're the epitome of unhussiness. You're--"

"I get it. I'm boring. But at least I'm not a hussy."

"Well, there is that."

Paula offered a strained smile. "Maybe I should've learned to fish. Maybe I should've been more adventurous."

"Hush! I've said it before, and I'll say it as many times as necessary until you listen. Cal loved you just as you are. He loved your sweetness and your positivity. He loved that you were an awful cook and that you had two left feet everywhere except on the dance floor. He loved how much you loved him."

Paula sniffled and her smile warmed. "You really are my bestest friend forever, Cassie Campbell."

"Ditto, Paula Jean Purdy Arnett."

CHAPTER EIGHTEEN

As the afternoon wore on, Paula and Cassie enjoyed their ringside seat to the colorful influx of jugglers pulling up to the office of the Happy Valley Motor Inn and Resort. While many of the cars and pickup trucks had campers in tow, some folks began filling up vacant rooms. Outside the office, people clustered in groups, exchanging handshakes and hugs while awaiting their turn to register. Paula and Cassie watched with amused smiles plastered on their faces as they drank more beer than they'd intended.

Paula nudged Cassie and pointed as Martha emerged from the office, wringing her hands, a look of worry on her face. Martha spotted Paula and Cassie then made a beeline to their perch at their picnic table and said, "I hate to ask a favor of you ladies, but McKenzie has yet to return from town, and we're getting a bit nervous. Melinda and I are stuck here, but would you two mind going into town to find her?"

Paula winced as she eyed three empty beer bottles on the table in front of her and the four in front of Cassie. "Oh, Martha, I… I'm afraid we've both gone over the legal limit to drive."

Martha's shoulders slumped. "I don't know what's gotten into that girl. We sent her off with one task, to bring back ice, and two hours later, she's missing in action, and she's not answering her cellphone. Of course, the cell service out here is awful, but still."

Cassie lifted her index finger. "Hey, what about Dr. Fields? We could go fetch him in from the lake and send him to find her."

"Oh! Great idea. You two don't mind?"

"Not at all," Paula said. "You go on back and help Melinda. We'll go find the doctor."

As Martha headed back to the office, Cassie gathered up their empty bottles and dropped them into a recycling bin on the path to the lake. "Shall we?" she asked, extending an elbow.

"Lead the way, friend," Paula said, linking her arm through Cassie's.

They wound their way through the campground and snaked the sinuous path to the lush green bank of Lake Toledo Bend. The heat hung over the water like a blanket and soon both women were perspiring like a pair of overworked pipefitters.

Cassie shaded her eyes with her hand as she peered out over the lake. "I hope he didn't venture too far from our fishing spot."

"Hey, is that him over there?" Paula asked, pointing at a lone man fishing about fifty yards from shore.

"Looks like it. How are we going to get his attention?"

Paula jumped up and down and waved her arms over her head. "Hey! Doc! Over here!"

Cassie rolled her eyes. "Totally ineffective."

"You have a better idea?"

Cassie picked up a good-sized rock, drew back, and launched it at the small boat. The women watched in horror as the rock narrowly missed Dr. Fields. He jerked as the rock flew in front of his nose, and in doing so, stood, overbalanced, and fell into the lake with a resounding splash.

Paula's hands flew to her mouth. "Oh no! You've gone and drowned the doctor!"

They watched helplessly as Mark sputtered to the surface and tried unsuccessfully to climb back into the boat.

"Damn, how do we help him?" Cassie asked.

"Look! There's a boat over there. C'mon."

They scrambled over to a small wooden rowboat resting upside down in the weeds on the shore, and with only a little difficulty, flipped it over to find a fat black snake beneath the hull.

"Holy crap!" Paula's voice could be heard across the lake as she ran backward.

"Sonofabitch!" Cassie followed Paula without hesitation.

The snake slithered into the lake unperturbed.

Paula held out her trembling hands. "Dammit, I think I'm having a heart attack! Look at me; I'm shaking like a leaf."

Cassie bent over and panted. "I hate snakes. Especially black, sneaky, hidden snakes."

As they caught their breath, Paula said, "I don't want to touch the boat now."

"But the doc!"

"Right, let's go."

They brushed debris out of the boat and eased its nose into the lake. Cassie positioned herself at the stern. "You get in. I'll push you to get started and jump in behind you."

"Okay." Paula climbed into the boat and positioned herself on a plank in the bow.

"Ready?" Cassie stepped forward.

"Ready."

With a hefty shove Cassie pushed the boat into the lake. Her attempt to jump into the boat fell short, and she barely caught herself before falling face first into the lake. "Crap! Sorry! You're on your own."

Paula gasped. "Wait! I don't have a paddle!"

"Here!" Cassie scrambled into the weeds and salvaged an old oar, then tossed it underhand.

It landed in the water beside the boat where Paula was able to snag it. She used every ounce of her strength to paddle to where Dr. Fields was watching with a bemused expression as he reclined in his own boat.

As she arrived at his side, her face fell. "Oh, you didn't drown."

Mark laughed. "You sound disappointed. Are you two drunk?"

"Maybe a little, but, in our defense, there was a snake."

"What are you doing out here?"

"We were trying to get your attention."

"Well, you definitely succeeded. But why?"

"Somebody needs to drive into town to find McKenzie. Martha and Melinda are up to their necks in jugglers, and as you noted, Cassie and I are drunk."

"Jugglers? You mean like circus folk?"

"That's right. The National Jugglers of America are holding a meeting here this weekend, and they're all checking in. McKenzie went into town to get supplies, and that was over two hours ago, and apparently they expected her back by now."

"Got it. Well, I'll go in. I have to go change clothes, though." He wrung the tail of his wet shirt.

"Oh, yeah. Sorry about that. It could've been worse, though. Cassie might've hit you with that rock."

"It's my own fault. I know better than to stand in one of these boats. It's kind of sweet that you came out to rescue me, though. Of course, I'm not sure I'd have thought it was sweet if that rock had hit me."

Paula covered her face with her hands. "I'd have been here sooner, but there was a snake."

"Yes, you mentioned that. That explains the noise."

"We hate snakes."

"Gotcha. I'm not all that fond of them either. Let's get back to the bank, and I'll go find the kid. Can you manage to make it back?"

Paula cleared her throat. "Well, I'm not the one who fell in."

Mark laughed and began paddling to shore while Paula made a broad turn and followed him. By the time she'd grounded her boat, Mark had disappeared into the trees, and Paula was a sweaty mess. "Do you think he was mad at us?" she asked Cassie.

Cassie giggled. "No. He looked amused. Dripping wet, but amused. He said something about wild women."

"Ha! Well, at least we accomplished what we intended."

Cassie held up her hand for a high five. "Well done, friend. Well done. Although, I think you're going to need a second shower."

They turned the boat over and tossed the paddle underneath it before trekking back to the campground. Since they'd been gone, the campsites had started to fill with fifth wheel trailers, Airstreams, pop-up campers, and even a Class A motorhome. People everywhere were glad-handing one another, hugging, giggling, and attaching hoses to campsite hookups.

Cassie lowered her voice. "Looks like a fun group of people. Maybe there is money to be made here without relying on fishermen."

"Maybe, but there has to be a way to bring fishermen back to Happy Valley."

"Hey there, young ladies," a friendly voice said. "You two new to the N.J.O.A.?"

"Who? Us?" asked Cassie, giving the big red headed man the once over.

"Yep! I reckon I know every member of our little group, and I would remember two pretty young ladies such as yourselves."

Paula felt Cassie tensing up, and said, "No sir, we aren't here for the juggling. We're just spending a few days on the lake."

"Well, I'm Zeke Fitzgerald. I'm the president of this outfit. Say, you wouldn't be the ladies Miss Melinda said would help judge our competition tonight would you?"

Cassie pursed her lips and raised an eyebrow. "Only if you stop calling us *ladies*. I'm Cassie and this is Paul—um, er, Patricia."

Zeke waited a moment before belting out a hearty guffaw. He laughed so long Paula feared Cassie was going to slug him. "I see," he finally said, as tears ran down his reddened cheeks. "I admire your forthrightness. You'll be a great judge, little, um, Cassie."

Paula relaxed as Cassie smiled her prettiest smile and said, "Why, thank you. While we're talking about juggling and such, I don't suppose anybody would be interested in giving me lessons?"

Zeke eyed Cassie. "You want to learn to juggle, eh? Why, I reckon I can teach ya. Wait until after tonight's doin's and if you still want to learn, then we'll get it done."

"What time should we be there?" Paula asked.

Zeke scratched his head. "Well, did Miss Melinda tell you we'd be doin' a big cookout? I reckon we'll start the cookin' around six and then the competition can commence at 7:00 or so. Be sure and bring your mosquito repellant."

"Will do!" Cassie said with a salute. She and Paula continued back to their picnic table.

As they neared the table, Paula lowered her voice. "Look. It looks like McKenzie made it back, and she brought a friend." They smiled as they approached McKenzie, Dr. Fields, and a handsome young man with the prettiest head of auburn hair curling just above his ears.

McKenzie nodded at them and said, "If you folks'll excuse me, I'd better get in there and help Mom and Gram before they send more troops out to find me."

"Good idea, young lady," Mark said. He stepped between Paula and Cassie and nodded toward the young man. "It seems Miss McKenzie had some car trouble and Jeffries here came to her rescue. He boosted her car and then followed her back to make sure she made it okay."

"Jeffries?" Paula said. "You must be Delilah's son!"

Cassie shook the boy's hand. "We ate supper at your mom's place last night."

Jeffries smiled. "Yes ma'am. Delilah is my mom. Hope you enjoyed your meal."

"Oh, it was fantastic. We understand you're studying to be a chef," Cassie said. "That's what I wish I'd done at your age."

"You could still do it," he said, suddenly serious. "We have several O.T.A.s in our class."

Cassie and Paula simultaneously asked, "O.T.A.s?"

Jeffries nodded. "Yes ma'am, older than average."

Paula burst out laughing, until she felt Cassie bristle beside her.

Cassie's face grew dark. "Older than average? Well, that just pisses me off! How dare they!"

Dr. Fields cleared his throat. "So, I hear you two are going to assist me in judging the juggling competition this evening."

"You got roped in, too?" Paula asked.

"Well, I'm staying here for free. I felt like I owed Melinda a little something for my room."

Paula raised an eyebrow. "Free?"

"Well, sort of." Mark kicked a pebble and shrugged, shoving his hands into the pockets of his cargo pants.

Cassie and Paula exchanged a look, but before either could say anything, Jeffries said, "I guess I'd better get back to the café. I'll be the one in trouble if I don't get there in time to help prep for this evening."

Cassie nodded. "Nice to meet you, Jeffries. Please let your mom know we'll be back for another meal before we leave the area."

"I'll do that. Um, McKenzie invited me to come back out after we close tonight. Maybe I'll see you all then."

Paula swatted a mosquito on her shoulder. "Sounds good; we'll look forward to seeing you then."

As Jeffries headed back to his car, Paula said, "Now, that's a nice young man."

Cassie popped open another beer. *"And* he can cook. And apparently, he can fix cars."

"Plus, he was courteous enough to make sure McKenzie got back home," Mark said.

Paula grabbed Cassie's beer and took a swig. "Hmm. Kind of the whole package, I'd say."

Cassie nodded and opened another beer. "Yup."

Mark gave her a sidelong look. "You think McKenzie might be interested in him?"

Paula nodded. "Could be. If I were her age, I'd sure notice him. And I definitely noticed him noticing her." As she smiled, a sudden rush of exhilaration overtook her, making her feel lighter and happier than she had in days. Then it hit her why she'd been so down. *Cal's dead. He's gone and here I am playing matchmaker and forgetting about my poor dead husband! What kind of widow am I?* Her face blanched. "Would you all excuse me? I think I'm going to go rest for a bit."

Paula went straight to her room, closed the drapes, and laid down on the happy fish comforter. *How could I have laughed and giggled and felt happiness out there when just a few days ago I buried my best friend? We were supposed to be together forever. Damn.* She squeezed her eyes closed, sniffled, and dabbed her tears with the sheet. "Am I a horrible woman, Cal?

As she drifted into a sleepy haze, paralyzing her between consciousness and oblivion, Cal's voice said, "Goldilocks, you're human. I love you, and I want you to be happy. So, be happy."

CHAPTER NINETEEN

The sound of running water stirred Paula from her slumber. She lay on the bed as Cassie finished in the shower, smiling in wonder at Cal's undeniable message. As weird as it seemed, she was certain that Cal was with her, urging her along on this journey.

When Cassie emerged from the bathroom wrapped in a thick towel, Paula sat up, a huge smile plastered across her face.

Cassie raised an eyebrow. "Wow, someone must've had a great nap."

"Someone did. I can't describe it. I just feel happy. Actually, I feel *unreasonably* happy. Maybe I don't know what Cal was thinking when he bought this place, but whatever it was, I know now that he did the right thing."

Cassie sat on the edge of Paula's bed and ran a comb through her wet hair. "I'm beginning to think you're right. It's like we both landed in our happy place. Who knew it would include rescuing fish and juggler judging?"

"Oh! I almost forgot about the jugglers! What time is it?"

Cassie squirted lotion in her hand then rubbed it between her palms and onto her legs. "Time for you to get ready for dinner. If you're planning on looking judge-like, you'd best get up and get ready."

Paula rubbed her eyes. "Did I sleep away the whole afternoon?"

"You did. I was going to pour a cold glass of water on your head if you weren't awake when I finished showering."

"Damn. I guess the combination of fishing, beer, and happiness knocked me out."

"Hurry and get ready. I'm starving.

In record time, Paula showered, dressed in a khaki skirt and a red tank top, dried her hair, and applied a tinted moisturizer and a bit of mascara.

Cassie wolf whistled. "Wow, you look like you're sixteen again."

"Look who's talking. You honestly don't look a day over eighteen, plus, you're stunning."

"Yeah. And you've got a bridge to sell me, too, right?"

"Stop. I'm serious. You could easily be a model for a health and fitness magazine.

A rosy blush crept up Cassie's neck and face. "If only we had agents, right? Okay. I guess we'll be the best-looking juggler judges ever. Let's go."

Arm in arm the two left the room, pausing to lock up before heading to the campground. The sounds of merriment, along with mouthwatering aromas of meat on a grill, lured them into the thick of the festivities as they followed the already familiar winding path.

Surveying the smiling participants, Paula said, "These are the happiest damned campers I've ever seen."

Cassie snorted a giggle. "Without a doubt."

They found Zeke engaged in a lively discussion with a group of three people. "Ladies!" he said before wincing. "I mean, Cassie, Patricia, thanks so much for agreeing to be judges. Come get something to eat. You'll be judging from the table we've set up over there." He gestured to a rectangular folding table placed facing the concrete slab which had been transformed into an impromptu stage. "Dr. Fields is already there. Come to think of it, I doubt we've ever had an actual doctor serve as a judge."

Mark was busy munching on a hamburger, and the ladies waved at him as they found their place in the food line behind a portly red-headed man with a stout moustache. The man turned to face them. "Evenin' ladies. My name's Zed. Are you fillies here to juggle or to judge?"

Paula giggled. "Zed, I'm Paula and this is my friend Cassie. We're here to judge tonight."

Zed stood back and motioned for them to go ahead of them. "Good enough. I'll be sure to put my best foot forward as a contestant, then."

After filling their plates, Cassie and Paula joined Mark. "Evening, Doc. You look pretty satisfied with yourself," Cassie said.

Mark patted his stomach and leaned back in his chair. "I don't know if they can juggle, but they can sure build a burger."

Cassie picked up her burger. "Too bad that's not what we're judging. I know good cooking when I taste it. I'm not so sure I'll be able to spot good juggling."

"Here's the list of criteria," Mark said, sliding sheets of paper to each of them.

"Thanks," Paula said, taking a bite of her burger. "Oh my! I didn't realize how hungry I was. This is excellent."

"Did they give us pencils or anything to write with?" Cassie asked, as she studied the paper.

Mark frowned. "Um, I don't think so. Maybe I should run over to the office and get some pencils from Melinda."

"No, I'll go," Cassie said. She stood and hurried off with her burger in hand before anyone could object.

Mark's eyes followed Cassie until she was out of sight. "Wow. She seems to only have two speeds: fast and faster."

Paula chuckled. "Ah, you noticed. I don't think I've seen her sit still for more than a few minutes at a time since we met in kindergarten." As they worked on more of their meals in silence, they observed the warm-up antics of the excited jugglers.

Mark breathed a heavy sigh after eating his last bite. "Ugh, Maybe I shouldn't have eaten the whole burger. So, are you having a good time here at Happy Valley?"

"Yes, actually. Much better than I could have imagined."

"You said your husband passed away recently. Do you mind me asking what happened?"

Paula cast her eyes down. "Car accident. He was alive, and then suddenly he wasn't."

"Oh. I'm so sorry. When was this?"

Tears burned behind her eyes. "It... It was last Sunday. His funeral was Wednesday. Does that make me awful? Here I am, laughing and joking, about to judge a juggling contest. And I just buried my husband."

"Hey, I'm an oncologist. I see all sorts of reactions to grief. Yours seems fairly healthy. But however you handle his death, it's okay. There really aren't any rules."

He touched her hand and they shared a smile. By the time Cassie returned with the pens, Paula and Mark were chatting away like old friends.

"Y'all ready for this?" Cassie asked.

"You bet," Paula said, clasping her hands. "Bring on the jugglers."

As if on cue, Zeke Fitzgerald emerged onto the concrete stage from the door of an adjacent motor home. "Welcome, everyone! It's so good to see our like-minded friends from far and wide. I hope you've all settled into your rooms or campsites here at the Happy Valley Motor Inn and Resort. Isn't this just the prettiest place? Be sure and stop by the office sometime this weekend and let Miss Melinda know how much you appreciate their hospitality." He cleared his throat. "Now, as is our custom we kick off our gathering with a friendly competition. Let's welcome our guest judges!" He peeked at the note in his hand. "Folks, I give you Patricia, Mark, and Cassie who've all graciously agreed to help us out here tonight."

A boisterous round of applause followed as the judges waved to the crowd.

Mark furrowed his brow. "Patricia? I'm sorry, I thought your name was Paula."

Paula's cheeks burned with fire and she cut her eyes to Cassie. "Um, yeah. Patricia Paula. That's my name."

Mark raised an eyebrow then turned toward the stage as the string of lights overhead dimmed and a bright spotlight flipped on, lighting the makeshift stage.

Zeke stepped to the side of the stage. "And now, without further ado, I present to you the best of the Natural Jugglers of America! First up, the Amazing Anabella!"

Anabella emerged, wearing a bright blue boa, a pair of gold hoop earrings, and nothing else. Paula, Cassie, and Mark exchanged wide-eyed, open-mouthed looks. Mark smacked his own forehead. "Oh! *Natural* jugglers. I get it now." They watched in amazement as the generously endowed Anabella manipulated a trio of bowling pins with ease, in a dazzling display of juggling virtuosity.

Paula nudged Mark and pointed to their criteria sheets. He in turn nudged Cassie and the three found themselves more focused on the juggler's technique than on her bare flesh.

"What in hell?" Cassie whispered.

"The N in N.J.O.A. doesn't stand for National. It's for Natural. As in Naked," Mark said under his breath.

Paula and Cassie exchanged glances and Paula's hand flew to her mouth to keep from giggling out loud.

After the performance was well underway, Mark snorted then attempted to turn it into clearing his throat. "Hey, I'm a doctor. I see naked people all the time. None of them are juggling when I see them, but still."

Paula choked on her drink and her cheeks burned. "How about jiggling?"

"Well, occasionally we'll get a jiggler. But never a juggler."

Cassie gave them a stern look. "C'mon y'all. Anabella just completed two multiplexed throws in succession. Make sure you note that on the form."

Paula and Mark snickered as they dutifully circled the appropriate words on their lists of criteria.

After Anabella took her bows, Zeke took the stage again. "Let's give Anabella another round of applause! She has really upped her performance from last year. Not bad for someone who took up the sport just a few years ago, am I right?"

The crowd clapped and cheered, interspersing the roar of applause with cries of "Well done!" and "Way to go!"

Zeke said, "Next, we have one of our founding members, Mr. Tate Alexander." The crowd hooted as Zeke exited and a spry gentleman who looked to be in his 80's took the stage holding three bowling balls. He wore a pair of bright green novelty sunglasses, but other than that he was naked as a jaybird. And where Anabella had juggled wordlessly, Tate kept up a comedy routine that had nothing to do with juggling or balls.

A repetitive thought kept nagging Paula that she *should* be appalled, but there was nothing lewd about the performance. In fact, Tate was so skilled at tossing and catching the heavy bowling balls while making the crowd laugh that she almost forgot his costume was his birthday suit.

Next, Zeke introduced a tiny, middle-aged Asian man named Lee. Paula held her breath and bit the insides of her cheeks to keep herself from laughing at Mark, who had covered his face in an effort to smother his uncontrollable snickers as soon as strains of the "Sugar Plum Fairy" from Tchaikovsky's *Nutcracker Suite* began playing on the boombox beside the stage.

As the evening progressed, one juggler after another crossed the stage, including Zed who captured their attention by juggling a set of long knives while blindfolded. Paula and Cassie watched through gaps between their fingers after they covered their faces at his first big throw.

The parade of jugglers continued. Some were old, some relatively young, some White, some Black, a few Latino, approximately half were women. There were skinny jugglers, heavy jugglers, short and tall jugglers. The only common thread was that they all juggled proficiently in the nude. At the judges' table, Paula, Cassie, and Mark marked their score sheets, then at Zeke's request, conferred among themselves to select a winner while the jugglers and their audience took an intermission for refreshments.

"What the hell was that?" Paula asked.

"A whole bunch of *nekkid* people," Cassie said.

Mark chuckled. "Friends, I'm a doctor, and I've *never* seen that many naked people consecutively before."

Cassie shook her head and grinned as she perused her review form. "Well, let's pick a winner. Wait, how many places will we give? Maybe there's a ribbon for first, second, and third."

"Where are they going to pin a ribbon?" giggled Paula, sending Mark over the edge.

"Hey, judges," Zeke said, breaking into their conference. "So, what did you think?"

"We think you could've warned us that the jugglers would be N-A-K-E-D," Cassie hissed.

"It was an experience I'll never forget," Mark said.

"Ditto," Paula said. "But, once I recovered from the shock, I really enjoyed it."

"Honestly, I thought you folks knew what you were getting into," Zeke said. "After all, we are the Natural Jugglers of America."

Paula threw back her head and laughed. "Yes, but McKenzie booked your group as the *National* Jugglers of America."

Zeke scratched his head. "Well, that makes no sense at all."

"McKenzie strikes again," Mark said, shaking his head while telling Zeke about the Furries convention that McKenzie had booked as the Funnies, thinking they were clowns or comedians. "I swear that girl must be dyslexic."

Zeke let out a guffaw then squared his sights on Cassie. "So, how about you, Miss Cassie? Still want to learn our craft?"

Cassie tapped her index finger to her temple. "Maybe," she said with a laugh.

Zeke shook his head with a smile. "So, do you all have us a winner?"

Paula held her score sheet against her chest. "We're close, but how many places do you award?"

"Just the one for first place. We'll have a more formal competition at the national championship in January where we break things down more into categories and places."

Cassie cut her eyes to the other judges. "Formal? Like, do they wear top hats?"

"Or tails?" Mark said, sending all of them into a fit of laughter.

Zeke let out a loud belly laugh. "No, but we'll have judges who are jugglers themselves and there'll be a great deal of pomp and circumstance. Miss Cassie, if you start working hard, you could enter."

"Let me think on that," Cassie said, blinking her eyes. "Okay, thought about it. Nope. No way."

"No? Well, let me know if you change your mind."

Mark silently solicited a nod from the ladies then said, "Okay, Zeke, I think we're in agreement as to who won tonight's competition."

"Terrific, let me assemble the jugglers and we can make the announcement. One of y'all will need to bring me the envelope when I ask for it."

Paula and Mark simultaneously pointed at Cassie, who responded with a resounding. "Noooooo!"

In the end, Mark took the envelope up to Zeke, who called the attendees to attention. "Friends in juggling, it gives me great pleasure to announce that after a two-year absence, everyone's best friend, Zed has won the competition. Thanks to our judges for picking up on Zed's amazing talent even when two of them were watching with their eyes partly closed."

At everyone's applause, the judges smiled and waved, then Paula put on her most serious deadpan face and looked at Mark. "He told us he was going to put his best foot forward. I'm not sure I ever looked at his feet."

CHAPTER TWENTY

As the festivities came to a close, Paula, Cassie, and Mark bid the jugglers goodnight and made their way, single file, back to the motor inn with the help of a flashlight. Darkness enveloped them, and the trio recounted the highlights of the evening to the accompaniment of a chorus of frogs.

Cassie giggled. "Who's gonna tell the 3M's about the naked stuff?"

Paula chuckled. "Not me! That sounds like a job for a physician."

Mark shrugged and said, "I don't mind doing it as long as you two back me up. Otherwise, I'm afraid they'd think I was joking."

"Be sure and tell them that Cassie's considering a club membership," Paula said, ducking when Cassie took a half-hearted swing at her.

As they neared the communal restrooms, an out of breath and clearly distraught McKenzie came barreling down the path and into Mark's arms. "It's Mom!" she said, attempting to catch her breath. "Hurry!"

Mark took off running, with McKenzie on his heels. Paula and Cassie trailed in their wake. "What if she's dying?" Paula asked, grabbing Cassie's hand.

Cassie squeezed Paula's fingers. "Let's not think about that. We'll just pray she'll be okay."

Before they reached the end of the tree-lined path, an ambulance's strobe lights lit up the parking area, urging the ladies into the clearing where Martha hugged a sobbing McKenzie. The women watched helplessly as Mark climbed into the ambulance behind the stretcher where Melinda lay.

Paula rested her hand on Martha's shoulder. "What can we do to help?"

Martha squeezed her eyes closed and pinched the bridge of her nose. "I... I'm just so afraid. She needs us and we need to be here."

Paula's tone was so authoritative, she almost surprised herself. "Go. Cassie and I can hold down the fort here. Just give us your cell number in case we need to contact you. We can handle this."

Indecision mixed with fear and relief flickered across Martha's face. "You'd do that? But you don't even know us."

Cassie grabbed Martha's shoulders. "And you don't know us. But Pau...tricia's right. We can handle this, and you need to be with your daughter."

McKenzie wiped her eyes on her sleeve and pulled at Martha's hand. "Gram, let's go! Mom needs us there."

Martha nodded. "I can't believe I'm doing this, but I'm going to put my faith in two complete strangers. Come on, let me show you where the keys are. If anyone wants to check in, just tell them we're full.

Better yet, I'll turn the *No Vacancy* sign on. That'll discourage all but the most desperate travelers. McKenzie, go grab my purse and keys."

"Where will they take your daughter?" Paula asked as they stepped inside the office. McKenzie ducked behind the door leading to the living quarters while Martha led Paula and Cassie behind the tall oak counter.

"Mercy General in Nacogdoches. It's an hour from here, but it's where Dr. Fields– Mark– practices." Martha scribbled hers and McKenzie's cell numbers on a sticky note. "You shouldn't need anything, but please call me if you run into any problems." She flipped a toggle switch and the neon *No Vacancy* sign lit up the window.

Cassie grabbed Martha's hand. "We'll be fine. Y'all just go."

Martha stepped toward the front door then turned back. "Oh! McKenzie just changed the sheets on the beds in our apartments this morning. Go ahead and bunk in there just in case anyone needs something. Besides you two and Mark, the only other guests are those with the juggling group. I think that's everything. Just—"

"Just go," Paula said, placing a gentle hand on Martha's shoulder. I promise everything here will be fine, and we'll call you if anything comes up that we can't handle.

Martha turned back toward the door then spun around again and grabbed Paula embracing her. "Thank you. Thank you both. You're like answers to a prayer."

McKenzie emerged from the back with an overnight bag, a small backpack, and Martha's purse. "Thank you, guys. Gram, let's go!"

Cassie joined Paula at the door, and they watched the worried pair of M's climb into an old Subaru and drive out to the road to follow in the wake of the ambulance.

CHAPTER TWENTY-ONE

Alone inside the A-frame office, Paula closed the front door and leaned against it as Cassie sagged against the counter. "I feel so guilty," Paula said. "Martha and McKenzie think we're angels instead of the sneaky spies we are."

Cassie's eyes lit up. You know, we could use this time to go through some of the resort's records. Maybe figure out what we can about Melinda's relationship with Cal."

"You mean snoop through their personal documents? That'd take this whole spy business to another level. I don't think that'd be right."

"So, you'd rather keep on not knowing? Let's recap. Melinda's last name is Arnett. She's about Cal's age and her daughter would be about the right age to be Cal's child."

Paula sat down hard on one of the upholstered chairs. "You don't really think McKenzie is Cal's, do you? She doesn't look anything like him."

"Yeah, but maybe Cal's genes weren't dominant?"

"I can't even think about the possibility that McKenzie is Cal's. I mean, I couldn't give him a child. Maybe Melinda could." Paula's voice caught in her throat. "And I guess *that* could explain everything."

Cassie sighed. "Even if that's the case, McKenzie would've been born before you and Cal even met. She's what, twenty? Twenty-one? You and Cal only met sixteen years ago."

"Yeah. But surely, he'd have told me about having an ex-wife and a child. Unless..."

"Unless what?"

"Unless he didn't want me to feel any worse about not giving him a child than I already did. He knew how emotional I got when other women my age were having babies and I was having miscarriages," Paula said with a hitch in her voice.

Cassie gave Paula a loving squeeze on the shoulder then meandered behind the counter and opened a drawer where she began rifling through a stack of papers. "Well, if he did keep secrets, maybe some of the answers are right here. You deserve to know."

Paula rubbed her temples. "I don't know that I can pry into Melinda's stuff in such an underhanded way."

"You don't have to. That's why I'm here."

Paula rose to her full five feet and five inches, her eyes narrowed. "No! Stop that right now! I'm not going to do anything to betray their trust and neither are you."

"Dammit, Paula. Isn't this what we came here to do? Where's that steel I heard in your voice yesterday when you ordered Delbert and me out of your house?"

"I didn't know Melinda then. And I hadn't had the dream yet."

Cassie's hands curled into fists at her side. "That damned dream of yours! It was just your subconscious trying to make you feel better about this whole situation. Cal no more came to you in a dream than Elvis riding a camel did."

Paula shook her head in defiance. "You don't have to believe me, but it was real! And Cal said they needed me. I don't think he meant they needed me to intrude on their privacy."

Cassie scowled and shoved the stack of paper back in the drawer. "Fine! I'm going to our room! You can take the first shift over here!" She stormed to the door and jerked it open, stomping outside where she forcefully pulled the door shut behind her. It was obvious she'd meant for it to slam, but the door closed behind her as if in slow motion. She huffed as she hurried across the courtyard, not looking back.

Paula flopped back in the chair, covering her face with her hands. *Oh mercy! If I wasn't so damn angry, that would've been hilarious. How in the world did I get to this place? A week ago, my life was as happy as a fairy tale. Six days ago, I got the call about Cal's accident. Three days ago, I buried him. Only a couple of hours ago, I was laughing so hard judging a crazy juggling competition that anyone watching would think I was the happiest woman alive. And now, I've pissed off my oldest and dearest friend because I'm protecting the woman Cal could have been secretly married to while he was married to me. What is wrong with me?* She closed her eyes and massaged her throbbing temples.

Moments later, she caught herself starting to doze but jerked herself awake. She stood and stretched her arms over her head, realizing just how alone she was in the unfamiliar surroundings. "Doesn't matter. I know I did the right thing. Going through Melinda's stuff is just wrong, regardless of the circumstances."

She stepped behind the counter and thumbed through the register. *Wait? Am I doing the same thing as Cassie? No, because this is part of the resort, and I'm just looking out for Cal's investment. Besides, it's technically mine now, anyway... Hmm. I'd have thought they'd have kept guest records in a computer, but they don't seem to have one. Dang, look at this big gap between bookings. Cal's investment might need to be liquidated, but I have to get to the truth before I can even begin to contemplate that eventuality.*

The bell over the office door rang, startling her from her thoughts. Zeke stepped in with a huge grin plastered on his face. "Well, hello there, Ms. Patricia Paula. Where's Ms. Melinda?"

"She's not here right now. There was a bit of an emergency. I'm watching the front desk for her until she or her mother gets back."

"Oh. I hope everything's okay."

"So do I. Is there something I could try to help you with?"

"Yes, we wondered if we could get some extra towels down at the campground. As you might expect, juggling in the buff works up quite a sweat. Towels come in mighty handy.

Paula hooted, then covered her mouth with both hands. "Sorry. That's a pretty vivid picture you painted there. Let me go look. I haven't been past the desk, but I'm guessing there's a linen closet somewhere close by.

Paula stepped through the curtain behind the desk down a narrow hallway with doors on each side. She opened the one on the left and found an office storage room crowded with file cabinets and stacked banker boxes. *Thank goodness Cassie didn't know about this!* She moved across the hall and found the laundry room with an abundance of white towels stamped with the acronym HVMI&R in blue, folded in perfect alignment, filling an entire wall of shelves. Sheets and fish-themed bedspreads like the ones in her room were stacked as neat as a pin on the opposite wall. She smiled in approval at how clean the commercial-sized washer and dryer were kept, and how orderly the bottles of detergent, bleach, and fabric softener appeared, stacked on a supply shelf next to the dryer.

"How many towels do you think you'll need?" she called out to Zeke.

"Oh, a dozen should do."

She grabbed one of several white plastic laundry baskets stacked under the folding table and loaded it with towels and washcloths. She returned to the office and said, "Here you go. If you need more there are plenty here."

"I'll tell you what, I'll send one of our group up here with our used linens in the morning, seeing as how it looks like you might need a little help here, being all alone."

Paula frowned. "Shoot. I hadn't even thought about that. Thanks. I need to remember to get the rooms taken care of in the morning. Hopefully Martha or McKenzie will be back, but I'll take care of things if they aren't."

"You let me know if any of us can help. There's more to the N.J.O.A. than meets the eye, you know," he said with a twinkle in his eye.

In spite of herself, Paula laughed. "I'll remember that. Thank you, Zeke." She watched as he left and as Jeffries passed him on the porch with a respectful nod of the head on his way in. *Wow, this is a regular Grand Central Station.*

"Hey Jeffries," she said when the young man stepped in and closed the office door.

"Hi, um... Sorry, ma'am, I don't remember your name."

She smiled, "It's Paula. I'm a guest here. I don't think we were officially introduced, but I heard your name earlier."

"Right!" Jeffries said, his face brightening with recognition. "When I followed McKenzie back here... Uh, I don't guess I could see her, could I?"

"I'm sorry, but she's not here. Her mom had to go to the hospital in Nacogdoches and McKenzie and her grandmother went to be with her."

"Oh, man. Is she going to be alright?"

"I think so. At least I hope so. Anyway, my friend and I offered to watch the office for them while they're gone."

"Will you let me know when you hear from them?"

"Sure," she said, passing him a pen and a yellow sticky pad. "Jot down your number and I'll call you tomorrow when I hear something."

He scribbled his name and number. "You can just text me, unless its bad news. For that I'd appreciate a call. Okay?"

"Okay. I promise, except our texts don't always seem to go through. There's bad reception here, I guess."

"Maybe just call me, too, okay? Just in case?"

"No problem. And I'll tell McKenzie you were looking for her."
He nodded and attempted a smile, though his brow was still wrinkled with concern. "Thanks. G'night, ma'am."

As soon as he left, Paula dialed the room she was sharing with Cassie, her fingers trembling.

In the middle of the first ring, Cassie answered and said, "I'm so sorry. I know you're right. It'd be wrong to go through the 3M's records, especially while they're in the middle of a crisis. We'll just have to figure another way to go about this."

Tears formed in Paula's eyes. "It's okay. I have to admit it's tempting to go through their files, but I just can't do that. I, uh... I was thinking that as soon as we know Melinda's okay, maybe it's time we just asked what her relationship with Cal was."

"Let's just take things one step at a time and hope they can all come home tomorrow."

Paula exhaled, releasing more pent-up emotions than she realized she'd been holding onto. "Oh! Speaking of which, Zeke came up and got some towels, and it reminded me that we're going to need to take care of business here tomorrow—like housekeeping and stuff."

"Yeah, I was thinking about that, too. Do they have any staff?"

"I have no idea. I guess we'll find out soon enough. If not, are you up for cleaning rooms?"

Cassie laughed. "Well, I was up for judging naked jugglers, so this should be a breeze. What have we gotten ourselves into?"

Paula felt a smile curving her lips and infiltrating her entire being. "I have no idea, but I'm willing to take on anything that comes my way. Hey, could you bring my pajamas and toiletries over, and maybe a change of clothes? Oh, and my purse?"

"Sure, but can I stay, too? I don't want you to be by yourself."

"Of course. I was hoping you'd say that."

CHAPTER TWENTY-TWO

While waiting for Cassie, Paula explored the hotel's living quarters and noted that the personal space was more than twice the size of the office, file room, and laundry facilities combined. She admired the smart functionality of the layout as well as its rustic charm.

She took an immediate dislike to the stuffed wide-mouthed bass over the den's fireplace because, just like Cal's swordfish, it seemed to watch her every move. But otherwise, she was enchanted by the many paintings and photos of scenic spots along the lake. Her eyes danced over a floor to ceiling bookcase, and she made a mental note to select a book to read later.

She wandered back to the bedrooms, peeking into the first room, and holding her breath as she flipped on the overhead light. Paula grinned at the sight of posters adorning the walls. *This has to be McKenzie's room.* She gently closed the door and moved to the next room.

She hesitated on the threshold, fumbling for the light switch. On a full-size bed lay what appeared to be a homemade quilt. Its gorgeous riot of color drew all the attention in the small room. *How lovely! Martha's room? I'll have to ask what that pattern is.* An oversized upholstered chair filled with quilting squares sat in the corner next to a card table and sewing frame.

She backed out of the room and poked her head in the final bedroom then flipped on the light. The walls were decorated with botanical paintings, and when she inspected them more closely, the artist's initials, M.M.A., nearly smacked her in the face. "Melinda M. Arnett." She started to allow her mind to wander to a dark place, but something caught her eye and interrupted her thoughts. She stepped closer to the bedside table, and her breath caught in her throat at the sight of so many pill bottles. "Oh, my, it's like a pharmacy in here." She wiped a tear from her cheek when the bell over the office door jingled.

Cassie's voice grew near. "Hey, where are you?"

Paula sat on the corner of the bed. "Back here in Melinda's room. Come down the hallway, through the great room, and make a right."

A moment later, Cassie dropped Paula's purse on the dresser. "Wow. This is nice."

"Yeah, it's lovely. Look closer at the paintings. I think Melinda might've painted most of them. Check out the initials."

Cassie squinted as she inspected the art then backed away. "Maybe. But they might be McKenzie's."

"I doubt it. These look like the work of a mature artist."

Cassie sat beside her and, following a minute of silence, touched Paula's shoulder. "You know you're my very best friend in the whole world, right? I mean, you're more than a friend. You're the sister I always wished Court had been."

Paula laughed, "I know. And you're the only sister I ever had. Better than a sister, really, because sisters fight, and until this evening, we never did."

"Oh, that? It wasn't much of a fight. I mean, I did make a dramatic exit, but heck, I couldn't even get the door to slam. Plus, there was no screaming or hair pulling, so it hardly qualified as a fight."

"Thank goodness. I think you could totally beat the crap out of me in a real fight."

"Of course, I could."

Paula chuckled. "I hope you brought our box of wine."

"That's why I'm your best friend."

CHAPTER TWENTY-THREE

Paula located the glassware in the kitchen and poured two glasses of wine. She and Cassie settled down in the den.

"This is really a cozy place," Cassie said from her place on a floral sofa.

"These ladies know how to make a house feel like home."

"They do," Paula said, walking about the room to survey the photos and objects d' art. "I really think most of these paintings are Melinda's. And I think the framed quilt squares are definitely Martha's."

Cassie stood and examined a mounted quilt square. "This is gorgeous. I wonder if McKenzie has contributed anything artistically to the décor?"

"I'm thinking maybe the little pottery pieces. There are several of them in her room, but rustic. Like a beginner with talent might've created them."

Cassie returned to her seat and sipped her wine. "We're sure assuming a lot."

"Yeah, seems we've done our share of assuming the past couple of days." Paula slipped into the chair across from Cassie and yawned.

Cassie looked at her watch. "Wow, it's only eleven. Feels like ages since we left the naked jugglers."

"Ah, the days of our innocence."

The phone rang and both women jumped. Cassie pushed the button to answer the call on speaker and cleared her throat. "Good evening. Happy Valley Motor Inn and Resort. Cassie Campbell speaking. How may I help you?"

"Oh, Cassie, you sound so professional. This is Martha. I hope I didn't wake you."

"No, not at all. You sound more upbeat than you did when you left here. I hope that means you have good news."

"Yes. Melinda is doing well. She just got dehydrated running around trying to make sure everything around the resort was ship shape for the jugglers, and she got a bit of bad news that sent her for a loop. Mark has her on an IV to get her hydrated, and she should be able to go home in the morning."

"Oh, that's wonderful." Cassie gave Paula a thumbs up.

"Anyway, if you two don't mind staying in our rooms tonight, McKenzie and I are going to take turns staying in the hospital's family housing facility next door while the other one takes a shift with Melinda. Hopefully Mark will release her before noon, and we can be home fairly early tomorrow.

"Of course, we'll stay, and don't worry. Is there anything we need to take care of in the morning?"

"Our housekeeper will be there around eight to start cleaning rooms. Her name's Ellie and she knows just what to do. You can tell her everything. Oh, and I remembered that the resort area needs towels. Would you mind taking some out there?"

"Zeke came up a while ago and got some, so that's covered."

"I knew you two were angels. Proof that God answers prayers."

Cassie's eyes filled with tears. "We're hardly angels, but we'll help any way we can. Just take care of Melinda."

"One other thing, don't forget to lock up. There's a sign you can put out beside the office door. It's underneath the counter—second shelf. It directs folks to call the house number if they need anything after hours."

"Okay, we'll go do that right now. Get some rest if you can."

"Will do. Thanks again and goodnight."

Cassie disconnected the call and sniffled as she wiped her red-rimmed eyes. "Thanks for not letting me be an ass earlier."

Paula hugged Cassie and said, "You're welcome. Come on. Do you want to see the rest of the house?"

After a quick tour, Cassie stopped to explore her favorite room in any house, the kitchen, looking through the pantry and refrigerator to check supplies. "I'll make us breakfast in the morning, okay?"

"Definitely okay."

"Glad that's settled. Now, how about some more wine?"

Full glasses in hand, they retired to the den where Cassie returned to her place on the sofa and Paula snuggled up in an overstuffed chair. Paula took a sip and asked, "Do you think the bad news Melinda heard has to do with Cal?"

Cassie kicked off her shoes and gathered her feet under her bottom. "Maybe. I wonder how she might've learned about his death, though. Would Delbert have called her?"

"Delbert! I forgot to call Delbert and let him know what we're up to. I kept meaning to, but my cellphone isn't working out here. Shoot. It's too late to call him tonight. It'd scare the crap out of him."

"Well, he's full of the stuff, so maybe it'd do him some good."

"Ha ha," Paula said with a straight face. "Just remind me to call him first thing in the morning. I'll ask if he contacted Melinda."

"And, if he did? How do we handle that? Does it make our job easier or tougher?

Paula ran her fingers through her hair. "Don't make me think about that tonight. I'll never sleep. Let's just take one step at a time. If she knows, we'll find out soon enough."

"Okay. No more speculating tonight. Are you ready to turn in yet? I'm exhausted."

"Me, too. My eyes are featuring alternating visions of naked jugglers and strobing ambulance lights. Oh! I promised I'd text Jeffries if there was good news about Melinda. He stopped by after work to see McKenzie"

"Ooooh. He just keeps looking more and more like a good guy, right?"

Paula chuckled. "He certainly seems like one." She composed a text then called and left a quick voicemail for Jeffries. "Okay, that's done. I'm thinking one of us should sleep in McKenzie's room and the other one in Martha's. Let's leave Melinda's quarters pristine so she can go right to bed tomorrow. I'll wash the sheets we sleep on, but they aren't as big a priority as Melinda's.

Cassie stood and yawned. "Good idea. I'll take Martha's if you don't mind. That quilt is calling to me."

"Perfect. I think there's just the one bathroom on that side of the house, though. Do you mind if I shower first?"

"I showered in our room while we were embroiled in our intense sisterly melee. Didn't you even notice that I don't smell like hamburgers, mosquito repellant, and sunscreen anymore?"

"Nope. You just smelled like my friend. Safe, loyal, and just a little like alcohol." Paula giggled as she hugged Cassie

"Ah, well, there's a new scent for a shampoo: *New Garnier Safe, Loyal, and Drunk.*

"They'd sell a million bottles in no time. Now, you go on to bed. I'll lock up and see you at breakfast in the morning."

CHAPTER TWENTY-FOUR

Paula slept through the night, disturbed by nothing more than sweet memories-turned-dreams of Cal. The one that most stuck with her when she woke was of the time they'd rented a canary yellow Mustang convertible and taken a road trip to Corpus Christie. She'd tied a lime green scarf around her hair and pretended she was a glamorous movie star from the fifties. As a result of that dream, she woke a few minutes after six, with a smile on her face and a feeling of peace. She pulled her robe on over her pajamas and headed to the kitchen in search of coffee.

She found Cassie bustling around in the sun-drenched kitchen. The unmistakable scent of bacon frying, along with the healing aroma of freshly brewed coffee and other tantalizing aromas, wafted through the living area putting an even bigger smile on Paula's face. "Oh, my goodness, Cassie, what have you created today?"

"It's a new thing I'm trying," Cassie said, waving a spatula over the cooktop grill. "I'm making French toast. I've dipped the bread into pancake batter before frying it. Lots of butter and cinnamon involved. Come forth, young woman, and try it."

After filling a cup with coffee, Paula sat at the counter and allowed Cassie to serve her a slice of French toast and two thick slices of bacon.

Paula added a generous pour of maple syrup before taking a bite. "Mmm, this is heavenly!" Her tastebuds danced in anticipation of the next scrumptious bite. *"This.* This is what life is all about."

"I know, right? The idea came to me in a dream last night."

"Ah ha! Now *you're* a believer in dreams."

"For sure. I think this stuff is a game changer. Maybe I'll open a café that specializes in breakfast and brunch. I'll create specialties like this, and people will drive from miles around just to experience my culinary excellence."

"Where, pray tell, will you build this fine establishment?"

"I don't know yet. Maybe wherever you are."

Paula froze, mid-bite, with her fork poised an inch from her mouth. "You keep talking like that and people are going to take you seriously. What makes you think I won't be in Dempsey?"

"Hmmm. Just a weird feeling I have. I think we've both outgrown Dempsey. What's there for you now that Cal is gone?"

"Well, you for one thing. And our friends. I mean there's Melvin and Sue Ann. Delbert and Sherry. The gals at church."

"But what if I wasn't there anymore? Would you stick around?" Paula's brow furrowed. "I don't want to think about a Dempsey without a Cassie in it. I refuse to think about it."

"Then hear me out. What if, after you reveal your ownership of the Happy Valley Resort and Motor Inn, we establish a dining facility here on the property. People would come here for brunch and stay to fish. And the folks who stayed here wouldn't have to go into town for a meal."

"You're assuming that I'd want to take on a managerial role here."
"Well, you do own the place."

"So Delbert says."

"Right. The only thing we don't know is why."

Paula bit her lip and set her fork on her plate. "You're right, but I can't just put the 3M's out on the street."

"You never know. Maybe they'd be relieved to be out from under this business. And Cal paid them a hefty amount for the place. Probably much more than it's worth, knowing Cal."

"Perhaps. I know I'm going to have to talk with Melinda, but I just don't want to do it while she's so vulnerable."

"Well, if she knows Cal's gone, if that's the bad news she got yesterday, I doubt anything else is going to shock her too much. Oh! Remember--you wanted to call Delbert."

Paula picked up her fork and swirled a square of French toast in syrup. "Right. Just let me finish this plateful of awesomeness. I don't want it to get cold."

Cassie served herself a piece of toast and the rest of the bacon. When she took a bite, her eyes rolled heavenward. "Wow! If I hadn't made this myself, I'd say it was the best food ever created on this or any other planet."

"Don't disqualify yourself from that vote. After all, you do have credentials as a judge now. It's definitely the best."

They both laughed until a knock on the office door made them jump. "Oh, I guess we'd better open up," Paula said.

Cassie stood. "You finish eating. I'll get it."

Not wanting to be left out, Paula shoved half a slice of bacon in her mouth and followed closely behind.

Cassie unlocked and opened the door. "Oh, hi. You must be Ellie, right?"

The woman standing on the porch hugged the teenage girl next to her to her side. "Yes. Who're you?"

Cassie stepped back to allow Ellie and the teenager into the office. "We're friends of Melinda's. She had to go to the hospital last night and McKenzie and Martha are there with her. We volunteered to look after the place for them."

"Oh, no! Is Miss Melinda alright?"

Cassie patted Ellie's shoulder. "Yes, she's going to be just fine. She should be home later today."

Ellie's lips quivered. "I just saw her yesterday. She looked a little tired, but I swear she was gettin' better after her last round of chemo." Tears welled in her eyes. "She and her mama and McKenzie have been so good to me and Lindsay." She nudged the girl forward. "This is my daughter, Lindsay, by the way. Anyway, they're good people. I pray for Melinda all the time."

Paula stepped forward and patted Ellie's shoulder. "Ellie, don't worry, really. Martha called last night and said Melinda was just dehydrated. She'll be back this afternoon and will need some rest. Let's not fret too much. Dr. Fields is taking really good care of her."

Ellie wiped her eyes on her sleeve and nodded. "Thanks. I guess I'll just get to cleaning the rooms, then. Is anyone checking out this morning?"

Paula looked at Cassie and shrugged. "We're not sure. How would we tell?"

Ellie walked behind the counter and opened the registration book.

"Have you had breakfast, yet?" Cassie asked Lindsay.

"No ma'am, but we brought a snack with us."

"I'm not a ma'am. Just call me Cassie."

"Yes ma'am."

Cassie's look of mock severity brought giggles from Lindsay. "Well, save that snack for later. I promise you've never had a breakfast like I make. Come on back while your mom and Paula figure out the chores. Ellie, Paula, can we bring you some coffee?"

"Yes, please," Ellie said.

Paula nodded. "Me, too." She said as the housekeeper pored over the register.

"See here," Ellie said, running her finger across a line of the book. "This Mr. Fitzgerald checked in yesterday and here's a note in column C saying he'll be leaving Monday morning. Looks like everyone in the register except for the folks in Room 23 will be gone in the morning."

"Oh, Cassie and I are staying in twenty-three."

"You're guests here? How'd you end up watching the place for the ladies?"

Paula felt her ears grow warm. "I guess we were just in the right place at the right time. The ambulance came for Melinda and we could see how torn Martha and McKenzie were about leaving, so we volunteered. It just seemed the right thing to do."

Ellie pursed her lips and raised a discerning eyebrow. "Well, you two must've made a big impression on them. They don't trust just anyone."

"I can understand that. It can't be easy running a place like this."

"That's for sure. I hope I'm not telling tales out of school here, but they almost went under not too long ago. Just between you and me, I thought I'd be looking for another job, and that'd mean a move to Nacogdoches, pulling Lindsay out of school here. I was worried sick."

So, it's likely that Cal was the one who saved them. But why? A pang stabbed Paula's heart, compelling her to probe for more. "So, uh, what changed? Do you know?"

"Not much, except that some old friend bailed them out. Miss Melinda didn't say, but I think maybe this friend bought the place and hired the ladies to run it. Sure wish I had friends like that."

Before Paula could pry further, Lindsay emerged from the living area with a huge grin on her face, a plate of bacon and French toast in one hand, and a small pitcher of syrup and two forks in the other. Cassie followed with two cups of coffee and napkins.

Lindsay set the plate on the counter. "Mama, you've *got* to try this breakfast Miss Cassie made!"

Ellie sniffed the air and smiled. "Believe I will. My stars, does that smell good!"

Lindsay took a bite and nodded. "Yeah, and it tastes even better than it smells."

Ellie took a seat on a stool behind the counter. She took a bite of French toast and her eyes twinkled. "Miss Cassie, you made this? Can I have the recipe?"

Cassie narrowed her eyes. "Yes, I did, and no, you may not. Of course, I guess I *could* tell you, but then I'd have to kill you."

At Ellie's look of horror, Cassie patted her on the arm and promised she'd let her in on the secret as long as she didn't tell anyone else.

A look of relief washed over Ellie, and she grinned. "You have my word," before taking another bite.

Cassie patted Elie's shoulder. "I'll write the recipe down for you before you leave today. So, how do we need to proceed here as far as cleaning the rooms? What's the routine?"

Ellie wiped her chin with a napkin. "Lindsay and I will handle all the rooms. We always do that part alone unless we're in a rush to turn them over, but there will be plenty of laundry if you're up for doing a few loads. And if one of you wouldn't mind going out to the campground and collecting the towels from the bathroom areas, that'd help a lot. But you can't do it too early because a lot of folks'll shower this morning."

Paula snapped her fingers. "That reminds me, Mr. Fitzgerald with the juggling group said he'd send someone up with their dirty towels this morning.

Ellie dunked a bite of bacon in syrup. "That was mighty nice of him. Someone'll still need to check around noon to see if there are more dirty towels. Course, a lot of the camping folks bring their own towels and such, but we'll still need to go out and clean the restrooms. Best to let them all get up and going first."

Cassie nodded. "Don't worry about cleaning our room. We didn't sleep out there last night. I showered so we need some towels, but I'll take those over later."

Paula nudged Cassie with her hip. "Would you mind taking my clothes and stuff back over when you go? I'm going to strip the beds here and get those sheets washed so they'll be ready for the 3M's when they get back."

Ellie raised an eyebrow. "Three Ems?"

Cassie collected the empty plate and silverware. "Yep, McKenzie, Melinda, Martha. Three M's."

Ellie nodded. "Hmmm. Guess that fits." She elbowed Lindsay to stand. "Okay, kiddo, time to get to work. Let's go grab some clean linens. Thank you for the breakfast, Miss Cassie."

The housekeepers headed to the linen supply room and Paula and Cassie returned to their respective borrowed rooms to tidy up. Paula gave her pajamas and toiletries to Cassie to take back to their room, then she stripped both beds. After a quick survey of each room, Paula headed to the laundry room and started a load then left to clean up the breakfast mess.

She stepped in the kitchen and gasped. *Dang, it looks like a tornado hit. Cassie, girl, as much as I love you, you sure do leave a mess.* She sighed and started wiping the table. "Oh, Cassie, Cassie, Cassie," she said to the kitchen at large.

"Paula, Paula, Paula," Cassie said from the door. "Are we doing everything in threes this morning?"

Paula glanced over her shoulder, "Hush up and come help clean this disaster you wrought."

Cassie stacked several dishes and set them in the sink. "When I have my own place, I'll have people to do the cleaning for me."

"Fair enough. Until then, I'll give you a hand, but mercy, you're a mess."

Cassie started washing a bowl. "Yes. Yes, I am. But then most artists are."

As they cleaned, Paula recounted what Ellie had told her about the 3M's close call with losing the resort.

Cassie wiped down the countertop. "So, obviously Cal was this good friend Ellie mentioned, right?"

"I think he must've been. It all fits. And doesn't that kind of tell us what we need to know? Surely Ellie would've mentioned this person being a romantic friend or even a boyfriend if she thought that was the case."

Cassie shook her head and started loading dishes in the dishwasher. "Maybe, maybe not. I don't think Ellie thinks in abstract terms. She's pretty black and white. Only if one of the 3M's told her specifically that the friend had been more than a friend would that have registered with her. Plus, that doesn't explain why Melinda is the Mrs. Arnett Cal purchased this place from."

"Okay, I'll give you that. Still, it makes me feel a little better."

The unmistakable voice of Zeke Fitzgerald rang out from the office. "Hello! I brought you some towels."

Paula hurried up front to find Zeke leaning on the counter next to a full basket of dirty towels. "Morning, Zeke. Thanks. How was everything last night?"

"Just perfect. We couldn't have asked for a better meeting place. This group only gets together two or three times a year, and we're all like family."

"Mind if I ask you something about your group?"

With a mischievous grin, Zeke said, "Why, Miss Patricia Paula – or is it Paula Patricia? I thought it was Miss Cassie who wanted to learn to juggle."

Paula felt herself blush. "Uh, no, I'm good, but what I need to know is... Well... Are the members of your group fully clothed when they aren't juggling? I mean other than when they're showering or bathing or—"

Zeke let out a hearty guffaw. "We aren't nudists, so yes, during most of our waking hours we're dressed like any other folks you might know."

"Then, why? Why juggle in the nude?"

Zeke composed his face, lowered his voice, and uttered three words, "Because we can."

Then it was Paula's turn to laugh. "I just wanted to know if the housekeeper and her teenaged daughter would get a shock when they went back to tidy up the showers and bathrooms."

"If they knock before entering, they should be just fine, Miss Paula Patricia."

"It's just Paula, really. There was some mix up with my name when we checked in, and Cassie's been teasing me about it ever since. Kind of like your group's being registered as the National Jugglers instead of Natural Jugglers. I'll clear it up with Melinda when she returns."

He nodded. "Sounds good! I wanted to speak to one of the ladies about reserving the place for next year. This is the best location we've ever had for our get together. It's not just anyplace that'll welcome naked jugglers."

"I understand. I'll make sure to mention it to Melinda, but remember, she doesn't likely know yet that you're not the *National* Jugglers."

"So, you said last night. That makes no sense at all. Who'd call a group National Jugglers of America? That's like saying *American* Jugglers of America."

Paula shrugged her shoulders. "I know, but it made sense to McKenzie. My point is, unless Dr. Fields thought to tell them, they might not realize that you're... natural."

He shook his head. "Don't that beat all? I'll be sure they understand when I reserve for next year."

"And Cassie and I will vouch for you. I don't know if that'll carry any weight, but it really was such fun. And eye-opening," she said with a wink.

"I like you, young lady, and your friend, too, even if she doesn't like being called a lady."

Paula rolled her eyes. "Yeah, that's her big pet peeve. And it'd really upset her if she knew that most people find her very ladylike. That is, when she isn't judging a nude juggling contest."

Zeke wiggled his eyebrows. "Say, speaking of ladies, some of the women in our group wondered if there's any shopping to be done in these parts."

Paula shook her head, "I'm not from here, and I've only been into town once. There is a great place to eat on Main street, though. Oaks on Main, I think it's called. If folks go, make sure they mention they're staying out here. Maybe talk it up a bit. I think Melinda would appreciate it. Just don't mention the nudity, please."

"For you Miss Paula, anything."

After Zeke left, Paula carried the towels back to the laundry room, then went to check on Cassie. The kitchen was spotless, but Cassie was nowhere to be found. Paula made a last inspection of the living quarters, making sure everything was just as the 3M's had left it, then glanced out the window and spotted Cassie sitting out on the back porch, a cup of coffee in hand.

Rather than joining Cassie on the back porch, she selected a Janet Evanovich book from the shelves in the den and took it to the front porch to read. A weathered wooden rocker sat midway between the office door and the corner of the building, and Paula figured it would be a great place from which to view the comings and goings of those staying at Happy Valley. The morning, while already warm, was still pleasant enough to enjoy rocking beneath the shade of the building's eaves.

She attempted to call Delbert before opening the book, but her connection was bad. *Surely, he won't be too worried, but I do need to get someone to look in on my houseplant soon. Poor Mabel might be missing my particular brand of neglect.*

Despite everything else going on, Paula surprised herself by becoming lost in the book, laughing over the antics of Lula and Grandma Mazur, while salivating over Ranger and Morelli. She barely noticed when Cassie joined her, pulling a rocker from around the corner.

"Hey, what're you reading?"

Paula held up her book.

"Oh man, I love those," Cassie said.

Paula nodded towards the cabin. "There were several in the great room if you want to go get one. I just know I'm a better reader than a fisherman, and a book keeps me from thinking too much."

Cassie nodded. "Any word from Martha or McKenzie yet?"

"No, but you know how hospitals work. They might say you'll be discharged early, but it never really happens that way."

"Truth."

Paula rocked and read while Cassie fidgeted. Soon, Lindsay pushed a laundry cart up the walkway and said, "Hey, y'all. I'm gonna drop these off."

"Do you need some help?" Paula asked.

"Oh, no, ma'am. Thanks."

Paula nodded. "Okay, just put them in the laundry room and I'll start that load next. Have you been out to the campgrounds yet?"

"No, ma'am, these are just from the rooms that we could get into, but it's most of them. These folks seem to be early risers. Best kind, Mama says."

"I can imagine," Cassie said. "How long have you and your mama worked out here?"

Lindsey's mouth pursed in concentration. "Mama's been cleaning places for a long time. I only help out during the summer and school breaks, but we've just been here since the ladies took over. Well, I better get going, or Mama'll be wonderin' if I fell in a hole or something."

Lindsay left, Paula returned to her book, and Cassie resumed fidgeting. Minutes later, Cassie stood and said, "If I don't get a Dr. Pepper soon, I might go crazy."

Paula chuckled. "Well, go into town and buy some. We need to buy bacon and eggs and stuff to replace what we ate for breakfast, anyway. I can hold down the fort while you're gone."

"You're sure you don't mind?"

"What? Of course not. I'm surprised you made it this long. Bring us back something for lunch so we don't have to keep eating their food."

"I'm going to go and clean up a bit and then I'll head into Happy Vale. I'd tell you to text me if you think of anything else you need, but I'm not sure the message would come through."

"Oh, while you're in town, will you see if you have enough of a connection to call Delbert?"

Cassie stretched her arms over her head. "Yeah, okay. I'll need your keys after I freshen up."

"They're on the dresser in the room."

"Okay, see ya later." She took off jogging toward their room without waiting for a reply.

Paula picked up Cassie's coffee cup and went inside. She washed their cups then headed to the laundry room.

Laundry had always been the one domestic chore Paula really enjoyed doing. Though the sheets fresh from the dryer smelled so good, she resisted the urge to bury her face into their warmth as she carried one set to McKenzie's room and the other to Martha's.

After making up both beds, she stopped at Melinda's door and bit her lip as she fought the urge to go in. After a moment's hesitation, she pushed the door open and headed straight to one of the paintings. She took in each one with meticulous inspection, looking for any clues they might give. "Did she ever paint you, Cal?" A tear rolled down her cheek before she even realized she was crying. She shook her head and wiped her face with her fingertips then left the room exactly as she found it.

She returned to the porch and her book, but was unable to concentrate, her thoughts wandering all over the place. *I wonder just how much the 3M's know? How am I ever going to come clean? Of course, if they know Cal died, they might be wondering what their futures hold, and if Melinda was having an affair with him, and discovers I was his wife, she might be too afraid to put me on the defensive about anything. A new owner of the hotel might result in considerable chaos in their lives, and if I can reassure them, they might just welcome my revelation. Or not. They might hate me.*

Paula shifted in her seat and folded her foot under her bottom. After rocking for a moment, she let out a deep sigh. *How do I even go about telling them who I am?* "Hi! *My name is really Paula Arnett and I'm still confused, like, were one of you married to my husband or what, and anyway, I think I own this place?*"

She blew air out through pursed lips. *Dammit, Cal, how could you put me in such an awkward situation? What were you thinking? Would you have eventually told me about Melinda and the other M's or did you just hope our worlds would never converge?*

The crunching of gravel under tires pulled her from her thoughts. She stood and watched as Martha's Subaru emerged from the highway and drove up to the office. Melinda sat up front with Mark driving, while Martha and McKenzie rode in back. Paula took a deep breath, put on her best forced smile, and went out to meet them.

CHAPTER TWENTY-FIVE

Paula stepped up to the car and opened Melinda's door. Martha got out of the backseat and helped her daughter to her feet.

Paula stepped aside. "Welcome home, Melinda. You're back earlier than we expected. We were so worried about you."

Melinda smiled. "I'm fine. It helps having the doctor as a friend."

Mark opened the trunk and helped McKenzie with the bags. He flashed a lopsided grin at Paula then nudged McKenzie. "Come on, kid. Let's get your mom into bed."

Melinda rolled her eyes. "Come on; I'm tired of being in bed. Is that really necessary?"

Mark raised an eyebrow. "Humor me. Stay in your room today and through the night, rest and drink lots of water, and we'll see how you're feeling in the morning."

Paula waited, but Melinda didn't put up much of a fight. Her too-white skin and dull eyes signaled that her body needed to rest.

Melinda sighed. "Whatever, you say, you big bully." She grabbed Paula's hand, giving it a gentle squeeze. "By the way, thank you and Cassie for looking after things for us. It was sure nice having Mom and McKenzie at the hospital so I didn't have to worry what trouble they might get into without me here to keep them in line."

Paula smiled, her eyes crinkling. "I'm glad we could help. Nothing much happened while you were gone. I'll catch them up on the few things that might be of interest."

"Again, thank you. I'll refund part of your bill to make up for putting you out."

Paula waved her hand. "Absolutely not. We still made use of your facilities."

"We'll see about that," Melinda said under her breath while Mark and McKenzie herded her toward her room. "Everybody keeps bossing me around."

Martha planted herself beside Paula and gave her an appraising look. "I think you and I need to talk."

Paula bit her lip. "Uh, okay." A knot formed in her stomach. *Crap, I wish Cassie was here! I hate confrontations. How can I even begin to explain things?*

"Let's go in the office where it's coo— Oh no! Not again."

Paula followed Martha's line of sight to a short, refurbished school bus pulling in off the highway. As soon as the bus stopped, the doors opened, disgorging a steady line of people carrying placards with slogans such as: "Keep Nudity at Home!" and "This is Happy Vale Not NudieVille!" and "Clothing is NOT Optional!"

Paula frowned. "What in the world?"

Martha clenched her teeth. "Mark told me about the nudists in our campground, but I guess you knew that. Nudists, of all things, here at Happy Valley! That's why I wanted to talk to you. I was going to apologize for sending you and Cassie out there. I'm so embarrassed. I had no idea."

Paula heaved a sigh of relief. "Please don't be embarrassed. They aren't really nudists. They, um... Well, they just juggle in the nude."

Martha tipped her head at the bus. "Do you really think that'll make a difference to *this* bunch?"

Twenty or more protesters formed a circle and began marching around the parking lot chanting, "Go Home, Perverts! Go Home, Perverts!"

An older, slightly built man with thinning gray hair broke from the group and approached the women. Martha stepped into the parking lot to meet him with Paula close on her heels.

The man folded his arms across his chest and scowled. "Ms. Murray, I'm sorry it's come to this again."

Martha's nostrils flared. "Reverend Davis, I don't think you're sorry at all! Whatever are you and your fine congregants doing at Happy Valley on this beautiful Sunday morning? Shouldn't you be preaching hellfire and damnation from behind the safety of your pulpit?"

"You know good and well what we're here about. You've got folks cavortin' in the nude back in that campground of yours. We thought those orgy havin' furry people were bad, but at least they were dressed! What are we s'posed to tell our young'uns about what y'all have got goin' on out here?"

Martha lifted her chin and clenched her fists. "Reverend, my daughter was in the hospital last night. My granddaughter and I were with her. I have no idea what you're talking about."

The man looked from Martha to Paula. "Well, who was in charge, then?"

Paula opened her mouth to answer, but Martha laid a hand on her arm and said, "Not that it's any of your concern, but we shut the front office down! It was an emergency!"

"Well, I'm sorry to hear that. Nevertheless, the fact remains you had people prancing around in your campground stark nekkid, and we want them gone. You, too, if you want the truth. Why, this place used to be one where we could bring our children to fish without worrying about devil worshippers and nudists and sex addicts running around in the woods."

The reverend's face reflected his pious anger, and without waiting for a reply, he spun on his heel and joined the other protestors, taking his place in their ranks. Their chant changed to, "Shame on you! Shame on you!"

Martha and Paula retreated to the shade of the porch and were soon joined by Mark. He rolled his eyes and snorted. "Don't tell me, the good members of the Triumphant Army of God are at it again."

Martha took a deep breath and folded her arms. "Yes, indeed. Apparently, they got word of the juggling nudist colony we're hosting."

"But how?" Paula asked.

Martha's eyes narrowed at the chanting group. "Likely the same way they learned about the Furries group we had awhile back—danged kids hanging out in the woods getting drunk and smoking pot. And word travels fast in a town this size."

The chants from the parking lot grew louder. "Nudies, Go Home! Nudies, Go Home!"

Two vehicles pulled up behind the bus and Martha covered her face with her hands. "Oh, no! Not more of 'em!"

Paula's stomach performed a series of flip flops as she took a closer look at the cars. "No, that's just Cassie and… Crap. Delbert." She rushed across the parking lot and cut through the protesters to meet Delbert as he exited his SUV. "What on earth are *you* doing here?" she asked.

Cassie, carrying two sacks of groceries, joined them. "I thought that oversized red tank in my rear-view mirror looked familiar. Don't you have better things to do than to come chasing after us?"

Sherry, Sue Ann, and Melvin stepped out of the SUV. Melvin took the packages from Cassie and said, I'm just along for the ride."

Sherry wagged her finger. "We've been worried sick about you, Paula Jean Arnett!"

"What about me? Wasn't anyone worried about me?" Cassie asked, an innocent smile on her pretty face.

Delbert shot Cassie a stern look. "To be honest, we thought *you* were on a job somewhere. Guess we should've known Paula wouldn't have gone anywhere without you. In fact, you probably instigated this."

Cassie's eyes narrowed. "Now hold on just a minute!"

The protestors' chants grew louder. "No More Nudes! No More Nudes!"

Sue Ann's anger visibly melted, and she hugged Paula then Cassie. "We really have been worried about you. Couldn't you have at least called?"

Paula hung her head. "We intended to. It was on our agenda, but we forgot, then when we got here, we had lousy reception. Honest. Cassie was going to try and call you from town."

Cassie nodded. "I did try. Multiple times."

Melvin patted Paula's shoulder. "Well, now what? Should we go somewhere to talk? I told you all that Paula would be just fine."

Paula took a deep breath. "We can't really leave while these protesters are harassing the 3M's, er, uh, I mean the resort owners."

Delbert drew himself up to his full six feet four inches. "Leave this to me." He stepped into the middle of the group and raised his voice. The chanting ceased as he said, "Ladies and gentlemen, as acting attorney for the Happy Valley Motor Inn and Resort and for its owner, Ms. Paula Jean Arnett, I hereby order you to cease and disperse before further legal action is taken against this group. You are trespassing on private property, and if you are not off the premises within exactly five minutes, both criminal and civil charges will be pursued against each and every one of you, both personally and as an organization. Consider this your only warning."

Reverend Davis took one step toward Delbert, but Delbert didn't back down, towering over the banty rooster reverend. The man of the cloth narrowed his eyes and shook his fist. "We'll leave, but this doesn't end here. We'll make sure no one *ever* stays in this place again! We'll shut you down one way or the other!" He motioned to his congregation to load up while leading them in singing "The Battle Hymn of the Republic." The group's dramatic exit was cut short while the bus driver had to navigate several turns backing up and pulling forward to maneuver around Paula's sedan and Delbert's SUV.

Once the bus turned out onto the highway, Paula threw her arms around Delbert's neck and said, "That was brilliant! It's great to have a lawyer for a friend."

Delbert patted her back and raised an eyebrow in mock disapproval. A hug won't get you out of trouble, young woman. Where can we go to talk?"

"Paula Jean Arnett?" At the sound of Martha's voice, Paula spun around. "Maybe we need to go on up to the cabin to talk. I think it's high time we got to know exactly who you are, *Patricia*.

CHAPTER TWENTY-SIX

Paula lagged behind Martha and Mark as they led the group to the office. Cassie and the rest of the Dempsey crew followed behind, whispering among themselves. Even as Paula tried to work out how to share her story with Martha, she couldn't help but feel a bit proud as she listened to her hometown friends admiring the Happy Valley grounds.

"Did y'all ever stay out here when you fished Toledo Bend?" Sherry asked the men.

"No, not here," Melvin said.

"Well, I, for one, wouldn't mind staying here. It's so peaceful and woodsy. Not like in Dempsey."

Sue Ann fanned her face with her hand. "Yes, nothing like Dempsey, is it? Mercy! Sure is humid, though,"

Too soon for Paula's unraveling nerves, the group was inside the office. "You all come on back," Martha said. "Mark, will you get some extra chairs out for our guests while I check on Melinda and McKenzie?"

Cassie carried the grocery bags as she followed Mark into the kitchen. Paula gestured for Sue Ann and Sherry to take a seat while Delbert and Melvin waited for the rest of the ladies to sit. When Mark returned with two chairs, Cassie followed him, carrying another. She joined Paula on the loveseat while Mark and the men from Dempsey perched on chairs.

Martha entered and sat in a yellow upholstered chair in the midst of Paula's friends. "They're both sound asleep, I think." She turned her attention to Paula. "Now, which is it? Patricia? Or Paula Arnett?"

Paula fought the urge to cry as she bit her bottom lip. She took a deep breath and said, "Martha, Mark, my name is Paula Arnett, and I was married to someone I believe you or Melinda might have known—Calvin Arnett."

Martha pursed her lips and nodded.

Paula's voice caught in her throat. "Cal and I have, had, that is we were married for over fifteen years." Tears pooled in her eyes and she sniffled. "Excuse me." Sherry dug into her purse and passed Paula a tissue. Paula dabbed at her eyes and said, "Thank you. Cal and I built a nice life in Dempsey, where these good people are from. By the way, that's Sherry and her husband Delbert. He's my lawyer. And this is Melvin and Sue Ann Atkins. They're all good friends. Anyway, Cal died suddenly, a week ago today. I... I just can't believe he's gone and I'm here. I'm so sorry!" She stood and her chest heaved as she sobbed. "Excuse me for a minute, please."

She ran to the washroom and splashed cool water on her face, then took some deep breaths before drying her red-rimmed eyes. Looking into the mirror, she whispered, "Cal, I could really use your support right now! Please help me find the right words."

"Goldilocks," she thought she heard, but nothing more.

"Cal? Is that all you've got right now?"

She blew her nose and cracked open the door. She heard Sherry ask, "Does she have to do this now? She's all torn up, poor thing."

"Poor girl," Sue Ann said.

Paula took a deep breath and headed back to the other room.

Cassie said, "She's been trying to get up the courage to talk to Melinda all morning. I think she wants to keep going, but she wasn't expecting to tell her story just yet, and not like this. It's just going to be hard."

Martha folded her arms over her chest. "I just don't want Melinda upset any more than she already is. This talk of Calvin Arnett is sure to bring back bad memories."

Paula cleared her throat, and all eyes turned to her. "I... I'm sorry, Martha. I was hoping to say this only once with Melinda present."

"Are you all talking about me?" Melinda asked from behind Paula. Paula turned, her heart hammering in her chest. Melinda offered a small smile and nod and said, "If you are, I'd like to be a part of the conversation."

Cassie stood and moved to the sofa between Sue Ann and Sherry. Mark stood, placing his hand on Melinda's forehead. "You really shouldn't be up," he said.

Melinda backed away from him and nudged Paula to the loveseat, taking a seat beside her. "I'm fine, worrywart. And it sounded like I needed to hear this. McKenzie, not so much. She's sleeping like a baby."

Paula sat and faced Melinda, "First, I think I need to apologize to you. You see, Cassie and I came down here to spy on you, or at least someone with the initial M."

Melinda laughed. "On me? Whatever for?"

"Um, as I was telling your mother, Cal Arnett was my husband, and—"

Melinda's hand covered her mouth as she gasped. "Oh! So, *you're* Goldilocks!"

Paula's chin quivered as she nodded. Fresh tears welled in her eyes and she mouthed, "Yes."

Melinda wrapped her arms around Paula and rubbed her back. "Aww, don't cry, Goldilocks. I can't begin to tell you how much Cal loved you."

CHAPTER TWENTY-SEVEN

As Paula and Melinda, bonded over the single word, "Goldilocks," everyone else looked on without saying a word.

After a minute, Martha broke the silence. "I don't understand what just happened."

Melinda grabbed two tissues and offered one to Paula. "Mama, I'll fill you in on everything later. Right now, I think Paula and I need to talk privately." Her eyes widened in surprise as she looked around the room. "Oh. Um, folks, I hate to be rude, and I really want to meet you all, but I think Paula and I could use some privacy."

Delbert stood and tipped his head. "Yes, good idea. Miss, Melinda, I'm Delbert Derryberry, a friend of Paula and Cal's. Say, how about I treat everyone to lunch while you two talk. That is, unless you need me to stay, Paula?"

Paula dried her tears and shook her head. "No. Y'all go on. Melinda and I need to talk with no interruptions."

Mark frowned. "I don't like the idea of leaving you alone after all you've been through these past few hours, Melinda. How about I stay and look after the front desk?

Melinda sighed. "Okay, but no interfering."

Cassie hugged Paula and whispered, "I'd tell you to call me if you need support, but we both know these cellphones are worthless out here."

Paula squeezed Cassie's hand. "I'll be fine. Why don't you take them to Delilah's place? Bring Melinda and me back something good to eat when you're done."

"I brought back sandwich fixings, but I didn't know we were going to host a whole army for lunch. At any rate, I won't turn down another meal from Delilah's place, especially if Delbert is paying."

Melinda patted Martha's shoulder. "Mama, could you bring something for McKenzie, too? She's going to be starving when she wakes up. Oh, and don't forget Mark."

Delbert stood by the door and tapped his watch. "I don't know about anyone else, but I'm hungry. Come on, guys; saddle up."

After everyone filed out of the den Melinda closed the door and took a seat. "Well, here we are: the two Mrs. Calvin Arnetts. Should I go first?"

Paula sniffled. "I think so. Can I get you anything to drink?"

As if on cue, Mark brought in two large glasses of iced water with slices of lemon. "I know, I know. No interference, but Melinda needs to stay hydrated. Watch her closely, okay, Paula? Come get me if she even looks a little bit wobbly."

Paula set her glass on a coaster. "I promise."

He grabbed a random book from the nearest shelf and disappeared into the office, closing the door behind him.

Melinda took a deep breath. "I... I'm going to tell you stuff that might be shocking to you. All I ask is that you let me get it all out, because I might chicken out if I have to think too much."

Paula's eyes grew wide, and she felt her chest tighten. *Cal, if you're here, please prepare me for whatever she's going to say.* She forced a smile. "I'm listening."

CHAPTER TWENTY-EIGHT

The hair on the back of Paula's neck stood on end as she waited to hear what Melinda had to say. After a long drink, Melinda asked, "Did Mama tell you that I had a twin sister named Marie?"

"Not in detail, but she mentioned it."

"Well, we were as different as night and day, even though we looked identical except for one tiny detail. Marie had a light brown, heart-shaped speckle on the back of her left hand. A birthmark. That's the only way our parents could tell us apart when we were babies. But as we grew, our personalities diverged so sharply that no one needed a birthmark to distinguish one of us from the other." Melinda coughed and took a sip of water.

"If you're not feeling up to this—"

"No, I'm okay. Honestly, I'm ready to share this with someone. So, Marie was all sweetness and light, outgoing and charming. Now, I was a little mouse, as Daddy used to say. Shy and reserved from the time I was very small. Marie and I got along most of the time, simply because the older we got, the less we had in common, so our paths went in totally different directions. We didn't have to compete on any level."

Paula's pulse raced. *Get to the part about Cal!*

Melinda smiled as if she could read Paula's mind. "We lived in a small town in Indiana, near Danville, about twenty miles west of Indianapolis. Daddy owned a grocery store, and Mama helped out as a checker and as his bookkeeper, but while we were growing up, she was home every day after school with milk and cookies. It was pretty perfect, although, sometimes, Marie and I both wished for a little space. Especially during our teenage years. In high school, Marie was the cheerleader, the prom and homecoming queen, star of the school theater class, and voted *Most Popular* in our class every single year. You get the picture."

Paula nodded and took a sip of water.

"And, I was her biggest fan. We looked alike, but I lacked her grace and her pizazz. I was a bookworm who read well into the night even after Mama threatened to ground me if I didn't go to sleep at a certain time. I was involved in band and art. Scenes I created were used as backdrops in Marie's plays. I captained the school's scholastic bowl team that won the state competition my senior year. My grades were always top notch. I was the valedictorian of my class and was offered several scholarships as a result. And, Marie was always *my* biggest fan." She took a sip of water. "Perfect, right?"

Paula nodded, hoping her face didn't betray her anxiety.

"Then I went to college in Illinois, and Marie stayed home and married her long-time boyfriend, Kyle Blair. Again, a familiar story—homecoming queen marries high school quarterback. They should've lived happily ever after, blah, blah, blah, only Kyle had aspirations to play college ball, and when he didn't get recruited by a single school, not even a junior college, he went to work for one of his father's car dealerships. The family owned several in and around Indianapolis. That's when the newlyweds' happily ever after was marred by Kyle's drinking and philandering. But my sister had been raised by two loving parents, and she was determined to make a go of her marriage. She never let on what was happening inside her home."

Paula felt her pulse speeding up at the mention of Illinois. *Cal went to school there!*

"I had no idea that she was so unhappy, or that Kyle was treating her so poorly. I was having the time of my life at the University of Illinois where I majored in art education. Finally, being the bookworm was paying off. There were so many people I identified with. I found the world outside of my little hometown so enriching. And then I fell in love..."

Paula took a drink, her hands shaking in anticipating of hearing Cal's name.

"...with my roommate, Ginger Jordan."

Paula choked on her water. "What?"

Melinda chuckled. "I gather you weren't expecting that."

"No," Paula said in a hoarse whisper. "Never in a million years, actually. I thought you were going to say—"

"Cal, right? No, sweetie, I fell head over heels with one of the most beautiful women I've ever known. And she loved me back. Honestly, Paula, I didn't even know what a homosexual or a lesbian was at that time. Gay was still a word that meant 'happy or light-hearted.' Our romance confused both of us. We didn't have Google back then, and it wasn't something we could just go ask the librarian about, so we spent nights in our room figuring out what it meant to be in love. You can't believe how many times I've rehearsed saying all this."

"I... I don't know what to say."

Melinda patted her hand. "It's okay. Just listen. Anyway, in public we gave each other a wide berth. We did our best to put a lot of distance between us during the daylight hours. Ginger was involved in drama, while I studied my butt off in the library and made the Dean's list every semester. Some people clean when they're troubled, but I study. And, I poured myself into my art, spending hours painting people and places around campus. Some of my stuff was pretty good, too, no doubt influenced by my infatuation with Ginger. Oh! I painted her, too. Without her knowledge. Hold on, I've got that painting tucked away in a drawer somewhere." She stood and left the room.

Paula's heart thumped so hard, she thought it might just burst right out of her chest. *Melinda? A lesbian? But she's so feminine, so pretty. How can she be gay? And where does Cal fit into this?* She felt as if her world had just been upended.

Moments later, Melinda returned with a rolled-up canvas. "I had to be stealthy. Thankfully, McKenzie's still out like a light. Poor kid didn't sleep at all last night, even over at the family housing facility."

"Does she know all of this?" Paula asked.

"Heavens, no! To her, I'm totally asexual. She'd flip out if she thought I'd ever been in love with *anyone,* let alone a woman. Mama doesn't know either, by the way."

"But—"

"Let's not get sidetracked," Melinda said, untying the string from the canvas. With care, she revealed her rendition of Ginger.

Goosebumps covered Paula's arms. "She's beautiful. And you're so talented."

Melinda shrugged her shoulders. "Thanks. I don't often paint people and I didn't come close to doing her justice. She looked like a fairy-tale princess, yards of strawberry blonde hair and the most beautiful skin, like porcelain. And she always seemed so sweet and innocent."

As Melinda rolled the canvas and retied it, Paula asked, "So what happened? Did you two stay together after college."

"No. Ginger was from an extremely wealthy family in Chicago. You know, international vacations, private jets, hobnobbing with the rich and powerful. Her dad was an investment banker or something like that, and her mom was queen of the charity circuit, throwing lavish parties where people paid thousands of dollars to attend. We came from totally different worlds."

"Oh. And that meant trouble?"

"Yes. We kept our relationship a secret for four years. We were madly in love. But as we neared graduation day, she tried to tell her parents that she'd fallen for someone at school, not even mentioning that this someone was a woman. They shut her down pretty quickly. Seems her parents had already picked out two suitable candidates for her to wed and they were going to allow her to choose one."

Paula gasped. "What?"

"I know, right? This wasn't that many years ago, but things were different then, especially for girls from her social circle. And, honestly at that time, what did we have to look forward to as a couple? Very few people were openly gay, and those who were risked a lot for daring to be themselves. Ginger didn't exactly have a strong personality, either. It broke her heart to tell me we had to end our affair. She cried buckets, and nothing I said or did could convince her she had other choices. In the end, Ginger put me away like I was a well-loved, but unstylish, pair of shoes. Get this—she asked me to be a bridesmaid in her big destination wedding! I declined, even though it meant giving up a dream trip to Paris.

A shiver traveled up Paula's spine. "Oh, I'm so sorry. So, what happened next?"

"I went on to graduate *summa cum laude* with a major in education and a minor in art. A broken heart, it seemed, did not diminish my need to study. If anything, it spurred me on. Studying shut out the memories and the thoughts of Ginger kissing someone else. I was hired by the school district in Champaign to teach in one of their high schools, and that was where I met Calvin."

Paula felt her body tense. "Was it love at first sight?"

Without hesitation, Melinda let out a hearty laugh. "No, oh no." She took Paula's hand and said, "You know, there is only one other person I've ever told that part of my story to, though."

"Cal?"

"Yes, Cal," Melinda said. She took a long drink of her water and leaned back with an amused look on her face.

Paula's knees trembled as she stood and grabbed Melinda's empty glass. "Here, let me go get you a refill. Just to keep Mark happy." A minute later, she returned with two full glasses and a few snickerdoodle cookies on a plate. "I thought we might need some energy for the rest of your story."

Melinda took a cookie and smiled. "Thank you. I think the hard part's done now. You have no idea how relieved I am that somebody else knows who I really am."

"But you married Cal. Doesn't that make you, um, *bi*?"

"Well, you're getting ahead of the story. Are you ready for the next part?"

"I... I think so."

Melinda took a drink of water and smiled. "I loved teaching art. My students weren't angels, but they were fun, and my days were long and tiring and fulfilling. The school where I taught was in an older building, but the staff was relatively young. A group of about twelve of us single teachers were deemed *The Wild Bunch* because we were all mavericks. There were so many inspiring teachers in that school, and I don't think it would surprise you to learn that Cal was one of them. Maybe the most inspiring of all of us." She cleared her throat.

"As you might imagine, Cal was the listener in the group. He never scoffed at another teacher's idea or problem, or a student's, for that matter. He could listen patiently and tell whether a person wanted help with a solution or just needed to talk. He became my best friend in the group, but I think a good many of The Wild Bunch felt the same way.

Paula's heart warmed. *Oh, Cal...*

Melinda nibbled a cookie. "We were all under thirty. I was just twenty-four when I started teaching at Chambers High. We got into a routine of going out on Friday nights as a group. If there was a home football game, we helped with concessions and cheered on the team, then went for drinks afterward. Or we'd meet at one of the group members' apartments to eat and drink and talk until well after the sun came up. None of us had much money. We were living on teachers' salaries, after all. But we didn't need much. It was the best time of my life up to that point.

Paula nodded. *And about Cal?*

"A few relationships were formed within 'The Wild Bunch'. But I was still confused about Ginger. I was still hurt, too. I wasn't ready for any kind of romantic involvement, let alone one with a man, but then

Cal stayed to help me clean up one night after the group left. He hadn't paired up either and it was almost like there was a pressure being applied by those who had. We talked as we cleaned, and I felt so comfortable with him. Maybe, I thought, this is what I'm supposed to have. Not fireworks and passion, but friendship and comfort. I let him kiss me."

Paula knew the moment her face gave her away. Even though she'd been preparing to hear all the details, it still stung, knowing that someone else had known Cal like that.

Melinda touched Paula's knee and offered a sweet smile. "Remember, Paula, he had no idea at the time that his Goldilocks was waiting for him in the future. If he had, he'd never have paid any attention to me. But you were, what? Twelve at the time and in Texas?"

Paula blushed and nodded, but she couldn't seem to make herself speak around the lump in her throat. Cal had loved this woman, and now, she could understand why.

Melinda patted Paula's hand. "So, we began doing stuff together outside of the group. Picnicking and boating at Lake of the Woods. Plays in Peoria. Movies at the Virginia Theatre in Champaign. Hiking at Turkey Creek State Park in Indiana. We held hands and shared popcorn and mosquito repellant. But—" She paused, to take a sip of water. "We never had sex. Not once during that whole courtship process. I didn't encourage him, and he never pushed me. After all, I was technically a virgin, and even though he was a couple of years older than me, he was old-fashioned like that. Honestly, I could've gone on with our relationship like that forever, but not Cal. He wanted to get married. He got down on one knee among the roses and asked one afternoon while we were exploring Allerton Park."

"He did?" Paula willed her chin to stop quivering.

"Paula, I should've said no, because I knew that I could never be the kind of wife he needed or deserved. But part of me wanted what other women my age had. I wanted what I thought my sister had. I wanted to be part of a forever couple, and Cal could give me that. So, I said yes, and the unstoppable wedding machinery clicked into high gear. We took a trip to my family's home where he made a show of asking my parents for their permission, and they both fell in love with him. We set a wedding date for the end of October, and Mama went to work planning it with Marie's help. I kept in touch by phone and with frequent trips home, but I let the two of them carry me through all of the preparations and arrangements. It was like someone I barely knew was getting married. That kind of event planning stuff was never really my thing, anyway, but part of me kept thinking that at some point, Cal would want to back out, that he'd see me for what I was. But he didn't." She grabbed a tissue and dabbed her moist eyes then offered a Kleenex to Paula.

"We were married on a beautiful autumn afternoon in the little Methodist church where Marie and I had been baptized. Thanks to Mama and Marie, everything went off without a hitch. Cal's mother, Eunice, came from Watseka. She was a kind woman, very much like Cal. He got his listening skills from her. I know you never got to meet her, but the two of you would've gotten on so well. I've got a photo of her somewhere. Have you ever seen a picture of her?"

"Yes, there's one on Cal's desk in his home office. She looked so pretty—all dressed up—Oh. I'll bet it was from your wedding day." She jumped to her feet. "Long navy-blue dress, with lacy sleeves down to here. Her hair done up in a French twist. Pearls around her neck and small diamond studs in her ears." Her knees buckled and she melted back into her seat. All that time there'd been a clue to Cal's previous marriage right in front of her eyes.

"Yes, that fits my memory of the day. She pulled me aside and told me she was so glad Cal had found the right woman," Melinda said with a sigh. "At least she never knew how I disappointed him. She had a slight stroke the January after we married. We brought her to live with us after that. I loved her, and those first few months with her in our home were the best of our marriage. While Eunice was in the house, I could use her as an excuse to get out of my—you know—*wifely duties.* I was always too tired or was afraid she'd hear us, or I wanted to stay up and watch television or play cards with her. Any other man probably would've lost his cool, but Cal was so patient."

"But surely you had sex. I mean—" Paula gestured to a photo of McKenzie.

Melinda chuckled. "We just barely made love on our honeymoon. We consummated the marriage, but I hated the act. I tried to hide my feelings, but it all felt so wrong, and Cal was no dummy. I couldn't help comparing him to Ginger, and I knew that wasn't fair."

"Oh, no."

"Eventually Eunice needed more care than we could provide. We found a nice nursing home close to us so one or both of us could visit every day. I invented new excuses, and Cal kind of gave up. He knew something was preventing me from being the wife he needed, but he loved me, and he wanted me in his life. He was the most decent man ever, and I loved him as much as I could."

Paula squeezed Melinda's hand. "I know you did. I can feel how much you cared for him and how torn you must have been...How hard those days must have been for you both."

"Yes, we still had good times, though, mostly centered around school, but we'd also go hiking and boating. I was actually the one who taught Cal to fish just like Daddy and Uncle James had taught me. He took it up enthusiastically, partly, I suspect, to give me some space. We might've gone on that way forever because he was so patient, but then two things happened...Come to think of it, this next part may be the hardest to tell. Would you mind getting me some more water and another cookie?"

Paula's heart threatened to jump out of her chest as she stood and collected their glasses and the cookie plate. When she returned, she asked, "Are you feeling okay? You know, we don't have to do this right now if you're not up to it."

Melinda took her glass and shook it to clink the ice cubes against the sides of the glass. "Actually, I feel better right now than I have in a long time. Lighter. All these secrets have kept me weighed down for far too long."

"Just promise me you'll stop if you need to."

"Thank you. You're sweet. It's easy to see why Cal was so enamored by you. Anyway, as I said, two things happened. First, Eunice passed away. She'd been an anchor of sorts for our marriage, and as long as we were busy caring for her and visiting her daily, we didn't have to work on us. Cal went into a funk. I could hardly blame him. His mother had died, and his wife was frigid. And we were just in our twenties. The future looked kind of bleak for both of us. Even then, we might've made it through, except—" She took a deep breath and fanned the tears from her eyes. "Except one Saturday, while Cal was on a field trip as a sponsor for the school's debate team, Ginger Jordan-Simmons showed up at my door. Paula, I wept the moment I saw her. She came into my apartment, took me in her arms, and we cried for ten minutes. I felt like I was getting my first drink of water after a million-mile march through the desert."

Paula felt a shiver run down her spine. "What was she doing there after all that time?"

"She and her husband, Darden, had had a huge fight. She said she hadn't been happy a day since we'd broken up and that all she wanted was to be with me. And, Paula, I couldn't resist her. We, um…. Well, I think maybe you can guess what happened that afternoon."

Paula, gulped, then nodded. "You don't have to tell me."

"Cal came home early and found us together. Not *together*, together, but sitting so close that there was no mistaking what our relationship was. He didn't get angry. Didn't yell. I think I'd have understood better if he had. He just closed the door and left. I didn't see him until we were both at school on Monday morning, and then he was polite. Polite. Paula, it broke my heart.

"Oh, no."

"Like a high schooler I sent him a note via a student, telling him we needed to talk. I told him I'd be home at four that afternoon. He met me there, and I told him all about Ginger. How much I'd loved her, but how much I loved him, too, just in a different way. We talked and cried. Cal, the listener as always, was so hurt, but at the same time, he finally had an answer to why I could never be what he needed. I can't imagine any other man in his position being so damned understanding. I deserved to be chastised and yelled at, while he just held me and told me he would always be there for me in whatever capacity I needed. All I had to do was ask. Lord knows, I didn't deserve Calvin Arnett, but you, Goldilocks, you did, and he deserved you. I'm so glad he found you."

Paula felt somehow like a weight of her own had been lifted. "So, you and Cal divorced, but did Ginger come back into your life for good?"

Melinda sighed. "Yes, Cal and I filed for divorce. There was no animosity. Of course, I couldn't tell my folks why we'd split. To this day, I think Mama believes Cal was unfaithful. I'm ashamed to say that, while I never said that was the reason, I never denied it either. I was a coward. I could never tell my family about Ginger or our relationship. Mama would be mortified if she knew I'd had an affair with a woman."

Paula felt a pang in her heart. *How sad.*

"And, no, Ginger did not come back into my life. Not for good, anyway. She used me, not just that time, but on several other occasions through the years. Any time her husband lost his temper with her, she'd run to me. Finally, I had enough and told her so. I haven't seen her since just after McKenzie was born."

Paula blinked and realized her cheeks were moist with tears. She dried them and said, "Wait a minute. So, Cal isn't McKenzie's father?"

Melinda leaned close and lowered her voice to a whisper. "Paula, Cal wasn't McKenzie's father. I'm not even her biological mother."

Paula felt the blood rush from her face, and her mouth opened then shut in confusion. Before she could respond, though, a loud knock at the cabin's back door startled both of them.

CHAPTER TWENTY-NINE

Paula jumped to her feet. "Do you want me to answer it?"

Melinda stood and headed toward the door. "No need." She opened the door with a smile and found Zeke Fitzgerald. "Oh, Mr. Fitzgerald. The office is up front."

"Yes, Miss Melinda," Zeke said, wringing his hat in his hands. "But there appears to be some trouble brewing up front, and I didn't want to get in the middle of things. There's a large crowd forming in the parking lot. I just thought you ought to know."

Melinda nodded. "Thank you for letting me know. I'll go check on it right now. Is there anything else?"

Scarlet patches bloomed on Zeke's neck. "I'm just afraid that my group is the cause of this whole mess. If you want, we can leave."

"What? How could that be? You've caused no disruption at all as far as I can tell. We want you here."

Zeke looked to Paula and asked, "Miss Paula, does Miss Melinda know what kind of jugglers we are?"

Paula bit her lip and cut her eyes to Melinda. "I'm sorry, there hasn't been an opportunity to tell you. Um, they aren't the *National* Jugglers of America, they're the *Natural* Jugglers. Natural, as in naked. But only when they're juggling."

Melinda raised her eyebrows. "Oh? Oh, no! Oh. Naked, eh?" Her hand covered her smile. "Oh dear. Still, Mr. Fitzgerald, your group is staying on my property, and you're my guests. You folks just stay right where you are. We'll handle this."

Zeke nodded. "Thank you, ma'am. Let me know if I can do anything to smooth this over. Looks like they've got tv cameras out front."

Melinda's face blanched. "Cameras? Oh, dear. Thank you, Mr. Fitzgerald. I'll keep your offer in mind." She gestured for him to go and closed the door behind him then turned to Paula. "I guess you'd better fill me in."

CHAPTER THIRTY

Paula gave Melinda a brief rundown on the juggling contest as they headed to the office. "Honestly, I was shocked that I wasn't shocked, but the whole thing was just so ridiculously unoffensive that I just went with the flow. We all did. Then when you had to go to the hospital, we forgot all about it. Mark told Martha, but I'm not even sure McKenzie knows. Then, this morning, after you went inside to rest, some preacher and his congregation showed up and—"

Melinda rolled her eyes. "Don't tell me. Reverend Davis?"

"Uh, yeah, I'm afraid so. They all had signs made up and started picketing, and chanting, and everything, until my friends from Dempsey showed up. Delbert, he's my attorney, told them to leave before he brought legal action against them for trespassing. It seemed to work, but now…."

Melinda wrinkled her nose. "Ugh! Those people! They just can't keep their noses out of everyone else's business. Reverend Davis has been a pain in my butt ever since we came here. Honestly, I think his main complaint is that we're women."

As the women entered the office, Mark turned around from peeking through the blinds. "No, he's not a pain in the butt; he's a pompous, uptight jackass who considers everyone else a sinner." His mouth was drawn into a line as he pulled down a section of blinds and moved to one side so they could all peer out. A news reporter and her cameraman lined up to take shots of the cabin and the rooms, while Reverend Davis and his busload of protestors planted themselves across the driveway.

Melinda's nostrils flared. You've got that right.... Hey, I recognize that reporter. She's with one of the stations in Nacogdoches."

Mark closed the blinds. "So, what are you doing in here anyway? You promised you'd rest."

"I've rested and I'm so hydrated that water's likely to come spouting out of my ears. Mr. Fitzgerald just told us about the brouhaha brewing out here."

Mark cut his eyes to Paula. "Uh, did he happen to tell you why?"

"No, but Paula did. It sounds pretty harmless. It's obvious that these news folks didn't just show up to take pictures of our resort; so, Reverend Davis must've reported last night's little contest. I guess he failed to report that the only way he could possibly know about it was if his delinquent son and his buddies were out trespassing in our woods again, drinking and spying on our guests. That's how they found out about the Furries, remember?"

Mark smirked and said, "Perhaps I should go out there and tell him, 'Physician, heal thyself.'"

Melinda rolled her eyes. "What, and deny me the pleasure? I doubt he'd appreciate us pointing that out, anyway." She sighed. "I guess I should go out there and give them what they want."

In unison, Paula and Mark said, "No!"

Paula grabbed the office phone, waving the receiver. "Let me call Delbert and try to get him back here. I'm sure they went to Oaks on Main to eat. Likely they're taking their time to give us some privacy."

Mark grabbed the phonebook from behind the counter and looked up the number. "That sounds like a great idea. Look, here's the number..."

"I feel like a coward waiting for someone else to do my job," Melinda said as Paula dialed.

Paula covered the receiver with her hand. "Delbert's my attorney, and while we aren't exactly at the end of your story, I think that means he's *our* attorney now... Oh! Yes, April, I'm looking for a customer named Delbert Derryberry. He's with a group of six, most of them from out of town... Oh, okay... Delbert, it's Paula..." Paula explained the commotion then cradled the receiver. "They're leaving now. They've already paid their check, and they should be here in a few minutes."

Mark rested his hand on the doorknob. "Melinda, you take it easy. I'm going to go tell that reporter she'll have her story shortly."

After he stepped out, Paula and Melinda peeked outside. As soon as Mark neared the reporter, the church group began chanting, "No Place for Perverts! No Place for Perverts!"

Melinda paced the length of the office then sighed. "Maybe I should go freshen up, especially if I'm going to be on TV."

Paula bit her lip. "Uh..."

"What is it?"

"Never mind. I don't know if I should even suggest such a thing."

"Suggest what? I just spilled my guts to you. You're the only living person who knows so many intimate details of my life. I think that entitles us to be frank with one another."

A look of relief washed over Paula and she said, "Well, I was just thinking that the reporter might be kinder to a woman who's obviously, uh, not in the best of health. I mean, it can't hurt to get the public's sympathy on our side, right? Besides, you don't want to take a chance on waking McKenzie up..."

Melinda took a deep breath and nodded. "I guess you're right. Your attorney will probably be here any minute now, anyway.

Paula mentally replayed Melinda's story and watched as the other woman thumbed through the register on the counter. Paula sighed. *So many questions still without answers. But I'm beginning to understand why Cal insisted that Melinda needs me. Still, what should I do about this place, or even about CalNet? Most importantly, how am I ever going to live without Cal?* She closed her eyes and smiled. *At least I know now he truly loved me and was never unfaithful.* She felt a lump form in her throat, and her eyes burned with pending tears.

She jumped when Melinda touched her arm and gestured out the window to Mark and the news people rising from their seats on the porch.

"Is this the cavalry we're waiting on?" Melinda asked, nodding toward two vehicles driving up the path.

Delbert honked his horn and drove his Suburban carrying the Dempsey Four through the gauntlet while Cassie and Martha followed in Paula's car. The Triumphant Army of God closed in around them, raising their fists and calling out epithets. Delbert parked as close to the office as he could get and ushered the women into the building. Cassie and Martha parked beside Room 23 and stormed over to join Mark on the porch.

Delbert opened the door to the office and motioned for Melinda and Paula to join him on the porch where they conferred. Once he was apprised of the situation, the three of them approached the reporter and her cameraman who was already filming the protestors.

The perky newswoman gamely attempted to maintain her on-camera banter while the protesters chanted, "Nude is Crude! Nude is Crude!" As Delbert and company approached, the journalist made a slashing motion across her throat to her coworker who lowered his camera.

She stepped closer to the trio. "Mrs. Arnett?" She looked between the women, but Delbert gave them a cautionary look before stepping forward.

He tipped his head to the reporter. "Excuse me, Ms..."

The reporter wore her best camera-ready smile. "I'm Jennifer Dodson with KNGD. And you are..."

"Delbert Derryberry, attorney at law," he said, offering her his card.

"I see, Mr. Derryberry. Are you Mrs. Arnett's legal representative?"

"I am here in that capacity."

"I'd like to interview Mrs. Arnett. Our viewers are interested in her side of the story."

"I'm afraid Mrs. Arnett is not well right now. In fact, her doctor has advised her to go back inside to rest, but I'm available for you to interview."

"But it won't take but a minute, and—"

"Ms. Dodson, at this time I cannot consent to Mrs. Arnett being interviewed. She spent last night in the hospital, you see, but perhaps at a later date she could talk to you. If you want an interview now, you'll only get me."

The reporter chewed on her lower lip for a second before saying, "Fine." She motioned to her cameraman to shoot the next footage with the cabin as the backdrop, getting film of Paula escorting Melinda inside.

She asked Delbert to repeat his name, and then turned to the camera. "Not much happens in sleepy Happy Vale, the government seat of Big Lake County, except for outstanding bass fishing and some good deer hunting. But today we're just outside of Happy Vale at the Happy Valley Motor Inn and Resort where a group of protesters led by Reverend Leroy Davis, pastor of the church known as the Triumphant Army of God is picketing the premises. Reverend Davis is concerned about what he terms, and I quote, 'an unsavory group of people parading around in the nude for all the world to see' at the resort. The owner of the resort, Mrs. Calvin Arnett, is unable to provide us with an interview at this time; however, her attorney, Delbert Derryberry has agreed to speak with us. Mr. Derryberry, is what Reverend Davis told us true?" She turned the microphone toward Delbert.

Delbert squared his shoulders. "Ms. Dodson, the Reverend Davis is currently trespassing on private property owned by Mrs. Calvin Arnett. I have called on Judge Driscoll of Big Lake County to issue an order for the Triumphant Army of God to cease and desist, and to remove themselves from my client's property immediately. I expect that order to arrive momentarily."

"But, Mr. Derryberry, what about the accusations Reverend Davis has made? Can you verify what group or groups are staying here?"

"That is a matter of privacy. My client is under no obligation to reveal who is or is not staying at the resort, nor what their business is here unless a law has been broken. I can, however, assure you that absolutely no laws have been breached and that the claim that guests here are, as you say, *parading around in the nude for all the world to see,* is a ridiculous and inflammatory allegation. Obviously, guests of the resort are contained to the private acreage you see here, including the lake. If, at any time, guests happened to be in the nude, and I'm not saying they were, I can guarantee with one hundred percent certainty that such activity would have taken place strictly in the presence of other consenting adults only, and that, if such were true, it could only be known to the good reverend or any of his congregants if they were trespassing on private property. I invite you to take a walk along the property line and film the posted warnings advising trespassers to stay off the property here. Now, if you'll excuse me, as I said earlier, my client spent the night in the hospital. She needs time to recover from her illness, and we need to focus on her well-being. Thank you." He turned away from the camera without waiting for a reply and headed toward the office.

Jennifer rushed after him and said, "Mr. Derryberry, how long have you been representing Mrs. Arnett?"

Delbert stopped in his tracks, looked over his shoulder, and smiled. "For at least the past fifteen years."

CHAPTER THIRTY-ONE

Paula paced back and forth while watching Delbert wrap up his interview. As they stepped into the office, she asked, "So, what do you think? Did it go okay?"

"Well, you heard what I told them. What did you think?"

"I thought you were great. Did you really file a motion with a local judge?"

"I'm about to right now. Is there a phone I can use? My cellphone hasn't had reception since we got to town."

Melinda said, "Of course, right this way."

Paula peeked outside. The news van pulled away and moments later, the church group stopped chanting, put down their signs, and began wiping the sweat off their faces. With a burst of inspiration, she headed to the kitchen and found Mark and Cassie pantomiming the jugglers for Martha, Melinda, and the Dempsey crew while summarizing the events of the contest.

Their audience laughed, encouraging Mark and Cassie to kick their act up a notch.

"You should've seen the guy who juggled knives blindfolded," Cassie said.

"You're one to talk," Mark laughed. "Cassie and Paula watched him like this." He placed his splayed hands over his eyes and scrunched up his face in a close approximation of the ladies' actions. "I watched with both eyes open in case I needed to provide medical assistance."

Martha and Melinda shook with laughter, while Sue Ann blushed and attempted to hide her giggles. Sherry had to wipe away the tears that formed in her eyes from laughing so much.

Paula grinned. "Friends, I hate to intrude on such an *obviously* exaggerated story..." she said with a wink, "...but I had an idea that might pay dividends in the future. Our protesters out there are looking a bit worse for the heat. What if we take some cold drinks out to them? You know, do unto others, and all that."

Sue Ann tilted her head. "Oooh, I like that idea!"

Martha stood and opened the refrigerator. "Let's do this! Cassie, would you mind filling that pitcher on the counter with ice and water? Paula, if you'll grab this tea pitcher, I'll make some lemonade, and if you gentlemen would be so kind, you could help us carry it outside."

Melvin stood next to Mark and said, "Of course."

Cassie secured the lid of the pitcher. "We also have cookies that I bought at the market this morning. You want to take some of those out, too?"

Paula opened a grocery bag and pulled out two bags of Mrs. Archer's Homemade Cookies. "Oh, yum. Good thinking."

Melinda grabbed a serving tray and arranged the cookies. "Okay, let's go make nice with these people."

Mark intervened, taking the tray from Melinda's hands. "Allow me. You need to take it easy."

Martha set a wooden spoon in the sink and snapped the lid on the lemonade pitcher. Alright, Sherry, there's a sleeve of paper cups in that cabinet, and, Sue Ann, if you'll grab that stack of napkins, we're ready. She led the procession through the office and across the parking lot to the picnic table under the oak tree.

While Sue Ann and Sherry filled cups, Paula grabbed Cassie's arm and headed toward the protesters. Under her breath, Paula said, "You're going to ooze charm, friend. *Ooze.*"

Cassie's eyes lit up. "Aye, aye, Cap'n!"

The protesters sounded as weary as they looked as they shuffled in a circle, half-heartedly chanting, "Nudists, nudists go away! Don't come around here to play!"

Paula made a beeline for their leader. "Reverend Davis, I don't believe we've been properly introduced. My name is Paula Arnett, and this is my dear friend, Cassie Campbell. We couldn't help but notice that your group looks tired and thirsty. We'd like to offer you all some refreshments."

The reverend sneered at Paula's outstretched hand as if she'd offered him a dead skunk. "We don't need your false charity, missy."

Cassie offered a beguiling smile and laid a gentle hand on his arm. "Are you sure, sir? I see some mighty tired looking ladies in your group. Why, you look like you're about to drop yourself, and you're a big strong man. I'm sure your friends here are faring much worse than you."

Even a self-righteous curmudgeon the likes of Reverend Davis couldn't resist the full effect of Cassie Campbell at her most charming. "Well," he muttered. "I don't guess it would hurt anything if they took a rest. They are doing the Lord's work after all, and they need their energy."

Cassie batted her eyelashes. "Exactly what I was thinking. Why don't you all come over to the shade? It's too hot to be marching out here without staying hydrated."

The reverend allowed Cassie to link her arm through his and guide him to the table, waving for his congregants to follow.

Paula stood back and introduced herself to each of them after they got a drink, asking about their families and their church.

Mark and Melvin moved several chairs from the porch into the shade, and Mark waved Melinda over. "Come and sit, Melinda. You've already been on your feet too long."

Melinda took a deep breath and touched the reverend's elbow. "Pastor, won't you come sit with me for a moment and talk? Mama, would you be so kind as to bring Reverend Davis something to drink?"

The preacher bristled, but Cassie pulled him by the elbow until he was in the chair next to Melinda's.

Paula watched as the hesitant protestors soon made themselves at home while Sue Ann and Sherry doled out refreshments. Paula struggled to hide a smile when the ladies began exchanging recipes and showing each other photos of their respective families with much oohing and ahhing over pictures of cute kids and puppies.

Paula hovered between that group and the one where Melinda was speaking earnestly with Reverend Davis. She could tell that the

Reverend, seemingly against his better judgement, was coming to an understanding with the other Mrs. Arnett. While she desperately wanted to know what they were talking about, she didn't want to upset the delicate balance that Melinda and Cassie had found with the preacher.

She joined Mark and Melvin on the porch. "I don't know about you," Melvin whispered, "but I could use a beer."

"I'll second that," Mark said through a tight smile.

Paula nodded. "I do, too, but I don't think it would be a good idea until we can get the good reverend to leave."

Mark said, "Yeah, I agree. I see Cassie has him wrapped around her little finger."

Paula chuckled. "She can be quite the little persuader when she needs to. Most men have difficulty saying no to that face."

Melvin snorted. "Not me. I'm immune to her. We grew up across the alley from each other. Her brother, Court, and I were best friends. Cassie was a little pain in the butt from the day she was born and didn't let up until…well, never."

Delbert came out of the office and pulled additional chairs over to where the others were seated. "Well, well, well. What have we here?"

"Hopefully a peace conference," Paula said.

Delbert raised an eyebrow. "Looks like you've got the perfect ambassador working on it. Too bad Cassie can't use her powers for good more often."

Melvin nodded. "Yep, already came to that conclusion. So, did you have any luck with the judge?"

"As a matter of fact, a deputy is going to bring an order for the Triumphant Army of God to vacate the premises. But it looks like that might not be necessary anymore."

Paula crossed her fingers. "Let's hope that between Melinda's calm demeanor and Cassie's charm, they might've bewitched the good reverend. Or at least soothed his troubled waters."

Delbert shifted his weight in his chair and faced Paula. "So, Goldilocks, tell me, how are you holding up? With all this going on, I almost forgot about you and all you must be dealing with."

Paula smiled. "I'm good, actually. Melinda cleared up a bunch of the mystery this morning. We haven't finished talking about it yet, but at least I'm pretty confident that Cal never cheated on me."

"I'm glad to hear that. Knowing Cal and how he felt about you, I couldn't imagine that being the case, but it's good to see you smiling again."

Mark raised an eyebrow. "So, what's with the Goldilocks thing? First you were Patricia, then Paula, and now Goldilocks? What are you and Cassie really doing here?"

Melvin and Delbert took turns telling the Goldilocks story, causing Paula to blush. She hung her head and said, "I don't know why he thought everything I did was *just right*. I'm starting to realize all the things I should've done for him that it's too late to do now."

Melvin chuckled. "Honey, Cal didn't *think* you were perfect, he was *positive* about it. Hell, he almost convinced all of us that you were. Good thing we'd all known you longer and knew better than to believe that bullshit." He slapped his knee and laughed while Delbert joined in.

Paula winced and lowered her voice. "Shhhh! Don't upset the good members of the Triumphant Army of God."

Mark said, "But that still doesn't answer why you're here."

Paula bit her lip. "Because my husband apparently bought this motel a few months before he died and never told me a thing about it. After he died, I learned that he bought it from a Mrs. Calvin Arnett. So, I thought maybe he had a second family or something. That's why Cassie and I came. To investigate."

Mark shook his head. "Wait, so you thought Melinda was your husband's what?"

"I don't know. Mistress. Secret wife."

Mark rolled his eyes. "You know that's crazy. Right?"

"Maybe. But how was I to know? I mean bigamy isn't unheard of. Anyway, I was in shock and felt helpless, so I decided to do something about it, and here I am."

Delbert flicked a stone with the toe of his boot. "I just wish you'd told me what you were planning to do. We really were worried about you. After you sent Cassie and me packing the other morning, I was concerned you'd do something really stupid. Looks like I was partly right."

"Cassie was with me the whole time."

Delbert frowned. "Yeah, well, we didn't know that, and I'm not sure it would've made me feel less worried or more so if I had known it."

Their heads turned when a sheriff's cruiser pulled in and parked behind the church bus. A deputy emerged from the car and scanned the area.

Delbert stood. "I'd best get out there before he interrupts Melinda and the reverend." Without waiting for a reply, he took off across the yard and met the lawman as he approached the group.

Paula kept her eyes on the reverend where he sat talking between Cassie and Melinda. He looked less perturbed, perhaps even slightly happy, but his face seemed to be one that carried a permanent scowl. *Unfortunate look for a man of God....*

Delbert spoke with the deputy for a few minutes, accepting a document from him. With a handshake and a shake of his head, he sent the deputy on his way. "Here's our cease and desist order," Delbert said, upon returning to the group. "We'll use it if we need to, but," he gestured at a remarkably happy looking Reverend Davis, "I don't think we'll need to. Still, maybe I need to go insert myself into the conversation."

"I'll join you," Paula said, standing.

"Reverend Davis," Cassie said as they approached, "you remember my friend Paula, and this is our friend, Delbert Derryberry."

"I remember both of them, young lady. Sir, I thought you were Mrs. Arnett's lawyer."

Paula exchanged a glance with Melinda and said, "He is both my friend, and my attorney. And he's just taken Melinda on as a client."

Delbert squared his shoulders. "Reverend Davis, it seems we got off on the wrong foot this morning. I apologize if I came on a little strong, but I assure you it was to protect Miss Melinda here."

The reverend nodded. "I appreciate that, sir. I certainly didn't know the whole story before my visit with these ladies. They've both assured me that they were unaware of the nature of the group stayin' on the property. I reckon they won't let such a thing happen again."

Paula recalled Zeke's desire to return for the group's next meeting, but she figured that was best left unsaid.

Cassie batted her eyelashes. "You see, we've explained to Reverend Davis that it's been difficult to make the resort work without renting to groups like the NJOA. He's going to start spreading the word on their church Facebook page so the *proper* kind of people from all over the state will know about us. Won't *that* be wonderful?"

Paula had to swallow a laugh.

The reverend stood and tipped his head. "Well, I s'pose I've taken up enough of your time this morning. I'm glad we had this talk. I'll be prayin' for you, Miss Melinda."

Melinda smiled. "I appreciate that. And if you and the missus ever want to come spend a couple of nights out here, I'll let you have a special rate. Any time of the year."

"Thank you," he said, shaking Melinda's hand. "We might just take you up on that."

Turning to Cassie he said, "Miss Campbell, I sure enjoyed getting to know you. Good luck with your catering bizness. You let us know when you're down this way and we'll order somethin' from you, maybe we could have you fix dinner for the annual members' meetin' or somethin'."

"I'd be honored to do so," Cassie said, patting his arm. "We'll be in touch."

"Miss Paula, Mr. Derryberry, pleasure to meet you," the reverend said before gathering his congregants.

Goodbyes were exchanged among Sue Ann, Sherry, Martha and the church ladies as the latter group loaded onto the bus.

"Whoever would've thought things would turn out this way?" Martha said as she joined Paula and company.

"They don't call her Goldilocks for nothing," Cassie said with a grin.

"It only worked because Reverend Davis fell for you two," Paula said, nodding at Cassie and Melinda.

Melinda blushed. "Well, it was mostly Cassie he was ogling, but we made a good team. All of us. The refreshments were a great idea, Paula. And, yes, it didn't hurt that the good preacher was smitten with Cassie. Thank you all. For the first time in ages I feel like maybe we've got a real chance of making Happy Valley profitable again."

Delbert held up his index finger. "Ah, about that—"

The smile vanished from Melinda's face. "Oh. I forgot."

Cassie stepped between them. "Hey y'all, we can hash this all out later. Some of these folks haven't eaten yet. Let's take care of their needs before we talk business."

Mark rested his hand on Melinda's back. "Good idea. Melinda needs to eat something and get in out of the heat. In fact, we all need to get out of the heat."

CHAPTER THIRTY-TWO

Paula followed Martha to the kitchen and helped warm the food from Delilah's. Tantalizing aromas soon permeated the home. When everyone had gathered around the table, Martha said, "Paula, your friends thought you'd like the special. Meat loaf, mashed potatoes and gravy, and fried okra. You've got a salad in the fridge and you'll find dressing on one of the shelves in the door."

Paula's mouth watered. "Oh, my friends know me too well. Fried okra is my one addiction."

"Mama, I only hope you know me that well," Melinda said. "I'd hate to have to arm wrestle Paula for her lunch."

"Of course! Your meal has everything Paula's does except I asked them to leave off the gravy. Actually, I think Melvin took your portion of gravy for himself."

"That I did," Melvin grinned.

Sue Ann rolled her eyes. "That man never turns down gravy. It's the one thing I have a terrible time fixing, but he never complains."

Martha passed a plate to Mark. "Doc, we got you the same thing. I hope that's okay."

Mark cut his eyes to Melvin and stifled a smile. "Absolutely. I just hope you didn't give my gravy away to Melvin here."

Melvin guffawed. "I angled for it, but Martha held firm."

"Should I wake up McKenzie?" Martha asked.

Melinda dressed her salad. "Not just yet. I want to visit with the group about the resort's future. I'm not sure I'm ready to let McKenzie in on the bigger picture yet."

Paula gave Melinda a sidelong look. Surely there were already too many secrets. Yet, Melinda knew McKenzie better, so she said nothing.

Cassie filled Paula, Melinda, and Mark in on the group's excursion to Oaks on Main. "I think we scored some points with the locals at lunch today," she said.

"How's that?" Melinda asked.

Martha picked up the story, "You know Jeffries followed McKenzie home the other afternoon. Anyway, he came out from the kitchen to talk to me after we got our food, and then his mom came out."

Cassie nodded. "That would be Delilah."

Martha nodded. "Yes, and they both asked after you, Melinda. They wanted to know if we needed anything, and this time I didn't brush them off like we have in the past. On the way into town, Cassie clued me in on how the locals viewed us. Apparently, they think we're standoffish at best, and devil worshippers at worst."

Melinda's eyes grew large. "Devil worshipers? That's the second time I've heard that today! How'd that get started?"

Cassie said, "When Paula and I ate there on our first night here, April, the little waitress there, told us that was the word around town."

Mark plunged his fork into his mashed potatoes. "I'm sure the good Reverend Davis had something to do with that nonsense."

Melinda's forehead creased. "No wonder people don't seem eager for us to succeed."

Martha nodded. "Anyway, when Delilah asked if we needed anything, I told her I was grateful for the offer, but that the thing we needed most was for people to spread the word about Happy Valley. That we love this area and people like Jeffries who have been so concerned about Melinda, but that we're realizing we can't do this alone. Then this amazon of a woman did the darndest thing. She *hugged* me, Melinda. Right in the middle of the café with half the town watching. You know me. Normally I'd shun a hug from a stranger, but with Delilah, it just seemed so natural."

"Natural? Like the jugglers?" Mark asked, between bites.

Martha chuckled and elbowed him in the ribs. "Not *that* kind of natural! Actually, she said she was sorry that she hadn't realized how difficult things had been for us, but that she was eager to help us fit in. And that, Melinda, if you need anything at all, you only need give her a call."

Cassie stood and refilled the tea glasses then set a plate of cookies on the table. "After that, darn near everyone in the place came over to meet Martha. Of course, they were curious about the rest of us, and we shook a lot of hands. After that, I'm fairly sure either Delbert or Melvin could run for city commissioner here and win in a landslide."

"Then, Paula called, and we hightailed it back here," Delbert finished.

Paula took her plate to the sink. "Well, I've learned quite a bit today, too. Okay, Melinda?"

Melinda nodded. "Be my guest."

Paula remained standing, her glass in hand. "My good friends from Dempsey, thank you all for being here. It feels so good to be loved and worried over by all of you. And my new friends, Melinda and Martha, thank you for your hospitality. Look at all the people you've opened your home up to in these past few hours. It's amazing that Calvin Arnett was able to bring us all together like this.

Martha snorted and rolled her eyes. "Indeed."

Melinda rested her hand on her mother's and said, "Mama, you don't know the whole story. Just listen."

Paula nodded at Melinda. "Last Sunday, almost exactly a week ago, I received a call from the state highway patrol. They'd responded to an accident involving my husband, and they told me an ambulance had taken him to Methodist Hospital in Lubbock. As you can imagine, I was a mess. Dempsey is well over an hour's drive to Lubbock, and by the time I arrived, it was too late. My Cal was gone."

Cassie stood and grabbed a tissue box, passing it first to Paula and then around the table. "You okay?"

"Yes," Paula said, her words catching in her throat. "The next three days were a blur. People coming over. Making funeral arrangements. All of my dear Dempsey friends were there to help. Cal was gone, but deep down I knew eventually I would be all right. I had wonderful memories and great friends to see me through. Then, Delbert came over and told me 'Surprise! Cal sold off everything but the house and bought a motel in southeast Texas. Not only that, he bought it from Mrs. Calvin Arnett.'"

"That's not exactly how I said it," Delbert protested.

Paula cast her eyes down. "No, but that's how it felt. I went over every torturous scenario in my head: Cal had a secret wife; Cal had a mistress; Cal had lost his ever-loving mind. You name it, I thought it. I wavered between being devastated by his death and decimated by his treachery. Melinda, I especially want you to know that before that day, I'd never looked through any of Cal's stuff, not his papers or anything, but after Delbert dropped that bomb on me, I went through Cal's desk with a fine-toothed comb. The only clue I found was a note that said: *'Calvin, I need you.'* It was signed *'M'* and the envelope in which it was stored had a Happy Vale address. When I put that together with what Delbert said about Cal buying a motel down here, I decided to go on the offensive. The rest you all pretty much know by now."

Martha did a double take. "So, *you* own Happy Valley now? Melinda, is that where you got the cash from to keep us going through the winter?"

"Yes, Mama. After I got my diagnosis, I knew we needed to do something to keep the place going. We didn't have any health insurance and I couldn't see a way out of it. Cal once told me that he'd do anything he could to help me. All I had to do was ask."

"But why?" Sherry asked. "What's *your* connection to Cal?"

Melinda cut her eyes to Paula and sighed. "Many years ago… Actually, a lifetime ago, Cal and I were married."

All eyes turned to Melinda and Sue Ann gasped. "What? But, why didn't he tell Paula? That doesn't sound like something Cal would just omit."

Melinda nodded. "It's a long story, and one that I've shared with Paula. She can relay parts of it to you when she's ready. I trust her to protect my secrets. Really, my marriage to Cal was so brief and so long ago, that I could see why he let it stay in the past with the cobwebs and dust. We parted as friends, and like I said he made me promise to let him help me if I ever needed it. And while I'd tried everything else, I could think of, nothing worked. Cal was my last resort. Without his help, I honestly don't know if I'd be here today.

"You all knew Cal and what a great listener he was. How he could make things right. After we parted, I honestly never thought I'd really need to take him up on his offer, but things got pretty desperate here. Paula and Cassie already know that my uncle who owned this place had gone a little crazy and stopped paying taxes on it before he died. Mama and I were able to satisfy the IRS after I inherited the place, and with the little bit of cash Uncle James had put aside, it looked like we might be able to make it profitable again. But then, I got sick. I prayed and prayed for an answer to our problems, and one night after sobbing into my pillow, I heard Cal's voice in my head."

Paula felt her eyes fill with tears.

Melinda sniffled and grabbed a tissue. "He said, 'Melinda, remember my promise.' I didn't question what I heard. Maybe my subconscious was bringing up old memories, or maybe it really was some kind of psychic telepathy, but I knew right then what I needed to do. I tracked him down through mutual friends we'd taught with in Illinois. One of the guys, Everett, had a number for him. When Cal answered the phone, he sounded exactly like the voice I'd heard in my head. We talked for almost an hour catching each other up on all that had happened since we parted ways. I was shocked to learn that he also lived here in Texas and he'd actually stayed not twenty miles from here on previous fishing trips."

Melvin nodded. "Yep. He was talking about Buck Parker's place on the other side of the lake."

Melinda continued, saying, "That's right. I told him about losing my sister, Marie, and my Dad. Mama, he said to give you a hug."

Martha snorted.

Melinda clasped her hands together and leaned forward. "I also told him about McKenzie and what a joy she's been all these years. He told me all about CalNet, but mostly he talked about you, Goldilocks. He said you were the most honest, smartest, most wonderful person in the world, and that you'd given him a reason to have a home again after all his years on the road."

"Pass me those tissues," Sherry whispered.

"I thought it was all exaggeration until I met you, Paula. But Cal was right. When I finally got up the courage to tell him what we were facing here—my cancer, the failing resort, the hurdles, all he said was, 'I can help.' I wouldn't let him just give me the money, even though he offered. Maybe that was stupid and if he had just given me money, Paula, you'd never have had to doubt Cal's love. But then we'd likely never have met any of you. I insisted that we come to an agreement that would perhaps pay off for him at some point in time, so we agreed that he would purchase Happy Valley and that I'd operate it for him until I could save up the money to buy it back. When Everett called me yesterday to tell me Cal had died, it hit me right in the gut. I went down hard. That, along with all of the stress and the heat is what sent me to the E.R."

Cassie reached for a tissue and dabbed her eyes. "We'd wondered if Cal's death was the bad news you'd gotten."

Melinda nodded. "While I was in the hospital last night, I realized I was going to have to contact Cal's wife, or his attorney, or someone who could help guide us through all of this. Did his death mean that Mama, McKenzie, and I would be out on the street? I never dreamed that Goldilocks didn't even know Cal had bought Happy Valley. I can only guess that he planned to tell you when the time was right. He actually mentioned bringing you down for a week, so maybe he was saving it for a surprise."

Paula wiped a tear from her cheek. "Maybe. I still can't quite understand why he didn't tell me he'd been married before."

After a pause Cassie said, "Remember what I told you on the road trip? That not everyone could be as honest as you, Paula? Maybe Cal was afraid of disappointing you, and that's why he didn't tell you about his marriage to Melinda in the first place. And then, when she called for help and he responded, he likely wondered how much to tell you about his unlikely purchase of a fishing resort in Happy Vale."

Paula hung her head. "I just hate that he died with such huge secrets. Knowing Cal, they probably weighed on him every day."

Everyone went silent, apparently wrestling with their own thoughts.

Moments later, a voice from the other side of the house said, "Mom? Where are you?"

"In here Mac," Melinda called.

McKenzie flung open the kitchen door, took a couple of steps, and then stopped. Her eyes grew large. "Whoa! Who are all these people? Did I miss something?"

"Not much," Mark said. "Just a group of protesters, an impromptu social gathering, naked jugglers, tv cameras."

"You know, the usual," added Melinda.

"Oh. Okay," McKenzie said. "What's for lunch? I'm starving."

CHAPTER THIRTY-THREE

Paula and her Dempsey friends followed Melinda and Mark to the living room. Mark hovered over Melinda as she sat, giving her the once over before saying, "Well, folks, I hate to break up a good party, but I have to get back to Nacogdoches. I don't know about the rest of you, but I have work to do tomorrow and patients to see. Melinda, please promise me you'll let someone else handle the details for a few days. Even if you don't feel like it, you *really* need to rest."

"Yes, Doctor Fields," she said, feigning a swoon.

After Mark left, Melvin looked at his watch. "Oh, I didn't realize how late it was getting. We need to get back on the road, too."

Paula frowned. "Surely you're not driving all the way back to Dempsey tonight."

Sherry cut her eyes to her husband and said, "Delbert promised that once we were assured that you were okay, we'd head back to Dallas to spend the night, then go on home early tomorrow."

Melvin wrapped an arm around Cassie's shoulder and said, "We called your rascal of a brother on our way down here and asked if he knew where you were. You know what he said?"

Cassie rolled her eyes. "Probably something like, 'Have I *ever* known what that girl's up to?'"

"You're pretty close, except his answer included some profanity. Anyway, he's in Dallas for a few days, and we're going to go take him to dinner tonight. I figure he'll be interested in knowing about your most recent shenanigans."

"Give the old coot a hug from me and tell him I'll call him on my way home."

Sherry and Sue Ann hugged Paula and Cassie then gathered their purses. "Is there anything you need us to do when we get home?" Sue Ann asked.

Paula clasped Sue Ann's hands. "My house plant, Mabel, would appreciate some water, I'm sure. She's on the windowsill over the kitchen sink. You know the garage code, right?"

Sue Ann patted her purse. "Yep, I have it stored in my phone."

Paula said, "Thanks. I can't think of anything else. The yard's going to need mowing when I get home. Ms. Stephens next door will throw a hissy fit if it grows too high."

Delbert draped an arm around Paula's shoulders. "Don't worry, I'll get someone over there to mow it so you don't have to. I know a couple of teenagers on my block that are suffering from the summertime blues.

"Paula, could I have a quick word with you and Melinda before we go?"

Paula and Melinda exchanged a look and each nodded.

Delbert tossed the car keys to Melvin. "Y'all go on and get the car cooled off. I won't be a minute."

After another round of hugs and handshakes and a called-out goodbye to Martha who came out of the kitchen to wish the travelers well, the living area emptied out except for Delbert and the two Mrs. Arnetts.

"Let's go into the office," Delbert said. "I sure didn't foresee how this day would go," he said, once they were in the hallway leading into the office area.

"Neither did I," Paula said. "I'm relieved, but I don't know what our next move should be. Any thoughts?"

"Well, you two need to figure out what exactly you want to do going forward. Paula, do you want to keep this resort and allow it to continue under Melinda's management? Do you want to honor Cal's arrangement with Melinda and give her the option to purchase it back? Do you want to get out from under it right away and look for an outside buyer for it? I'm sure there are other options that we just haven't thought about. When are you planning on coming home?"

Paula glanced at Melinda. "We booked the room through Friday, so we have time to explore some possibilities. And, if it's okay with Melinda, maybe I can give her a hand while I'm here and see what's involved in running a place like this."

Melinda offered a tentative smile. "I'd appreciate that. And I'd love to have you around a few more days. You can get to know the place and see what plans we discussed before my diagnosis. And if you end up allowing us to stay here, maybe you can be our guide to dealing with people in a small Texas town. When we got here, we were just trying to be self-sufficient, and apparently, they thought we were snobs, at best and devil worshipers, at worst."

"Of course, I'd be happy to do that. You know, Delbert, Cassie might want to go home with y'all. She might not want to stay now that we discovered what we came for."

"I heard that, Paula Jean Arnett," Cassie said, having returned from saying her goodbyes. "I'm not going anywhere unless you run me off."

"Well, that settles it," Delbert said. He looked at Melinda and Paula. "You two figure out what you want to do about this place." He turned to face Cassie and pointed a stern finger at her chest. "You stay out of trouble."

"No promises, you old Aggie," she said. After he hugged Paula and shook hands with Melinda, Cassie escorted him to the car.

CHAPTER THIRTY-FOUR

With Delbert and Cassie gone, Paula held her breath as she studied Melinda. Replaying their earlier conversation in her mind, she finally felt free. Free from the feeling of betrayal she'd been carrying ever since she'd learned there was another Mrs. Arnett. *Melinda's such a sweet soul. No wonder Cal felt the need to help her.*

"Well," Melinda said, breaking the silence.

"Yes. Well," Paula repeated. "Let's not talk about any more serious stuff today. We've got until Friday to hash this out. You've promised Mark you'll rest, and I promised I'd take care of the laundry that Ellie and Lindsey brought in. It kind of got pushed to the back of my mind."

"Oh, that's not necessary. McKenzie can take care of that."

"It's okay. I actually enjoy doing laundry."

"Really?"

"I know. Weird, right? It calms me down. Cal always said it was my hobby."

Melinda giggled. "We need to get you a better hobby, then. But, thank you. I'm sure McKenzie will appreciate the help."

Paula smiled and patted Melinda's shoulder. "Try and get some rest, okay?"

Melinda pulled her in for a hug. "I will. Thank you again. I can't tell you how much lighter I feel after our talk. I might finally be able to actually rest."

"You deserve to rest well," Paula said, shooing Melinda in the direction of the bedroom.

Satisfied that Melinda was on her way to a nap, Paula stepped into the kitchen. "Martha, Melinda went to lie down and I'll be in the laundry room if you need me."

McKenzie stood. "I can take care of the laundry."

Paula waved her hand. "No, there's no need for that, hon. I promised Ellie I'd take care of it."

Martha tossed a dishtowel to McKenzie. "Alright, then, you can help me dry, kiddo."

Paula had barely started the laundry chores when Cassie poked her head into the laundry room. "Need a hand?"

"Sure," Paula said, stepping to the side of the folding table.

Cassie grabbed a towel and shook it by the corners before creasing it. "So, any thoughts?"

"I'm trying not to have any right now. That's the beauty of laundry."

"Ah. That's how I feel about cooking."

For a while the two friends folded towels in silence. Cassie began singing "Shall we gather at the river," and Paula hummed along, enjoying the sound of Cassie's voice, the mindless activity, and the smell of freshly laundered linens.

When they switched to folding sheets, Cassie watched in amazement as Paula produced a precisely folded fitted sheet. "And you said you have no talents," Cassie laughed.

"Well, you know my mom was a stickler about stuff like folding sheets and making beds. Understanding the complexities of the perfect fitted sheet and crisp hospital corners were the cornerstones of my domestic education. She never taught me to cook, but I can make a bed with the best of them."

"I remember. She was the sweetest thing unless you didn't properly make your bed, then whoa! Katy bar the door."

Paula laughed. "Now, *your* mom was totally laid back. I've always loved Dolores. She's such a hoot. Have you talked to her recently?"

"Not since we started on this adventure. She and Daddy are somewhere wandering the country in their RV. The last I talked to them they were in South Dakota. I told them about Cal, and they said to give you their love. I'm sure they'll be in touch."

"They sent a beautiful floral spray to the funeral home. Oh! That reminds me, I still have a ton of thank you notes to write."

Cassie pursed her lips and turned a pillowcase right-side out. "Those can wait a week or two. And, I can help if you'd like."

"Thanks, but I think that's something I need to do personally. I'm sure there are still folks I need to notify, too—business associates, and such. Cal touched a lot of lives."

Cassie took one end of a flat sheet and waited for Paula to pick up the other. "I noticed Martha didn't seem to be a big fan of her former son-in-law. I can't think of any enemies Cal might've had through the years, but Martha's reaction to the mention of his name was pretty strong."

Paula brought her end of the sheet to meet Cassie's. Without meeting her eyes, she said, "Martha is under the impression that Cal wasn't faithful to Melinda, and her daughter didn't disabuse her of that notion."

Cassie laid the sheet on a growing stack. "So, Cal *wasn't* unfaithful, but Melinda let her mother think that was the case? How awful. I thought better of her than that."

"Well, don't judge. There were extenuating circumstances. I totally understand why things played out as they did. Just trust me on this, okay?"

Cassie raised an eyebrow. "What *can* you tell?"

"I'm trying to decide how much I can repeat without breaking her confidence. They were young and both teachers in Champaign. I think they just weren't ready to be in a long-term relationship yet."

"You know you're a lousy liar, Goldilocks. It's none of my business, so I'll just trust your judgement.

After they finished the folding, Paula found Martha working on a quilt block at the kitchen table. "Hey, I just wanted to tell you we're done. Cassie and I are going to our room now. Thanks for letting me take care of the laundry."

Martha chuckled. "That's a phrase I don't think I've ever heard around here, or anywhere for that matter." The smile melted from her face. "I'm glad Melinda was able to talk with you. That girl keeps all of her thoughts in her head. Maybe one day she'll feel like she can share them with me."

"Maybe. I hope she will. When Cassie and I were on our way down here, I was furious with this mysterious M in Cal's note, but from almost the first time I met all of you, I couldn't help but like you. Even before I knew Melinda's story, I decided that Cal must've had a good reason for buying this place."

"I never thought about it being Cal who put up the money," Martha said, laying her quilting square on the table. "Maybe I've been wrong about him all these years, but I'm not ready to forgive him for what he did to my daughter."

Paula bit her lip and considered her response. After a moment of silence, she said, "I didn't know *that* Cal. I've just known *my* Cal, and he was old-fashioned and stubborn, but he was also loving, and giving, and decent. As Melinda said earlier, there's more to their story than anyone else probably knows.

Martha lifted an eyebrow. "Well then, dear. I'm going to take your word on that. For now, anyway. Thank you again for your help."

Paula left Martha to her work and went back through the office and across the parking lot toward her room. Several of the jugglers, fully clothed, were sitting in the shade around the picnic table where members of the Triumphant Army of God had assembled only a short time ago.

"Hey!" one of the women called out. "Weren't you one of our judges last night?"

Paula smiled and made her way to the table, waving at Zed and Anabella as she approached. "I did have that privilege. I have to say, I wasn't prepared for the nudity, but the juggling was outstanding."

"Told you I'd put my best foot forward. Guess it paid off," Zed said with a laugh.

Paula's cheeks turned red. "I was a nervous wreck watching you. I mean, one slip of a knife and—"

"And a bull becomes a steer!" Zed laughed.

The woman next to Zed smacked his arm and said, "You're certainly full of bull. Guess that makes you an expert."

Anabella snickered. "You and your friends looked pretty shocked when I started my act. We didn't know until afterward that you all weren't prepared for our particular brand of juggling. It was priceless, though, to see you all with your mouths hanging open and your eyes bulging. You did a good job even so. Still, I can't imagine why this old fart won," she said, nudging Zed.

"Charm and talent, my dears. Charm and talent," Zed said to a laughing audience.

Another juggler offered Paula a beer and a place at the table, but Paula declined saying, "Thanks, but I'll take you up on that another time. Right now, a long nap is calling me." She waved and headed to her room. It felt like a lifetime since she'd slept there, dreaming that sweet dream of Cal. She'd expected to find Cassie inside, but the room was empty.

Within minutes, Paula was curled up under the bedspread with the air conditioner on full blast. Wishing she'd brought the Evanovich book was her last fleeting thought before she was out like a light.

CHAPTER THIRTY-FIVE

The light of the setting sun beaming through the crack between the drapes drew Paula from her nap. She wiped a bit of drool from the corner of her mouth and listened to see if Cassie was in the bathroom. Except for the muffled sound of birds singing, there was only silence. *Where's that girl gotten to?* Paula checked her cellphone. *No messages. This part of Texas must be where text messages go to die.*

The room's analog alarm clock told her it was almost six p.m. She showered and dressed in a white t-shirt and jean shorts. For the first time since the funeral, she took the time to dry and style her hair. She applied tinted moisturizer, a dusting of blush, and mascara. After standing back to admire her reflection in the mirror, she added her favorite earrings, a souvenir of a trip she'd taken with Cal to Scotland several years ago. For what felt like the first time in ages, a well-rested woman with few worry lines looked back at her. She tried out a smile, and it felt good.

Paula's heart ached for Cal, and she suspected that wasn't ever going to completely fade away. She hoped it wouldn't anyway. He'd meant too much to her for the past fifteen years, and hearing Melinda's story made her love him even more. She hugged her arms to her chest, and surprising herself said, "Thank you, Cal." And even though he didn't answer, Paula knew he'd heard.

She stuffed her room key in her pocket, grabbed the can of mosquito repellant, and left to find Cassie. The picnic tables were empty, so Paula headed to the office where McKenzie was behind the desk, engaged in a sudoku puzzle.

McKenzie looked up. "Oh, hi, Patricia. Is everything okay?"

Paula flinched. "Oh, uh, my name's actually Paula, not Patricia. My friend, Cassie, was just playing one of her little tricks when she introduced me before."

"Hmm. Okay. Do you need any help?"

"I'm looking for my friend. Have you seen her?"

"No ma'am. But you might check back in the campground. Mom and Gram went back there a little while ago. Maybe Cassie went with them."

"You're okay up here by yourself?"

"Sure, I do it all the time. Oh, by the way, I'm really sorry about the naked jugglers. Honest I thought they were regular clothes wearing jugglers. I didn't know anyone juggled in the nude."

Paula laughed, "Neither did we. Although, I have to say it was an interesting experience."

McKenzie shivered. "I'll bet! Glad I wasn't a judge."

"I'm glad you weren't either." She turned to leave, stopped, and turned around. "I've been meaning to ask, are you on vacation from school?"

McKenzie closed her puzzle book. "Nah. I went to a junior college in Indiana, but I wasn't sure what I wanted to do. Then then we moved down here and Mom got sick, I figured I'd help out until she didn't need me anymore."

"Have you decided what you want to do now?"

"I'm trying to choose between being a massage therapist or an esthetician. Do you think that's silly of me?"

"Absolutely not. Is there a school nearby where you could take those courses if you had the opportunity?"

"There's one in Tyler. It's a couple of hours away, though. I'd either need a better car or a place to stay there during the week. But first, we've got to get Mom well."

Paula smiled. "She's very lucky to have you as a daughter."

"Thank you, Ms. Paula," McKenzie said, blushing and raising a hand to brush her hair out of her face. It was then that Paula noticed the heart-shaped speckle on the back of McKenzie's left hand. It looked exactly as Melinda had described her twin sister's birthmark.

Feeling as if she might have solved another piece of the 3M's puzzle, Paula left the office and encountered Jeffries walking across the parking lot. "Hi Jeffries," she smiled. "You aren't helping out at your mom's place tonight?

He grinned and tipped his head. "Hello, Ms. Paula. We close after the noon meal on Sundays, and we're closed on Mondays. It's the only time Mom gets a break. Say, is McKenzie around?"

"She is. In fact, she's in the office holding down the fort right now, and I'd bet she'd enjoy some company."

His smile widened. "Cool, thanks. I'll go see if I can help out or something."

Paula watched Jeffries jog up the stairs to the office and heard McKenzie say, "Oh, hi!" before the door closed behind him. She could almost feel the blush on the girl's face.

As she headed down to the campground, Paula found herself smiling and humming along with a familiar folk song she heard playing in the distance. As she neared the lake, the strains of an acoustic guitar grew louder. The smell of barbecue drew her onward until she emerged at the edge of the camp.

Several fully clothed jugglers called out greetings, and she waved and returned their friendly smiles. Wandering through clusters of friends chatting about this or that, Paula searched for a glimpse of Cassie's dark hair. She thought she saw Melinda seated in a folding chair on the far side of the camp and made her way toward her, hoping Cassie would be close. When she neared, she realized Martha was hovering over her daughter, and the two were engaged in what appeared to be an intense conversation. *Oops!* Paula spun on her heel and bumped into Zeke. "Oh, excuse me. Oh, hey there."

"Hey, yourself, Ms. Paula," Zeke said, matching her smile with one of his own. "Glad you could join us this evening. Cassie told us you were sleeping."

"I took an epic nap, it seems. So, have you seen Cassie recently?"

"*Seen* her? You could say that. Watch this."

Paula held up her hand. "Wait. Please tell me she's not juggling naked."

Zeke stifled a chortle and knocked on the door of his motorhome. "Judge for yourself. Ms. Campbell, you've got an audience." He cued the guitar player who began playing a Spanish flamenco song.

Paula steeled herself for what she might see, but when Cassie emerged from the camper, she had on the same khaki shorts and Longhorn t-shirt she'd worn all day.

With a Mona Lisa smile, Cassie floated down the steps of the motor home, a multi-colored bean bag style ball in each hand. She curtsied to Paula and the others who'd gathered in a semi-circle. "My first performance is dedicated to my dearest friend, Paula Arnett," she said. "Bet you thought I was going to be stark naked, right?"

Along with the audience, Paula laughed. Out of the corner of her eye, she saw Melinda and Martha headed over, and she waved at them to join her, securing a chair for Melinda.

"I've been working on this routine for approximately…" Cassie checked her watch… "two and a half hours. The first hour of which was mainly spent learning to do this…" She let the ball in her right hand fall to the ground before tossing the other one above her head and catching it in her opposite hand. She then tossed it in the opposite direction and caught it again. After ten successful tosses, she gripped the ball and curtsied to the tune of wild applause.

She raised her eyebrows. "Exciting stuff, right?" she said, to a chorus of laughter. She curtsied again and picked up the second bag. "The next forty-five minutes were spent learning to do this…." As the first ball left her hand and began to descend, she threw the second one and caught both in the opposite hands. "Wait. I forgot to keep them going."

On her next attempt, she kept both balls in the air for six successive throws before dropping one. "Hold on, I can do better than that." Settling into a determined stance, she tossed the balls from hand to hand for twenty throws before catching them both in one hand. A thunderous round of applause rang throughout the campsite.

Anabella left her spot in the doorway of her RV and descended the steps. "Folks, you ain't seen nothing yet." She tossed a third ball to Cassie.

Cassie took a deep breath and settled two balls in her right hand and one in her left. After two false starts and one fit of giggles, she kept a three-ball cascade in the air for nearly a minute. The onlookers applauded and cheered as she placed her arm across her waist and bowed. "Thanks, guys. This was so much fun."

Zeke stepped beside her and looked to the crowd. "Folks, I'd say we have us a juggling prodigy on our hands. It's the damndest thing I've ever seen. This little la—er, uh, sorry, *Cassie* picked up juggling like nobody I've ever known, and y'all know I've seen a whole lot. I expect it won't be long before we see her at future N.J.O.A. gatherings."

Cassie held up her hand and laughed. "Nah, I think I'll keep my clothes on for the time being, thank you very much, but I *have* learned to never say never."

Zeke clapped her on the back. "Well, if you change your mind, you'll always have a place with us."

"Thanks, Zeke. And thank you to my patient teacher, Anabella."

Anabella stepped forward, grabbed Cassie's hand, and took a bow. She pulled her aside and said, "I have something for you. These were given to me last year when I was a beginner." She held out a small drawstring bag that held three bean bag balls.

Cassie hugged Anabella and Zeke. "Thank you both. I'll keep practicing."

"I hope so," Anabella said.

After receiving back pats and words of encouragement from many of the assembled jugglers, Cassie made her way to Paula. "What'd you think?" she asked.

Paula beamed as she hugged her friend. "You're amazing! But then, you've always been the athletic one in this friendship. I shouldn't be at all surprised."

Melinda and Martha joined them. "I, for one, am thoroughly impressed," Martha said.

"Me, too," Melinda said. "When I get some of my energy back, maybe you can teach me to juggle."

"Then I'd better practice, practice, practice," Cassie said, her eyes twinkling.

Zeke approached the women and touched Martha's shoulder. "We'd love to have you all stay for supper, Ms. Martha. The guys cooked a brisket and there's more than enough for everyone. Whaddya say?"

Martha's hand rested on her chest. "Well, I'd love to. How about it, Melinda?"

"I guess I could be persuaded," she winked. "Actually, I've been smelling that brisket all afternoon and if you hadn't invited us, I'd likely have just made myself a place at the table anyway."

Zeke threw back his head and laughed. "How about you two?" he asked Paula and Cassie.

"We wouldn't miss it," Paula said.

Cassie nodded. "Darn straight. Count us in. Thanks."

The women followed Zeke to the barbecue pit where Zed and several other men were tending the brisket. "Have you ladies met my ornery baby brother, Zed, yet?" Zeke asked.

Paula stood beside Zeke. "Cassie and I have. I guess we should've figured you two were brothers."

Zed nudged his brother who said, "Our mom named our oldest brother Zane after Zane Grey, the writer. She liked the Z sound so much that we all got stuck with it. Our baby sister is Zinnia. I think maybe she got the worst of it."

"Do they juggle, too?" Cassie asked.

Zeke laughed. "Oh, no! We don't dare tell Zane or Zinnia about our hobby. They're a lot like the members of that group you had marching around up front earlier."

Martha covered her mouth. "Oh, dear!"

Zed nodded. "Right. They're good people, but they see everything strictly in black and white. Dressed and undressed."

A buffet table set up in the center of the camp was laden with steaming pans of pork and beans, corn on the cob, and mashed potatoes, along with a large bowl of German potato salad. There was a fresh garden salad, as well as a huge basket of bread, bowls of pickles and jalapeno peppers, and various condiments including three red squeeze bottles of different kinds of barbecue sauce, and a fourth one with ketchup. An oversized aluminum foil pan nearly overflowing with brisket completed the tableau. Red plastic cups filled with water or iced tea took up a separate table, with two oversized washtubs, one packed with ice cold beer, the other with a variety of soft drinks, sitting on the ground at the end.

"Ladies, first," Zeke insisted, and for once Cassie didn't scowl at his choice of words. She gracefully accepted all of the accolades the servers doled out with the food as she passed through the line, and when the women, hands laden with food and drink, found an empty picnic table, Paula claimed the spot beside Cassie, telling her she'd never gotten to eat next to a real celebrity before.

"That's just not true," Cassie said, taking a bite of brisket. "You got to eat across from the Mattress King of the Texas Panhandle at last year's Relay for Life."

"Oh yeah, I'd completely forgotten about that."

Melinda smiled, her eyes twinkling. "I sense a story."

"Paula was the chairperson for our county's Relay for Life event, and for at least a year she looked high and low for someone of note to come address the participants at the kick-off banquet on Friday night," Cassie said.

Paula laughed. "Yeah, believe it or not, Dempsey County is not exactly a magnet for the rich and famous."

"At least not for the famous," Cassie corrected her. "We do have some wealthy folks there."

Paula nodded. "True, but none of them was suitable for a keynote speaker. I was having a devil of a time trying to find someone, anyone, who would come get the event kicked off with a bang."

"That's when Sue Ann told us that her aunt Nedra from Amarillo was married to a famous guy. It seems her husband, Richard King, was always on television, according to the aunt," Cassie said.

"And so he was, but as the owner of a discount mattress warehouse store. He did all these crazy commercials dressed like a king, crown and all. I know I should have done some research, but I was getting worried that I'd be the one doing the speaking, and no one wanted that. I'd already invited him to speak when I discovered all the details of his fame, and I didn't have the heart to cancel his appearance. Besides, by that time the Relay for Life was just days away, and there really was no one else I could've gotten."

Cassie nodded and plunged her fork onto a pile of potato salad. "Well, as it turned out, he was quite a funny guy, and he was a cancer survivor himself, so his opening speech was very moving."

Paula grimaced. "Of course, in the middle of his speech, he tried to sell us all a mattress. He'd even brought a trailer full of mattresses with him from Amarillo. I was so embarrassed. So was Sue Ann."

Cassie threw back her head and laughed. "Even so, I'm pretty sure he sold a couple of mattresses that weekend. *And* he got to sit with Paula and Cal at dinner that night where I believe he might've sold one more."

"Cal always was a pushover," Paula said, squirting a bit of barbecue sauce on her brisket.

"And how do you say 'no' to a guy wearing a robe and a crown?" Cassie asked.

"He was pretty charming at that. Sold us a full-sized mattress and we didn't even own a full-sized bed! We ended up donating it to Habitat for Humanity, I think."

Cassie winked. "So, I guess I'm the *second* celebrity you've eaten dinner with, and I'm not even going to try and sell you a mattress."

Martha laughed and wiped the corners of her eyes with her napkin. "You two should be a comedy team. Of course, you have no reason to know this, but Melinda was a bit of a celebrity back in Indiana."

Cassie steepled her fingers under her chin. "Oh, really? Do tell."

Melinda's face turned crimson. "Mama!"

Paula set her fork beside her plate. "Come on. It can't be worse than booking a mattress salesman to address a charity event."

Martha sat up straight and lifted her chin. "I'll have you know my daughter was the five-time champion hog caller of Hendricks County, Indiana."

Melinda grinned and hung her head. "It would've been six times, but I got strep throat my senior year in high school and had to withdraw."

"What proof do we have of this feat?" Cassie asked with a gleam in her eye. "I mean, I could claim to have won a cow patty tossing contest, and you'd never know if I was telling the truth or not."

"I've got her trophies in my closet," Martha said. "She wanted to throw them out when we moved, but I wasn't about to have any of that nonsense."

"Still, I think we need some verification right now," Cassie said, turning in her seat. "Hey Zeke, did you know we have a five-time hog-calling champ in our midst?"

Zeke wandered over. "Oh? Which of you lovely ladies hold that honor?" Three fingers pointed at Melinda, and his lips curled into a wide smile. "Oh? Miss Melinda. How about a demonstration? I've never actually known a hog-calling champ."

Melinda waved her hand. "Oh, this really isn't the time or place."

"You mean you're too embarrassed to call a pretend hog in front of a group of people who juggle naked?" Zeke asked.

Melinda laughed. "Well, when you put it that way...."

Zeke whistled through his fingers. "Folks, can I have your attention?"

Melinda covered her face with her hands. Through clenched teeth, she said, "Mama, I cannot believe you did this to me!"

Zeke raised his voice. "Ladies, and Gentleman, it seems we have an actual hog-calling champion in our midst, and she's agreed to demonstrate her talents for us. It's none other than the owner of the Happy Valley Motor Inn and Resort, Ms. Melinda Arnett. Give her a hand, y'all!"

Melinda shook her head and stood. "Ack. I don't believe I'm about to do this. Okay, everyone, I'm pretty rusty. I haven't done this since I was a junior in high school."

"You can do it," Cassie said.

Melinda blew out a breath, made a megaphone of her hands around her mouth, and yelled, "Soooeeee! Soooeeee!" accompanied by realistic pig sounds. The crowd clapped and cheered in delight. Melinda took a bow before making a quick return to her seat.

Zeke clasped his hands together. "That was terrific! Folks, we need to teach Melinda to juggle. Can you imagine a routine set to a hog call?" The crowd's laughter nearly drowned out their applause.

Melinda's face turned a deeper shade of scarlet. Under her breath, she said, "It'll be a cold day in hell..."

Zeke sat beside Martha. "I want to tell you ladies that this has been, by far, the best get-together our group has ever had. I told Ms. Paula that we'd like to go ahead and reserve the campground for next year, but I didn't know if she's had time to relay that information to you yet, Ms. Melinda."

Paula winced. "Sorry, I haven't had the chance."

Melinda said, "Oh. Uh, we had a bit of a dustup with a local church group today over the nudity. I actually had to promise them that we'd screen our groups more thoroughly in the future."

The smile melted from Zeke's face. "I was afraid we were the cause of the problem. I'm really sorry for the trouble we caused. I guess we should've known this place was too good to be true."

Melinda reached across Martha and patted his hand. "You didn't let me finish. I said *I* made that promise. But, the fact of the matter is, *I'm* not the owner of Happy Valley anymore. And the new owner never made such a promise."

Paula's eyes widened. "Oh! That's right. Zeke, as the new owner of Happy Valley Motor Inn and Resort, I'd love to have you come back next year. Before you leave tomorrow, stop by the office and we'll get your dates reserved."

Zeke raised his eyebrows. "Really? Why, don't that beat all! Ms. Paula, you're the new owner? Well, I'll be! Isn't that a hoot?"

Paula took a deep breath. "I'm still getting used to being part of something this incredible. But I'm certain of one thing—all of you are welcome back next year. In the meantime, we'll work on finding a way to keep the nosy local teenagers from sneaking through the woods to spy on our guests."

Zeke stood and clapped Paula on the back. "Thank you, Ms. Paula. Let me go tell everyone the good news." He left and flitted from table to table. Everywhere he went applause broke out.

Paula's smile widened as she watched the others finish their meals. "You know, I've been brainstorming a lot about ways to get this place on its feet," she said.

Melinda sipped her tea. "But we agreed to not discuss business tonight, right? This has been such a lovely evening. I don't want to get my brain all wrapped up in details this close to bedtime."

Paula took a long swig of her Shiner Bock. "I did say we needed a break, didn't I? Sorry. I'm just excited now about the future. Just a few days ago I didn't think I had anything to look forward to."

Cassie patted Paula's hand. "It's been a whirlwind, hasn't it? It's good to see you with color in your cheeks again."

"The makeup helped, eh?"

Martha wiped her mouth and stood, before collecting the ladies' empty plates. "If you gals'll excuse me, I need to go take a plate to McKenzie."

Paula swatted a mosquito and said, "You might want to take two. When I came out here, Jeffries was just joining her in the office." She pulled a small bottle of mosquito repellant from her back pocket and sprayed her own arms then passed the bottle to Melinda.

"Always prepared, aren't you?" Cassie said.

Paula shrugged her shoulders. "Not always, but my nap helped clear my mind a bit."

Melinda sprayed herself then passed the bottle to Cassie. "So, have you two known each other your whole lives?"

"Since we were five," Cassie said.

Paula opened a fresh beer. "Yep. She claimed me on the first day in Mrs. Toliver's kindergarten class, and I never could get rid of her after that. Not that I ever wanted to."

Melinda placed a hand over her heart. "Aww, that's sweet. Marie was my closest friend. We didn't actually do much together socially, but growing up, we told each other everything. I never really had a need for a friend until I left for college, and then, well…"

Paula sensed Melinda's sudden discomfort. "Um, oh, Cassie, remember that time in the sixth grade when we decided we weren't going to be best friends anymore?"

Melinda raised an eyebrow. "What brought that about?"

Paula shrugged. "I'm not sure. It's not like we were fighting or anything. We just decided it was time to broaden our horizons. I think that's how Cassie put it, anyway. It lasted maybe seven days. We were both miserable. We allowed a few others into our tight knit circle after that—Sue Ann and Sherry were two of them. But speaking for myself, no one has ever been as close to me as Cassie. She knows every one of my secrets, and I'm fairly sure I know all of hers."

Cassie looked between Melinda and Paula. "Well, maybe not *all* of them. That's what makes them secrets, right?" Cassie had laughed after that, but Paula was left wondering what she'd meant.

She turned her head when several campers pulled out instruments and an impromptu jam session broke out. She moved to the opposite side of the table so she could see what was going on, and she, Cassie, and Melinda sat in comfortable silence as one of the guitarists played

"Brown Eyed Girl." In the background, a chorus of bullfrogs filled in the spaces between the notes.

A couple got up to dance and were soon joined by others. Zeke came over and extended his hand to Paula. She shook her head, then at his persistence, accepted his request and allowed him to lead her to the dance floor. Cassie and Melinda clapped and tapped their feet as Paula and Zeke showed the younger campers how it was done. The next guitarist played "Crazy Little Thing Called Love," and Zed tapped Zeke on the shoulder to cut in. Song after song found Paula dancing with one partner after another while Cassie and Melinda managed to turn down their own offers, electing to watch from their seats.

After the better part of an hour, Paula begged off and went in search of a cold beer, putting it to her forehead before unscrewing the top. "Mercy, that was fun!" she said, rejoining Melinda and Cassie.

"You're a good dancer." Melinda said. "I mean *really* good."

Cassie patted Paula's hand. "That and laundry are her primary talents. Cal always loved to dance with our Paula."

The smile on Paula's face softened. "It makes me sad that I'll never get to dance with Cal again, but just the act of dancing made me feel close to him. Melinda, did you and Cal dance often?"

Melinda shook her head. "Mercy, no. I have two left feet and absolutely no sense of rhythm… Wait, actually, we did try once when the Wild Bunch put on a fundraising dance. The music was from the Big Band era, as I recall."

Cassie opened a new beer. "The Wild Bunch?"

Melinda nodded. "That's what we called ourselves back when we were all young teachers in Champaign. Actually, I think our principal coined the term after we came up with some wild scheme to motivate our students. Our school was in a low-income neighborhood, and the kids mostly came from single parent homes. Most of them had jobs outside of school and very little parental supervision, so we had to think outside the box to get them to care about their futures. Anyway, the nickname stuck, and we did a whole lot of good, but we also had a really good time." She sighed. "Those were the best days."

Paula sensed that Cassie wanted to ask more but thought better of it. "I guess the dancing didn't work out well, then?"

Melinda chuckled. "You could say that. We were trying to do a foxtrot or a waltz or some such old-fashioned dance, and my feet got all tangled up with a guy dancing behind us and we both went down! I sprained my ankle and the other guy was furious with me. Cal came to my rescue, though, and took responsibility for the whole thing. He was so good at smoothing over rough situations, wasn't he?"

"Indeed, he was," Paula said, lifting her bottle. "To Cal, who loved us and took care of us."

Cassie and Melinda, tears in their eyes, raised their drinks. "'Til the very end," Melinda said.

Cassie nodded. "Amen."

CHAPTER THIRTY-SIX

When the musicians took a break, Melinda stood and yawned. "Oh, pardon me. It's been quite a day. If you ladies will excuse me, I need to hit the hay. These folks will all be checking out early tomorrow, so I'd better get my beauty rest."

Paula squeezed Melinda's hand. "Remember, we'll be around to help. Take all the time you need to rest."

"That sounds good, but still, I'm ready to call it a night. It's been a crazy couple of days. We're not used to such mayhem around here."

Cassie covered her mouth and yawned. "Yeah, I'm tired, too. I didn't take a two hour nap this afternoon like *some* people I know."

"Y'all go on then. I want to have a word with Zeke, and then I'll be along."

After Cassie and Melinda left the campsite, Paula sat for a moment breathing in the night, enjoying the steady chorus of frogs competing with crickets. The carpet of stars overhead reminded her of stories her mother had told her when she was very young. Her mother had said that each star represented someone who loved her even though they'd never met her. Her grandparents and great grandparents, on and on until the beginning of time. That as long as Paula could see the stars, she'd never be alone. Paula looked for the star that might represent Cal and found one shining brighter than the others. Surely, that was Cal.

In the end, Paula didn't have to go looking for Zeke. He found her there, a smile on her face and tears in her eyes. "Ms. Paula, I hope you're okay."

She smiled at Zeke, and told him she was, pointing to the star that she'd picked out as Cal's. "See that star?" She asked. "I think maybe that's my husband looking down on me. Wishing me well."

"If you believe that, then I am sure it is. Of course, I think that's Venus you're looking at. Not a star."

She put her index finger to her lips. "Shhh. I want to believe it's Cal."

"Then I'll believe that, too," he said, sitting beside her.

"I don't know if I'd told you that he passed away a week ago today. Just about this time of day, too. And here I am. Dancing and laughing and I don't feel awful about that. And that in itself makes me feel awful."

Zeke looked down and cleared his throat. "Ms. Paula, I lost my wife of thirty-five years, let's see, six years it'll be in September. Nearly that whole first year, I sat like a hermit in my house. During that time, I was as mean as a one-eyed, three-legged bulldog to everyone, including my two children and three precious grandkids. Every single one of them I pushed away. Even Zed, my oldest friend in the whole world, couldn't help me grieve. I was mad at God. Mad at life itself. I just wanted to die so I could be with my Beth. Every night, I'd sit on my back porch rocking back and forth, back and forth, in the rocker that was the twin to Beth's. The two of us had spent countless hours rocking there, side by side, over the years. Every night I'd rock, and I'd beg God to take me. And when He didn't, it just made me madder.

"Then one late summer evening, on a night kind of like this one, I was sitting out on the porch rocking like I did every night. There was no breeze, just the crickets chirping and the June bugs flirting with the porch light. I tell you, Ms. Paula, I felt a presence come onto the porch, just like Beth used to come out to join me once the kitchen had been tidied after a meal. That presence sat in Beth's rocker, and that rocker began to rock, back and forth, back and forth, in time with mine. Peace filled me, and I knew that Beth was still with me, just in a different way."

Paula's eyes grew wide. "Then what?"

"Well, I felt like a big ol' fool after that. I was embarrassed about the time I'd wasted being angry at the world. Thank goodness my family hadn't given up on me. I called the kids that very night and told them how much I loved them. I spoke to each of my grands and apologized. The youngest, Emily, was only five, but you know what she said?"

Paula, a lump in her throat, shook her head no.

"She said, 'Grandpa, I missed you more than pasghetti,' and that child does love spaghetti. I reckon that's the best declaration of love I've ever heard."

Paula's eyes filled with tears. "The best."

"Now, what I'm tryin' to say here is, I didn't do anyone, including myself, a bit of good that year. What a waste it was. Elizabeth wouldn't have wanted that, and I don't think your husband would expect you to put on black clothes and sad feelings to hide away from the world. If you don't mind my saying, a man who'd married a woman like you, someone who is good and decent and obviously full of light, would never have wanted you to hide yourself away. I'm sure he was dancing here with you tonight."

Paula sniffled and smiled through her tears. "Oh, Zeke. Thank you. You know, Cal came to me in a dream a few days ago. Actually, it was more than a dream. It was like your experience with Beth. He was right here," she said, her hand over her heart.

He nodded. "I believe that with my whole being, Ms. Paula. Those we love and those who love us are never truly gone. They are a part of us, and nothing can change that. You keep being yourself, and don't let grief or someone else's idea of how you should grieve keep you from living. Not even for one second."

"Zeke, Cal would've liked you. He wouldn't have understood the nude juggling thing, but he would've definitely appreciated your take on life."

They shared a tearful laugh, and Paula gave him a hug. "If anyone had told me a week ago that I'd be here in Happy Vale, Texas, crying and laughing with someone whose hobby is juggling in the nude, I'd have told them they were nuts."

"I reckon we might all be a little bit nuts but only in the best way, Ms. Paula."

"Thank you again. You enjoy the rest of your stay here. Hopefully I'll get to see you tomorrow when y'all check out."

Zeke took her hand in his. "I promise I won't leave without saying goodbye to you. I'll leave you my contact information so you can holler at me any old time. Who knows? You might even decide to take up juggling."

"Well, that's not likely, but I might just call you anyway. You know, to talk about life. Goodnight, Zeke."

"Night, Ms. Paula."

She turned the flashlight on her cellphone on and started down the path to her room. Halfway there, she realized she'd forgotten to talk to Zeke about an idea she'd been formulating. *Shoot. Oh well. I'll see him in the morning.*

The moon was high in the mid-summer sky, and the Cal star watched over her all the way to her room. She entered on tiptoes, hoping not to wake Cassie, but as it turned out her friend was sitting up in bed, watching an old movie on the television.

"I was starting to get worried," Cassie said.

"I'm sorry. Zeke and I had a good talk. Not about what I wanted to talk to him about, but a good one by any measure. I'll be sad to see them leave."

"Same here," Cassie said, yawning. "Here's the remote. I'm going to sleep." Within moments, soft snoring came from her side of the room.

Paula chuckled and headed for the shower. Once in bed, she turned the TV channel until she found John Wayne and Maureen O'Hara in "The Quiet Man." Cal had never approved of watching television in bed, so Paula felt slightly guilty for doing so. Still, this had been one of Cal's favorite movies, and she watched it to the end before turning off the TV and dreaming sweet dreams of dancing with her love.

CHAPTER THIRTY-SEVEN

The squeak of a drawer opening brought an abrupt end to Paula's dream of dancing under the stars with Cal. She opened one eye to see Cassie picking out clothes for the day. "Can't you see I'm sleeping here?" Paula said as she pulled the sheet over her head.

"If you're talking to me, you're not sleeping. Get up, Goldilocks."

Paula burrowed under the covers and mumbled, "I don't wanna."

"You're going to miss saying goodbye to the jugglers. Come on. Get up."

Paula rubbed the sleep from her eyes and threw back the sheets. "I forgot. Don't leave without me." She shuffled to the sink, splashed water on her face, and ran a brush through her hair. She created a lopsided ponytail then traded her pajamas for khaki shorts and a black tank top.

Cassie, dressed in a gray University of Texas t-shirt, had taken the time to put on makeup and arrange her hair in a neater version of a ponytail. She gave Paula the once over and said, "Well, I *guess* you'll do. Let's go tell them goodbye."

"Wait, I can't find my left flip flop," Paula said, getting on her hands and knees beside her bed. "Shoot. Where'd I fling that thing when I came in last night?"

Cassie nosed around the room and said, "Here it is behind the bathroom door."

"Thanks. I guess I might've had too many beers last night."

"You think? Let's go."

Paula stuck her room key in her pocket and shut the door behind them. She and Cassie headed toward the office and were surprised to find nearly all of the N.J.O.A. members gathered on and around the parking lot, saying their goodbyes. When they noticed Paula and Cassie, there were friendly waves and greetings.

Anabella hurried over and hugged Cassie. "You keep practicing, okay?" She lowered her voice to a whisper and handed Cassie a scrap of paper. "Here's my number. If you ever decide to join the N.J.O.A., give me a call. The first time is a little scary, but I've found it's actually good for the soul. I don't even need my anti-depressants anymore."

Cassie chuckled. "Thanks. I'll remember that."

Paula found Zeke and Zed saying their goodbyes to Melinda and Martha near the office door. "Do you mind if I give you a hug?" Paula asked Zeke.

Zeke clutched at his chest. "Mind? Young lady, I'd be heartbroken if you didn't."

After embracing the man, she asked, "Did you get your dates booked for next year?"

"Yes, ma'am. We'll be back next July."

She winked. "Excellent. I'll make a special point to be here then, just in case you need an experienced judge."

Zeke laughed. "I'm always looking for seasoned judges."

"Could I ask a favor of you?"

"Sure, Ms. Paula. You name it."

"Well, Melinda and Martha and I would sure love it if you'd spread the word about Happy Valley. In fact, last night, I had an idea." She nodded at Martha. "I haven't cleared this with our bookkeeper yet, but I have a feeling she'll go along. If we get at least ten new bookings that are referred by you or anyone with your group, we'll give the N.J.O.A. a discount on your next stay. Of course, I'll have to work out the numbers with Martha, but I think we can come up with something that will benefit all of us."

Martha chewed on her bottom lip before nodding. "We can definitely do that."

Zeke gave Paula a one-armed hug. "I'll be more than happy to tell folks about this place. Here, take my card in case you need to get in touch with me." He handed her a business card, and she looked it over before shoving it in her back pocket. "Ms. Paula, would you walk with me to my truck? I need to ask *you* something."

"Of course."

When they got to his vehicle, he ducked his head, "Would you... I mean..."

Paula froze. *Crap! He's going to ask me out.* She cleared her throat. "Um, Zeke, you know my husband just pass—"

"Would you speak on my behalf to Ms. Martha? She isn't married or anything is she? I've been trying all weekend to get up the courage to talk to her alone."

Paula, exhaled and grinned, laying a hand on his arm "Martha is a widow. I can't really speak for her because I don't know her that well, but I don't think she'd mind hearing from you. In fact, I think she'd like that a lot."

"Thank you, Ms. Paula. I just find her very attractive. I haven't wanted the company of a woman since Beth passed, but for Martha, I might have to make an exception."

"I'll definitely mention your interest in her. Kind of pave the way."

"You'd do that?"

"Of course. I have your number," Paula said, patting his card in her back pocket. "I'll let you know if she's warm to the idea."

Zeke hugged her again. "Thank you, Ms. Paula. Thank you so much."

Paula watched Zeke get into his truck and turn the rig around with ease. They waved at each other until he was out of sight.

"Did he hit on you?" Cassie asked when Paula returned to the office.

Paul grinned. "No. Just my bad luck. It seems Zeke has his hopes set on another woman."

"Would it happen to be the same woman Zed seems to favor?" Cassie asked, nodding at Zed who appeared to be entranced with Martha.

Paula clasped her hands. "Oh, good heavens! This could be a problem."

CHAPTER THIRTY-EIGHT

As the last juggler drove away, Paula followed Martha to the office to observe and learn what she could. After Martha filed the paperwork for the last of the N.J.O.A. guests, she asked, "Where's Cassie?"

Paula closed the file drawer. "She's making us all some lunch."

"What a sweet girl. She loves to cook, doesn't she?"

"Yes, she always has. Hey, what did you think of Zeke?"

"Him? He was nice. They all were."

"I think so, too. Anyway, he wanted me to see how you might feel about going out with him."

Martha let out a little gasp. "Really? I can't imagine what he'd see in me."

Paula grinned. "He told me he thinks you're very attractive, but he was too shy to talk to you alone."

Martha laughed. "What? *I'm* more intimidating to him than taking off his clothes and juggling in front of a crowd?"

"Apparently so. He's actually a widower and hasn't dated since his wife passed away a few years ago. So, would you mind if he got in touch with you sometime? I have his contact information."

Martha bit her lip. "Well, this is certainly unexpected. Let me think on it, okay? I married my husband straight out of high school. Never even looked at another man in all the years since. The thought of actually going on a date is a scary proposition."

"I understand. And, well, like I said, Zeke knows, too. I guess all three of us are in this club together."

Martha flipped the guest registry closed and set her pen in its slot under the counter, then patted Paula's hand. "Well, I promise to give it some serious thought. He's a fine-looking man."

"He is at that. Maybe he'll teach you to juggle."

"Oh my! I think I'll just stick to quilting."

"I've been meaning to ask; did you make all the quilts in your room?"

"I did most of the work, but a couple are the products of a quilting group I belonged to at the Seniors' Center back in Plainfield. The girls and I had the best time stitching and matching squares, designing and gossiping. I sure do miss those ladies. In fact, the quilt on my bed was a going away gift from the group. I treasure it above all my other possessions."

"It's gorgeous. What's that pattern called?"

"It's a Double Irish Chain. We come from Scotch-Irish stock, you know, so it holds a great deal of meaning to me."

"I don't suppose you'd be interested in teaching me how to quilt, would you?"

Martha hugged Paula to her side. "Are you kidding? I'd love to. Neither Melinda nor McKenzie seem to have any interest in quilting or sewing of any kind. It'd be nice to pass on my knowledge to someone else. Especially since you're almost family."

Tears formed in Paula's eyes. "Really? Martha, I can't tell you how much it means to me to have you say that. Thank you so much. You know, I lost both my parents soon after Cal and I were married, and as far as siblings, Cassie's the closest thing I've got. Now, with Cal gone, I just… Well, I almost feel like an orphan. I know you didn't really care for Cal and that must sound kind of silly from someone my age, but just… Well, thank you."

Martha placed her hands on Paula's shoulders. "Paula, my daughter and I had a long talk yesterday. She told me she'd let Cal take the blame for their failed marriage all these years when that wasn't the case at all. So, it seems I've been too hard on Calvin Arnett all this time, and for that I apologize. I just wish I could've thanked him for helping us."

"There's no apology necessary. When you're working with limited information, it's easy to jump to the wrong conclusions. Just look at Cassie and me. If we hadn't read that note from Melinda and immediately thought the worst of Cal, we'd never have made this trip. And I'd known him and trusted him for more than fifteen years. You knew him for a much shorter time, so surely you can be forgiven for thinking the worst."

Martha squeezed Paula's hand and stepped away. "Thank you for that." She cleared her throat. "Now, back to business. After we finish the books for a big group, we typically start on the laundry. But it looks like Ellie must be running behind. The first load of towels should be going by now. I'd send McKenzie out to look for them, but her mom let her take today off. She's out with that nice young man this morning."

"Jeffries? I really like him. How about if I go check on Ellie? She might welcome some help."

"You wouldn't mind?"

"Not at all. I need to get a feel for every part of this operation, right?"

Martha pursed her lips. "I guess that depends on your intentions. Are we going to be sent packing while you run the place?"

Paula took a deep breath. "Martha, I don't know what my plans are yet, but I do know one thing—this will *always* be your place, too, as long as you want it to be. After all, Cal didn't buy it for me. He bought it to help Melinda, and I'll honor that for as long as she, and you, and even McKenzie, want to be a part of Happy Valley."

Martha grabbed a worn tissue from her pocket and dabbed her eyes. "I'm sorry. I've been worried sick since I learned that we no longer owned the place. Thank you, Paula. You've really put my mind at ease." She pulled Paula into her arms and sniffled as they embraced. The phone rang and Martha said, "I'd better get that."

Paula stepped toward the door. "I'll go find Ellie." She headed outside and wandered to the campground, searching until she heard movement in the ladies' side of the community shower and bathroom. "Ellie, it's me, Paula."

Ellie stepped from around a shower stall. "Hi, there. I saw Ms. Melinda this morning. She looked rosy-cheeked."

"Doesn't she? It's amazing what enough rest and hydration will do. I came to see if you needed any help."

"Oh, thank you. Lindsey didn't feel well this morning, so I'm on my own. If you wouldn't mind taking this load of towels up to the laundry room, I'd sure appreciate it." She rolled a bin filled with towels toward the door. "There's a box of disposable gloves on my cart. You'll want to wear some before touching these."

Paula found the gloves and pulled them on. "Do you want me to bring out some fresh towels right away?"

"No, ma'am. We don't put them out until someone checks in; otherwise, they start to smell stale. This danged humidity affects everything, you know."

"I guess I hadn't thought of that. Is there anything else you need me to do?

"Nope, that'll help a bunch, and I can just keep on cleaning."

"Cassie's fixing lunch. You're welcome to come up and take a break and eat with us. It's bound to be just as good as her French toast was."

"Thanks, but I'm afraid I can't today. Not if I want to get finished by four. I brought a lunch and I'll eat out here under that oak over yonder. It'll save me some time, plus, it's the only place on the property that gets good reception."

Paula looked where Ellie pointed at an ancient gnarly oak. "Oh?"

"Yes, ma'am. I call that Clyde's Oak, 'cause it looks like my uncle Clyde."

"I see. I guess I'd have had to have known your uncle to see any resemblance."

Ellie chuckled. "He was not a handsome man, that's for sure."

Paula laughed. *Maybe she has a sense of humor after all.*

CHAPTER THIRTY-NINE

Paula returned to the office, started a load of towels, then followed the sound of laughter to the kitchen. Martha and Melinda sat at the table as Cassie served one of her favorite specialties—homemade chicken salad on fresh bread.

Melinda took a bite and looked up. "Hey, Paula, come join us. I was just about to ask Cassie how she creates such delicious meals yet stays so slender."

Paula filled a glass with tea and pulled up a chair. "She's a fidgeter. There's no telling how many calories Cassie burns a day just by fidgeting."

Cassie set a plate with a sandwich and pickle spear in front of Paula then propped herself against a bar stool and picked up her own sandwich. "That's true, but I *am* really careful about the ingredients I use. Usually, anyway. Sometimes I get carried away, but this recipe is on the skinny side. Now, yesterday's French toast that you didn't get to experience, that's a different story. I'll make it for you in the morning if you'd like."

"Mmm, yes, please," Melinda said, biting into the second half of her sandwich.

Martha nodded with a full mouth. "Yes, me, too. Excuse me." She grabbed a napkin and wiped her mouth before she took the next bite.

Paula bit into her pickle spear. "Cassie's chicken salad is one of my favorites. Did you put everything but the kitchen sink in these?"

Cassie smiled. "Try it and see. I think you'll approve."

Paula took a huge bite. "Mmm, let's see... I taste apples, walnuts, a hint of onion, and just enough mayonnaise to hold it all together. "Oh, yes! Perfect as always."

Cassie stood. "Anyone need a refill? Oh, and there are chips. I forgot to set them out." She hurried to the pantry, grabbed a bag of chips, and set it on the table before topping off everyone's glass.

Paula chuckled. "See what I mean? She fidgets. Always busy."

Cassie moved her plate and sat next to Melinda. "I don't fidget. I'm just efficiently inefficient. Or vice versa. I forget."

Paula took a handful of chips from the bag. "I brought a load of towels up from the campground. Ellie's working alone today."

"Did you invite her to eat with us?" Cassie asked.

"I did, but she's looking forward to eating lunch under a tree that reminds her of her Uncle Clyde. And before you ask, don't. It's just a tree as far as I can tell."

Martha laughed, "Ellie has some unusual ideas, but she's good as gold. I don't know what we'd have done if she hadn't come looking for work."

"That's true," Melinda said, wiping her mouth. "At first, Mom, Mac, and I were trying to take care of all the cleaning. I kind of knew what to do having spent summers here with Uncle James and Aunt Chloe, but it sure wasn't something I was good at or enjoyed. Ellie seems to thrive on it. She showed up one day out of the blue and asked if we needed a housekeeper. Honestly, we couldn't actually afford one, but she works on an as-needed basis, and not many people are willing to do that."

Paula raised an eyebrow. "So, she doesn't earn a paycheck unless you have business, and business is spotty, right?"

Martha held up her palms. "No, not exactly. We pay her a small monthly salary. When we aren't busy, which is most of the time, she'll come out and look over the unused rooms and freshen them up in case we have drop-ins. Then we pay her more when we have guests, but it's not enough for her to make ends meet. She also cleans several homes in the area during the week, since our guests are usually only here on the weekends. Occasionally, we get drop-ins, but it's pretty hit and miss."

Cassie asked, "Besides the flyers at the rest stops, what kind of advertising do you do?"

Melinda looked at Martha, "Not much, really. We have the website, but it's not all that effective."

Paula swallowed her last bite of sandwich. "When I was trying to connect the dots before Cassie and I decided to come down here, I Googled *'motels in Happy Vale,'* and this place didn't even appear in my browser. It wasn't until I typed in *'Happy Valley'* that I got a hit."

"Shoot," Melinda said. "That explains a lot. We thought we could set up the site ourselves. I guess we should've hired someone."

Paula looked to Cassie. "Hey, don't you have a regular catering client that does website design?"

Cassie stood. "Yep, hold on. I'll go get my cellphone."

Paula watched Cassie hurry toward the lobby then said, "Melinda, you sure look refreshed this morning."

Melinda smiled. "Thanks, I feel so much better. Between the rest I got in the hospital and the way you all pampered me yesterday, I feel like a new woman. Plus, it helps that I got so much off my chest yesterday."

Martha eyed her daughter and pursed her lips. "I just don't understand why you don't feel comfortable talking to me about whatever's on your mind."

"It's just hard, Mom. I promise one day you'll know the whole story."

Paula bit her tongue. It wasn't her place to tell Melinda how to deal with the past. Cassie had been right—not everyone had the freedom to be as honest as Paula was. She just knew that Martha would love her daughter regardless. Sure, knowing that Melinda had been involved with a woman would be a shock initially, but anyone could see how much Martha loved her daughter. Paula was certain nothing would change that. She did have one big question, though, that she thought could be answered, even though Paula was fairly sure she knew part of the answer.

"Melinda, can you tell me about McKenzie's parents? I think I might've figured some of it out, but I've made too many wrong assumptions these past few days."

Melinda looked at Martha. "Mama, do you mind? Paula was afraid that Cal was Mac's father, so I told her that she's not even biologically mine."

Martha shook her head. "I just can't listen, but you do what you need to. I just can't." She dabbed her eyes with her napkin and rushed out.

Paula's eyes widened. "Oh, I'm so sorry. I had no idea it was such a painful topic. Please forgive me for even bringing it up."

Before Melinda could respond, Cassie returned with her phone. "Hey y'all, I have that contact we were talking about…where's Martha?"

Melinda cleared her throat. "Uh, Mama had to step out for a while. I think she needed to rest."

As a rosy blush crept to Melinda's neck, Paula hung her head and said, "I stuck my foot in my mouth and upset her."

Melinda rested her hand on Paula's. "That's not true. Actually, she didn't want to hear what I'm about to tell Paula. But you're welcome to stay."

Cassie pulled out a chair. "Are you sure? This sounds serious."

Paula tapped Cassie's chair with her foot. "Go ahead and sit down. Melinda's about to tell us part of her story."

Cassie took her seat beside Paula and for once, didn't fidget.

CHAPTER FORTY

Paula held her breath as Melinda turned her attention to Cassie. Melinda took a deep breath and said, "Paula knows I married Cal while we were teachers in Champaign. I loved him, but not like a woman should love her husband. Or maybe, because I was in love with someone else, someone I wasn't supposed to love, I tried to pour that love into Cal, but I could never give him everything he deserved. Anyway, we divorced and he, being Cal, made me promise that if I ever needed anything, all I had to do was ask. Looking back, I think he knew I was setting out on a difficult journey. It's understandable that Paula would want to know about McKenzie—if she was Cal's. That's about the time the church protesters got here and interrupted us. As we headed out to confront them, I told Paula that not only was McKenzie *not* Cal's daughter, she's not my biological daughter either."

Cassie looked between Paula and Melinda. "Oh. So, she's adopted."

Melinda sighed. "Not quite. I mean, technically, yes. I'm legally her mother, and of course, I couldn't love her any more than if I'd given birth to her. But she's my sister Marie's child."

Paula jiggled the ice in her glass. "I thought she might be. Last night when I was talking to her, I noticed a little heart-shaped birthmark just like you told me your sister had."

Melinda nodded. "Yep. It's exactly like Marie's. Same shape. Same spot. Same hand."

"Does McKenzie have any idea about this?" Paula asked.

Melinda cast her eyes down. "No. I know she deserves to know – has every right to know. But I just can't do it. Not yet anyway. Not after all we've been through."

Cassie squeezed Melinda's arm. "Aww, you poor thing. You've really had a rough time of it, haven't you?"

Melinda forced a smile. "Cassie, when I went off to college, Marie stayed in Indiana and married her high school sweetheart. I thought they had the perfect relationship, but those years were terrible for Marie. Kyle didn't get any offers to play college ball on a scholarship, and he wasn't a great student. So, he had no choice but to get a job at one of his dad's car dealerships. But despite his financial success, he just couldn't let go of his football glory days. Marie was determined to have a happy marriage like our parents, so she put up with his drinking and fooling around. I don't think he was ever physically abusive to her, but he ground my beautiful sister down until she didn't have a bit of self-esteem left. And she never spoke of this to any of us. I think she blamed herself for tying him down, when, if the idiot had had any brains, he'd have realized that Marie was the best thing that ever happened to him."

Cassie's voice caught in her throat. "Poor kid. If she was anything at all like you, she deserved way better."

Melinda sighed. "My sister was the most decent person I ever knew. She had such a big heart and a good soul. She was so talented.

It still breaks my heart that she wasted it all on Kyle Blair. He was an awful husband... an awful human being, really. He refused to take responsibility for anyone or anything. After Cal and I divorced, I intended to stay in Champaign and teach, but at the end of that school year, Mama called and said that Marie was four months pregnant. But what should have been joyous news was a nightmare for my sister. Kyle accused Marie of having an affair. He claimed the baby belonged to someone else, and he refused to raise another man's child. Mama was concerned for Marie's well-being, so I packed up all of my belongings and moved back to Indiana. I got a teaching job in Avon, and Marie moved into an apartment with me. Kyle wanted a divorce, and Marie reluctantly agreed. Yet, as awful as her life had been with him, she refused to give up hope that once the baby was born, he'd come to his senses."

Cassie stood and filled her empty glass with iced tea, then topped off Melinda's and Paula's. "That's so sad. I'm so sorry. At least she had you there with her."

Melinda sipped her tea. "Thanks for this. Marie and I grew closer than we'd ever been before. We decorated the nursery in a woodland creature theme. It had owls and rabbits, turtles and raccoons, all peacefully coexisting. It was kind of magical. I went with her to Lamaze and learned how to coach her through the birthing process. With both of us being divorced, we now had something in common. We'd often sit up late into the night talking about the baby and our dreams for her or him. Still, she couldn't give up the notion that once the baby came, Kyle would be smitten. I wasn't optimistic, but she didn't want to hear it."

Melinda stared out the window. "She went into labor on a Wednesday afternoon. I called Mama and Daddy—they were traveling, and they started for home. After nine hours of labor, Marie delivered a beautiful baby girl. I was the first to hold her, and I was the one who placed her in her mother's arms. She was so perfect. Marie had already decided on a name: McKenzie Kyle Blair. She was convinced that with Kyle's name in there, he'd *have* to acknowledge her as his child."

Paula's eyes filled with tears. "But, he didn't, did he?"

"No. I called him. Marie called him. Even Mama and Daddy called him. I think Daddy even went over to try and shame him into doing the right thing, but Kyle refused to be moved. If he'd even gotten a glimpse of sweet little McKenzie, he'd have been hooked. She had the sweetest fuzzy black hair and huge, dark eyes framed by black lashes in a perfectly round face. She was adorable. And I swear she smiled at me from the beginning. She was such an easygoing baby, but Kyle never knew that. He didn't *want* to know that. He even refused to take a blood test to determine if he was the father, and Marie didn't want to force him. I tried to get her to go to his parents for help, but I think she hoped that if she played nice, he'd eventually finally come around. When he didn't, she was defeated. When it was finally apparent to my sister that Kyle wasn't coming back, she went into a downward spiral. Looking back now, I realize that she likely had postpartum depression. We didn't call it that back then, just the baby blues, but she began to struggle just to get out of bed every day. I took over for nearly all of McKenzie's care. Mama helped a lot while I was at work, but I'd frequently come home to find McKenzie crying her little heart out and Marie curled up in her own bed in a fetal position."

Melinda took a deep breath and hung her head as tears formed in her eyes. She grabbed a napkin from the middle of the table and dabbed her nose then sniffled. "One day, Mama had to leave before I got home from work. The place was quiet when I opened the door. I checked on McKenzie first, as I did every day. She was asleep with her little thumb in her mouth and a sweet smile on her little lips. I smoothed her hair and kissed her cheek, then I headed to Marie's room. I knocked, and when she didn't respond, I opened the door.

"She was lying on top of the coverlet, dressed in a pretty nightgown, her hair brushed and spread on the pillow. There was an empty bottle of pills on the table beside her bed and a note to me propped up against a lamp. In the note, she asked me to take good care of McKenzie. She said she knew I'd be a wonderful mother and she thanked me for trying to help. I called an ambulance, but I knew she was already gone. The paramedics worked on her, but, of course, it was too late. Mama and Daddy got there almost as soon as the ambulance. None of us could understand how Marie, our perfect Marie, could have taken her own life. We all spent the next several days, weeks, and even years berating ourselves for not seeing how depressed she was. It was a nightmare. Even now, I'll sometimes find myself wondering if there was anything I could have done to change things, and I know Mama does, too. We both believe that Daddy carried a huge burden of guilt to his grave, lamenting that he hadn't done right by his little girl. He was never the same after her death. In fact, none of us has ever fully recovered.

Tears streamed down Paula's cheeks. "Oh, Melinda. I didn't know your sister, but I know you and I know Martha. I don't think anything you could've done or said would've made a difference to Marie. I'm sure you were as supportive as you possibly could've been."

"We tell ourselves that, and then we think back on things we'd say to her like, 'This will pass,' or, 'Everyone gets down in the dumps now and again.' We just didn't realize how alone and sad she felt, even while we were trying our best to help."

The three women sat, wrapped up in their own thoughts, until Cassie stood and said, "Look at us. We're all a mess. I'm going to go find us some tissues."

When she returned, Melinda took a tissue and wiped her eyes. "Mom and Dad wanted to adopt McKenzie, but I argued that they'd raised their children. Besides, Marie specifically named me in her note. She knew that McKenzie and I already had a strong bond. And while single parent adoption wasn't a common thing in those days, the judge took Marie's wishes into consideration, and I became the mother of that precious child."

Paula sniffled and grabbed a tissue. "Has she ever asked who her father is?"

Melinda bit her lip. "We've kind of led her to believe her father is dead. Part of the reason we left Indiana last year was that Kyle – who by then had remarried and divorced twice more and had another child whom he refused to acknowledge – developed a huge drinking problem and started telling everyone that McKenzie was his. I don't know if it was the result of guilt or what, but all of a sudden, he decided that she was the only one of his children that really mattered. Mama and I were looking into moving to another part of the state to get away from him when Uncle James died and left me Happy Valley. And here we are."

CHAPTER FORTY-ONE

Paula's eyes darted from Melinda to Cassie and back again. Heat rose to her cheeks as she said, "I'm really sorry, Melinda. I sure hope I didn't upset Martha too much by asking about McKenzie."

Melinda let out a deep sigh and stood, stretching her arms over her head. "It's okay; you didn't know. I'm sure she's not angry; it's just that Marie's suicide is still a painful subject. If you'll excuse me, I think I'd better go check on her."

Cassie stood and pulled Melinda into her arms. "Oh sweetie, I can't even imagine. You go on. Paula and I'll clean up in here."

Melinda looked over her shoulder at Paula as she rested her hand on the doorknob. "Have you already told Cassie the details of my relationship with Cal?"

Paula narrowed her eyes. "No, I gave you my word."

Melinda offered a small smile. "Thanks. I knew from all Cal told me about his Goldilocks that I could trust you. But I'm so tired of keeping secrets. You have my permission to tell her everything. I don't know many women who could go without telling their best friend something so salacious, but I just feel like I'm ready to let go of holding onto it so tightly, if you know what I mean."

Paula bit her lip. "Does that mean you're ready to tell Martha?"

Melinda visibly tensed. "Oh, heavens, I don't know. Soon. Maybe. Perhaps I'll get up the courage while you two are here, in case I need moral support."

Cassie dabbed her eyes with a napkin then rested her hand on Melinda's shoulder. "You don't owe me any explanations, but we will be here to support you."

After Melinda left, Paula and Cassie cleared the table and wiped the counter. Cassie started running water over the dirty dishes when Paula said, "I'm going to go start the next load of laundry. Do you need any more help?"

Cassie added soap to the water. "Nah, I'm fine. I think I'd like to go out and get some fresh air when I finish here. Feels like I've been sitting still all day."

Paula chuckled. "That's my Cassie. Fidgety as ever." She headed to the laundry room, started a new load in the wash, and transferred the wet linens to the dryer. *Maybe I'll go take another look at those books.* As she passed through the office, she meandered past the counter. The guest register caught her eye, so she planted herself on one of the high stools behind the desk and thumbed through the pages. *I feel awful that I upset Martha so much. She and Melinda have both experienced such an unbearable loss, yet, they've kept on going.*

As she studied the number of guests the resort had hosted over the last quarter Paula wondered how she'd have handled Cal's death if he had killed himself. Certainly, she thought, she wouldn't have experienced the joys she'd had these past few days. The weight of a loved one's death was heavy enough without the burden of knowing the death had been self-inflicted. She wondered if Marie had visited her loved ones in dreams. Paula would never ask, but maybe someday Martha or Melinda would mention it if she had.

The bell over the door rang and Paula looked up to see Delilah Oaks coming into the office with a picnic basket sized bag. "Delilah! What an unexpected surprise. What brings you here?"

Delilah closed the door and smiled. "Hello, yourself. It's Paula, right?"

Paula smiled. "Good memory. It's so good to see you. One of these days I'm going to find the time to make it back out to your restaurant."

Delilah set the bag on the counter. "You're always welcome there. You know, after Jeffries told me about McKenzie's mom having to spend the night in the hospital, I wanted to do something to help. For me, that means cooking. There's enough food in here for a couple of meals—fried chicken, potato salad, green beans, and an apple pie."

"Aww, that's so sweet. Thank you. I know Melinda will truly appreciate it. I believe she's indisposed right now, but I'm sure she'll want to call and thank you once she sees all this. Um, I've been wanting to talk to you. Do you have a moment?"

Delilah kicked her foot back and rested her elbows on the counter. "Sure. I'm not in any hurry. What's up?"

Paula stepped around the desk to the chairs in the reception area and gestured for Delilah to join her. "I wanted to let you know that we didn't technically tell you everything the other night when we met. My friend, Cassie, and I came here on a fact-finding mission. To make a long story short, unbeknownst to me, my late husband was friends with the family who owned Happy Valley, and when Melinda started her cancer treatments, he helped her out by purchasing the resort here and, uh, he died before they had the opportunity to buy it back. Soooo, it seems I am now the owner of this fine establishment."

Delilah's eyes grew wide. "Oh, my goodness! And you had no idea? What are you planning to do?"

Paula shrugged. "To be honest, I haven't thought that far ahead yet. I do know that I want Melinda and her mother to continue as management, but beyond that, I haven't a clue. I've just started looking over the books, and it's not hard to see that this place needs a powerful marketing campaign to get it up to its full potential. With Melinda being sick, she's had her hands full, so they've been barely hanging on here since they took the place over. That's why I specifically wanted to talk to you. I noticed that you've got quite a thriving business in town, and that doesn't happen by accident. I have *some* ideas to boost our visibility and get more people out here, but since you're here, I hoped maybe you'd be willing to share some suggestions."

"Me? Well, certainly. It's not easy for outsiders to come into a small town like Happy Vale and be accepted by the locals. For single women, it's even harder. I was born here, married my high school sweetheart, and still had to scramble to get the Oaks up and running, and it was harder, still to make a profit. Hmm... Off the top of my head I'd suggest that you join the Chamber of Commerce. It's filled with a lot of old fogies, and some of the businesses here haven't changed one iota since the last world war, but the new chamber manager is a young woman with big ideas for the county. I'll get you her name.

Paula stood and grabbed a pen and pad from the counter then started jotting notes. "Thanks. That's a great idea."

"Oh! And you might want to join the Rotary Club or the Lions Club and make some connections that way. I'm a Rotary Club member, and I can invite you and Melinda to a meeting. Also, I'll bet there's a local association for bass fishermen. You might look into getting a membership with them. But, since this is a motel *and* fishing camp, you're going to need to advertise all over the state and maybe even in some national publications. People who live here have their spots they like to fish, but you want to draw people in from Dallas and Houston and even up in the panhandle."

"These are all great ideas. We need to build community connections, but we also have to fish the larger pond.

Delilah threw her head back and laughed. "Pun intended? Word of mouth is pretty powerful around here, but I don't think that's anything you didn't already know. The thing to remember about a small town is it remains small because kids grow up and don't have any reason to stay. That means those kids and their families are likely in the big cities and they have friends there that would like to come experience nature on the weekends. So…"

Paula's face lit up. "Of course! Give the locals a reason to like us, and they tell their kids, and their kids mention us to their friends. Wow, you've just given me a great idea. Maybe even *ten* great ideas."

"I'm glad to help, but you're also right about looking at ways of reaching folks through other avenues. My place doesn't have to do that, but we could work out some mutually beneficial advertising, like folks who stay out here could get a discount on their meal at our place and vice versa." Delilah took a card out of a case in her purse and gestured for Paula's pen. "Here's my home number. If you have any questions or ideas you want to bounce off me, feel free to give me a call."

"Thank you! I love your ideas. I just hope you don't regret giving me your number—my questions may be coming fast and furious for a while. I'm so happy you came by today. The food alone is awesome, but you just put the cherry on top.

Delilah stood. "Well, thank *you.* Listen, you've got my number now. I need to get home. Jeffries has to head back to Dallas tomorrow, and if I know my son, he hasn't even started his laundry yet. He really likes McKenzie, by the way, and she seems like a sweetie."

Paula stood and held the door open. "She's the sweetest, but then your Jeffries is a perfect gentleman. They're pretty cute together."

"Thank you. He is a good kid. I just want him to get finished with school before he makes any big decisions, if you know what I mean."

Paula nodded, "Oh, I get it. I don't have any kids of my own, but still...."

Delilah left and the phone rang. Paula shoved Delilah's card in her pocket and picked up the receiver. "Good afternoon. Happy Valley Motor Inn and Resort. How may I help you? ...Oh, a reservation? Please hold for a moment while I transfer you to our reservations desk." She pushed the hold button and scurried down the hallway then knocked on Martha's door.

Melinda cracked the door open without saying a word. Her eyes were red, and her face stained with tears. Paula peeked over Melinda's shoulder and saw Martha seated next to the craft table, attacking a quilt square. Paula grimaced. "Uh, Melinda, I hate to bother you, but there's a call from someone wanting to book a room. Do you mind showing me what to do?"

Melinda wiped her eyes with the back of her hand as she stepped into the corridor and closed the door behind her. "Not at all. Did you put the call on hold?"

They hurried to the office. "Yes, I told them I was transferring them to reservations. So, you're reservations."

Melinda winked at Paula and picked up the phone. "This is Melinda in reservations. How may I help you? ...Yes, we are right on Lake

Toledo Bend. ...Fishing? You bet. ...Great! What dates do you have in mind?" She flipped open the planner to the last week of July.

Paula looked over Melinda's shoulder. *There aren't* any *entries at all that week.*

Melinda cleared her throat. "Let's see, it looks like we have several rooms available for check-in on the twenty-seventh and departing on the thirtieth, but if you prefer a campsite or trailer hook-up, we can help you out with that, as well."

Paula scribbled a quick note and pushed it in front of Melinda: *"Ask how they found out about us."*

Melinda nodded. "Let's see, you need two king rooms. How many guests will be staying in each room? ...Two adults?" Melinda gave them pricing information then took their names and credit card number. "Got it. Thank you for choosing Happy Valley Motor Inn and Resort. May I ask how you learned about us?" A smile spread across her face. "Yes, he is a hoot. Again, we thank you for your business. We'll look forward to meeting you on the twenty-seventh."

She cradled the receiver and her eyes danced as she turned to face Paula. "You're not going to believe this... It was Zeke! They met Zeke at a restaurant in Denton, and apparently he told everyone in the place about us."

Paula clasped her hands. "That's our boy! Let's make sure and credit two referrals to the N.J.O.A. Martha and I promised them a discount if the club sent at least ten referrals our way before their next event here."

"Oh, okay. I'm going to need a better system to keep up with stuff like that."

The women jumped when the phone rang. Melinda took the call and made another reservation. When she hung up, she said, "Wow, that's another referral from Zeke now. This one's for the first week in August."

Paula offered a delighted grin. "Very cool! I knew Zeke would be just the kind of cheerleader we needed... Oh! Hold on, I hear the dryer buzzing..." She spun on her heel and headed to the laundry room. She began to fold towels and closed her eyes as she inhaled their fresh, clean scent. *Hmm. Delilah's suggestions were terrific. I almost want to just jump in and take the reins, but I just don't know how much of the day-to-day business here I'm really willing to take on. I don't know. Maybe Cassie's right. Things in Dempsey have changed. Without Cal there, would my memories of us together comfort or stifle me?*

Her thoughts wandered back to the day after Cal died. A friend from church called to express her sympathy. She was in her early seventies and had been widowed for a couple of years. "Paula," she'd said, "don't make any quick decisions right now. They're bound to be all tied up in your grief and you might regret them later." She went on to explain how, at her children's urging, she'd sold her home a month after her husband's death and moved in with her daughter's family. She soon realized that relinquishing her independence was a colossal mistake. "I love my kids, don't get me wrong, but I feel like I'm a freeloader. I'd give *anything* to have my own home again."

Paula folded the last of the towels, stacking them beside the others on the shelves. She knew her situation was different than her friend's had been. Paula was much younger and didn't have children urging her to do anything. *My home's in Dempsey, filled with memories of life with Cal. Selling it would feel like giving up everything we had together. I'm not ready to do that yet. Still, it is awfully big, and even though it's paid for, I'll still be responsible for property taxes and H.O.A. dues. Of course, Delbert can help me with that stuff, but it's still daunting. I really wish I'd taken a greater interest in our finances.* She let out a deep sigh and cleaned the lint trap. *I already love it here. But do I love it like a teenage girl loves a boy she's met on summer vacation? Will this infatuation wane once summer's over? I guess only time will tell. Maybe I can keep the Dempsey house and still come here every couple of months. I'm sure with a little coaching, there's a lot I could handle over the internet.*

She turned off the light in the laundry room and stopped by the office where Melinda was checking in a man, a very pregnant woman, and a little girl who was busy playing a game on a tablet. Paula smiled watching how Melinda seemed to truly enjoy interacting with guests.

Melinda reached for a key on the peg board and, seeing Paula, smiled. "Oh! I didn't see you there. These are the Grahams. They were passing through and decided to spend a night with us. Would you mind checking with Ellie to see if Room 12 is available?"

"I'd be happy to. I'll be right back." Paula winked at the little girl and took the key to room from its hook on the wall. She trotted over to the room, looking for signs of Ellie. She recalled that the housekeeper had planned to be finished by four. It was half past the hour, but it wouldn't hurt to make sure the room was good to go. She wondered if Zeke had also had a hand in this couple's decision to seek out Happy Valley. It might be his way of showing off for Martha, but Paula didn't care.

The room was spotless, but lacked towels, so Paula made a note to bring some back over for the Grahams. On her way back to the office, she walked past a black SUV and waved at the driver who gave her a long, hard look. Maybe another of Zeke's referrals, she thought with a smile. "Room twelve is ready to go," Paula said, entering the office. "I'm just going to grab some towels fresh out of the dryer for you."

Melinda closed the guest register. "Paula, Mr. Graham says they ran into a fellow by the name of Zeke at a rest stop outside of Dallas. He says Mr. Zeke recommended us highly."

Paula resisted the urge to give a fist pump. "Oh, that's wonderful. Mr. Zeke is one of our favorite guests. We're so happy you decided to stay with us."

Mrs. Graham rubbed her protruding belly and nodded to her daughter. "We're taking Sophia here on a road trip. She's about to become a big sister, and we wanted to do something fun with her before the baby gets here."

Melinda said, "What a great idea. When are you due?"

Mrs. Graham winced and held her back. "Not for three weeks. Sophia here was a week late, so I'm not expecting any surprises."

Mr. Graham grabbed his daughter's hand. "I vote for no surprises."

Paula said, "Me, too, if my vote's worth anything. I'll be over in a minute with your towels." She rushed to the laundry room and grabbed a few sets of towels then hurried back through the empty office.

As she crossed the parking lot, the driver of the SUV focused on his cellphone, shaking it in apparent frustration. He appeared to be yelling at the phone, but not into it. She held her breath and strained to hear what he was so obviously upset about.

She handed off the towels to Mrs. Graham and smiled at Sophia who was twirling, arms spread, as she belted out a song from *Frozen*. Paula smiled to herself as she headed to her own room to see if Cassie was there. Seeing that the dark room was empty, she locked the door and headed back toward the office.

Melinda opened the office door and waved for Paula to hurry. When Paula stepped in, Melinda asked, "Would you mind watching the office for a few minutes? I need to go smooth things over with Mama."

"Of course, go ahead. Hey, does Ellie have a walkie talkie?"

"No, but that's a great idea. It sure would save us all some steps." Melinda stepped toward the door to the residential section then spun around. "Paula, I just want you to know how much I appreciate you. You've brought something to this place that's been missing since we got here. For the first time in months, I feel hopeful."

Paula blushed. "I just wish I'd been open from the beginning instead of all the subterfuge. I should've known I could trust Cal. I just wish he'd have told me about you when we got married. All our secrets just slowed us down."

Melinda's lungs deflated. "I know what you're trying to tell me, Paula. It's time to come clean on all accounts. I'm just so afraid of how Mama's going to react once she knows the truth. She can be very unyielding in her beliefs, and it's going to be a kick in the gut when she finds out who I really am. She's been my rock my whole life, and the truth could rip us apart."

"But what is *not* telling her doing to *you?* Carrying such a huge secret can't be good for your health. You've suffered with this for so long, not being able to be who you really are." Paula stepped closer and rested her hand on Melinda's arm. "It's easy to see how much Martha loves you. She might not understand or approve, but I just know she'd never stop loving you. I'm positive nothing could ever change that."

Melinda took a shaky breath. "Okay. You've convinced me. I'm going to bare my soul to Mama right now."

"Not without a hug first," Paula said, wrapping her arms around Melinda and giving her a firm embrace. "I wish you the best of luck. I'll be with you in spirit."

Melinda took a deep breath and nodded. "Thanks. Here goes nothing."

Paula said a little prayer for Melinda and Martha before taking her place on a stool behind the desk. She was nervous for Melinda and anxious about Martha's reaction, but couldn't help but believe that Melinda was doing the right thing by telling her mother the truth.

Trying to distract herself, Paula thumbed through the reservations calendar. *Hmm. Compared to past months, the near future already looks so much brighter. I wonder when prime bass fishing season is? Filling the resort then needs to be a major priority. What can we do to draw fishermen here?*

The phone interrupted her thoughts, and she was soon busy taking a steady stream of reservations, all resulting from Zeke's personal brand of marketing expertise. In between calls, her smile grew wider. *This is awesome! Maybe we should make Zeke Fitzgerald our official ambassador.*

CHAPTER FORTY-TWO

Paula had completely forgotten about the man in the SUV from the parking lot until he entered the office. "Hello there," she said, offering a warm smile. "How can I help you?"

The man, dressed in tan pants and a fitted black polo shirt, looked to be in his mid-forties. In a deep voice, he said, "Yes, I'm looking for some place to stay for a couple of nights. Have you got any vacancies?"

"We certainly do. How many guests will be staying with us?"

"Just me, but if you've got a room with a king bed, I'll take it."

Paula perused the list of rooms. "We've got a king suite if you need the extra room, but we have a standard king, as well."

"Standard'll be fine. You take American Express?"

She slid a document across the counter to him. "Yes, sir. If you'll just fill out the registration form, I'll get the keys to Room 18 for you."

"If I decide to fish, do I need a permit?"

She dug through an envelope under the counter and handed him a worn photocopy. "Yes sir. Here's a printout of local retailers who can sell you a license."

"Thanks. Is there a place I can buy liquor in town?"

"Well, this is a dry county, but if you go into Hemphill about eight miles out on the other side of town, there's a bait shop that sells beer and fishing licenses. One stop shopping."

His shoulders slumped as he sighed and took his wallet out of his back pocket. "Thanks." He handed his credit card to her.

Paula scanned the registration form and swiped his credit card. "Thank you, Mr. Townes. Let me know if you need anything else. Here's your key and your receipt." She stepped around the counter and opened the door. "Your room is just across the parking lot. And to find the lake, if you follow the path right there all the way back, there's no way you'll miss it. We also have picnic tables and grills and even fishing gear you can borrow if you didn't bring your own."

The man shoved the receipt in his back pocket and walked out the door. His aloofness was strange, Paula thought. Her experience with fisherman was that they tended to be eager to talk about their sport, and this guy, Eric Townes, didn't seem all that enthusiastic. She read over his registration information. The form indicated his home address was in Illinois. Maybe he was stressed out from being on the road, and a couple of days on the lake would help him relax.

She smacked her forehead with the palm of her hand. "Dang. I forgot to ask how he heard about us." Upon hearing her own voice out loud, she cringed. *Oops. Well, I need to take him some towels. I'll ask him then.* She activated the answering machine before grabbing some towels from the laundry room, then she rushed across the lot to his room. As she neared his open door, the agitation in his voice stopped her in her tracks. She held her breath and squeezed herself against the wall as she listened.

"All right, Mr. Blair, I think I found the right place. Happy Valley something, right? A real hick joint if I ever saw one. I had to call on the phone in my room, the cell connection is so lousy here… Okay, my preliminary report is that the broad at the front desk doesn't look anything like anyone in the photo you gave me… Naw, this one's short and blonde. Cute, but she's too old to be the kid and not old enough to be the ex-wife's sister… No, I didn't ask. I just checked in. I thought you wanted me to be stealthy… Yes, I know I'm on your dime, but give me some credit. I know what I'm doing. We don't want to spook them…"

Paula's heart raced as she backed away from the door, being careful not to kick up any gravel or otherwise alert Mr. Townes to her presence. She tiptoe-sprinted to the office and, once inside, leaned her back against the door as she caught her breath. *Broad, indeed! Wait. Wasn't Blair the name of McKenzie's father? If this rat's working for Kyle Blair, he must be up to no good!* She started pacing and, thinking out loud, said, "Dammit, Cassie, where are you?"

As if on cue, Cassie stepped in the office door and froze in her tracks. "Whoa! Someone's ramped up this afternoon."

Paula raised her finger to her lips. "Shhh! Where have you been? Never mind. Come here!" She grabbed Cassie's wrist and pulled her out to the porch. "Don't be obvious about it but look at the black SUV next to Room 18."

"So?"

Paula pushed Cassie into a rocking chair then sat beside her. "Act like we're having a conversation."

"We *are* having a conversation."

"I know, but let's look like we're having one about something other than the man in Room 18, so laugh every now and then, even if it isn't funny."

Cassie raised an eyebrow as she threw back her head and laughed. "Good enough?"

"Perfect. Listen, and laugh. The guy is from Illinois. He checked in for two days. Asked about fishing licenses and beer."

Cassie laughed. "Imagine that!"

"I went to take him some towels. Ellie doesn't put towels in the room until a guest checks in, so they won't smell mildew-y, not the guests, the towels. Due to the humidity, you know."

Cassie chuckled and slapped her knee. "Darned humidity. That's hilarious."

"When I got to Room 18, I overheard him talking on the phone to someone named Mr. Blair. Cassie, I think he was talking to McKenzie's biological father! The man said he was trying to be stealthy. He told this Mr. Blair that I was too short and blonde to be his daughter or his ex-wife's sister."

Cassie remained silent as her eyes grew wide.

"Laugh, Cassie."

"I can't. This is serious. Have you told Melinda yet?"

Paula laughed like she was in the front row of a stand-up comedy act. Several seconds later, Cassie slapped Paula's arm and said, "Enough! Cut it out. Did you tell Melinda yet?"

"Melinda's busy telling Martha everything she told me yesterday."

"That doesn't matter right now. If McKenzie's well-being is threatened, Melinda and Martha would want to know. Go interrupt them!"

"You're right. Will you stay here and watch Room 18 for me? I want to know if this guy leaves and, if he does, where he goes."

"Give me your keys and if he goes anywhere, I'll tail him."

"They're in my purse in the room. Be careful."

Paula rushed inside and knocked on Martha's door.

"Please, go away," Martha said in a tear-filled voice.

Paula took a deep breath. "I would, but this is urgent! I need to talk to you both right away! It's about McKenzie."

Melinda opened the door and wiped a tear from her red-rimmed eyes. "What is it?"

Paula looked from Melinda to Martha and back again. "I think Kyle Blair is stalking her."

CHAPTER FORTY-THREE

Paula held her breath as she waited for Melinda's and Martha's reactions.

Martha's jaw hung open. She stood, then fell back into her chair. "But, how?"

Melinda handed Martha a glass of water from the dresser. "Mama, plenty of people in Plainfield knew about Uncle James's place down here. It wouldn't take a rocket scientist to figure out where we went when we left Indiana. I just didn't think Kyle would ever go out of his way to even try. He doesn't normally demonstrate that level of ambition."

Martha sipped her water then her eyes bored a hole into Paula. "What makes you think Kyle is stalking my granddaughter?"

Paula bit her lip and took a deep breath. "When I was outside earlier, I spotted a stranger in a black SUV... After he checked in, he needed towels... I overheard his phone call to a Mr. Blair ... And that's why I've got Cassie out there keeping an eye on him right now." She leaned against the door jamb and wiped tiny beads of perspiration from her brow.

Melinda's legs refused to hold her as she crumpled to the bed's edge. "Damn. What do we do now?"

"Cassie's watching him? I hope you told her to be careful," Martha said.

"I did. She knows that's important. I mean, I don't think this guy is dangerous, really, but Kyle sent him to be stealthy, and I don't like the sound of that."

Melinda's face blanched. "Is McKenzie home yet?"

Paula shook her head. "Not yet. Maybe we should call her and tell her to stay where she is."

Martha frowned. "But she has no idea about Kyle. What reason could we possibly give her?"

Paula thought a minute before sitting on the edge of Martha's bed, "She's still out with Jeffries. What if we called Delilah and gave her a very brief account of the situation? We could get her to invite McKenzie for dinner to keep her away from the resort until after dark...."

Melinda's eyes brightened. "Yes! And we can ask her to tell Jeffries to drive McKenzie to the back door when they get here."

Paula nodded. "That could work, or I could go pick her up at Delilah's place once it's dark out. Either way, we don't want her coming home in full daylight. This guy has a photo of her and of you, Melinda. Maybe even one of Martha. I think you should all stay out of sight until he's gone."

Melinda ran her fingers through her short, wispy hair. "I can't believe this is happening. We've tried so hard to keep that bastard out of my baby's life."

Martha stood and moved to the other side of her daughter then sat next to her and enfolded her in a hug. "Listen, we don't even know what this Townes fellow wants. Let's try not to worry until we find out for certain."

A tear rolled down Melinda's cheek. "But, how do we find that out?"

"We'll think of something."

Melinda sniffled. "Mama, I'm so sorry. I really picked a crappy day to lay everything on you, and now this."

Martha straightened her shoulders and forced a smile. "It's okay. Let's get through the present, then, if we have to, we'll deal with the past. All that matters to me right now is that you and McKenzie are safe."

Paula's eyes lit up. "Hey! Don't forget, we have a secret weapon by the name of Cassie Campbell, femme fatale. The Reverend Davis couldn't resist her charms, and I'm willing to bet that Eric Townes won't be able to either. Let me run out and stop her before she goes into town to follow him. One of you need to call Delilah and tell her what's going on and see if she can get Jeffries to bring McKenzie there if he hasn't already." She dug Delilah's card out of her pocket and handed it to Martha. "Delilah brought food over earlier today, and I put it in the fridge. Let me go catch Cassie then I'll man the front desk. You two lay low, and maybe I should call Delbert when I get back."

Melinda bit her lip. "Actually, that's a great idea. I'm sure we could use every resource we have available. Thank you."

Paula headed out as Melinda drew the drapes. Paula made a mental note to shut all of the blinds and curtains throughout the house as soon as she'd talked to Cassie. *Crap! I still need to take towels to that jerk! Wait! Of course! That could distract Townes so he doesn't see Cassie going between the office and our room, and it'll also give her another chance to look him over.*

Paula cracked open the office door. "Psst! Come in here! Hurry!"

Cassie stood, stretched her arms over head, and yawned as she meandered into the office. As soon as she closed the door, they peeked out the blinds. "He hasn't left his room. What did Melinda and Martha say?"

Paula stepped away from the window. "They were understandably upset, but as we talked, I had an idea. I've got a little job for you…"

CHAPTER FORTY-FOUR

Paula, armed with a generous stack of towels and wash cloths, knocked on the door to Room 18. "Mr. Townes, I have some fresh towels for you."

Silence.

Crap. What if he knows I eavesdropped? What if he bugged the office and knows I warned Melinda and Martha? What if—"

The door flew open and a shirtless Eric Townes scowled and grabbed the towels. He grumbled something under his breath and started to close the door.

Paula stepped backward and nearly bumped into Cassie. "Oh, Ms. Campbell, pardon me. I didn't see you there." She turned to face Cassie but kept an eye on Eric's door. She stifled a smile as she caught him peeking through the narrow crack in the door. She winked at Cassie and raised her voice. "I'm so glad we got a chance to talk this afternoon. It gets awfully lonely out here."

Cassie tilted her head and giggled. She drawled, "Oh, I know what you mean. That's the most I've laughed since I kicked that two-timing jackass out of my house. I'm lonely, but the freedom from his bullshit is exhilarating. Say, I'm thinking about going into town later for dinner and maybe have a glass of wine or three." She pulled on the scooped neck of her t-shirt and fanned it against her chest. "Whew! Sure is hot out here! I think I'm going to go take a nice shower and see if I can cool off."

Paula peeked at Townes and could tell he was hooked. *Cassie's bait worked again.* She smiled. "That sounds like a good idea. Just let me know if you need anything."

"Thank you, Ms. Arnett."

"Please, call me Paula."

"I'll do that. And I'm Cassie, by the way."

"Okay, Cassie. I'll see ya later."

Cassie waved her fingertips as she continued to fan her cleavage and headed to her room.

Paula strolled toward Room 17 until she heard Townes close his door. She giggled to herself and gave a tiny fist pump. *Yessss!* She returned to the office and checked the answering machine. After returning two calls for reservations, she made her rounds through the house, shutting all the curtains and blinds. When she was done, she tapped Martha's door. "It's safe for you two to come out now."

Both emerged, obviously frazzled. They all headed to the kitchen and Melinda said, "We talked to Delilah. McKenzie's already called to tell me she was having dinner at the Oaks's home and that Jeffries will bring her home after. She sounded so upbeat and carefree. Sometimes, I forget that we pulled her away from all of her friends just when she was getting her adult life started."

Martha filled three glasses with iced tea. "Melinda, that child has always been happiest when she's wherever you are, but it is good to see her with someone her own age."

Paula picked up a glass and took a sip. "What'd you tell Delilah?"

Melinda shrugged her shoulders. "The truth. At least as much as I could tell in a ten-minute phone call. I said that McKenzie's biological father, who never even acknowledged her existence until a few months ago and who she knows nothing about, is now trying to worm his way into her life by hiring an investigator to spy on her."

Paula chewed on her bottom lip. "That sums it up nicely. I'm about to go set the hook a little deeper. If my plan works, Townes will follow Cassie into town. If he does, I'm going to run over to my room and get some of my things. I'll spend the night on your couch, if that's all right. That way I can answer the door if Townes needs anything."

Melinda waved her hand. "No! You're not sleeping on the couch. McKenzie can do that, and you can have her bed."

Paula shook her head. "I wouldn't dream of doing that. Besides, we don't want her to wonder what's going on. I can sleep out in the living room, and she'll likely never even know I'm there. When I get back from my room, I'll tell you what Cassie and I have planned for Eric Townes."

CHAPTER FORTY-FIVE

Paula sat on the front porch, waiting. She checked her watch. *Seven o'clock.* A flash of blue caught her eye, and she looked up as Cassie emerged from their room wearing the dress and heels Paula had packed for herself. *Wow. That dress doesn't look quite as demure on Cassie as it does on me.*

"Holy cow," Paula said under her breath. The dress clung to Cassie's curves and exposed more of her legs and cleavage than Paula would have ever felt comfortable revealing. *Look out, Mr. Townes!*

The women's plan was flexible, depending on whether Eric exited his room immediately or not. Paula counted on him having taken a shower. She knew he hadn't left his room since she'd delivered his towels.

Cassie tossed her purse in Paula's car then took her time as she looked around, feigning concern over some forgotten item. She strolled to the office, sashaying her hips as she walked.

Paula kept her eye on Eric's room as she stood and headed toward Cassie. They met halfway so they could speak in normal tones, yet perhaps still capture Eric's attention – or be heard by him if his interest was already piqued. Paula raised her eyebrows as the women met. "Wow! You sure look pretty tonight, Cassie. You have big plans?"

Cassie rested her hand on her hip, hiking up the dress's hem another three inches. "I was hoping you might be able to recommend a place to eat. Somewhere quiet where I can enjoy a glass or two of wine.

"Hmm..." Paula furrowed her brow and pretended to think of a place, when in fact she'd asked Melinda for a suggestion just a few minutes earlier. She tapped her finger to her temple as she sneaked a glance to Room 18. "Yes, let's see... Oh, I know. On Monday nights, a lot of places are closed around here. But I'm certain The Mighty Fin's is open. It's nothing fancy, but they have a great wine selection, and their grilled steaks are the best."

"Sounds perfect," Cassie giggled. "At least the wine part."

Paula gave her directions to The Mighty Fin's using broad gestures. "It's easy to find, just go through Happy Vale and then all the way through Hemphill. There's a bait and tackle shop on the right just before a fairly long bridge. Go over that bridge and your destination is just on the other side of that. It'll be on your left. Be sure and tell them Ms. Arnett from Happy Valley sent you."

"Thanks. That sounds easy enough," Cassie said with a smile." I guess you have to work? I could sure use some company."

"Aww, another time, perhaps. But it's just me here tonight, and you know what they say: No rest for the wicked." Paula chuckled. "I hope you have a nice time."

"Oh, I intend to." Cassie's slow, deliberate walk to the Cadillac showed off every inch of her long, shapely legs. She grabbed a tube of lipstick and a compact out of her purse and looked in the mirror as she dotted her pouty lips with fresh color, then she climbed into the front seat and started the engine.

A flicker of Eric's curtains informed Paula that they'd hit pay dirt. She stood back as Cassie backed out of the parking spot and headed toward the highway. Paula suppressed a grin. "C'mon little fishy," she said under her breath. "Come out and play."

CHAPTER FORTY-SIX

Paula peeked through a crack in the office blinds. Within moments of Cassie pulling onto the highway, the door to Room 18 flew open, and Eric stepped out dressed in a navy jacket and tan slacks. Paula held her breath as he took a couple of steps toward the office then spun on his heel and got in his SUV. *Yes!* Her eyes followed his SUV as he pulled out of the drive and turned in the direction Cassie had taken.

She hustled over to her room and gathered her pajamas, toiletries, a change of clothes, and other essentials then composed a quick text to Cassie telling her to be on the lookout for Townes then watched as the message stuck in the queue. *Crap. I forgot about the spotty service here. Hopefully this'll go through soon.*

Stowing her stuff beneath the reception desk, Paula went out on the porch to survey the property. The family from room 12 waved as they pulled out of their covered parking place, likely in search of dinner. It really was a shame there wasn't a place at Happy Valley, or even within ten miles, where guests could grab a meal. Cassie was already mulling over a remedy for that, but Paula didn't think she'd seriously undertake such a project. And yet, when she'd started Campbell's Catering five years ago everyone had told her she was nuts, and today it was by all measures the most successful business of its kind in the Texas panhandle. Cassie turned away more business than most other catering outfits in the area booked simply because her calendar was always full. So, maybe she shouldn't try to pour cold water on Cassie's idea. If she was totally honest with herself, Paula figured that on some level she was jealous of Cassie's tenacity and independence. Perhaps she could borrow some of Cassie's grit now that Cal was gone. She was certainly going to need it.

Satisfied that Eric wasn't returning any time soon, Paula headed back inside and wandered to the kitchen. Martha stood in front of the microwave, heating the food Delilah had brought. "Are you hungry?" Martha asked.

Paula peeked down the hall. "Always. Where's Melinda? Is she okay?"

"She's just worried sick. I sent her to lay down while I got dinner ready. Would you like some wine?"

"Sure. I'll even pour, but only if you'll join me. Red or white?"

"How 'bout Chardonnay?"

After pouring two glasses, Paula got out some plates and flatware and set the table for three.

Martha, her mouth drawn in a thin line, sat across from her. "Things just need to heat up a bit, but I want to ask you a couple of questions before I call Melinda to dinner. Okay?"

"Sure. I'll answer what I can."

"Melinda told you about... well... about this woman she took up with during college?"

"Ginger? Yes, she did."

Martha's voice caught in her throat. "Paula, I didn't raise my daughters to do such sinful things. I just... I don't know what to do now. I feel like such a failure as a parent. My Marie took her own life, and now I learn that Melinda is a, a homosexual. I'm not sure I can handle any of this."

Paula moved around the table and placed an arm around Martha, letting the older woman cry as long as she needed. When Martha ran out of tears, Paula said, "First, let me tell you what I told Melinda about Marie's death. Neither of you is to blame for the decision she made all those years ago. She had to have been deeply depressed to have done such a thing. And I think you believe, as I do, in a loving God who opened His arms to Marie the minute she passed. So, while that's a horrific and painful time in your mind, in that instant, Marie found an everlasting peace. As for Melinda, I have to confess I was shocked. I mean she could have seriously knocked me over with a feather. I was prepared to dislike her as the other woman in Cal's life, but I never dreamed that her relationship with another woman was responsible for ending their marriage."

Martha sniffled and grabbed a napkin then dabbed her eyes. "But—"

"But, while I've only known Melinda for a ridiculously short time, I can tell that she's a decent, caring, loving person. She wouldn't do anything on purpose to hurt you. That's why through all these years, she hasn't sought out the company of someone she might want to share her life with, knowing how that might affect you. I don't know many people who could or would make such a sacrifice.

"And it's not like she chose to be in a same-sex relationship. She just fell in love. When she tried to deny herself that kind of love to make a go of a relationship with Cal, she was miserable. And I'm sure Melinda will tell you, if she hasn't already, what a wonderful man he was."

Martha squeezed her hands into fists and pounded the table once, her face contorted in obvious pain. "But it's a sin!"

Paula took a deep breath. "When I fell in love with Cal, my parents weren't happy at first. He was thirty-five; I was twenty. They couldn't understand why I couldn't find someone my own age. But, Martha, I couldn't help loving him."

"But—"

"Please let me finish. I know it's not the same thing. But love is love. Did I plan on falling in love with a man fifteen years older than me? No. And I know he never thought he'd become involved with a twenty-year-old college student. But love insisted, and love won out."

"Still, I can't condone homosexual behavior."

"But you *can* love your daughter. She's still Melinda. You changed her diapers. Dried her tears. Held her hand and bandaged skinned knees. You've watched her grow up to be this beautiful, determined woman and you've seen the devotion and love she gave to Marie and how she has put her life second to raise McKenzie. You raised a really fine daughter, Martha. One that any mother would be proud of. Please remember that."

Martha nodded but her lips remained pressed in a tight line as she stood. "I'd better get this food on the table. Would you mind telling Melinda it's ready?"

Paula squeezed Martha's arm and stood before impulsively kissing her on the top of the head. "I'll do that." On her way to Melinda's room, Paula detoured to check on the office where all was quiet. She looked out the window, noting that neither Townes nor Cassie had yet returned to Happy Valley. A quick check of her phone yielded no text messages. The inability to keep in touch with Cassie over these next few hours was going to drive her insane if she didn't keep busy;

although, something Ellie had mentioned earlier kept tugging at her memory.

She knocked on Melinda's door then thought she heard the shower running. She sat on the sofa and waited while Martha's concerns weighed on her. *I can't believe I pushed Melinda to come out to her mother, and now this. There goes my damn Goldilocks syndrome again. No secrets allowed. Everything has to be just right. Damn.*

"Cal? Now what?" Paula whispered. She didn't expect a response, but just asking calmed her. What was that Melinda had said about Cal? That he had had been good at determining who just needed to vent and who needed advice? Something like that. Maybe he knew Paula was just trying to work everything out in her own mind. And, she thought wryly, this kind of thinking might mean I'm losing it.

Melinda emerged from her bedroom with a smile on her face. She blew out a breath and said, "I am so glad that's all out. Have you talked to Mama?"

Paula glanced toward the kitchen and nodded. "Yes, I was sitting here wondering if I'd ruined your life by urging you to tell her everything."

"No. It's going to be difficult for her. For me, too, but my goodness, I finally feel like I'm free. *Really* free."

Paula smiled as she stood. "Let's go get some of Delilah's fried chicken. Martha has everything ready for us."

Melinda took a deep breath. "Let me go first, okay?"

"You bet."

Paula waited a couple of minutes then headed to the kitchen. Melinda was hugging her mother and Martha seemed more relaxed.

They sat and began eating in awkward silence until Paula said, "Mmm. This is delicious."

Melinda laughed. "After all we've been through today, that's your only comment?"

"Sorry," Paula said, "but Delilah's fried chicken is better than any medicine."

Even Martha had to laugh then before asking, "Have you heard anything from Cassie?"

"No. Damned lack of connectivity. I thought I might call The Mighty Fin's and have her paged."

Melinda scooped some potato salad onto her plate. "But if Cassie's with Townes, we may not want to interrupt them, or he might lose interest and move along. But I think Fin's has better phone reception than we do, so you might try texting her again."

Paula composed a text asking how Cassie was enjoying her meal, then she turned her attention back to her fried chicken. Seconds later, her phone dinged and said, *"Great meal. Good company."*

"Look!" Paula squealed. "I think she's caught a big old fish. Now, I just want her back safely."

Melinda took a sip of wine. "Me, too. So, what's the plan?"

"Cassie and I discussed several options depending on how the evening goes. The main thing, in my opinion, is for her to discover Townes's intentions. Like, what does Kyle want him to do? Is he on a fact-finding mission or does he plan on accosting McKenzie or harming any of you?"

Melinda took a deep breath. "I've been wracking my brain as to why Kyle, who was a complete asshole during Marie's pregnancy and for the first nineteen years of McKenzie's life, would've suddenly developed paternal feelings for her. All this time has passed, and he hasn't wanted anything to do with her, and now she's important enough for him to have sent someone to find her? I just don't get it."

"Could he have developed a conscience after all this time?" Paula asked.

Martha snorted. "Hardly."

Melinda rolled her eyes. "He's a textbook narcissist. He can be charming. He certainly fooled all of us. But in the end, it's all about him."

Paula nodded. "I just wondered if he possibly wanted to make up for the years he was absent."

Martha snorted, "If that were the case, he would've contacted us when we lived just twenty miles away instead of telling every person in every bar in three counties about her. No, whatever he's got on his mind, it's not philanthropic."

Paula nodded and took a sip of wine. "Well, once we learn what Townes's intentions are, we can make a more informed decision. If he's just looking to deliver a message, I can take that on your behalf and tell him I bought the motel from you and that you only contact me occasionally. Then you can decide how to proceed. But, if Cassie feels like he's planning something more sinister, then I think we have to notify the authorities. I haven't called Delbert yet, but I will if we need some legal advice on this. For starters, did Kyle actually relinquish his parental rights legally when you adopted McKenzie? Or did his refusal to acknowledge her count as giving up his rights?"

Melinda refilled her wine glass. "He didn't contest the adoption." We gave him every opportunity to be in McKenzie's life, but he refused."

Paula nodded. "There's something else we need to consider here, though. McKenzie is an adult. Shouldn't she have a say in deciding if she wants Kyle to be in her life?"

Martha raised her hand. "No, not where that snake is concerned."

Melinda's eyes watered. "Mama, McKenzie does need to be told the truth. I've known her whole life that this day would come."

Martha folded her arms across her chest and shook her head, "Well, I don't like it. I think we're just borrowing trouble if we tell her now."

Paula wanted badly to caution Martha that not telling McKenzie the truth might cause more harm than telling her would, but figured she'd offered up enough advice for one day.

Melinda grabbed Martha's hand. "Mama, we won't tell her tonight, but for her own sake and safety, we need to do it soon. I'd certainly prefer for you to be a part of that conversation, but I'll do it either with or without you."

Martha said a word that shocked Paula as the older woman stood and threw her napkin onto the table in front of Melinda's place, "Do whatever you want; it seems you always have anyway. I won't be a part of it. Any of it." She stormed out of the kitchen, slamming the door behind her.

"Well," Melinda said. "I didn't even know my mother knew that word, let alone how to use it in context."

Paula bit her lip. "I can't help feeling like this is all my fault."

"No. None of it is. We've kept too many secrets in this family for too many years, and now they're all threatening to cause us a world of hurt unless we face up to them."

The bell from the front office rang. Melinda started to stand, but Paula caught her arm. "Wait. Remember, you still have to stay hidden until we know what Townes is up to. I'll go."

Grateful to have a reason to leave the hot zone, Paula hurried to the office where Mr. Graham stood wringing his hands. "Help!" he said with abject fear in his eyes. "It's Julie. Her water just broke. Where's the nearest hospital?"

CHAPTER FORTY-SEVEN

Just looking at the frantic man, Paula's heart raced. Flustered, she turned one way then another, then froze in her tracks. "Hey! Martha, Melinda, somebody! Help, please!"

Martha rushed up from the back. "What's up?"

Paula's mouth went dry. "One of our guests is in labor!"

Mr. Graham stepped forward. "My wife's eight months pregnant and her water just broke! Can you point me to the nearest hospital?"

Melinda stepped into the office as Martha said, "Where's your wife now? How far apart are her contractions?"

Mr. Graham ran his finger through his hair. "She's in the car. We'd just got back from dinner when her water broke. She hasn't had any contractions yet, but her back's been hurting all afternoon."

Martha slid the phone toward Paula. "Paula, call 9-1-1. The paramedics can be here in less than ten minutes and they can decide where she needs to go. Melinda, go get your room ready. She can relax in there until the ambulance arrives. Mr. Graham, take me to your wife."

As Paula dialed, the Graham's little girl stepped inside and said, "Daddy, Mommy said hurry!"

As he trailed Martha out of the office, Mr. Graham got Paula's attention. "Ma'am, can Sophia please sit in here with you?"

Paula offered a reassuring smile. "Of course." She gave the resort's address to the operator then hung up the phone. "Hi, Sophia. My name's Paula."

The door flung open and Martha and Mr. Graham escorted Mrs. Graham in. Mrs. Graham winced and held her belly as she doubled over.

Mr. Graham's face blanched. "Breathe, Julie, honey. Try to hold on. Help is on the way."

"Try not to push," Martha said as she guided Julie to the bedroom.

Sophia raced after her parents and Paula caught the child by the hand. "Sweetie, why don't you wait out here with me. Your Mommy and Daddy are busy right now. Would you like to help me take care of the office? I could sure use a helper like you." Paula searched the child's wide, blue eyes which were busy scanning the room. *Hurry up, ambulance!*

Sophia's eyes grew wide and she nodded. "I help Mommy all the time."

"I'll bet you're a great helper," Paula said, wondering what activity might keep Sophia occupied. Her experience with small children was limited to occasional turns in the church nursery. Paula looked under the counter and found a stack of paper and a pen. A bit more rummaging resulted in the discovery of a wooden clipboard. "Would you like to draw a picture for your Mommy?"

Again, Sophia nodded. Paula inserted paper into the clip and helped the child into one of the reception room chairs. While Paula watched anxiously for the ambulance, Sophia drew a large circle with two skinny lines underneath, topped that with a smaller circle and added eyes, several strings of hair, and a mouth. After thinking for a bit, she added a third circle inside the large one.

"This is Mommy," Sophia said, pointing to the larger circle. "And this little teeny tiny thing inside of Mommy's tummy is my new baby sister."

Sophia, her little tongue sticking out of her mouth in concentration, added an elongated circle with stick legs to the picture. "This is Daddy."

Paula stifled a grin. "And, where are you?"

Sophia furrowed her brow. "I'm right here with you."

Paula bit her lip to keep from laughing. "Yes, you are." *Duh.* Paula thought she heard sirens, and hoped it wasn't just her imagination. The strobe of red lights soon filled the parking lot and Sophia's eyes went wide again. "It's just the doctors," Paula told her. "They're here to help your Mommy have your baby sister."

"Can I go help her, too?"

"I don't know. We'll ask the doctors if it's okay, but first, you sit right here, and I'll show them where to go. Can you do that?"

"Okay. Can I make another picture?"

"Sure. Make as many as you want, sweetie."

Paula opened the door onto the humid night. A huge yellow moon hovered above the resort. *I should've known it'd be a full moon.*

A man in a blue jumpsuit emerged from the ambulance, with a similarly clad young woman at his heels. They unloaded a gurney and raced to the office door. The woman asked, "Where's our patient?"

Paula stepped aside. "Here, I'll show you. Sophia, just stay put for a minute while I take the doctors to see your Mom." She led them through the short hallway and into the great room then stood aside. "Mrs. Graham is through that door. Can I do anything to help?"

"No ma'am. We've got this." The duo charged into the room without waiting for a response.

Paula returned to the office and found Sophia drawing on the wall behind her chair. Paula stopped in her tracks and gasped. "Oh, honey, we can't draw on the walls."

Sophia continued her picture. "Yes, we can. It's easy, see?"

Paula put her face in her hands. *Duh again.* "Well, can you tell me about your picture?"

"That's you sitting on the chair. I got lonely.

"Well, I'm back now, so you won't need to draw any more friends. If you promise to draw only on the paper and not on the wall, I'll go get us some milk and cookies from the kitchen."

"Hmm. Okay."

Paula glanced across the parking lot and noted that Cassie and Mr. Townes were both still gone. She was dismayed yet unsurprised by the lack of a message from Cassie.

She hurried to the kitchen and returned a minute later to find Sophia sitting on the floor with the clipboard in her lap and a pile of circle drawings all around her. Paula raised an eyebrow. "Wow, you've been really busy. Would you like to come sit up on the counter and have your snack?"

"Will you help me?"

"Of course. When I was your age my favorite thing was to sit on the table to eat."

"Didn't you have any toys when you were a little girl?" Sophia asked, frowning.

"Well, yes, but I still liked to sit on the table."

Paula and Sophia were practicing dipping their cookies in the milk, When Melinda and Martha entered the office. Both of the M's looked a little dazed. Paula gave them a quizzical look, and Martha held up two fingers.

"Twins?" Paula mouthed.

A huge grin formed on Melinda's face and Martha beamed as she said, "One of each kind. They're perfect. Small, but healthy."

Paula's jaw dropped open. "How incredible! I take it they weren't expecting twins."

Melinda shook her head. "No, it was a total surprise. Kind of like when my girls arrived."

Melinda hugged her mother, "You were a champ in there, Mama. Paula, the paramedics didn't make it until right before the second one was crowning."

Paula's eyes grew large. "You mean Martha delivered the first one?"

"She sure did. Just like a pro!"

Martha eased herself into the nearest chair. "Could one of you get me a glass of wine? I'm a bit shaky here."

Paula hurried to the kitchen, located three glasses, and poured wine for Martha, Melinda, and herself. "Shall we toast?" she asked when she returned.

Melinda raised her glass. "To Mama for going above and beyond the hospitality required of an innkeeper and doing it beautifully." Melinda said, raising a glass.

"To Martha," Paula said, raising her glass.

Sophia raised her milk glass to clink against the others' and asked, "Can I go see my Mommy now?"

Melinda helped the child down from the counter and took her hand. "It was pretty crowded in there earlier, but I'll bet your Mommy is ready to see you, too. Why don't you walk back there with me?"

"Okay." Sophia skipped as they headed back.

Paula watched them go then said, "I wouldn't have had the faintest idea how to deliver a baby. How'd you do it?"

"That baby girl was already on her way by the time we got Julie into bed. All I had to do was play catch. The hard part was knowing what to do with the umbilical cord, but Mr. Graham took over for that. I almost forgot about the placenta." Martha's face went white. "Oh my! I feel faint."

"Put your head between your knees." Paula raced to the bathroom, got a wet cloth, then returned and placed it on the back of Martha's neck. "Here. Sit still and keep this on."

Martha took a deep breath. "Thanks. It's helping already.

Paula looked up just as two sets of headlights pulled into the parking lot. "Oh! It's Cassie!" Before Martha could reply, Cassie and Eric were headed to the office. Paula's heart leapt into her throat. "Martha, I think we need to move you into the living room. Cassie and Eric Townes are headed this way."

"Okay, I'm feeling a little better now. Can I lean on you as far as the couch, though?"

"Of course."

Paula got Martha settled then hurried back to the office as Cassie rushed through the front door. Cassie's face was void of color. "What's happened? Is it Melinda?"

"We had babies. Twins."

"What? Who did?"

"Some guests. Um... You didn't meet them." Paula shot a wary glance at Eric, who'd entered the office behind Cassie. "They checked in before, uh, *him.*"

"Oh. Where's Melinda?"

"She took the Grahams' little girl, Sophia, in to meet her new siblings."

"How about McKenzie?"

Paula looked at Cassie like she'd lost her mind. Weren't they trying to keep McKenzie out of sight while Eric Townes was around?

Cassie pulled Eric by the wrist and smiled. "I promise, it's all okay. They just need to listen to what he has to say."

Eric leaned on the counter. "Ms. Arnett? Paula? I don't know where you got the idea that I intended any harm to McKenzie or her mom, but nothing could be further from the truth. Cassie can fill you in on the details, but it really *is* all going to be fine."

Paula narrowed her eyes. "Well, McKenzie is still with her friend, Jeffries. Martha's in the living room. She's pretty wobbly. She delivered the first baby before the ambulance even arrived."

Cassie's eyes lit up. "Honest?"

Paula grinned and nodded. "I guess it was overwhelming. And awesome. Cassie, you can come on back, but Mr. Townes, you probably need to stay here. Have a seat. I'll go check on Martha and see if she's up for a talk. This all might be better discussed in the morning, though. Today has had more than its share of craziness."

As Paula and Cassie entered the sitting room, the paramedics emerged from Melinda's room with Mrs. Graham on the gurney. Mr. Graham, looking dazed and proud, followed snuggling one of the tiny bundles. Melinda smiled from ear to ear as she brought up the rear, holding the other.

Melinda stopped on her way out and asked, "Paula, could you watch Sophia for a minute? She's going to stay with us tonight. I'll be right back."

"Of course." Paula went to Melinda's room and found Sophia sitting on the bed, her arms folded across her chest. Paula sat beside the girl and smoothed her hair. "Congratulations, Sophia! How exciting! You're a big sister now."

"I only wanted a baby sister, and Mommy says we can't give the brother back," Sophia pouted.

"Well, think of it this way, maybe your Daddy needs a boy to help him the way you help Mommy."

Sophia wrinkled her nose. "Daddy doesn't work. He just drives a car."

"Maybe your baby brother can help him do that."

"Babies can't drive, Miss Paula."

Paula took a deep breath and smiled. *Duh, again.* "I'll bet before long you'll love your brother as much as you love your sister."

"Nope."

"Miss Melinda told me you're going to have a sleepover with us tonight. How about I go and get one of my t-shirts for you to sleep in? Would that be okay?"

Sophia nodded.

"You can come with me if you'd like, or you can stay here with Miss Melinda."

The child slipped her hand in Paula's, and they headed to the living room.

Melinda, having handed off her precious cargo returned to the living room. "Paula, who is that man out there? He said he was waiting on you."

Paula's hand flew to her mouth. "Oh, crap. Sit down for a minute. That's Eric Townes."

"The man who's looking for McKenzie?"

"None other. I told him to stay there until Cassie could fill us in on her evening. She's assured me that Mr. Townes's motives are not sinister, but I think maybe there's been enough excitement for one day—even the good kind."

Melinda nodded. "I couldn't agree more. It's late and I'm exhausted. Let's get McKenzie home and get everyone settled. We can deal with him in the morning. Would you mind telling him?"

"Of course not. Sophia and I were headed over to my room to get her a t-shirt to sleep in, but maybe she can wear something of yours or McKenzie's."

Melinda's eyes sparkled as she leaned down to Sophia's level. "Of course. I know the perfect shirt. Let's go, Sophia."

For a second, Paula thought Sophia was going to insist on going with her, but finally she nodded and took Melinda's hand.

Eric Townes was seated right where she'd left him, looking at his cellphone. He looked up as she sat beside him. She cleared her throat. "Mr. Townes, I talked to Melinda and told her that Cassie assured me that you aren't the big bad wolf."

He chuckled. "It's Eric, and I'm one of the good guys, I promise. But after talking to Cassie I can see why you might've come to a different conclusion."

"The thing is, we've had a really emotional day around here, and even if you are the bearer of good news, Melinda would really prefer to wait until tomorrow to hear it. And you are here for another night anyway, so..."

He nodded. "I get it. I've accomplished my main task which was to locate Ms. Arnett and McKenzie. Actually, McKenzie is the reason I'm here, but my client didn't want me to do an end-around and give her mom a reason to bolt. I didn't count on you also being Mrs. Arnett. It threw me for a loop."

"That's a whole different matter," Paula said. She was dying to know the whole story, but it could wait until the morning. "We've got some work to do around here tonight before we can rest, so why don't we plan on giving you a call in the morning when the key players are ready to meet?

He stood then extended his hand and shook hers. "I understand. I'm sorry you thought I was up to no good, but I admire your protective instincts. We'll get off to a better start tomorrow."

Paula clasped his hand in both of hers and looked into his grey eyes. "Trust me when I say the past week has been the most emotional of my entire life. I guess I just overreacted. Hopefully, I'll have my wits about me when we meet again. Goodnight."

"Goodnight. I'll see you tomorrow."

She locked the door behind him and straightened up the office, gathering Sophia's drawings before putting the clipboard back underneath the counter. She eyed the drawing on the wall and couldn't help but smile. "Cal, what a day."

She thought she heard his voice whisper, "You're doing good work, Goldilocks. Everything is almost just right."

CHAPTER FORTY-EIGHT

McKenzie arrived through the back door just minutes after Eric Townes left the office. She was bubbling over with excitement about how she and Jeffries had spent their day, too wrapped up in her own thoughts to inquire as to why she'd had to come in the back door. While Melinda and Cassie, with Sophia's help, spent the better part of an hour getting Melinda's bedroom back in order after its turn as a delivery room, Paula and Martha heard all the details of McKenzie's date.

It was "Jeffries this," and "Jeffries that," for ten solid minutes. Apparently, Jeffries could do everything but walk on water, and it seemed that McKenzie thought he might even be able to do that. He'd made them a picnic lunch and taken her to his favorite spot on the lake. Did they know he could play guitar and was in a band called *Chef's Choice*? No? Well he was. And he could sing beautifully. Then his mom, she's SO nice, had invited them to dinner and their house was big, but cozy, not fancy, but they did have a pool, and she was glad she'd packed a swimsuit for the day, because they went swimming and had supper out by the pool." By the time McKenzie drew a breath, Paula was a bit dizzy and half in love with Jeffries herself.

"Whew!" Martha said. "Sounds like you had quite an eventful day."

"Gram, it was the second-best day of my whole life."

Paula smiled. "Oh? What was the first best day?"

"When Mom told us that we wouldn't have to leave Happy Valley."

Paula's heart warmed. *Cal, she's got you to thank for that.*

McKenzie folded her hands on the table and said, "So, I guess it was a quiet day around here, huh?"

Paula and Martha exchanged glances and Paula said, "Well, your gram delivered a baby girl about an hour ago, but besides that, it was quiet. Right, Martha?"

Martha nodded, stifling a smile. "Yep. Really quiet. But the baby was a twin and the paramedics arrived in time to deliver the second one. All in your mom's bedroom."

McKenzie laughed. "You guys can't possibly think I'm *that* gullible."

Melinda and Sophia entered the kitchen as if on cue. Melinda kissed McKenzie's forehead and said, "Sweetie, this is Sophia. Sophia, this is my daughter, McKenzie. Sophia's going to borrow your bunny rabbit t-shirt to sleep in tonight, okay?"

McKenzie raised an eyebrow. "Ohhh-kaaay."

Sophia leaned in close to her and, in a confidential tone, said, "Did you know I'm a big sister now? My mommy had two babies. A girl baby and a boy baby. I only wanted the girl, but Mommy says we have to keep them both. Can I sleep in your room tonight?"

"Sure, you can. Mom?"

Melinda smoothed Sophia's hair. "Why don't you get your stuff out of your bedroom while I get Sophia settled. You can bunk with me. I want to hear all about your day."

"Really? You just won't believe how awesome it was."

Paula and Martha exchanged a look and Martha said, "Yes, we can vouch for its awesomeness."

Paula craned her neck and looked down the hall. "Has anyone seen Cassie?"

Melinda said, "Oh, she went back to your room. I told her you'd be along in a bit."

Sophia attached herself to McKenzie like a tick to a hound. McKenzie said, "Come on, kiddo. Let's get ready for bed." Everyone had to give Sophia a goodnight kiss before she would close her eyes, but once she was settled, she was asleep in less than a minute.

Melinda walked Paula to the front door. "Thanks again. I don't know how we'd have handled all this without your help."

Paula grabbed her tote bag from behind the registration counter and said, "It was my pleasure. Since I don't need to sleep on your sofa tonight, if McKenzie would rather sleep there it's already made up."

"Actually, I think she and I will enjoy talking over her date. Plus, we have other stuff to discuss."

Paula rested her hand on Melinda's arm. "It's been an awfully long day. You're not planning on telling her everything tonight, are you?"

"No, not everything, but I do want her to be prepared for whatever Mr. Townes has to say tomorrow. By the way, what'd you tell him?"

"Just that we'd call his room in the morning whenever you're ready to talk."

"That'll work," Melinda said as she yawned. "Oh, excuse me. You go get some sleep. We may need you to watch the front office tomorrow if you're up for that."

"Absolutely." Paula gave Melinda a hug and said, "You get some rest, too."

"I will."

Outside the door, Paula heard Melinda turn the lock behind her. Across the parking lot it seemed as if Cassie had left a light on for her, and she noticed that room 18 was still lit up. With a smile, she wondered if Eric Townes had been smitten by her friend. Heaven knows he wouldn't be the first man who had been, and certainly not the last. Hopefully, Cassie would tell her everything tonight. An owl hooted overhead reminding Paula to look up and search for the Cal star. Only when she was sure she'd found it did she open the door to her room.

Cassie was already snoring softly, while on the television, Humphrey Bogart toasted a dewy-eyed Ingrid Bergman, calling her "kid." Paula took a shower, letting the day's events wash down the drain. So much had happened in such a short space of time, she couldn't imagine that her busy mind would allow her to rest. She crawled into bed and fell almost instantly to sleep, though, to a piano playing "As Time Goes By."

CHAPTER FORTY-NINE

The following morning, Paula woke to the chatter of a local TV morning show's dialog mixed with the sound of Cassie singing in the shower. Paula attempted to roll over and catch a few more minutes of sleep, but bolted upright when she heard the reporter say, "Last night, the Happy Valley Motor Inn and Resort, located near Happy Vale saw its share of action." Paula held her breath and braced herself for news about the Triumphant Army of God. She rubbed her eyes and focused on the television where a reporter stood outside the Happy Vale hospital. A banner at the bottom of the screen identified him as Dean Rawlings.

Dean smiled and said, "Yes, a family of three checked in, but before their stay was complete, their family grew into a family of five when their twins were born, turning a small fishing resort outside of Happy Vale into a maternity ward. At least for a brief time."

The camera panned over to include Mr. Graham. Dean said, "We're standing outside the Happy Vale Medical Center with Dallas resident, Alex Graham, the proud father of the twins. How are you this morning, Alex?"

Looking haggard but proud, Alex said, "Happy, grateful, and a little shocked."

"Shocked?"

"Yes! We had no idea she was carrying twins."

"Oh! That must have been a big surprise."

"You can't imagine!"

"So, tell us, what happened last evening?"

"My wife, Julie and I thought we'd treat our three-year-old daughter, Sophia, to a road trip before the baby arrived. We knew we had plenty of time, so we checked into the Happy Valley Motor Inn and Resort yesterday to do some fishing and exploring. After dinner last night, Julie went into labor right outside the resort, and the wonderful ladies there took charge, taking us into their home."

"So, the paramedics arrived in the nick of time and delivered the twins?"

"Oh, no. Only our baby boy. Ms. Martha at the resort delivered our baby girl before the paramedics could get there."

"Incredible. And what are you naming your new twins?"

"We're still trying to decide on a name for our son. We didn't know we'd have a boy. We'd originally planned to name our daughter Wendy, but since Martha was our angel last night, we're going with Martha Wendy Graham. Can I just say thank you to Ms. Martha and everyone at Happy Valley Motor Inn and Resort?"

"I think you just did, Alex. Thanks for your time and best of luck with your expanded family. Let us know when you choose a boy's name. By the way, my name's Dean, if you want to borrow that. Now, back to Allison in the newsroom."

Paula turned when Cassie said, "Well I'll be darned." She started to comb her hair.

Paula smiled. "Pretty cool, huh? I hope the M's had their television on. But even if they didn't, these small news stations tend to repeat their local stories throughout the day."

Cassie pulled her hair into a ponytail. "Go get dressed and we'll let Martha know about her new namesake."

Paula applied a bit of tinted moisturizer and blush, then brushed her hair, and pulled it into a ponytail. She put on her jean capris and a blue t-shirt, checked her appearance in the mirror and said, "Okay, I'm ready." They turned off the TV and headed out.

As they headed to the office, Paula said, "I was hoping you'd still be awake when I came in last night so you could tell me about your little date with Mr. Townes."

Cassie chuckled. "Let's just say he succumbed to my charms, but about midway through the evening, I realized he was a decent guy, and I couldn't keep up the charade. I hated leading him on."

"I hope, for the 3M's sake, he is the good guy he claims to be."

"He seemed genuine to me," Cassie said as they entered the office.

McKenzie and Sophia were manning the front desk.

Paula smiled. "Good morning, McKenzie. Who's this helping you?"

Sophia sat up straight. "'Member me, Paula? I'm Sophia." The three-year-old's face held tell-tale signs of donut and milk around her mouth.

"Well, you sure are! Did you have a good night?"

"I slept in Kenzie's bed, and now I'm eating breffest on the counter. See?"

McKenzie shrugged her shoulders. "She spent part of the night in my bed, anyway. She crawled in bed with Mom and me around two. Isn't that right, Sophia?"

"Uh huh. I got lonely. Hey, Paula, I get to see my new baby sister today. Daddy called me on the big telephone and said so. He's coming to get me."

"How exciting!" Paula said.

"What about your baby brother?" Cassie asked.

Sophia narrowed her eyes. "Do I know you? I'm not s'posed to talk to strangers."

Paula nudged Cassie forward. "This is my friend, Cassie. I promise she isn't a stranger."

Sophia nodded. "Okay, I guess I have to see the brother. But I don't think I'll like him."

Cassie offered a smile. "I have a big brother named Court. I don't like him sometimes, but most of the time I do."

This seemed like news Sophia could use. She nodded thoughtfully and went back to helping McKenzie between bites of donut.

"Where's your mom," Paula asked McKenzie.

"She and Gram are in the kitchen. At least they were a few minutes ago."

On their way to the kitchen, Paula leaned close to Cassie and said, "Melinda planned to tell McKenzie about her parentage last night. She seemed awfully calm just now for someone who just learned the person she thought was her mom isn't."

Cassie nodded. "Maybe Melinda decided to wait to hear what Eric has to say."

They stopped outside the kitchen door and Cassie asked, "By the way, have you decided what your role is going to be here?"

Paula bit her lip. "No. But to tell the truth, so much has happened that I really haven't spent too much time thinking about it. The smart thing to do would be to look at the financial records, but my heart wants a say in it, too."

"And you can't forget about CalNet."

"Trust me, I haven't. I can't carry on Cal's work, but it's definitely on my mind. I think I need to find just the right person to take over for him. Cal's name is tied in with that company, and I don't want that name disrespected."

They headed into the kitchen where Melinda and Martha sat at the pine table talking over coffee and donuts. Paula filled a coffee cup. "Morning, ladies."

Cassie grabbed her Dr. Pepper out of the refrigerator then sat and selected a donut. Before she bit into it, she winced. "Oops! I keep forgetting this isn't my kitchen. I hope you don't mind that I've made myself at home."

"Not at all," Melinda said, pushing the donuts toward Paula. "It feels like you belong here. *Both* of you."

Paula took a chocolate donut and asked, "Did you have the talk with McKenzie last night?"

Melinda cupped her hands around her coffee mug. "No. I thought about what you said. Let Mama and me talk to Mr. Townes first, then we'll decide what and how much to tell McKenzie. Besides, she was bubbling over with excitement. I just couldn't dampen that. According to my daughter, Jeffries has a halo. And wings."

Martha and Paula exchanged glances then burst out laughing. Paula said, "After hearing about him yesterday, I told Martha I was half in love with him myself."

Melinda's eyes twinkled. "She talked non-stop for at least an hour after we got into bed. Finally, I had to put on the brakes and tell her we could continue tomorrow. And then little Miss Sophia joined us in the middle of the night. It's been awhile since I shared a bed with a three-year-old. I feel like I've been kicked in the ribs by a small mule. Her dad is coming to get her after lunch today."

Paula chuckled. "Yes, she told us. Hey, that reminds me, Alex Graham was on the local news this morning. He mentioned Happy Valley and told them about Martha delivering their daughter. Martha, they're naming her after you."

Martha's jaw dropped open. "Oh, my! Surely they wouldn't do that to a little baby girl."

Cassie laughed. "Well, they did. Her name is Martha Wendy Graham. They still haven't decided on a name for the boy."

"Well, I'll be!" Martha said, clearly pleased.

Paula broke her donut in half. "They probably shouldn't let Sophia name her brother. It'll be Mud if she has a say in it."

Melinda giggled. "That child! She really says the darndest things."

Cassie took another donut. "I'm really sorry I didn't wake up early enough to cook breakfast for everyone. I'll do that tomorrow if you'd like. We kind of slept in this morning."

Melinda nodded. "That'd be wonderful, thank you. Mark's planning on coming over tonight, so he could check out your special breakfast, too."

Paula raised an eyebrow. "On a Tuesday night?"

Melinda said, "Yeah, he generally comes over on Tuesday evenings. He checks on me then he spends Wednesdays fishing. He doesn't keep office hours on Wednesdays, so unless there's an emergency he spends the day with us. When he called to confirm that his room would be available, he asked about you two. He wanted to make sure he saw you both before you left.

"How sweet," Paula said. She nudged Cassie in the ribs and said, "I'm pretty sure he's single, right Melinda?"

"He had a lady friend, but I haven't heard him mention her for a while, so...."

Cassie wrinkled her nose. "Sorry. Not my type."

Paula sighed. "If *he's* not your type, I give up."

Cassie bristled. "Good."

Martha stood and rinsed out her cup. "So, when and where do we want to talk to Mr. Townes?"

Melinda looked at the wall clock. "It's still early, Mama. What if we invited him back to the campground to talk? That way we won't be interrupted. Paula, Cassie, you're welcome to join us."

Cassie licked chocolate off her thumb. "I've already heard what he has to say. I'll stay up here and help McKenzie deal with Sophia. It's too bad the cellphone reception is so spotty out here. I think Eric might want to include another party in this conversation."

Paula's face lit up. "I know! We should meet with him out by Clyde's tree. Ellie said it's the only place on the property that has good phone connectivity."

Melinda furrowed her brow. "You're kidding. There's a tree on the property that boosts our phone signals?"

Paula shrugged her shoulders. "I don't know why it works. I just know what Ellie said, and she doesn't joke."

"Can you find this tree?" Martha asked.

Paula nodded. "Yes, I'm sure I can. She calls it Clyde's tree because it looks like her Uncle Clyde."

Martha sighed. "Then let's call Mr. Townes and get him to meet us outside his room. I'm ready to find out why he's here. Enough with the secrets."

Melinda stood and hugged her mom. "I agree, Mama. There's been too many for too long. Let's start unraveling them all."

CHAPTER FIFTY

Paula met Eric outside his room. She looked him over and half-smiled. *He looks much more agreeable than I remember him being yesterday afternoon. Maybe it's just that my perception of him has changed.*

He wiggled his eyebrows. "So, have you decided I'm not evil personified?"

She folded her arms across her chest. "Well, you did refer to me as a 'broad' when I overheard your conversation yesterday. I don't know about the women you're used to doing business with, but here in Texas men don't refer to women in such terms."

"My apologies. I had no idea I was being monitored."

"Still, it certainly didn't make a good first impression."

"Point taken. So, why are we meeting at the campground?"

"Melinda, that is Mrs. Arnett, wanted some privacy. She and her mother want to hear your story before they decide to get McKenzie involved. They're very protective of her, and from what I hear, it sounds like they should be. Your client hasn't always been the most stand up kind of guy, you know."

"How do you know who my client is?"

"I heard you call him Mr. Blair."

"So you did. You'd make an awful spy, you know. Maybe your pal Cassie could show you a thing or two."

Paula rolled her eyes. "Yeah, yeah. Come on." She led him to the picnic table closest to Clyde's tree. "Here, help me move this underneath the tree. We'll get better phone reception there."

He picked up one end of the table and grinned. "And all the way here I thought you were planning to bash my head in and throw me in the lake."

She nodded. "Well, we still haven't heard your news, and the day's still young. That lake isn't going anywhere anytime soon, and there *are* plenty of fist-sized rocks around."

He laughed as he hoisted the bulk of the weight of the table and moved it to the shade of the oak.

As they set it down, Paula brushed her hands on her pants and said, "Seriously, though, Happy Valley is a cellular dead zone. The housekeeper told me she sits out here on her break because she gets the best reception here."

"Good to know, but I won't let my guard down just yet."

Martha and Melinda showed up, bearing glasses of iced tea for everyone. "You must be Mr. Townes," Martha said.

Paula passed a glass of tea to Eric and said, "Yes, Mr. Townes, this is Martha and her daughter Melinda Arnett." He shook their hands.

Melinda sat at the table and said, "So, Paula told us you're working for Kyle Blair, but Cassie claims you're one of the good guys. Pardon me for saying so, but I don't see how both can be true."

Eric took a long drink, "This is good. Thank you. First, let me apologize for the misunderstanding. Paula... may I call you Paula?"

"Of course."

"Paula heard me talking on the phone to my client who is indeed Mr. Blair. But, it's not Kyle Blair I work for. It's his brother, Kevin."

Martha raised an eyebrow. "Kevin? But why would Kevin have you looking for us? I recall him as a cute little guy, maybe ten, eleven years old, when my daughter married his brother."

"Kevin and Kyle's dad, Andrew, died last month. Kyle was eliminated from the will years ago. It seems Andrew never approved of his behavior, so he named Kevin executor and charged him with the task of locating Kyle's children. The younger one, a boy named Grant, lives in Illinois with his mother and stepfather, but Kevin couldn't locate McKenzie, so he hired me to find her."

Martha pursed her lips. "Oh? For what purpose?"

Melinda held up her hand. "Mr. Townes, we would really prefer that McKenzie not know that her father never wanted her. I don't know how that might affect her."

Eric nodded. "Actually, my client considered that. He put the money Andrew set aside for McKenzie into a trust that you, Melinda, can draw on for expenses McKenzie might incur for education or basically anything for her future. If you decide to tell her, control of the trust can be transferred to her."

Melinda raised an eyebrow. "Money?"

"Yes, ma'am. Andrew Blair left each of his grandchildren over a million dollars. Of course, it'll be somewhat less when inheritance taxes are calculated, but I'm sure it'll still be a sizeable amount."

Disbelief, shock, wonder, and amazement played across Melinda's and Martha's faces.

Tears formed in Martha's eyes and she said, "Well, I'll be."

Melinda bit her lip. "Mr. Townes, we need to think about exactly how to handle this. It seems wrong that McKenzie would inherit this money without knowing its source, and we've always led her to believe that her father is deceased."

"You know she wants to go to massage therapy school, don't you?" Paula asked.

Martha raised her eyebrows. "She's never mentioned that to me. Has she told you, Melinda?"

"No. I just know she wasn't enjoying her classes at the community college. She's never been much into academics."

Paula nodded. "I asked her a couple of days ago what her plans for the future were, and she said she'd considered becoming a massage therapist or an esthetician, but first, she said her mother needed to be well."

"Oh!" Melinda said, a hitch in her voice. "My sweet girl."

Eric pulled his cellphone out of his pocket. "So, now that I told you everything, Kevin would like to speak with you on FaceTime while we're out here. Maybe he can help you decide." He dialed a number and the call was answered almost immediately by a forty-something man with pleasant features and a mouth that looked as if it smiled easily. "Mr. Blair, I have Melinda Arnett and her mother here. They've just learned about the trust but are unsure about how to proceed. I'm going to hand the phone over to Melinda now."

Melinda took the phone and smiled into the screen. "Hello, Kevin. My how you've grown. The last time I saw you was when Marie married your brother."

"I'm sad to say I don't remember much from that day. I was a kid and they made me dress up. All I wanted was to take that tuxedo off and play in the park."

Melinda laughed. "I don't blame you one bit. Just so you know, my mother, Martha is here, too, and so is our friend, Paula Arnett."

Kevin nodded, "Morning, ladies glad to talk to you. Melinda, I'm so sorry for the way my brother treated your sister and his daughter. I remember Mom and Dad arguing about his behavior. Neither of them approved, but they weren't ones for ruffling feathers. Keeping up appearances was really important to them back then, especially to Mom. Thankfully, Dad had the foresight to set aside money for Kyle's offspring and to make a will that would, in some small way, benefit his grandchildren. It breaks my heart that he never got to know them, and they never knew my dad. He was such a wonderful Papa to my three children."

Martha wiped the corners of her eyes. "I remember your father as being a decent man. And your mother was always so kind. I'm so sorry you lost them."

Kevin shrugged. "My folks were ashamed that Kyle chose the path he did, but in some ways, they made it too easy for him to neglect his responsibilities. As a parent myself, I understand how that could happen. The best we can do is give our children the tools to succeed, but we don't get to decide how they live."

Martha rested her hand on Melinda's shoulder. "No, we don't. All we can do is love them."

He nodded. "So, I hope you'll let McKenzie know that she has an Uncle Kevin who'd love to get to know her. My wife, Trina and our two children would love to welcome another member to our family. But, if you choose not to tell her about us, that money is still there for you to draw on, Melinda. The only restriction is that it be used for McKenzie."

Melinda nodded. She looked at Martha and said, "How can we possibly not tell her?"

Martha hugged her daughter and said, "We'll get back to you, Kevin. Soon. And thank you."

"You're very welcome. And I'm sorry that Mr. Townes's intentions came off as sinister. It's just that I was afraid you'd be tempted to run if you thought a Blair was looking for you."

Melinda nodded. "We understand. It's all good. We'll be talking to you soon."

Eric took the phone from Melinda and stepped away to speak to his client. When he returned, he said, "See, ladies? I told you I'm not a bad guy."

Melinda smiled. "You certainly aren't. Now, I just need to figure out how to tell my daughter."

CHAPTER FIFTY-ONE

Paula and the M's left Eric talking on his phone under the Clyde tree, and walked in silence back to the office where Ellie was just arriving.

When she saw Ellie, Melinda's face couldn't conceal her enthusiasm. "We had a bit of excitement out here last night."

Ellie's eyes twinkled. "Yes, I saw on the news where Miss Martha delivered a baby here last night. I wish I'd been here for that."

"Me, too," Martha said. "You could've delivered it instead of me."

Ellie nodded. "I reckon I could've, at that. I've pulled calves and birthed pigs all my life."

Martha raised her eyebrows. "Wow. Well, if we ever have another such occurrence here, we'll know who to call."

Melinda said, "Don't worry about cleaning room twelve until this afternoon. The Graham family left their stuff here when Mrs. Graham went to the hospital, but someone should be here to pick it up later.

"So, do I just need to clean Rooms 18 and 23, then? Lindsey didn't come with me today, but I can call her if she needs to come out."

Melinda nodded. "Yes, just the two rooms, plus we had a camper pull in yesterday afternoon. But be sure and stop by the office before you leave today to check the calendar. Things are looking up, and Happy Valley is going to be considerably busier in the next few months."

Ellie's face brightened. "That's wonderful." Without waiting for a response, she set out toward the guest rooms.

As Paula, Martha, and Melinda entered the office, McKenzie looked frustrated. "Where have you all been?" she asked. "The phone has been ringing non-stop since you left. We are seriously busy."

Melinda grabbed her daughter's hands. "And that's great news! Did you remember to ask everyone how they heard about us?"

"Um, not every time. Most of them told me it was someone with red hair named Zeke."

Melinda high-fived Paula. "Awesome! That's Mr. Fitzgerald, from the juggling group you booked. He's really doing a magnificent job spreading the word about us. Say, how about you take a break and let Paula watch the office for a while? Your Gram and I have something to talk to you about."

McKenzie shrugged her shoulders. "Okay. Miss Paula, Miss Cassie took Sophia back to wash her face and brush her hair. We washed her clothes from yesterday, so she'll be ready when her dad comes. Sophia was getting restless, so Miss Cassie is keeping her occupied. That kid is a handful."

After the 3M's left the office, Paula glanced at the artwork Sophia had contributed to the decor just last night and silently agreed. It seemed no one else had noticed the drawing Sophia had made of Paula yet, and she hoped it might stay for a little while longer. *If I squint, those circles on top of circles do look like me.*

Paula situated herself behind the reception desk and fished the Evanovich book from beneath, flipping to her bookmark. After reading and re-reading the same paragraph multiple times, she realized her mind wasn't on the book, so she put it away.

Her mind wandered to the events of the morning. *A million dollars. Handled properly, that'll be a life changer for McKenzie. And if McKenzie is free to pursue her dreams, then Melinda and Martha might want to reexamine theirs. I guess I'm also at a crossroad of sorts. I need to make time to really consider my own future. If Cassie's serious about moving away from Dempsey, do I really want to stay there? So many ifs.*

Paula jumped when Sophia bounced into the office followed by a bedraggled Cassie. Sophia wore a grin as wide as her face. "Hey, Paula? Can I help you?"

Paula lifted the child to the countertop. "Sure, Sophia. Hop up here and we can draw some more pictures."

"Can I make one for my new sister?"

Paula pulled out the clipboard. "Of course. Would it be okay if I make one for your little brother?"

Sophia gave a curt nod and started drawing.

Cassie leaned against the counter. "Someone got restless, and for once it wasn't me. Now I know how exhausting my fidgeting must seem to others."

Paula chuckled. "I'm used to your fidgeting. But I'm not sure I'd manage that well with our little friend here if I had her full-time."

Cassie ruffled Sophia's hair, "No wonder my parents hit the road as soon as I was out of the house. It's a wonder they didn't leave when I was three."

Paula laughed. "And just think, she's only one of three the Grahams get to deal with now."

"Oh, boy, are they in for a ride! So, you haven't told me… what'd you think about what Eric had to say?"

"I sat there with my mouth open, mostly. A million dollars… that's incredible."

"He didn't tell me the details, just that McKenzie was a beneficiary in her grandfather's will. That's a big responsibility for someone her age. Did the M's say how they were going to handle it?"

"Right now, they're talking to McKenzie about everything. I know I've been pushing for Melinda to not keep secrets, but now I just hope McKenzie receives it well."

"She's a good kid. It's obvious how much she and Melinda love each other. I'm certain that their love will get them through anything. Either way, I guess we'll find out soon enough."

The phone interrupted Paula's doubts, and she soon became busy taking reservations and answering questions about Happy Valley Motor Inn and Resort. She enjoyed the give and take with callers and imagined she would really enjoy doing customer service on a more regular basis.

Cassie showed Sophia how to draw a hand turkey. Soon, Sophia's hands were covered in ink while page upon page was filled with a variety of vague turkey shapes.

When Paula finally had a break, she admired Sophia's artwork. "Look, Paula, this one is a girl turkey for my baby sister and this one is a boy turkey for my baby brother."

Paula gave an approving nod at the nearly identical turkey pictures. The only discernable difference was that the girl turkey had long hair while the boy had none. "I'm sure your new sister and brother will be happy that you drew pictures for them."

Sophia nodded and continued drawing.

Paula looked to Cassie. "That's progress, anyway. How'd you get her to draw one for the b-o-y?"

"It just happened. I guess she's coming to terms with her new normal."

While Sophia continued to draw Paula remembered to ask Cassie about her catering client who specialized in web design. "We kind of got sidetracked yesterday. You said you'd located the number for the woman who designs websites?"

Cassie nodded. "I did more than that. Her name's Roslyn Dames, and I gave her a call this morning while Little Bit here was engaged in playing hide-and-seek in the living room. She hid; I didn't seek."

"Cool. So, what'd you find out?"

"Roslyn owes me a favor. I've catered two big events for her, both on extremely short notice. No one in Fort Worth would even consider either of the jobs because she waited so long to find a caterer, but I agreed to take on the events and they turned out spectacularly."

"How'd she find out about you?"

"Um, a friend from college was dating her at the time. They've since parted. Amicably, thank goodness. Anyway, she told me she'd gladly take on Happy Valley and be willing to barter with you. Maybe a room for a week or something like that in exchange for her expertise. I'm supposed to sit down with Melinda and you and decide what kind of look y'all have in mind, and what you want out of the site, then we can give Roslyn a call."

"That is awesome. Thank you so much. You probably haven't had a chance to tell Melinda yet, have you?"

"No. I thought that could be good news at dinner tonight. Speaking of eating, I think I'll take Sophia back and see what we can scrounge up for lunch."

"There's food left over from dinner last night. Delilah brought enough yesterday for several meals. Don't make anything too heavy, though. Remember Mark's coming for dinner tonight."

"Then we'll go see what we can do with the remains. I'll go shopping for dinner after Little Bit's dad picks her up."

"You two fidget monsters go take care of lunch, then."

"Sophia, you want to bring your pictures back to the kitchen and help me fix us some lunch?" Cassie asked.

"Let me finish this feather," Sophia said, concentrating on another turkey.

Cassie waited until Sophia was done. "Come on, kid. Let's take the paper with us and you can draw some more while I work."

"Can I draw a kitten now? I'm tired of turkeys all the time," Sophia said as she followed Cassie out of the room.

Paula laughed and was glad Cassie was on Sophia duty. She tried to go back to her book, but it was no use. Her mind was buzzing with ideas.

Paula took out a piece of paper and began making notes:

1. *Join the Chamber of Commerce [get the lady's name from Delilah]*
2. *Sit down with Melinda and Martha & go over the financial reports*
3. *Decide what they want the website to look like and do*
4. *CalNet!!!??? *Important! Look at this soon!**
5. *Plan a fishing event for locals -- maybe a kids' fishing derby?*
6. *Join the Rotary or Lions Club*
7. *Decide...* ☹

Decide what? To leave Dempsey and move to Happy Vale and take over day to day operations of the resort? To sell the resort and get back to my old life? What old life? Leave everything as is and visit periodically?

Paula flung her pen on the counter. "Why? Why is this so hard?"

She blew air out through her pursed lips and ran her fingers through her hair, mussing her ponytail. *I guess I need to keep things in perspective. At least I don't have to tell my grown child that her biological mother committed suicide and her biological father's a deadbeat who never wanted anything to do with her.* She pulled the band out of her hair and smoothed her locks just as the phone rang, startling her. *Crap!* "Good morning. Happy Valley—"

"Miss Paula, is that you? Dad-gummed if you don't sound just as perty as a church bell on a Sunday morning.

The familiar voice brought a smile to her heart. "Zeke! It's so good to hear your voice. How are you doing?"

"Miss Paula, if I were doing any better, they'd have to proclaim me King of Oklahoma. How are you doing?"

"Truthfully? You've made us very busy here. I'm not sure what you did before you retired, but you should have been in advertising."

When Zeke laughed, Paula imagined his head thrown back in pure abandon. He said, "I'm always glad to help out. You ladies, and Miss Cassie, are pretty special. Speaking of which, did you happen to mention me favorably to Miss Martha?"

Paula stifled a grin. "Oh, were you serious about that?"

Zeke let out a belly laugh. "I'm always serious about matters of the heart, young lady."

"I thought that might be the case. So... I told Martha that she'd caught your eye, and she promised she'd think about getting to know you better. But things have been crazy here since you left. I don't think she's had two minutes to think about much of anything. As a matter of fact, last night, she delivered a baby right here in the house!"

"Well, I'll be. She's a remarkable woman, that Martha."

"That, she is."

"To tell the truth, I didn't call just to yammer. The minute I got home, I was homesick for Happy Valley, so I thought, what's keeping me from paying a visit on my own? I want to book a room for July thirtieth."

Yesss! Paula's heart soared. She opened the guest register and said, "We'd be honored to have you back. I'll even give you the preferred customer rate."

"None of that. Let's save my discount for the N.J.O.A. next year. I'd like a king bed for three nights. Maybe more, but we'll play that by ear."

"Of course. I do have a room with a king available for three nights beginning on the thirtieth of July."

"Alrighty then. I'm looking forward to seeing you all again. Do you need my credit card number to hold the room?"

Paula didn't have the heart to tell him that she and Cassie would be leaving before he arrived, but she figured he wasn't actually coming to see them anyway. *As long as Martha's here, he'll be happy.* "There's no need for that in your case. I've got you all booked. And, I promise I'll touch base with Martha again. We're hoping today will hold fewer surprises. Speaking of which, do you want your visit to be one? A surprise, I mean?

"Hmmm. Maybe. If she gives you the go ahead to let me court her, then I'll decide."

"Sounds like a plan."

Zeke cleared his throat. "Alrighty, then. I'll let you go now. I hope your day is as sweet as you are, Miss Paula."

Paula couldn't help but smile. "Zeke Fitzgerald, you'd better watch it, or I'll be arm wrestling Martha for your affections."

Zeke let out a hearty guffaw. "Goodbye, young lady."

"Goodbye, Zeke."

The remainder of the morning passed quickly. Ellie brought in the dirty linens and started the washing machine. Paula followed her to the laundry room and said, "I'll be happy to put those in the dryer later for you."

Ellie frowned. "No, ma'am. I need to earn my pay, Miss Paula, and there's just the few to take care of."

Paula winced. *Crap. I never considered that I've been undermining Ellie's job by taking on the hotel's laundry.* "Of course. Just let me know if I can do anything to help."

"Yes, ma'am. I'll go make up the beds and check the campground restroom, then I'll be back up to finish the laundry."

Paula snapped her fingers. "Oh! Before I forget... there might be a gentleman out next to the Clyde tree. We told him about the better phone reception out there. I just didn't want you to be startled to see someone in your spot."

Ellie nodded. "Thanks for that. I'd hate to accidentally shoot a guest."

Paula's jaw dropped open. "Uh, that would certainly be a mistake."

"It sure would. Mostly because I'd be the one to have to clean up the mess."

When Ellie grinned, Paula knew she'd been had. Her heartrate slowed and she smiled. "Okay, I'll stay out of your business. You've obviously done this without my help for a long time."

After Ellie left, Paula reviewed her notes and added one more item: Let Ellie do the laundry or risk being shot!

CHAPTER FIFTY-TWO

Paula rose from her place behind the registration desk and went out to meet Alex Graham when he arrived just before noon, looking tired, but happy. "Mr. Graham, I'm sure you don't remember me from yesterday, what with all the excitement. I'm Paula Arnett, one of the owners of Happy Valley. Congratulations on your new little ones."

"Thank you, Paula. I don't know what we'd have done without you all. I'm ready to collect Sophia and get her out of your hair. She can be overwhelming."

"Aww, we enjoyed her so much. Follow me. I believe she's back in the kitchen helping my friend fix lunch."

They headed inside and found Sophia on the kitchen counter stirring a bowl of brownie mix.

Cassie put a casserole in the oven and said, "Sophia, look who I see."

Sophia looked up and her face brightened. "Daddy! Look, I'm cooking, and I've been drawing pictures and I slept in a big girl bed almost all night all by myself."

Alex's eyes filled with tears. "You're all grown up now, aren't you?"

Sophia frowned. "No, Daddy. See, I'm still your little girl."

She reached for him and he scooped her into his arms, ignoring the chocolate she smeared on his shirt. He twirled her in a circle and said, "Are you ready to pack up our stuff and go see Mommy and the new babies? The doctors say we can take them home today."

"I need to finish these brownies first. They're for you and Mommy."

Cassie pushed the bowl away from the counter's edge. "We can watch her while you go pack. In fact, you can stay for lunch with us if you'd like."

He set Sophia on the ground. "Thanks. I'll let you watch Sophia while I go pack, but we need to get back to check Julie and the babies out of the hospital. I'd like to take a quick shower, though, and change my clothes if you don't mind watching her for a few minutes longer." He pulled his shirt away from his chest. "I seem to have picked up a chocolate smear or two."

After Alex left, Paula helped Sophia finish her brownies and put them into the oven for her. "There. Hopefully they'll be ready when your daddy comes back."

"Any word from the 3M's yet?" Cassie asked.

Paula shrugged. "Not a peep. They've been in Melinda's room a long time. But I'm sure McKenzie's got a lot of questions for them to answer. Oh! Zeke called. He wants to come back on the thirtieth. He's sweet on Martha."

Cassie chuckled. "Yes, I remember you mentioning that." She pulled some leftover chicken out of the fridge. "Come here, Little Bit.

We can make a to-go lunch for your dad while your brownies bake." She looked to Paula, "You know he likely hasn't had a decent meal since all this started. I used most of the chicken making the casserole, but there were a couple of pieces left, along with an extra dinner roll. He can eat those and drive at the same time."

Sophia wrinkled her nose. "I want a peanut butter and jelly."

Paula grabbed the bread and said, "I think I can manage that."

Cassie poured a glass of milk and said, "Come on, kid. Let's eat."

"You're a natural at this mommy stuff," Paula said.

"Yeah, but just in the short term. This one's going bye-bye soon, and that makes all the difference."

The office bell rang and Paula headed to the front desk. Eric Townes stepped inside, wearing a tropical print shirt and cargo shorts. A Chicago Cubs cap topped off his ensemble.

Paula looked him up and down. "Hmm, I didn't take you for a Cubs fan. I probably would've mistrusted you even more."

He placed his right hand over his heart. "Oh, no! Don't tell me you're a Sox fan."

"Only by marriage. My husband grew up in Illinois. The White Sox had his heart."

"Had?"

"Yes. He passed away recently. A quick pang stabbed her heart. "Uh, what can I do for you, Mr. Townes?"

"Please, call me Eric. And, my condolences. I was just wondering if there's any news I can relay back to Mr. Blair, and if not, I hoped maybe I could borrow some of that fishing gear you mentioned when I checked in."

Paula smiled. "Martha and Melinda have been talking to McKenzie ever since we left you, so there's no news yet on that front. I'll be happy to show you where the gear is, but we don't have any bait."

"That's okay. I picked up some beer and bait when I got my fishing license this morning. One stop shopping, just as you told me."

"And here I thought you hadn't listened to anything I said."

"To the contrary, I hung on every word."

She attempted to conceal her grin as she rolled her eyes. She grabbed the keys to the shed and turned the answering machine on. "Come on and follow me. When you're done fishing, just leave the gear on the porch and let one of us know. We'll put it away for you." She unlocked the storage shed and allowed him to select his gear.

He grabbed a pole and tackle and said, "No problem. Listen, I'm really sorry I called you a broad yesterday. I was tired and cranky. My flight had been delayed and there was a mix up with my rental car. Normally I'm really a considerate guy, and my mother would throttle me if she ever heard me use such a word for a woman."

She chuckled. "It's okay. You're forgiven. Mostly because you also said I was cute."

A smile formed on his face. "Oh? And here I was thinking *you* hadn't listened to a word *I* said other than the one I shouldn't have."

Paula laughed, "I was hanging on to every word, too, you know. Good luck fishing today."

As he headed down the path, she locked up the shed and hurried back to the office. The heavenly scent of brownies baking wafted in from the kitchen and made her mouth water. *Maybe we should bake fresh cookies to give guests upon check-in. I know other hotels do that.* She added the idea to her list of notes. *Yeah, this'll add a nice, homey touch to our website advertising.*

She clicked her pen off and on a few times while she studied her list. *Of course, fishermen probably aren't as concerned with homemade cookies as they are with catching fish and drinking beer. I wonder what it would take to be able to sell beer and bait here on site. I'm sure we'd have to apply for a special alcohol license.* She added her thoughts to her list.

8. Fresh baked cookies for guests?
9. Check how to sell beer and bait

She leaned on the counter and her face lit up. *Oh! I need to see how to get more reliable cellphone service out here. Is something like that even possible? It won't hurt to check.* She added to her list:

10. Cellphone booster?

Soon, her mind wandered, and she began doodling in the margins. When she realized what she had done, she found a series of question marks all around the page. Big ones, small ones, elaborate and plain. *Like Sophia, I'm tired of drawing turkeys. It's time to make a decision about my future.*

CHAPTER FIFTY-THREE

Paula continued to kick around ideas of how to improve the inn's business. As she was deep in thought, Alex Graham stepped in and said, "Excuse me."

Snapped out of her trance, she jumped and clutched her chest. "Oh! No, excuse me, Mr. Graham. I'm sorry. I was a million miles away. Are you all packed and ready to go?"

He flashed a quick smile. "I am, but could I leave you my card so you can contact me in case I left anything behind? Let me borrow a pen, and I'll add my personal number and email. I'll gladly pay the shipping for anything you find. I double and triple-checked, but Julie packs more make-up than a department store, and I'm sure I've probably missed something."

She passed a pen across the desk then added his card to the ones in her pocket. "Don't worry. I'll let our housekeeper know to keep an eye out for anything you might've left behind."

They turned as Cassie and Sophia entered the office, each carrying a package. Sophia wore a proud smile as she approached him. "Daddy, look my brownies are cooked."

Cassie chuckled. "Sophia's a good little assistant. She taste-tested one and declared them to be *duper-super.*"

Alex gave a serious nod as he stifled a smile. "Well, if she says so, I'm sure they are. Thank you, Sophia."

Cassie passed a package covered in foil to him. "Here's a light lunch to take with you. It's just leftovers, but we thought you might want something for the road. Sophia's already had a peanut butter sandwich."

He accepted the package and shook his head. "Honestly, I don't know how to thank you all. I can't imagine how this would've played out if we'd stayed at a chain motel somewhere along our route."

Paula shrugged. "You don't need to thank us. Just come back when you can really enjoy Happy Valley and tell your friends about us."

"That I can do. Listen, I don't want to presume too much, but I couldn't help but notice that you didn't have many guests other than us."

Paula bit her lip. "Yes. It's a long story, but things are starting to look up."

Alex grabbed his daughter's hand. "Well, when you get a chance, look at my card and get in touch. I have some ideas for you. Sophia, let's go, sweetie."

Cassie and Paula escorted the Grahams to their car, and after Sophia gave them multiple hugs and kisses, Alex buckled her into her car seat. The women waved until the car was out of sight.

"What a sweet family," Paula said.

Cassie nodded. "Whose lives are about to get incredibly crazy. Hey, how about some lunch? I made a casserole out of the leftover chicken, and I threw together a salad."

"Perfect. Do you think we should tell the 3M's it's ready?"

"No. They'll get hungry soon enough and join us when they're ready. Besides, there's no way they can't smell the brownies. That ought to bring them out soon enough." She headed toward the kitchen and Paula followed.

Paula filled two glasses with ice. "If you'll make a list, I'll run into town and shop for dinner tonight. I haven't gotten away since we got here."

"Sure, but I can go with you."

"Would it hurt your feelings if I said I needed to go by myself?"

"Well, no, I don't guess so. As long as you bring me a Dr. Pepper with ice in it. But, is everything okay?"

"Yes, it's absolutely okay. I just need to make a decision about the future, but I can't do that while I'm surrounded by this place. I've got a feeling that Happy Valley Motor Inn and Resort is clouding my thinking."

"Grab us some plates and I'll get the food on the table." Cassie tossed the salad. "I understand what you mean about this place, though. I'm not nearly as fidgety here as I am in Dempsey."

Paula nearly choked on a sip of tea. "I hadn't noticed, but if you say so."

"Seriously? I can't believe you haven't noticed that I went almost an entire day without a Dr. Pepper. It has to be the Happy Valley influence."

Paula rolled her eyes. "I'm sure."

Cassie took the casserole out of the oven as the kitchen door opened. Martha entered with red-rimmed eyes, but a smile on her face. "Something sure smells good."

Paula set the plates on the table and ran to hug Martha. "Are you okay?"

Martha gave Paula a squeeze. "Yes, dear, thank you. My girls are just washing their faces. They'll be in shortly."

Cassie set the food on the table. "Come on and grab a seat. I just made a light lunch. Surely it'll tide us over until dinner."

Paula filled three more glasses and grabbed more plates and silverware. *I hope the smile on Martha's face is a good omen.*

The aroma of chicken mixed with the tangy smell of salad dressing, and Cassie said, "Maybe we should wait on the others."

"It smells so good," Martha said. "I'll try to wait, but no promises."

Within a few minutes, both Melinda and McKenzie joined them at the table. Like Martha, they both showed evidence of having cried, but there were also tentative smiles.

"What smells so wonderful?" Melinda asked.

Cassie scooped food onto everyone's plate and said, "It's just leftovers. I thought I'd transform last night's fried chicken into a casserole. I'm curious to know what you think."

Martha took a large bite and smiled. "Oh, this is divine! You must be antsy to get back to work."

Cassie nodded. "Yes, and no. Frankly, I'm worn out. It's difficult to keep good help. I was actually able to take this break because my sous chef, Janet, and her mom decided to go out on their own."

Paula frowned and grabbed Cassie's hand. "I didn't realize that. You should have told me."

Cassie blinked back a tear. "You've had enough on your own plate without having to worry about me. Anyway, I can't say that I blame her. Janet's seen how many jobs I've turned down."

"How long have you been cooking?" Melinda asked, stabbing her salad with her fork.

"I've been cooking my whole life. And I've worked for other caterers before, but I've owned my own catering business for five years now. It's been fun, but I've run myself ragged."

McKenzie shoved a bite of casserole in her mouth and said, "Mmm!" then gave a thumbs up.

Martha chuckled, "Mmm is right. I would have never even thought to transform fried chicken into a casserole like this. My taste buds are still looking forward to that breakfast you promised."

Cassie's eyes lit up. "I'll be happy to make that in the morning. I hope everyone likes French toast. I'll make enough for Dr. Fields too."

Martha nodded. "Yes, he should be here by five this evening, but he doesn't usually hang around for breakfast. He's always in too big a hurry to fish."

Cassie raised an eyebrow. "When I cook, I feed everyone. Maybe we should call him and let him know he's invited to breakfast tomorrow as well as supper tonight."

Melinda scraped the last bite of casserole from her plate. "He usually calls before he leaves Nacogdoches, mainly to make sure we haven't booked his room. Like *that's* ever happened."

Paula waved her finger at Melinda. "It could happen someday soon, though. We have a lot of new bookings for the next few weeks, mostly due to Zeke Fitzgerald's propensity for talking to strangers. By the way, Martha, he called this afternoon and asked if you've considered his offer."

A noticeable blush crept up Martha's neck and settled on her cheeks, giving her a bright, rosy glow. She bit her lip and said, "Tell him I've agreed to his offer, and I look forward to discussing it with him further."

Paula suppressed a grin. "Maybe you should just call him yourself. I've got his number if you want it."

Martha gave a sideways glance to Melinda and said, "No. No, that's all right. You can call him."

Paula nodded. "I can do that."

The office phone rang, and Martha stood. "I'll get it," she said as she bustled out the door.

When she returned a few moments later she was smiling. "That was Mark. He'll be here around five, and he said *he's* cooking dinner for *us*. He said he's got a surprise and he hopes that all of us will join him."

McKenzie narrowed her eyes and her lips formed a thin, white line. "Oh joy. Another surprise." No one spoke until McKenzie added, "Hey, where's Sophia?"

Paula said, "Her dad picked her up about an hour ago. He was so appreciative of how Martha and Melinda handled the whole labor and delivery thing, but he also promised to tell everyone he knows about Happy Valley. He said he wanted to help out however he could."

Cassie stood and brought a platter of brownies to the table. "He also told you to look at his card."

Paula furrowed her brow. "Oh, yeah, I forgot." She dug the cards out of her back pocket and waggled one in front of Martha. "This one's Zeke's."

Martha blushed and waved her hand.

Paula patted Martha's shoulder. "And this one is Alex's." She examined the card. "Well, I'll be. This says he's the director of a marketing agency. Actually, it looks like it's either his business or his family's business. Look." She passed the card around.

GMS
Graham Marketing Solutions
Dallas, Texas
Alex Graham, Director

Melinda inspected the card and fingered the raised lettering. "Wow. And he said he wants to help us?"

Paula nodded. "He did. And I've got a feeling his terms will be quite favorable."

Cassie took a brownie and pushed the platter toward the middle of the table. "Don't forget, I spoke to my client who does web design. Her name is Roslyn Dames. She owes me a couple of favors, and she said she'd be happy to design a new site for you. You just need to decide what you want it to look like and what you want it to do."

Melinda grimaced. "Can we afford her?"

A smile spread across Cassie's face. "Yes. She's actually interested in trading out services, such as a room here for a weekend or two in exchange for her work."

Melinda's eyes lit up. "That's exciting. If we can get our name out there and have a productive website, I think we may have a real chance of success."

Paula stood and started collecting empty plates. "I'm going to run into town and get some supplies for breakfast. Cassie, why don't you make a list of ingredients you need while I clean the kitchen."

"I can go to the store," Martha said.

Paula stacked the dishes in the sink. "That's okay. I haven't been into town since we got here, and I'd like to go explore a bit. If you all need anything, let me know."

McKenzie stood and took the dirty glasses to the sink. "I'll clean the kitchen. I just feel like doing something normal. Mom, do I have to talk to this Mr. Townes?"

Melinda forced a smile. "Only if you want to, sweetie. I can handle it if you like, but it's up to you."

McKenzie squirted soap on a dish sponge. "This adulting isn't as easy as I thought it would be."

Paula stifled a smile and said, "Mr. Townes went fishing before lunch. Do you want to be told when he returns the fishing gear?"

McKenzie bit her lip. "Yeah, I guess so. Mom, Gram, would you guys come with me?"

Melinda stood and rubbed McKenzie's back. "Of course, we will. You don't have to adult alone."

Melinda gestured for Paula to follow her to the office. As they got to the front desk, Paula said, "You know, when things start getting busier around here, you might need to hire someone to help out. Especially if McKenzie starts school."

Melinda nodded. "Yeah, I've been thinking about that, too. If that's what she wants to do, I'd love for her to go to school. I'd also like to put Ellie on full-time."

"Would you and Martha sit down with me sometime tomorrow or Thursday so we can look over the books? I don't even know what Cal paid for this place or what it costs to operate."

"Absolutely. In fact, I'd wondered why you hadn't already asked. Mom's the one you really want to talk to, but I'll sit in, too."

"Cal handled all of our finances, right down to the penny. I never had a single worry in that regard, and now I feel totally unprepared to handle what I'll need to do to keep my own house going, let alone the business of an entire fishing resort."

Melinda took a deep breath and bit the inside of her cheek. "Have you considered selling your house? Maybe you want to move out here."

Paula sighed. "Actually, I have thought about it, but it makes me sad to think about it for too long. I have so many memories of Cal there. The house still smells like him."

Melinda wrapped her arms around Paula. "Aww, I'm sorry. I shouldn't have even suggested it."

Paula fanned her eyes. "Don't feel bad. I keep going 'round and 'round in my head wondering what to do. Selling the house is always the part that gets me right here," she said, placing a palm on her chest.

"Mama went through that when we left Indiana. She cried for a week when the house she and Daddy shared sold. You might ask her how she feels now."

Paula wiped a tear from her cheek. "I will. I really like Martha. Heck, I love you all. I can't believe I didn't even know you all last week, and now I feel like you're my family."

Melinda squeezed Paula's hand. "And that might be the thing that helps you decide. As far as I'm concerned, you *are* family. Surely there's a name for our relationship? Wives-in-law?"

Paula laughed. "The Ex and the Missus?"

Cassie stepped in and raised an eyebrow. "You both seem to be in a great mood. What'd I miss?"

Paula smiled. "We're trying to decide what our relationship should be called."

Cassie folded her arms. "Friends won't do?"

Paula shrugged. "I guess it'll have to do until we can come up with something more descriptive. Melinda already nixed Sister Wives."

Cassie giggled. "Girl, you definitely need to get out of here for a while. Here's your list."

CHAPTER FIFTY-FOUR

Paula asked Melinda if she needed anything from the store before heading to Room 23 to pick up her purse. Behind the wheel of her sedan, Paula felt a weight lift from her that she hadn't realized she'd been carrying. Being alone in the car made her feel more in charge of her own life than she'd been for the past two weeks. In what she'd begun thinking of as her 'old life' Paula knew she'd become accustomed to being alone, happy with being by herself all day with the company of a good book.

If not for Cal and Cassie, she probably would've been just fine avoiding most social contact. And they both had traveled for their careers frequently enough that Paula often didn't interact with anyone much during the week except for trips to the grocery store. Of course, she attended Sunday church services, and occasionally went to Bible study, but she was always content to be home.

She smiled as she passed the Welcome to Happy Vale sign. *It's almost as if* Cal *manipulated me into ending up at Happy Valley Motor Inn and Resort in Happy Vale, Texas, where I'd have no choice but to deal with people on a daily basis.* She chuckled. "And oddly enough, I think I like it."

Paula drove down Main Street, a pleasant oak-lined road with a variety of small shops, including a women's clothing boutique, a small bookstore, a quaint furniture store, a locally-owned grocery store, a law firm, the local newspaper, and the familiar Oaks on Main.

As she cruised down the street, her head turning back and forth to inspect each business and the numerous people walking in and out of shops and down the sidewalks on each side of the road, a shiver traveled up her spine when she got to the end of Main and saw a majestic three-story red brick edifice with columns gracing both sides of the entrance under a marble sign that said *"Big Lake County Courthouse."*

The courthouse lawn hosted a farmers' market which was in full swing. Every parking spot was taken, so she turned around and parked across the street from Delilah's place. She turned off the car then perused Cassie's list to see what might be available at the farmer's market. She laughed when she came to the last item in all capital letters: *"GIANT SIZED DR. PEPPER WITH ICE."* She feigned a grimace and rolled her eyes. *Heaven help me if I forget that!*

More than two dozen vendors stood or lounged beneath the shade of their respective stands behind tables laden with cardboard cartons of homegrown vegetables and fruits. As she walked toward the market, her eyes darted between the tables of local crafts, the stand of homemade cheeses, and the colorful table featuring an assortment of flowers.

She glanced at her list then stood still as her eyes searched for any booths that might have items she needed. *Good. I think they'll have a lot of what I need here.* She craned her neck as she wove her way through the small crowd of people lined up at various stands. Some gave her a look that let her know she was not recognized as a part of the normal crowd. She shook off her feelings of self-consciousness and acknowledged any curious looks with a smile and a nod of the head or a hello. *Small towns. I belong in Dempsey. I wonder what it would take for me to belong here?*

After mentally checking off the items she knew would be available there, she headed back up Main Street to the grocery store where she picked up several items. As she headed back to her car, she paid careful attention to the businesses lining the road. She smiled to herself. *Everything here seems so well kept. These folks must take a great deal of pride in their community.*

She locked her groceries in the trunk of her car and then headed back to the cheese stand at the farmer's market. On the advice of the vendor, she selected a cheese that would pair well with white wine and another to go with red.

She headed to the flower booth and inhaled the mixture of scents coming from the colorful buds, bringing a smile to her face. A young man behind the counter said, "Hi. Can I help you?"

Paula stepped closer. "Yes, actually. Would it be possible for you to put together a bouquet for me? I have some other purchases to make, and I'd like to pick up the flowers afterward, if that's okay."

He tugged at his Happy Vale High cap. "My mom usually does the bouquets. She had to run home to take care of my sister, but I'll be happy to give it a shot."

"I'm sure you'll do a better job than I could. I'll even let you pick them out for me. I'm just looking for something colorful and sunny."

"Okay, I'll see what I can do. You want to come back in about fifteen minutes?"

She smiled. "That'll be fine." She headed to a few other booths and purchased the remaining items on her list then checked her watch. *The flowers should be ready about now.* As she spun on her heel to head back to the flower booth, she bumped into a man. "Oh! Excuse me."

The man offered a playful smile. "Fancy meeting you here."

She shifted her packages in her arms and then looked up at him as her lips curved into a smile.

"Mr. Townes. I see you came in from the lake."

"It's Eric, remember? And, yes, I got tired of catching a whole lot of nothing. Besides, since I didn't take anything out there to eat, I'm pretty much starving now. I don't suppose you'd like to grab a bite with me?"

She bit her lip. "Oh, thank you for the offer, but I'm sorry, I can't. I'm buying groceries for the resort and I need to get back. However, I can recommend a café." With a nod of the head, she gestured. "Oaks on Main. I promise you won't be disappointed. A friend of mine, Delilah Oaks, owns and runs it, so if you see her, please mention that I sent you."

"You've sold me. I'll be sure to tell her. Oh, by the way, I spoke to McKenzie before I left."

"Really? How'd that go?"

"She was totally chill, as the young people say. It's really sad that her father never acknowledged her."

"It is sad, but she is one resilient kid. I hope she'll develop a relationship with her uncle and her cousins in the future."

"She asked about them. I haven't met Kevin's wife or kids, but I've dealt with him for business purposes for a number of years now, and, like I told McKenzie, he really is a stand-up guy."

"That's wonderful. I have no doubt she'll end up meeting them. Hey, I don't want to keep you. You go have lunch at Oaks. But be careful. You might not want to go back to Illinois once you taste Delilah's cooking."

Eric glanced at the farmers hawking their goods and lowered his voice. "I'm sure there's no chance of that happening. I'm purely a city boy."

She laughed and rearranged her packages in her arms. "Okay, well, enjoy your lunch anyway."

He nodded. "Will do." He hurried up the road toward Oaks on Main and Paula hustled over to her car.

She stuffed her packages in the trunk then rushed back to the flower stand. When she saw the pink and purple zinnias mixed with baby's breath and greenery in a mason jar, she clasped her hands to her chest. "Oh, this is gorgeous! Are you here every Tuesday?"

The boy nodded. "One of the family brings flowers in for the market. We're here on Tuesdays and in Hemphill on Saturdays. Usually it's my mom and little sister. Dad comes sometimes. I hardly ever help out at the stand 'cause of baseball," he said, tipping his cap.

"Well, I'll tell the ladies out at Happy Valley Motor Inn and Resort about your flowers. I'd like to keep some in the office every day to brighten up the place. Do you happen to have a card?"

"No, ma'am, but I'll be happy to jot down our info for you." He tore a piece of floral tissue off a roll and scribbled down the flower stand's name and a phone number.

She read the note and said, "So, are you one of the Burkes in Burkes Bouquets?"

"Yes, ma'am. I'm Noah Burke."

"It's nice to meet you, Noah. I'll be sure and mention Burkes Bouquets to my friends." Paula turned to leave then spun back around. "Noah, could you direct me to a convenience store where I can buy a Dr. Pepper fountain drink?"

"Sure. If you're headed back toward the Happy Valley resort, there's a Quik Shop on the right side of the highway just after the big water tower. You know where I'm talking about?"

A look of recognition washed over her face. "Oh, yes. There's a big pasture there."

"Right."

"Perfect. Thank you so much." On her way back to her car she couldn't help but smile.

Paula retraced her route and as she passed Eric's SUV parked in front of Delilah's place, she wished she'd taken time to browse around in some of the shops before buying her groceries, but she knew she'd be back to Happy Vale another time. *I've made too many connections here to not return.*

After stopping for Cassie's beverage of choice, Paula drove on to the resort. Pulling into the entrance, she felt as if she were returning home. *It's not necessarily home in the same way that Dempsey is home, but here, I feel so welcome, and it's like I'm part of something bigger than myself.* She parked in front of the office next to a pickup truck with a fishing boat, displaying Louisiana tags. As she headed inside, Cassie met her in the office and snatched the Dr. Pepper from Paula's hand.

Martha stood behind the counter chatting with a couple of men dressed in full fishing gear. She nodded at Paula and said, "Personally, I'm not much of a fisherman, but Paula here caught a fish her first go around."

Paula shrugged. "To be honest, that was an accident. I didn't even know what I was doing. You're bound to catch something."

The men laughed and one said, "At this point we just want to kick back and have a few beers today. Catching something would just be a bonus."

Martha turned her attention to Paula. "McKenzie took some fresh towels over to their rooms already. They're in five and seven."

Paula offered the men a smile. "Welcome to Happy Valley, and good luck on the lake."

After the men left, Martha took the packages from Paula's arms and headed toward the kitchen, while Paula stepped outside and gathered the remainder of her purchases. She went back in and set the bouquet at the end of the registration desk, just as Melinda entered the office. "Oh, Melinda, I hope you don't mind. These were so pretty; I just couldn't resist."

Melinda smelled the flowers. "Of course, I don't mind. I know most fisherman might not notice, but I appreciate having something pretty to look at. Thank you."

"You're welcome. I found them at the farmers' market down on the courthouse lawn. They had a lot of nice-looking produce, crafts, cheeses, and other stuff there. Have you ever been?"

"No. McKenzie did once when we first moved here, but she said everyone looked at her like she didn't belong. In her words, she said they made her feel like an outsider. So, we just go to the grocery store."

"I noticed that when I first got there, too, but once I started saying hello to people, they warmed right up to me. You might want to try again. It seems like a great place to get to know the locals. They had so many nice things there, you might even consider setting up your own booth and selling some of your paintings or your mom's quilts."

"Wow. I never thought of that. What a great idea. Maybe we could even sell some fishing lures or something to try to drum up more business for the resort."

"That's a great idea. I'd better go put these berries and cheeses away. The berries are for breakfast, and since we have no idea what Mark's cooking for supper, at least we'll have something to fall back on that we know we can eat."

Melinda laughed. "I'm just curious as to what his surprise is. Heaven knows we've had more than our share of surprises these past few days."

Paula nodded. "That's the truth." She headed to the kitchen where she found Martha and Cassie relaxing. She put the cheese in the refrigerator and passed the berries to Cassie.

Cassie's eyes grew large, "Look how luscious these are! Set them next to the sink and I'll wash them in a bit."

Paula poured herself a glass of juice, "Melinda and I were just wondering what Mark's surprise might be."

Martha took a sip of coffee. "Maybe he's finally getting married. He's had a lady friend in his life for quite some time, although we have yet to meet her."

Cassie twisted her drinking straw, "Maybe he's going to declare his love for Melinda. I mean, he's her doctor now, but he won't always be. Maybe he's going to tell her he's broken it off with this other woman and wants to start seeing her."

Martha cut her eyes to Paula. "I doubt he'd tell all of us before talking to Melinda. Plus, it wouldn't be like him to spring that on her in front of others, and anyway, she's never expressed any romantic interest in him."

Cassie's cheeks flushed. "I guess you're right. That wouldn't exactly be something he'd just throw out there."

The ladies bandied a few ideas back and forth until they became outrageous: Mark was going to quit medicine and become a rodeo clown. He'd been selected for the astronaut training program and was moving to Houston. Paula suggested that a major television network had approached him about doing a reality tv show titled, "Hunky, MD."

Martha and Cassie cackled, and Cassie shook her head. "I don't find him hunky at all."

Martha frowned. "Neither do I. His hair's too long for my taste, and his smile is lopsided."

Paula bit her lip. "I guess hunky is in the eye of the beholder. Personally, I think he's adorable."

McKenzie entered and headed to the refrigerator. "Who's adorable?"

"Paula thinks Dr. Fields is a hunk," Martha said.

McKenzie wrinkled her nose. "Ewww. I mean, I guess for an old guy he's okay, but ewww. Is there anything here for me to snack on? I don't think I can wait until Dr. Hunky gets here to cook."

Paula shook her head, "Please don't tell him I called him that."

McKenzie grinned. "I'll try not to."

"Why don't you go take over the front desk for your mom," Martha said. "I'll bring you a snack."

After McKenzie left, Paula said, "I ran into Eric Townes while I was out shopping. He told me he'd spoken to McKenzie."

Martha stood and opened the refrigerator. "I don't think it's hit her yet what all of this could mean for her. An expanded family. A huge inheritance. She has choices today that she didn't yesterday, and as much as I adore my granddaughter, I'm not blind to her little idiosyncrasies. She's gullible, for one thing. I'd hate for someone to take advantage of her."

Cassie rattled the ice in her drink. "What did she say when she learned about the money?"

Tears welled in Martha's eyes. "She sat there for a long time without saying anything. Just nodded and smiled. Then she turned to Melinda and said, 'Mom, this means you don't have to worry about any of your medical bills now.'"

Paula pressed her hand to her heart. "Oh my. Most kids her age would have already thought of a shopping list a mile long."

Cassie fanned her eyes and blinked back a tear. "I sure would have."

Martha gave a playful smirk to Cassie and said, "You'd have spent it all on soft drinks."

Cassie grinned. "Maybe not all of it." She put the back of her hand over her forehead and, emulating Scarlet O'Hara, said, "But, as God is my witness, I'd never go thirsty again."

Melinda opened the door. "Hey what's everyone doing in here? We have a perfectly good living room."

Martha closed the refrigerator door. "I'm looking for something for your daughter to eat. She thinks she's starving."

Cassie stood. "Let me whip up something for McKenzie to tide her over until Dr. Hunky arrives.

Melinda raised an eyebrow. "Dr. Hunky? Are you talking about Mark? A hunk?" Melinda threw back her head and let out a hearty guffaw. "Are we being serious?"

Scarlet patches traveled from Paula's neck to her cheeks. "Okay, okay. You've all weighed in. But a girl's entitled to her opinion."

Melinda's eyes twinkled. "Ah. I see you're the source of Dr. Fields's new nickname."

Paula bit her lip. "Please, let's not allow that to go beyond this kitchen, okay?"

Martha winked. "Dr. Hunky will never know, will he?"

Cassie raised her hand in the Girl Scout salute, "Never. Scout's honor."

Paula raised an eyebrow and giggled. "What do you mean Scout's honor? You were a Brownie troop dropout. And what's worse, you convinced me to drop out with you."

Cassie grabbed a knife and started chopping vegetables. "If you'll recall, I was upset that they wouldn't let me work on my cooking badge in Brownie scouts. Just think, I might be a world class chef if they hadn't held me back."

Paula pursed her lips and steepled her fingers under her chin. "Yeah, and I might be able to properly catch and release a fish if we hadn't dropped out."

Martha shook her head and laughed. "Oh, you two... Melinda, how did we entertain ourselves before Paula and Cassie entered our lives?"

Melinda wiped her eyes as she laughed, then she sobered. "I honestly don't know. It's sure going to be quiet around here when you two leave on Friday."

CHAPTER FIFTY-FIVE

At the thought of leaving Happy Valley, a lump of sorrow settled in Paula's heart, weighing her down. After Cassie prepared a snack of finger sandwiches and a small crudité platter, Melinda took the plate to McKenzie in the office while Paula and Martha headed to the living room. Paula asked, "Do you think tomorrow we could make time to go over the books?"

As they sat, Martha said, "Of course. We wondered why you hadn't already asked."

Melinda joined them as Paula said, "Finances were never my thing. Cal handled it all. It's like I told Melinda, I just barely know what it takes to keep my house running. And while this trip has been wonderful and I'm so happy that we came down here and found you all, I've been in denial about what needs to be done back home in my real life. Not to mention figuring out what I need to do with Cal's business." Paula buried her head in her hands. "Frankly, I get a headache just thinking about it."

Melinda rubbed Paula's shoulder. "You've been so good at brainstorming ways to help business here, I just figured you'd put the same thinking to work for yourself."

Paula shrugged. "I guess it's just that forest for the trees thing. I mean, here I'm removed. It's like the things I dream up for the resort are on a different level. Everything feels a little magical here. But my home and the bills there are concrete. I don't know where to start." Her eyes burned and she was astonished to realize how close she was to tears. "Plus, I just miss Cal so much. I can go for a while without thinking about what I've lost. The resort helps so much with that, keeping me busy and productive, but any time I let my guard down, there's an empty space where Cal used to be."

Martha moved to the couch and gathered Paula into a hug. "I'm so sorry." She pulled back and looked Paula in the eyes. "I've been where you are. I *know* the way the loss sneaks up and punches you in the gut, sometimes out of the clear, blue sky, and I understand the feelings of guilt for being happy, even for just a moment. I know people say things that are hurtful without meaning to, and other people don't know what to say at all. It is true that time will ease your pain, but the amount of time necessary for that to happen is different for everyone. I still hurt so bad when I think of Marie. Time hasn't eased that pain much at all. When my husband Jerry passed, I think my heart was already so broken that his loss just got absorbed in my sorrow over my daughter."

Melinda reached across Paula and patted Martha's hand. "Mama, look at you, though, talking about Marie. You couldn't do that a month ago."

Martha's eyes glistened as she smiled. "I guess you're right. See, Paula? Marie's been gone for more than twenty years, and it's only been recently than I can even give myself permission to talk about her. To forgive her. Because I was angry at her and that got all mixed up with the sadness. Oh, listen to me go on. I'm sorry I hijacked your thoughts."

Paula swallowed the lump in her throat and smiled. "No, don't be sorry. I think you're exactly right. We each have to grieve in our own way and our own time. You know, Zeke said something along those lines to me after the cookout the other night. As a matter of fact, I think I'll head outside and give him a call about that project you and I discussed earlier."

Martha gave a bashful blush. "I think that's a good idea."

CHAPTER FIFTY-SIX

Paula refilled her tea glass and headed out the back door into the heat of the day and meandered down the path to the campground. Stifled by the humidity, she took a long sip of her drink and fanned her face with her hand. Under the shade of Clyde's tree, she fished Zeke's card out of her back pocket before taking a seat on the edge of the picnic table.

While she waited for Zeke to answer, Paula watched the men who'd checked in earlier fish from their boat. The way they laughed with one another and their obvious camaraderie reminded her of Cal and Delbert and brought a smile to her face.

"Hello?"

Her head snapped away from the lake. "Oh! Zeke? This is Paula Arnett from Happy Valley."

"Well, what a lovely surprise! How are you, Miss Paula?"

"I'm fine, thank you."

"So am I. Especially now that I have the pleasure of talking to you."

"Um, I just called to let you know that I talked to Martha." She could almost feel him holding his breath.

"Oh? You don't say. And?"

She couldn't repress a grin. "And she'd welcome a call from you."

The smile in Zeke's voice was apparent, "Well, I'll be. You just made me happier than a pig rolling in his own private mud hole."

She giggled. "I didn't tell her you'd made a reservation. I figured you could tell her when you two talked."

"Oh? Do you think I could call her right now? I mean, do you think it's too soon?"

Paula laughed. "Zeke, I think right now would be a great time for you to call." She read off Martha's home number, and he repeated it back to her.

He blew out a nervous breath. "Whew. Now I'm nervous."

She is, too, Zeke. I think you'll both be okay once you start talking. That first step is always the hardest, right?"

"You've got that right. Okay, here goes nothing. Thank you, Miss Paula."

"You're more than welcome. I'll talk to you later. Break a leg."

Paula took a deep breath and dialed Delbert's number then sighed when the call went directly to his voice mail. "Hi, Delbert, it's Paula. Can you please call me back as soon as you get a moment? I'll be going over the books with Martha tomorrow, and I need to talk some stuff over with you first. If you can't reach my cell, please call the office here and I'll call you back. Thanks."

A whoop from the lake caught her attention as she disconnected the call, and she looked up in time to see one of the anglers pull a huge fish in. *Wow!* Her phone rang, startling her. "Oh, hello?"

"Hey there, Goldilocks. It's Delbert. How are you?"

She answered with a shaky laugh. "Confused. And I need someone who can unconfuse me."

He chuckled. "You're sure I'm the one you want to talk to? Cassie probably wouldn't approve."

"You're probably right. She never did trust a Texas Aggie to have much sense."

"Point taken. So, what's up?"

She sighed. "Everything. I mean, I just love this place so much. The whole family has welcomed me with open arms, but I just don't know what to do."

"Well, hon, what are your options? Have you made a list?"

"Kind of, but it didn't help much."

"Well, let's make one together. I'll write and then I'll send you a text of our thoughts."

"Well, here's how I see it: I can go back to Dempsey, live in that big house that still feels like Cal. That's still full of our life together. Or I could sell the house and move down here to help with the resort full-time. The thing is, I feel needed here, you know? But, either way, I still need to do something with CalNet, and I have to do that before anything else."

"First off, you know I'm partial to you coming back here. Sherry and I would miss the heck out of you if you moved. But, that aside, I'm not sure you should make any big decisions about the future just yet. Come on home, at least for now, and we'll discuss your options on CalNet. As for relocating, if, down the line, you decide you want to leave Dempsey, Sherry and I will do everything in our power to help you transition if that's what you really want. Besides, I'm just itching to fish that beautiful, big lake you've got there, and it'd be awfully nice to stay with friends when I do."

Paula smiled into the phone. "Thanks for supporting me. I'm pretty sure I know what I want to do now. It's not cut and dried, but I think I can have my cake and eat it, too."

Delbert let out a chortle. "I swear, I never did understand that saying. If someone gives me cake, I'm damned sure gonna eat it."

"I know, right? By the way, you haven't happened to have been by my house, have you?"

"No, but Sherry and Sue Ann went over yesterday. They watered your plant, Margaret."

"Mabel," Paula corrected.

"Whatever. They watered it. Said everything looked good. Melvin's nephew, Daryl, mowed your lawn. He said Ms. Stephens from next door came asking about you."

She rolled her eyes. "That doesn't surprise me. I'm sure she's just itching to know where I am. It's a wonder she hasn't called the police to check on me."

"If she has, it hasn't gotten back to me. By now, she's probably worn a path in her carpet peeking out her window at your place."

She chuckled. "Well, I'd be surprised if she didn't. Anyway, thanks for letting me think out loud. And for not pressuring me one way or the other."

"No problem. Hey, tell Cassie that Court said she'd better come see him soon. You, too, by the way. He was plenty pissed to learn y'all drove through Dallas and didn't even call."

She winced. "That was my fault. To tell you the truth, we didn't even mention Court. I sort of railroaded Cassie the whole trip."

"Now, I find that hard to believe. Nobody railroads that girl."

She laughed. "When I get home, I'll catch you up on all the stuff that's happened since you guys were here. This place was humming for a while. And we've been busy making some marketing plans that I think will really make a difference. Oh, I almost forgot... I'm going to sit down with Martha tomorrow and look over the books. Can you imagine me looking at financials? Cal would have a good laugh over that."

Delbert's tone grew serious. "You're wrong. Paula, he only handled that stuff because he didn't want you to have a worry in the world. It wasn't because he didn't think you weren't smart enough to handle it. He just had some old-fashioned ideas, but I guess I don't have to tell you that."

She swatted at a fly. "I guess I never really thought about it. It was just the way we did things, but I really feel like a fish out of water right now."

"Aww, just remember you can do anything, Goldilocks. Trust your instincts. Listen, I'd better go. Sherry's on the other line. I'm sure she's wanting me to stop by the store on my way home."

"Okay, thanks. Give her my love."

"Will do, as long as you promise to give Cassie some grief."

Paula chuckled, "For you I will." After the call ended, she sat for a while, watching the fishermen and listening to her instincts.

CHAPTER FIFTY-SEVEN

Paula wiped the sweat from her brow with the back of her hand then wrinkled her nose. *Yuck! I need a shower.* She headed over to her room and heard the water running. Apparently, Cassie had the same idea. She looked at her clean bed then pulled her sticky shirt from her chest and grimaced. She grabbed a beer from the fridge then stepped outside and sat in a metal chair under the shade of the roof's overhang.

Two cars pulled in, one towing a camper. After both drivers checked in at the office the car with the camper headed down to the campground and the other vehicle pulled over to Room Four. Moments later, Dr. Fields pulled in. Like a voyeur, she watched as he parked in front of the office and stepped around to the trunk of his car, where he collected several grocery bags. *True, he's no Harrison Ford, but still, there's something attractive about him.* She bit her lip as she continued to watch his every move. As he closed the car trunk and turned sideways to head inside it struck her: *Holy cow! He looks a lot like Cal!*

Paula stood, her jaw hanging open. *Could it be? Maybe I'm wr— No, I was right. He definitely bears a strong resemblance to Cal. That explains why I find him so hunky.* She downed the rest of the beer and headed inside.

Cassie stood in front of the mirror, dabbing on eye shadow. "Hey, there. Did you get lost?"

Paula took some clean clothes out of the dresser. "I was on the phone. I called Zeke, then I spoke to Delbert. Apparently, Court's not happy that we didn't stop in Dallas on our way through."

Cassie rolled her eyes. "I didn't even know he was in town. Besides, we were on a mission. I'll call him tomorrow and tell him we're heading home Friday and that if we get the opportunity we'll stop by and visit then."

Paula plucked a couple of clean towels from the counter. "Hey, you know how I think Mark is kind of good looking?"

Cassie smirked. "You mean Dr. Hunky?"

"Well, he just drove in and I realized something."

"What's that?"

"Think about it. He looks like someone."

Cassie's eyes widened. "Oh, my goodness! I didn't notice it before, either. He looks like Cal! I mean, the way Cal looked when you guys got married."

Paula sniffled and blinked back a tear. "I don't know why I didn't see it sooner. I wonder why Melinda never noticed."

"Maybe she did. Or maybe Cal changed after they divorced."

"Maybe. Or maybe she never paid much attention to Cal in the first place," Paula said as she disappeared into the bathroom.

When Paula emerged after her shower, she found Cassie propped up in bed, watching television. Cassie looked up and clicked the remote to mute the volume, then raised an eyebrow. "Okay. You've hooked me. Why wouldn't Melinda have paid attention to her own husband?"

Paula pulled on a denim skirt and red tank top, then combed her hair as she told Melinda's story about her unrequited love for Ginger.

Cassie steepled her fingers under her chin and cast her eyes down. After a moment, she pursed her lips and nodded. "I see. That explains a lot."

Paula sat on the end of her bed and rubbed lotion on her legs. "I know. I never thought I'd even know, much less genuinely like, someone who is, well, a lesbian."

Cassie took a deep breath. "Um… that's not exactly true. After all, you know me."

Paula giggled, but as she studied Cassie, the smile melted from Paula's face. "What?"

"I've wanted to tell you for years."

Paula's jaw dropped open. "Why haven't you?"

"I guess I was just afraid to lose your friendship. I thought you'd look at me differently… you know, treat me differently if you knew."

Paula sat mutely, trying to process Cassie's words. She recalled how she'd counseled Martha. Now she felt like a hypocrite. She'd had no idea what Martha was experiencing. "But I would *know!*" Paula insisted. "How could I not have known?"

"Because you don't have anything to hide. You're Goldilocks. You don't have secrets, and you never think anyone else does either. To be honest, you kind of look down on those who can't be just like you."

"What? I do not," Paula fumed. "Why would you say something like that?"

Cassie moved across the space between the beds to sit beside Paula. "Maybe 'look down on' was the wrong term. You're no snob. It's just that you cannot fathom anyone keeping secrets. Hell, you fainted when you tried to keep who you were from the 3M's. And the thought of denying who you were never entered your mind when Martha confronted you. Most everyone else I know would've tried to keep up the ruse for as long as possible.

Paula sniffled. "I had no idea."

Cassie grabbed a tissue for herself and one for Paula. "Remember when I told you that not everyone has the same freedom you have to be totally honest? I was speaking for myself as well as for Cal. Can you imagine what I'd have gone through in Dempsey if word had leaked out that I was gay? I've wanted to tell you a million times over the years, but I didn't want you to look at me like you're looking at me right now."

Paula dabbed her red-rimmed eyes. "I, uh, I think I need some time to process this. Would you mind?" Paula's chin quivered as she nodded toward the door.

Cassie's jaw tightened. "Do you want me to get my own room? I'll do it if you're uncomfortable sharing a room with me now."

Paula's eyes widened, then she laughed. "What? Oh, heavens, no! Cassie, I still love you as much as ever! You're my best friend... You're my *sister*. I just need time to reflect on how I could have been so blind all these years. I wish you could have felt comfortable enough to tell me. Of course, I realize now that I probably didn't make it easy. Gosh, so many things in our past make sense now. Honest, I just need a little time by myself to wrap my head around this."

They hugged through their tears then Cassie stood. "I love you, too, girl. If it weren't for you, I'd have left Dempsey years ago. I'll give you some space. Besides, I really need a—"

"Dr. Pepper. I know. Go on; take the car. I'll be along in a bit."

They hugged again, then Cassie grabbed the car keys. "This is such a weight off my shoulders. I've both hoped for and dreaded this day since sixth grade – since I had a word to put with my feelings."

Paula squeezed Cassie's hand. "One day, you can tell me everything. I'm just not quite ready for that yet."

As Cassie left, Paula flopped onto her bed and stared at the ceiling. "Cal, did you think I couldn't forgive your secrets, too?"

Paula closed her eyes and images from her childhood ran through her mind. Cassie had been right there beside her since they were five. They'd played Barbies together, but they'd also played army. When they'd gotten old enough to start noticing boys, Cassie had been just as interested as Paula had been. But even though she was attractive and popular, Cassie's dating life was lackluster. *She used to go out with Seth Boone. He was one of the best-looking guys in high school. Quarterback of the football team. She even went to prom and homecoming with him. They were a cute couple. All of us hoped they'd continue to date after high school, but he went to Texas Tech. Now that I think of it, Cassie went to UT, even though most of her family had attended Texas Tech for generations. I was always hurt that she didn't go to Tech with me, but maybe she was attempting to explore who she was.*

Tears formed in her eyes. "Maybe I've been holding Cassie back all these years. If so, that would just break my heart. Oh Cal, don't let me mess this up. I feel like I don't know anything anymore."

CHAPTER FIFTY-EIGHT

After a time, Paula got up, washed her face, and put on some makeup. Her hair was going all directions, but instead of putting it into a ponytail she brushed it out and dug through her bag until she found a headband. It was lime green, and didn't match her red blouse, but right then it suited her mood.

She forced a smile as she examined herself in the mirror. She grabbed several Shiner Bocks from the refrigerator and headed toward the office.

On her way over, Paula noticed several of the rooms had cars parked underneath the car ports. The place wasn't full, but it was a far cry from empty. Martha was watching over the desk when Paula entered. She nodded at the beers in Paula's hand and said, "I've always wondered what those taste like."

Paula leaned on the counter. "They taste just like heaven. Sweet, but not heavy or hoppy. I'll stick one in the fridge for you, and we have plenty more in the room."

"I might just try one," Martha said. "I seem to be branching out these days."

Paula grinned, "Oh?"

Martha peeked over her shoulder and lowered her voice. "I have a date with Zeke. He's coming back on the thirtieth to stay a few days. But I guess you already knew that, didn't you?"

"I would have told you earlier, but Zeke wasn't sure if he wanted it to be a surprise visit or not."

A rosy blush brightened Martha's cheeks. "I feel just like a schoolgirl. I have no idea of what to wear or say."

"Aww. Just be yourself. Besides, Zeke'll probably do most of the talking. He certainly doesn't seem to be shy."

Martha laughed, "You're certainly right about that."

The ladies turned their heads when Mark appeared in the corridor doorway. He dried his hands on a dishtowel and said, "Hi, Paula. I thought I heard your voice."

Heat rose to Paula's cheeks as she studied his face, looking for more resemblances to Cal. "We heard you were cooking. I have to be around for that." As he threw back his head and laughed, she saw more of Cal in him than ever.

Mark stepped closer to the desk. "And Martha, what is it I hear about you practicing medicine without a license? Should I be worried?"

Martha grabbed the dishtowel from his hand, and with a playful scowl, swatted him with it. "Oh, stop. You have no idea how much I wished you would have been here."

"Delivering babies is hardly my specialty, but I'm sure in a pinch, I could pull it off." He looked to Paula. "Mmm, Shiner Bocks. You want me to put those in the fridge for you?"

Paula felt herself blush. "No, I'll walk on back with you. I want to see if I left my book back there."

He stepped aside and gestured toward the corridor. "After you."

As Paula loaded the beer into the refrigerator, she giggled at the inordinate amount of grocery bags covering the table and counter. "Did you bring all of this food? There's enough here for all of Happy Vale."

He offered a sheepish grin. "I couldn't decide what I wanted to cook, and I just kept buying stuff."

She offered him a beer then popped the top off of another bottle and took a sip. "We've all been speculating about your surprise."

"I had a feeling that would be the case."

She raised an eyebrow. "I don't guess you'd give me a hint?"

Frowning, he fumbled in a drawer full of utensils. With a flourish he pulled out a garlic press and smiled. "Nope."

She folded her arms and poked out her lips in a pout.

Undeterred, he rinsed a basket of tomatoes and said, "Melinda is sure going to miss you two. You've been good for her."

"I hope that's true. It seems like we've been on a roller coaster ever since we got here. I was afraid you thought we were wearing her out."

Mark stopped dicing an onion and looked into Paula's eyes. "I, uh, hope you plan to visit often. I mean, for Melinda's sake, but, well, I'd like to see you again, too. I mean, well, after you've had some time to grieve. I just—never mind. Oh, hell. Forget all that. I just hope I get to become better acquainted with you. And with Cassie, too, of course."

Paula held her breath. *Is he's saying he's interested in me? I thought Martha said he had a lady friend.* She cleared her throat. "Of course. I mean I imagine I'll visit as often as possible. In the past few days, this place has grown on me so much, that I've got a feeling I'll be making the trip here regularly."

"I'm glad to hear it. Would you mind if I gave you my number? You could give me a call anytime. Just to talk."

Paula's heart did a little dance. "Of course. That would be nice."

He resumed dicing onions. "I'll be sure to give it to you after dinner."

She turned away so he wouldn't mistake her piqued interest for something more. "Ooooh, you've brought a bottle of champagne!"

"There should be two bottles. It's a very good surprise. Now, leave me alone so I can focus on cooking."

"I could help for the price of a hint."

"No, thanks. Go on. I've got this."

"Okay, but if you really need help cooking, let me know and I'll send Cassie in."

He waved a hand at her. "Shoo. I'll call you when dinner's ready."

No one was in the main living area, and both Melinda's and McKenzie's doors were closed. Paula stood at the back door looking out the window, wondering if Mark really was interested in getting to know her better. She couldn't wrap her head around that, not with Cal gone only a week. Paula went out on the back porch and sat in one of the rockers there and took a deep drink of her beer.

She was anxious for Cassie to return, but nervous at the same time. A great deal depended on how Cassie perceived Paula's greeting upon her arrival. The truth was, Paula thought, if she was honest with herself, she did feel differently about her friend. How could she not? But her feelings weren't negative, if anything they were a mix of hurt that Cassie hadn't felt like she could confide in her and relief that she finally had. Right at that moment Paula wanted nothing more than to hug Cassie and tell her that whatever adventure she had in mind for the future she should just do it, no matter where it took her. Not to worry about Paula, just worry about her own future. That Cal's death was proof enough that life was too short to put off finding someone to love and be loved by in return. She'd had that with Cal. How could she live with herself if she got in the way of Cassie having the same opportunity?

At that moment, as if on cue Cassie stepped outside Shiner Bock in hand. "Hey, girl."

Paula smiled, and she gestured to the chair beside her. "Hey. I was just thinking of you."

Cassie sat and took a swig of beer. "Oh? Something good, I hope."

"Quite good. I love you and I want you to love whoever you want to without worrying what others might think about you. You have my support, no matter who you are with. If you think you've outgrown Dempsey, then I want you to go where you can be yourself and be happy. Hell, I have a car and I know how to buy a plane ticket. Just because we live in different places doesn't mean we can't stay close."

"Part of me wants to go off and start a new life. Live in a city where my chances are greater for finding someone to love. But another part of me says that I can't go chasing love. I kind of did that when I went to U.T. If you haven't guessed by now, that's why I didn't go to Tech, even though I wanted nothing more than to room with my best friend. That felt like the only way I could distance myself from everyone's idea of who I was supposed to be."

Paula bit her lip. "Did you…were you able to find acceptance there?"

Cassie took a deep breath. "Yes. There were some girls, and even a boy or two. I dated, but there was no one I really clicked with. I began to wonder if there was something wrong with me. Seth called me at least once a week, but I never felt anything for him more than friendship. I went out with a girl named Holly for about a month, but she wasn't the one either. And when you found Cal, I felt more desolate than ever. I knew then that I didn't want anything less than what you two had together. At the time, that didn't seem even remotely possible. It still doesn't."

Paula took Cassie's hand and said, "No matter what you decide, where you go, what you do, who you love, I'll be in your corner. After all these years, you cannot unclaim me. You're my sister and I love you."

"I love you, too," Cassie said, squeezing Paula's hand. "And thank you."

They heard a curse through the kitchen window and Cassie laughed. "Maybe I need to go see how Dr. Hunky is doing."

The color drained from Paula's face. "Please do *not* let him hear you call him that!"

Cassie stuck out her tongue as she stood, then without another word, headed inside.

CHAPTER FIFTY-NINE

Paula counted the colors in the sky as the sun headed West. She held her breath when she heard Cassie and Mark laughing in the kitchen. *Crap! I hope to hell she didn't call him Dr. Hunky!* She craned her neck and listened, hoping to make out their words, but all she heard was the beating of her own heart.

Moments later, Melinda emerged from the campground, an easel and small canvas in hand and a black bag slung over her shoulder. Paula waved at her and Melinda approached the porch, set up her easel, and set the canvas on it. She shooed a fly as she sat. "Hey. Wouldn't you rather be inside with the air conditioning?"

Paula inspected the watercolor of the lake with two fishermen in a boat enjoying a hearty laugh. "Nah. I've been banished from the kitchen, and I came out here to clear my head."

Melinda edged to the front of her seat. "Oh? Would you rather I left?"

"What? No, no, of course not. Please stay. Wow, this painting is incredible! These are the two guys who checked in this morning, right? I watched them fish earlier."

"It is. I don't often paint people, but I loved their colorful shirts and hats, not to mention their obvious enjoyment. I was thinking that something like this might be just the thing to sell at the farmer's market."

"That's a terrific idea! But, if you don't mind, I'd like to buy this one. These two remind me of Cal and Delbert."

"Then it's yours. As soon as it's dry, I'll wrap it up for you."

"What? No, only if I can pay you for it."

"Paula, you've already paid for this painting a hundred times over. This one's yours."

"I... Thank you. Hey, speaking of people who remind me of Cal, have you ever noticed that Dr. Fields bears a strong resemblance to him?"

Melinda sat back in her chair and furrowed her brow as she gazed up at the clouds. "Hmm... You know, now that you mention it, I guess he does. I always thought he had a look of familiarity, but I could never put my finger on it. I think it's his eyes and that jawline. Come to think of it, that lopsided smile resembles Cal's, too. I'll be darned. You'd think an artist would've noticed the similarities way before now. Maybe that's why I don't paint people often." A clash of pans from the kitchen caused them to turn. Melinda offered a playful smirk. "Has Dr. Hunky started cooking yet?"

A scarlet blush rose up Paula's chest to her cheeks. "I really wish I'd never called him that. At least now we know why I find him attractive, right? And he started cooking about a half hour ago. I believe Cassie's in there helping."

Melinda stood. "I'm going in and clean up a bit before dinner. Is my mom still in the office?"

"She was earlier. I haven't seen McKenzie."

"Oh, McKenzie's out at Clyde's tree talking to you-know-who."

A broad grin stretched across Paula's face. "Jeffries, I presume."

"By the sound of her voice, I'm certain it's him. She's not the giggling sort, and I distinctly heard at least two giggles."

"Ah, love, sweet love."

Melinda held up her hand and gave an exaggerated cringe. "Don't say that. I'm not ready for her to fall in love."

"Neither were my parents when I met Cal, and I was just about McKenzie's age."

Melinda raised an eyebrow then chuckled. "Okay, now I'm really going to go clean up. Would you mind fetching Mac? I've been watching that bank of clouds over there. They're building quickly now, and I'd hate for her to get caught down by the lake when the lightning starts."

"I don't mind at all." Paula stood and followed a butterfly down the path to the lake where she found McKenzie lost in thought. "Earth to McKenzie."

McKenzie turned and a look of recognition washed over her face. She sighed. "Oh, hi, Paula. Were you ever in love?"

"I certainly was. I'll tell you about it one day. Your mom wanted me to fetch you. She's worried about those clouds."

McKenzie looked up, "Wow, I didn't even notice."

The two fishermen approached. "Looks like we need to get inside for a bit," the shorter man said.

The taller one said, "Yeah, it looks like we're gonna have a real gullywasher. Can you ladies suggest a good place for dinner?"

Without hesitation, McKenzie said, "Oaks on Main. It's right downtown in Happy Vale."

Paula stifled a grin. "I agree. You can't beat Delilah's cooking."

The men thanked them and they parted company at the office. Paula and McKenzie ducked under the porch as a flash of lightning hit nearby, followed by a boom of thunder and a deluge of rain.

McKenzie cringed. "Eww, that was close!"

Paula hugged herself as she struggled to see through the driving sheets of water. "Yes, *too* close. That storm is moving fast."

Melinda met them inside the door and said, "Thank goodness you two made it inside. I have a feeling that lightning hit somewhere on the property."

A loud crack of thunder and a flash of lightning arrived in the same instant, causing the lights to flicker then go dark. Each distinct tick of a nearby wall clock echoed through the room, melding with the cacophony of rain hitting the roof.

Cassie stepped out of the kitchen with a lit candle in each hand. "Wow, what a downpour! At this rate, we'll need a boat to get back over to our room tonight."

Melinda's eyes sparkled. "We'll find room for you two over here if it doesn't clear up by then. Do we need a backup plan for dinner?"

Cassie offered Melinda a candle. "Actually, we just finished. Dr. Hunky... I mean the visiting chef is about ready to put food on the table."

Paula felt herself blush. She folded her arms and narrowed her eyes. "Shh!"

Cassie chuckled. "Sorry, I couldn't resist. Don't worry, he can't hear me. He's busy dishing up food by the light of his cellphone. Melinda these were the only candles I could find."

Melinda said, "You guys go ahead into the dining room. Mac, you grab some candles from your room. I'll go get mom."

CHAPTER SIXTY

Paula and Cassie headed to the dining room and began dividing a stack of plates and silverware and setting each place. Paula lowered her voice. "I don't guess you got a hint as to Mark's surprise?"

Cassie shook her head. "Not even a teeny one. That man is totally immune to my charms."

Martha's voice wafted in from the front. "Ellie just showed up to watch the office. Was that your doing?"

Melinda sounded perplexed. "No. I wonder if McKenzie called her."

Paula heard McKenzie close the door to her room. "Called who?" McKenzie asked.

Martha's voice grew closer as she said, "Ellie. She said she got a call to come in and watch the desk for the evening."

"Why would I call her?" McKenzie asked, setting an armload of candles on the table.

Mark carried in a large covered pot and set it in the center of the table. "I called her. I told her I'd pay her to answer the phones and watch the office so we could have an uninterrupted dinner."

As Martha and Melinda lit candles, Cassie said, "Let me go grab the potatoes and salad."

"How can I help?" Paula asked.

Mark arranged the candles around the room. "Would you get the bread? It's warming on top of the range. Oh, get the butter, too, please."

Paula gave a jaunty salute and headed to the kitchen. Her heart soared as she counted her blessings. She was so pleased to be part of this evening with friends and an impending surprise. When she returned with a warm loaf of garlic bread and the butter dish, she took the empty seat next to Mark and across from Cassie.

Mark cleared his throat and raised his glass. "I took the liberty of pouring everyone a glass of champagne. Would you all please join me in a toast?"

The women raised their glasses and Paula shivered in anticipation. She smiled at Cassie who grinned back.

Mark took a deep breath. "I was going to make you all wait until after dinner for the surprise, but I'm not sure I have that kind of patience, so here goes. To Melinda Arnett. My favorite patient, even though I'm not supposed to have favorites." He waited for the women's laughter to die down and his eyes filled with tears. "Again, to Melinda," he paused and composed himself. "Whose cancer is in remission."

Melinda's eyes grew wide. "What?"

Tears streamed down Martha's face. "Oh, Melinda!"

McKenzie jumped up and hugged her mother. "Mom!"

Paula's heart swelled as she watched the obvious joy and relief evident in the faces of the 3M's. Tears stung her own eyes. "To Melinda!" she said, sniffling. Cassie clinked her glass, then Mark, then they all took turns clinking and toasting Melinda.

Melinda beamed as she stood and raised her glass. "I never doubted you'd get me through this, Mark. Not once. Here's a toast to you, dear Dr. Fields, for never making me feel like a patient, but always like a cherished friend. God sent me here at just the right time so I could have you as my doctor."

"To Mark!" Cassie said, followed by a chorus of the other women raising their glasses again and toasting Mark.

A flickering candle illuminated Mark's blush. He gave a lopsided grin and said, "Uh, let's eat before all this food gets cold." He removed the lid from the pot and waved his hand over it. "I give you my famous chicken cacciatore. Pass your plates and I'll serve everyone."

Paula said little as she took in the excitement and let the conversation flow around her. The candlelight granted a cozy intimacy and at that moment, she never wanted to leave the Happy Valley Motor Inn and Resort or the family seated around the table.

When everyone oohed and ahhed over Mark's dinner he shrugged and said, "I'd like to take all the credit, but honestly, without Cassie's assistance, we'd be eating cold cuts. I'd never have gotten this ready before we lost power without her."

"You can be my sous chef any time," Cassie said.

Mark raised an eyebrow. "Wait, you were *my* sous chef."

Cassie grinned and wiggled her eyebrows. "Only this once."

McKenzie raised her glass. "To Cassie."

"To Cassie," the others echoed.

Melinda, still smiling, raised her glass again. "To my mother and my daughter, who sacrificed so much while I was going through chemo and radiation. You two... You two cared for me without making me feel like a burden. I never had to worry about a thing getting done around here, not once. To McKenzie, my heart, and to Mama, my soul."

As Melinda sipped her champagne, there wasn't a dry eye in the room. Mark sniffed as he stood and said, "Excuse me. I've got another bottle of champagne in the kitchen."

When Mark returned and refilled everyone's glasses, Melinda said, "I have one more toast to make. To Cal Arnett. He'll never know now how much his generosity unburdened my mind and allowed me to concentrate on getting well. But any toast to Cal is a toast to his wife, his love, Paula. Paula, you've brought hope to Happy Valley Motor Inn and Resort. Goldilocks, Cal was right about you. You do make everything just right."

Paula fanned her tear-filled eyes and choked back the lump in her throat. "Thank you. I wish more than anything he was here to share this meal and to hear the good news. But you know what he'd say?"

"I do," Cassie said. "Eat up!"

Paula nodded. "Exactly."

As she ate, Paula's heart was bursting with happiness. Between the steady tattoo of rain beating on the roof and forks clinking, she enjoyed the break in conversation as she recalled her initial rage at learning Cal had likely deceived her by purchasing a small-town resort from another Mrs. Arnett. She laughed at herself. *That seems like such a long time ago, now. Cal, I'm sorry I ever doubted you. Your passing left me a whole new family to fill the void.* She shook herself from her reverie when she realized Melinda was speaking...

Melinda cut her eyes to Mark. "I'll never forget the first time I met you. I said to myself *surely, he's not old enough to be a doctor.* To be honest, I thought you were an intern."

Mark tipped his head. "Well, thank you, ma'am. I am known for my boyish good looks."

Cassie guffawed and Paula glared at her. *Don't you dare tell him about this Dr. Hunky business!*

Over a dessert of key lime cheesecake, Mark said, "Well, I'm thrilled that Melinda's officially in remission, but I'm afraid I'm going to have to come up with some fake malady for her to be treated for now. I'm going to miss my stays here."

Melinda waved her hand. "Mark Fields! You know you always have a room here free of charge. There's no way I could ever repay you for what you've done for me." She grimaced then cut her eyes to Paula. "Of course, I'm not the owner anymore."

A somber look washed over Paula's face as she turned to Mark. "Oh, I'm afraid I can't be as generous as Melinda. You see, I'm a hardcore businesswoman. Starting now, we're going to have to charge you triple what you currently pay for a room."

McKenzie furrowed her brow and gasped. "But you can't—"

Martha's eyes twinkled as she reached across the table and patted McKenzie's hand. "Three times nothing is what, Mac?"

A look of understanding washed over McKenzie's face. "Oh. Still nothing. Dang, Paula, you really had me going for a minute."

Paula winked at McKenzie then found herself winking at everyone. The champagne had gone straight to her head. When she winked at Mark, he winked back and smiled that lopsided smile that reminded her of Cal. Her heart stuttered. It was almost like having Cal right there beside her. Looking across the table at Cassie, Paula could tell that her friend knew exactly what was going through her mind.

As everyone scraped the last crumbs of cheesecake from their plates, the lights popped on. Martha wiped her mouth then stood. "Mark, dinner was delicious, and the reason for it was even better. If you folks'll excuse me, I'd better go warm up a plate for Ellie." She filled a plate then headed to the kitchen.

CHAPTER SIXTY-ONE

As Paula stood, the effects of the champagne put a wobble in her stance. "I'll go clean the kitchen. If there's anything I know about my friend Cassie, it's that she's made a mess in there."

With feigned surprise, Cassie clutched her chest. "Well, I never. Moi? Make a mess?"

Paula grinned. "Yes, you, but the results are always worth it."

Cassie tipped her head. "Damned straight!"

McKenzie leaned forward in her seat. "You want me to help, Paula?"

Mark stood and collected a few dessert plates. "No, kiddo, you stay here and let me help her. I supervised the clean up as we worked. It's not nearly as messy as Paula imagines."

As Paula and Mark entered the kitchen, she looked around. "Hmm, you were right. This isn't nearly as messy as I feared. Maybe Cassie needs to hire you full time."

Mark scraped the plates into the sink. "That woman is something else. She turns all that extra energy into magic in the kitchen, but I'm not sure I'd want to be under her watchful eye on a regular basis. She's kind of intense."

Paula laughed. "Kind of?" She told him about how even in kindergarten Cassie took charge and announced that they were going to be best friends. "I was afraid to say no, so here we are."

He flipped on the garbage disposal. "And you wouldn't have it any other way."

"Not even for a billion dollars."

They worked in harmony to the gentle patter of the rain. When they finished, he started the dishwasher and said, "Thanks for the help."

Paula dried her hands on a dishtowel. "Thank *you* for the dinner. Did Cassie already invite you to breakfast in the morning? She's making one of her newest specialties."

"Must've slipped her mind."

"Then consider this your invitation. I know she planned on feeding you. We'd already discussed the exclusive guest list."

Mark leaned against the counter. "Exclusive? Wow. I feel like a V.I.P."

"Truthfully, she said she'd feed anyone in the vicinity, so...."

He stuck out his bottom lip in an exaggerated pout. "Fine. Keep me from feeling special. Here I thought I was somebody."

"Oh, you're *definitely* somebody." As Paula heard her own words escape her lips she blushed. "Uh, I mean, we're *all* somebody, after all."

He folded his arms and grinned.

Paula looked down and wished her heart would stop racing. "Uh, I'd better go see if Cassie's still here. She might've returned to our room without me."

Mark followed her out to the living area and blew out a lone candle. "Hmm, I guess we're the last two standing."

"Somehow, I don't think so. Maybe they're in the office."

They headed to the office and found the 3M's huddled around a tearful Ellie. Mark stepped toward Ellie, his concern evident on his face. "Is everything all right?"

Ellie wrapped her arms around him and sobbed. "Thank you, Dr. Fields. Thank you for getting Miss Melinda well."

Mark patted Ellie's back and let her cry. "Hey, she's a tough cookie. It'd take more than a little cancer to keep Melinda down."

"I know that now. I was just worried, 'cause you know these Yankee women aren't as sturdy as us Texas girls are. She must be at least part Texan."

Paula disguised her unexpected laugh with a cough. She eyed Melinda and Martha who both covered their mouths and attempted to conceal their smiles.

Ellie sniffled and let go of Mark. "I didn't mean to say that out loud."

Everyone laughed and, after Ellie said her goodnights, Mark escorted her out. Paula hugged Melinda. "I'm so happy for you. Hey, don't forget about breakfast tomorrow."

McKenzie hugged Martha. "Cassie already told us. I'll even get up early for that. Maybe I should go to bed now so I'll be up in time. Man, what a day!" She hugged Melinda. "Goodnight, Mom. Gram. G'night, Paula." She smiled as she headed toward her room.

Paula leaned on the front desk. "Wow, I can't imagine that girl's got room in her stomach to even think about breakfast after such a meal. I just wanted to remind you because Cassie'll be using your kitchen, after all."

Martha touched Paula's arm. "Somehow, it feels like she belongs there."

Paula laughed. "Cassie's at home in any kitchen. She's cooked more meals in mine than I have over the years, and that's no exaggeration. Cal always said when he married me, he got her as a bonus."

"So, they were close?" Melinda asked.

Paula crossed her fingers. "Like this. She told me that in some ways, Cal knew her better than I did...." Her voice trailed off with the sudden realization that somehow Cal had known Cassie's secret. Whether she'd told him, or he'd guessed, Paula didn't know. And he had still loved her. Somehow that made his passing even more devastating. Paula was glad now that she knew and could be Cassie's shield and confidant.

Melinda set her hand on Paula's. "Paula? You all right?"

Paula choked back a lump in her throat. "Yes. I was just thinking about what we've lost now that Cal's gone. So many shared experiences."

Martha gave a knowing nod. "But the memories are there. I tell you what, next time you come, bring some of Cal's favorite clothes. We'll make you a memory quilt."

Tears burned behind Paula's eyes as she smiled. "I'd like that a lot," she whispered.

"Of course, it'll take more than one visit, that is unless you decide you want to stay here full-time," Martha said with a wink.

"Actually, Mark's news helped me come to a decision, but I'll be here plenty, regardless. You'll be begging me to go home."

Melinda said, "As far as I'm concerned, you are home."

Martha nodded. "I'll second that."

Paula clasped Melinda's hands, then Martha's. "Thank you. Both of you. Hey, are we still okay to look over the books in the morning?"

Mark came back in as Martha said, "Let's plan on it after breakfast."

Paula stifled a yawn. "Oh, excuse me. That sounds good. I'd better get to bed."

Mark gestured toward the door. "You want me to walk you to your room?"

Paula waved her hand. "That's not necessary. It's stopped raining, right?"

"Just a little sprinkle now," he said. "I'll follow you out anyway. It's awfully dark out there."

Melinda and Martha sent them off for the night with reminders not to be late for breakfast.

Clouds still dominated the night sky, blocking out the moon and stars. Paula gazed up and sighed when she realized there'd be no sighting of the Cal star.

"You okay?" Mark asked.

"Just a bit melancholy."

"Melancholy, eh? Surely there's a cure for that nowadays."

Paula laughed and pointed at the heavens. "I can't see my star tonight."

"You have a star?"

"Sort of." Paula didn't know why, but she was hesitant to tell Mark that it was her Cal star.

He looked up. "Just because it's not visible to us right now doesn't mean it isn't there. It'll be there whether you see it or not. In fact, someone somewhere is likely looking up at your star right now."

Paula crossed her arms and hugged herself as she searched the sky. "I hope so. I hope it's as comforting to that person as it is to me."

Mark took a deep breath. "I—uh, I'll see you in the morning. G'night, Paula."

She felt his eyes on her until she reached her door. It wasn't until she turned and waved that he turned in the opposite direction and headed toward his own room.

CHAPTER SIXTY-TWO

As Paula stepped in her room, the lights and television were on, and she heard Cassie singing in the shower. Paula took off her makeup, brushed her teeth, and changed into her pajamas.

She stuffed her dirty clothes in a bag and under her breath said, "Tomorrow I have to pack." The thought made her so sad she thought she might cry again. *No, stop. I've got a lot to be thankful for. I'm going home with my best friend. Poor, neglected Mable will be glad to see me. Hey! Maybe I'll get a pet!* Her lips curved into a satisfied smile as she got under her covers and propped herself against the headboard. "Yes, I'll definitely adopt a pet!" She recalled a conversation she'd had with Cal when she'd said she wanted a dog and he'd insisted that a pet would just be a hindrance to their frequent travels. *Cal, you were the one who did most of the traveling. I would've welcomed the presence of a furry companion in your absence.*

Cassie stepped out of the bathroom and dried her hair with a towel. "Well, you look lost in thought. What's going on?"

Paula hugged her knees. "I was just thinking that as soon as we get back to Dempsey, I'm going to adopt a pet."

"Good for you. Dog? Cat?"

"I'm not sure yet. I'll have to see what my options are."

Cassie ran a comb through her hair. "I never understood Cal's aversion to having a pet. Must've been some holdover from childhood."

"Maybe. But I'm beginning to realize that for fifteen years I did almost everything Cal decided I should do. Like eating only in the kitchen or dining room. Going to bed when he decided it was time to go to bed. He didn't ask much of me, so I was glad to give in on stuff like that. I miss him something awful, but I'm not going to miss some of the things he insisted on."

Cassie pumped her fist. "Girl Power!"

Paula offered a subdued echo. "Girl Power."

Cassie brushed her teeth, then turned out the lights and climbed into bed. She clicked off the television and said, "Do you feel like this has been both the longest week and the shortest week in the history of weeks?"

Paula let out a deep sigh. "Actually, the last two weeks have felt that way. Some moments it feels like Cal's been gone for years. Other times, it feels like I lost him only minutes ago. I suspect when we get back home, it'll all feel immediate again."

After moments of silence, Cassie said, "I called Court to see if he'd be home on Friday, but he didn't answer. I left a message, but I have a feeling he's in the air somewhere."

"I'd like to see him. How long's it been since he was in Dempsey? Three years."

"No, only one, but you and Cal were on vacation the last time he visited. Oh, I forgot to tell you, while I was out by Clyde's tree to call Court, I also spoke to Mom and Dad. I told them all about Happy Valley and your new status as owner, and what an excellent spot it is for RV's. They're going to do some word of mouth advertising, and they're calling tomorrow to make reservations for September."

Paula's heart leapt. "Yay. Maybe we should plan to be here when they come."

"Yes!"

A few moments of silence passed, and Paula asked, "Do your parents know?"

"About?"

"You."

"Oh, that. I think Mom suspects, but it would never cross Daddy's mind. Court knows, though. He's even tried setting me up on dates."

Paula took a deep breath. "Cal knew, didn't he?"

Cassie took a moment to answer. "Yes. I didn't tell him, but one night at the Unruly Longhorn, you were out dancing with someone. Melvin, maybe. Cal and I sat talking while we drank our beers. After a few men asked me to dance and I turned them down, Cal just looked at me and asked if I was gay. Just like that. He wasn't being flippant or using it as a slur, he was interested in knowing the truth. I told him I thought I was probably was, but that as long as I lived in Dempsey I'd likely never know. He just smiled a beautifully sad lopsided smile, we clinked our beers, and he told me that he loved me like a sister. He said if I ever needed him, he'd be there to help."

Paula's chest heaved as her tears threatened to fall. "That man. No wonder I loved him."

Cassie sniffled. "But now he won't be here."

Paula reached a hand across the divide and took Cassie's hand in hers. "But I'm here in his place. I want to make you the same promise. And he *is* still here, even if we can't see him."

Cassie squeezed Paula's hand before letting it go. "Sweet dreams, Goldilocks. I have to get up early to cook."

"Wake me when you get up and I'll help you."

Paula thought she heard Cassie snort in reply, but maybe it was the beginning of a snore. Either way, she soon succumbed to sleep as the gentle rhythm of rain pattered against the roof.

CHAPTER SIXTY-THREE

The next morning, Paula woke, showered, dressed, and applied some makeup, then shook Cassie's shoulder. "C'mon, chef, let's get a move on."

Cassie opened one eye, glanced at the clock on the bedside stand, and grumbled as she rose. Ten minutes later, she was ready to meet the kitchen head on.

"What can I do to help?" Paula asked as they stepped out of their room into the muggy air.

Cassie maintained her gaze on the office door. "Stay out of the kitchen."

Paula chuckled. "Aye, aye. Gladly. Hey, don't forget I'll be going over the books with Martha after breakfast. But maybe for lunch or dinner, you and I could eat at Delilah's. Kind of let her place be our bookends to the week."

"Yeah, I'd like that."

As they stepped into the office, Martha looked up from behind the registration counter, an open accounts binder in front of her. "Oh, good morning."

Cassie forged onward toward the kitchen. "Morning. I'll bring you both some coffee in a few minutes."

Paula leaned across the counter. "Good morning. Is that the accounting?"

Martha started to roll her eyes, then offered a forced smile. "That it is. I'm just looking them over again before we sit down to talk later."

"Don't you enjoy keeping the books?"

Martha sighed. "The truth? I've never enjoyed bookkeeping. When my husband and I had the grocery store, he decided that I was going to keep the books. So, I did. I took a few courses at the community college and learned the basics. Plus, I had a good friend who kept books for a local hardware store who let me call whenever I had a question, but I'd much rather be doing something creative."

"So, if you don't like it, why do you do it?"

"I guess when Melinda inherited this place, it was just assumed that I'd pick up the accounting role."

Paula bit her lip. "Then, would you be insulted or relieved if I hired an outside firm to handle the books in the future?"

Martha's eyes widened, and her smile took over her entire face. "I would hug you, and I don't hug just anyone."

Paula laughed. "I can always use a hug."

Martha grabbed a tissue and dabbed her eyes. "I'm tired, Paula. I love being here with my girls, but I'm ready to retire and relax. Maybe travel some more like Jerry and I did before Marie died. And now, knowing that Melinda is well and McKenzie can afford to start on her own adventures, I feel like I can finally do some living of my own."

"Does Melinda know how you feel?"

"I've hinted a few times but never said anything outright."

"Maybe later when we discuss the books, it'd be a good time for you to bring it up."

Martha smiled. "It might be at that."

Paula yawned. "Excuse me. I don't think I can wait on Cassie for that coffee. Do you want me to grab you a cup?"

"No, thanks. I'll be there in a few minutes. I want to finish reviewing this."

"Okay." Paula headed to the kitchen and filled a cup. "What happened? You forget about us?"

Cassie cracked an egg on the side of a bowl and tossed the shell on the garbage. "What? Oh, I'm sorry. I had a sort of a flash of an idea for a new dinner side dish and I wanted to write it down before I lost it. I guess I got in my cooking zone after that."

"No problem. You want any help?"

Cassie began beating her egg mixture. "Nope. Just go somewhere and relax, and I'll call you when it's ready."

Paula saluted. "Yes, ma'am." She giggled as she headed toward the living room where she found Melinda and Mark. "Good morning. Mind if I join you?"

Melinda patted a spot on the couch beside her. "Of course not. I was just telling Mark about Mac's inheritance."

"And your plot to find out what this Townes guy was up to. I'm sorry I missed the fun," Mark said.

Paula laughed. "Don't forget the twins' births. Things were hopping while you were away doing important doctor stuff."

Cassie poked her head out of the kitchen, "Hey, y'all, let's eat in here. The first slices of French toast are about to come off the grill and the bacon is ready. Come and get it."

Paula said, "You guys go ahead. I'll go tell Martha and McKenzie it's ready." She knocked on McKenzie's bedroom door, but there was no answer. Martha said she'd be along soon, so Paula headed to the kitchen where Melinda and Mark were each taking their first bite.

Melinda's eyes rolled back in her head. "Oh, my goodness! Where, oh where have you been all my life?"

Cassie laughed as she handed a plate to Paula. "Are you talking to me or to the food?"

"Both," Melinda said, plunging her fork into another bite.

Paula sat by Mark and took a bite. "Mmmm! This is even better than I remembered."

Melinda stifled a giggle as she caught Paula's attention. She gestured with her head at Mark who was shoveling in his food so fast, his arm was practically a blur. Both women started laughing and he looked up, a mouthful of food in his cheek and another on his fork, poised to plunge into a pool of syrup. "What? Can't a man enjoy his breakfast?"

Paula's eyes twinkled. "Obviously a man can. Breathe, doctor! Breathe!"

The office bell rang and moments later, Martha and Eric Townes came into the kitchen. Martha stepped aside. "Eric was about to check out. I thought maybe you'd like to say goodbye."

Cassie stood. "Hi, Eric. Have a seat and I'll fix you a plate."

Before Eric answered, Melinda said, "Don't waste your time telling her no. Cassie feeds everyone."

He took the seat across from Paula and introduced himself to Mark before saying, "Well, okay. But I don't have long. My flight out of Shreveport leaves at 12:30."

Martha sat and Cassie offered her and Eric a plate. Martha nodded. "Thanks, dear. Don't worry, Mr. Townes, you'll make it with time to spare."

When McKenzie came in Cassie said, "Oh, let me fix you a plate."

McKenzie sat beside Martha. "Thanks. I thought I heard you, Mr. Townes. I've been thinking. I'd like to talk to my Uncle Kevin."

Eric fished a card out of his wallet and offered it to McKenzie. "He'll be happy to hear that. I'll let him know he can expect your call." He took a bite. "Wow! This is amazing."

Cassie set a plate in front of McKenzie then returned to her seat. "Thanks. It's my own invention."

Melinda eyed McKenzie. "Are you sure you're ready to call your uncle? You know that's a genie you can't put back in the bottle."

"I know, Mom. I'm sure. He sounds like a nice man, and I've always wanted uncles and aunts and cousins. I used to pretend I had them like the other kids my age."

Eric took another bite and shook his head. "You sure you made this, Cassie? I might just have to take you home with me."

Cassie laughed. "Oh, stop."

"You're fishing today, right Mark?" Martha asked.

Mark nodded as he wiped his mouth with his napkin. "I am. Anyone want to join me?" He looked around the table, but no one volunteered. He held up his hands. "Okay, I can take the hint. I'll go be the hunter and bring home something for the little ladies to cook later."

Cassie raised an eyebrow and shot him a dirty look. "Beg your pardon?"

Mark laughed and raised his hands in surrender. "Kidding. I'm just kidding. I'll go fish. Alone. By myself." He stood and rinsed his dirty dishes. "Cassie, thanks for a delicious breakfast. Mr. Townes, safe travels. Ladies, I'll see you later." He whistled as he headed out.

A minute later, Eric patted his belly and stood. "I don't know when I've had such a phenomenal meal. Cassie, if you ever change your mind and get up to Chicago, I'll be happy to have you cook for me again."

She stood and swatted him with a dishtowel. "Very funny. Have a good trip. Okay, everybody out. I need to get this kitchen cleaned."

As everyone else headed toward the office, Eric shook the ladies' hands. "Thanks again. I hope I see all of you again someday. Maybe I'll come down and stay on my own dime."

"You'd be welcome any time," Melinda said. "Come in the fall when it's not so blooming hot out."

"I'll remember that."

As McKenzie perched behind the office desk, Martha gathered the accounting ledger. "Paula, Melinda, let's go tackle these books."

CHAPTER SIXTY-FOUR

Until Paula sat down with the resort's books, she'd dreaded the mere thought of it. But Martha laid everything out in a way that Paula could understand at a glance how desperate times had been before Melinda felt she had no other option than to contact Cal. The infusion of cash he'd provided put the resort in the black, but without an increase in revenues, they wouldn't be able to stay there forever.

Paula pulled her list out of her pocket. "Thank you for making this so easy for me to wrap my head around. I had some ideas the other day. Some of them are just things I need to do to wrap up Cal's interests, but I jotted down some things we might do to help increase business here." She unfolded the paper and smoothed it with her hands. "Here, what do you think?"

1. Join the Chamber of Commerce [get the lady's name from Delilah]
2. Sit down with Melinda and Martha & go over the financial reports
3. Decide what they want the website to look like and do
4. CalNet!!!??? *Important! Look at this soon!*
5. Plan a fishing event for locals -- maybe a kids' fishing derby?
6. Join the Rotary or Lions Club
7. Decide... ☹

8. Let Ellie do the laundry or risk being shot!
9. Fresh baked cookies for guests?
10. Check how to sell beer and bait
11. Cellphone booster?

Martha ran her finger down the page as she read it aloud. After reading number eight, she giggled. "What's this? Is Ellie packing heat now?" The women laughed and Martha said, "Oh! Don't forget to add Alex Graham's name to this list. Remember, he said he could offer some help."

Melinda raised her eyebrow. "Yes! And also the farmer's market."

Paula added the items:

12. Alex Graham, GMS
13. Farmer's market presence

Paula clicked off her pen and said, "None of these alone will make a huge difference, but if we're persistent and consistent, I think Happy Valley has a real chance."

Melinda rested her hand on Paula's arm. "I already feel much better about our future here. Now, with my clean bill of health and McKenzie's future being more secure...and with *you* here with us, I just *know* we can make it."

Cassie stepped out of the kitchen. "I'm done cleaning. Let me know when you're ready to head into town."

Paula stood and stretched her arms over her head. "I think we're done here. Right?"

Martha winked at Paula. "Yes, and I think now's as good as time as any for me to have that little talk with Melinda."

Paula offered an encouraging smile. "Of course. Can we get you two anything while we're out?"

Melinda looked at Martha then shrugged. "No, thanks. You two have fun."

On their way out, they asked McKenzie if she needed anything. "Um, maybe a new sudoku book," she said, holding up an almost completed puzzle book.

A while later, after they'd parked in front of the gazebo on Main Street, they stopped to look at a commemorative plaque displayed in a bed of roses. "In Memory of Those Who Gave All" was engraved in large letters on the top with a list underneath of Big Lake County's service men and women who'd died serving their country. Cassie took a deep breath. Look, this goes all the way back to World War I."

The mood was somber as they silently read through the names until Paula said, "Look! There's Stanley Jeffries Oaks in the list of the Korean conflict casualties."

Cassie raised her eyebrows. "Wow. I guess we know now where Jeffries got his name."

In the bookstore, after finding a sudoku book for McKenzie, they chatted with the owner and mentioned the resort. The owner clasped her hands and said, "Oh, yes, a friend of mine, Delilah Oaks, was telling me about those ladies out there just yesterday. She says they're just as sweet as can be."

When they visited the gift shop to purchase some trinkets for their Dempsey friends as well as for Martha and Melinda, the store owner said, "My friend who owns Oaks on Main told me about those sweet ladies out at the motor inn. I was actually planning on taking them a goodie basket this week. I know it's too late for a welcome basket, but I can still show them some support."

Through with their shopping, Paula and Cassie returned to the car and took a short driving tour of Happy Vale then drove through Hemphill and past Mighty Fin's, before turning around and heading back to Delilah's. After they placed their order, Delilah delivered their soup and sandwich specials and sat with them. "Hi. It's good to see you both again. So, you're really going home tomorrow?"

Paula sighed. "I have to. Until last night, I really wasn't certain I would, but I think Melinda has everything well in hand now. They don't really need me here."

Delilah took a drink of tea. "You'll be back soon, though, right?"

"Oh, without a doubt. My gut is telling me to keep from doing anything drastic for at least a while. Well, my gut and a couple of friends who've been where I am and regretted their hasty decisions."

Delilah nodded. "How 'bout you, Cassie?"

Cassie sipped a spoonful of soup. "I'll go where Paula goes. For a while, anyway."

One of the kitchen staff called Delilah and she stood. "Oh, I'd better go. You ladies stop by next time you're here."

After their meal, they drove to a gas station where Paula filled the car up with gas while Cassie scored her beverage of choice, before heading back to the motel. Paula honked the horn when they saw Mark leave the office, and he did an about-face, meeting them as they got out of the car.

His smile widened. "I was afraid I was going to miss telling you two goodbye."

Cassie sipped her Dr. Pepper. "You're not leaving so soon?"

He sighed. "Yes, my office called and one of my patients is having some issues. I planned on having dinner with you all again tonight, but I'm going to have to hit the road."

Cassie set her drink on the hood of the car and hugged him. "Aww, we hate to see you go. I'm sorry I tried to hit you with a rock."

His eyes crinkled at the corners as he laughed. "I'm glad you missed."

Paula extended her hand to shake his, but as he grabbed her hand, he pulled her close and hugged her. He patted her back and said, "I hope you come back soon."

Paula bit her lip as she stepped out of his embrace. "We will." Her heart raced, and she maintained her cautious smile. *Stupid heart.*

He stepped backward. "Well, you two have a safe drive home." He nodded at Paula. "Call me." He waved then spun on his heel and left without waiting for a reply.

Cassie sipped her drink. "Looks like someone's interested in you."

"Oh, he's just concerned about me; that's all."

"I understand that you're not ready yet, but someday you will be. Cal wouldn't want you to live a nun's life."

"But what if that's what I want?"

Cassie hugged Paula to her side. "If that's what you really want, I'll join the convent with you. I wonder if they're taking Protestants these days?"

Paula laughed. "You'd probably charm them into letting you join, regardless, and then you'd convince them to let me be your mascot or something."

Cassie nodded with an air of confidence. "Yep. That could work."

CHAPTER SIXTY-FIVE

A few hours later, Paula was packing when Cassie entered their room and said, "Hey, I was out practicing my juggling and I found where the lightning struck last night."

Paula grimaced. "Where? Is it bad?"

"You'll have to see for yourself. Come on…" As they headed toward a picnic table, she said, "There it is. Do you see it?"

Paula stood still and squinted as she looked all around. Her eyes opened wide as she fixed her gaze on the Clyde tree. "Oh. He's got two scorched circle eyes and a slashed mouth. Dang. That's either cool or creepy. I'll bet Ellie will have some story to tell, won't she?"

As they laughed about the tree and how it made them feel as if someone was watching them, Martha joined them. Her eyes twinkled as she waved a small sheet of scrap paper. "Hello, ladies. Cassie, I booked a reservation for a lovely sounding couple. Let's see, Ron and Dolores Campbell for the first week in September. Ring a bell?"

Cassie smiled. "Aww, I spoke to my folks yesterday and they said they'd be calling. You might as well put me down for a room the same week."

Paula smiled. "Me, too."

Martha clasped her hands to her chest. "Wonderful! That gives me something exciting to look forward to. By the way, I spoke with Melinda about turning the bookkeeping over to a professional. She gave the idea two thumbs up. I feel such a sense of freedom now. Maybe with my free time I'll take a little trip to Dempsey to visit you girls. I really hate to see you two go."

Cassie hugged Martha. "You're welcome there any time."

Paula squeezed Martha's hand. "Ditto. You're welcome to stay at my house. I have plenty of room, and once I write my thank you notes and get Cal's company sorted out, I'll probably have plenty of free time."

"Well, thank you. I might do just that. Listen, if you don't have other plans, Melinda and I thought it'd be fun to have a cookout out here tonight."

Cassie shoved her hands in her pockets. "I'm in. Do we need anything from the store?"

"Melinda is at the store right now. Hot dogs and s'mores sound all right?

Paula raised her eyebrows. "Sounds perfect. We'll be over as soon as we finish packing."

They took a few steps, then Cassie stopped and turned around. "Oh, we have some extra beer and wine. We'll bring it with us."

"Sounds great," Martha said, waving.

Back in their room, as Paula and Cassie packed, a knock at the door disturbed them. Cassie opened the door and McKenzie stepped inside.

She set two newspaper-wrapped boxes on the desk and said, "Dr. Fields asked me to give these to you. I've got to go help get stuff ready for the cookout. I'll see you soon." She hurried off without waiting for a reply.

Cassie tossed Paula's gift to her and examined her own. "I wonder what this could be."

"Open it."

"You first."

Paula laughed as she peeled off the paper and revealed a paperback. "Look. It's 'Angling for Amateurs.'" She flipped open the cover. "Oh, and it's inscribed... *'To Paula from Mark, may all your future fishing adventures be as exciting as your first.'*"

Cassie snorted. "Now that's hilarious."

Paula thumbed through the book's pages and found Mark's business card with his phone number written on the back. She fought the urge to grin as she stuffed it back in the book's binding. *This'll make a good bookmark until I'm ready to give him a call.* She stuffed the book in her suitcase before Cassie could see the card. "Your turn."

Cassie hefted her box. "Hmm, mine's kind of heavy." She tore off the wrapping, opened the box, and guffawed. "Ha! Look, it's my very own rock!" She took the rock out and showed Paula the funny face painted on the gray stone. "Oh, there's a card. *'From Mark to Cassie, I'm glad your aim was off. Please don't practice.'*"

Paula giggled. "Now these are souvenirs to savor."

Cassie tossed the rock into her suitcase. "This'll make a nice paperweight. He must've borrowed some paint from Melinda. I'm going to name it Dr. Hunky."

Paula rolled her eyes. "Dr. Chunky would suit it better. Are you ready to head down to the cookout?"

"Definitely." Cassie grabbed the beer cooler and Paula collected the gifts she'd bought in town for the 3M's. They took in all of Mother Nature's sights and sounds on their way down the path.

Paula's eyes danced back and forth between the trees surrounding the grill as she and Cassie took a seat. "What are these? Fairy lights? Y'all really went all out for this shindig."

Melinda stoked the charcoal. "McKenzie and I did that earlier. We just couldn't let you two leave without a special send off. I know there's nothing better than a hot dog roasted over a campfire, but with the storm last night, there wasn't any dry wood. I hope this is okay."

"It's perfect," Paula said, passing out beer. "Where are the others?"

"Mama should be here any minute, but McKenzie had a better offer at the last minute. She might drop by for s'mores later, but I wouldn't count on it."

Martha soon joined them and helped herself to a Shiner Bock. After she took her first sip, Paula raised her bottle and said, "I love this place. I love you ladies. And I even love Clyde here, even if he is a bit creepy with those new eyes of his. To Happy Valley Motor Inn and Resort. The best people and the best trees."

Cassie raised her bottle. "Hear, hear!"

The catchlight of the fairy lights twinkled in Melinda's eyes. She lifted her bottle and said, "Thank you, both. You've certainly made an impact on us and on this resort. I feel like I've found two sisters."

Martha raised her drink. "And I have two new daughters, one of whom can cook."

Melinda shot her mother a playful scowl. "Mama, I cook!"

"Yes, and I love you in spite of that."

Paula stood and moved close to the grill. "That's okay, I'm not much of a cook either. However, I do know how to roast a hot dog. Who's hungry?"

After Martha finished her second hot dog, she brushed the crumbs from her lap. "Oh, I have to stop. I haven't even had a s'more yet. But I will have one more of these Shiner Bocks. So good."

Paula chuckled. "I told you they were the best. You're an official Texan now."

As Cassie stood and made s'mores for everyone, the women shared stories of Cal and Paula's heart ached for him. As she swallowed the lump in her throat, she said, "I know when I get home all sorts of memories are going to flood in. This week has been a welcome distraction. I just wish it could last forever."

Martha stood and retrieved a package from the picnic table. "Paula, when I lost Marie, I thought I'd never recover. But every day I forced myself to get up, to engage in life. When my husband passed, I was sad, but I knew then that I was strong enough to endure. Look at you and what you've done this week. We might have provided a distraction, but you leant your strength to us. You're going to have moments of sadness so dark that you think you'll never see the sun again, but you'll also experience joy because you were so loved. It's those memories that get you through." She handed the package to Paula. "Here, I made you something."

Tears flooded Paula's eyes when she unwrapped a framed quilt square and read the embroidered words: *'When someone you love becomes a memory, the memory becomes a treasure.'* She traced the words with her fingertip. "Oh, Martha, thank you! It's so lovely. I bought something for each of you, too, at the little boutique downtown." She stood and gave Martha and Melinda cups with matching saucers and lids.

Melinda admired her cup painted with forget-me-nots then looked to Martha's adorned with a quilt motif. "Thank you. These are so pretty."

Martha nodded and dabbed her eyes with her napkin. "I love this. I'll think of you every morning when I have my coffee."

Melinda cleared her throat. "Paula, my gift to you is the painting you saw yesterday. It's dry now, so you can pick it up on the way back to your room tonight. Cassie, I wanted you to have a painting I did a few months ago of a red-winged black bird. I painted it ages ago, but it always seemed to need a special someone to make it their own. I think that someone is you."

Martha passed another wrapped package to Cassie. "And I got you this. It's a book on juggling."

Tears welled in Cassie's eyes. "Thank you both. I'm afraid I didn't get anything for anyone except for some sudoku books for McKenzie."

"You cooked some wonderful meals for us. Those were gifts," Martha said.

Melinda nodded. "And you were good entertainment. Just watching you flit from pillar to post is a show in itself."

Cassie blushed. "I do have my talents."

Paula nodded. "She sings, too. Beautifully."

After minimal urging, Cassie thought for a moment, then sat up straight and sang Dolly Parton's version of "I Will Always Love You." When she finished, there was complete silence.

"Oh, my," Melinda whispered.

Martha stood and hugged Cassie. "Sweetie, that was the prettiest thing I've heard in a long time."

Paula smiled through the tears that streamed down her cheeks. "I told you she could sing." After another half hour of girl talk, she looked at her watch and said, "Well, I'm afraid we need to hit the hay. I want to get an early start in the morning."

They all worked to clean up the remnants of their meal and make sure the fire in the grill was out before they headed to the office. As they reached the kitchen and put the food away, Cassie hugged Melinda and said. "Thank you again. For everything. I'm so glad you weren't Cal's hussy." She headed out without waiting for a reply.

Melinda shook her head. "That girl's something else." She motioned for Paula to follow her to her room, then gave her the paintings for her and Cassie.

Tears formed in Paula's eyes when she saw the canvas again. "This just looks so much like Cal. Thank you so much. I will miss you, Mrs. Arnett."

"And I will miss you, Mrs. Arnett. Promise you'll call when you and Cassie get home."

"I promise. And let's talk often. You go out and sit by Clyde and we'll have weekly meetings on FaceTime."

"Definitely. Is there any particular reason you need to leave so early in the morning?

Paula sighed. "Yeah, there's something I feel I must do, and I want to get home before sunset. It's time I began taking charge of my life."

As she made her way to Room 23 for the last time, Paula had no trouble finding the Cal star. Her heart soared. She paused in her walk and asked, "Did I do everything just right this time, Cal?" Even when there was no reply, she felt as if Cal was smiling on her.

She entered her room and wasn't surprised to find Cassie already asleep. She placed their paintings on top of the dresser then took a shower and crawled into bed. *As much as I hate leaving Happy Valley, I'm looking forward to being in my own bed tomorrow night.* A soft smile creased her lips as she drifted off to sweet dreams.

CHAPTER SIXTY-SIX

As the sun peeked over the horizon the next morning, Paula sat waiting in the passenger seat of her car for Cassie to emerge from the convenience store with a box of donuts and a beverage for each of them. Once behind the wheel, Cassie dug into the box of donuts before handing it, and a cup of coffee, off to Paula. She started the car and took a big sip of her Dr. Pepper. "What was that saying we're supposed to repeat?"

Paula smiled. "Off again, on again, gone again, Flanagan."

Cassie started the car. "It sure seemed to bring us good luck this week. I don't mind saying it nearly as much this time."

With the sedan headed toward Dempsey, Paula was anxious to get home.

After a long silence, Cassie asked, "Do you want me to hang out at the house with you for a few days?"

Paula turned in her seat to face her friend. "No offense, but I'm ready for some solitude. I've got a lot of things running through my mind, though, and if I need to talk, I know who to call."

A silent moment passed, then Cassie asked, "You mean me, right?"

Paula laughed, "Who else?"

"Maybe... a certain doctor?"

Paula waved her hand and rolled her eyes. "Nah. Maybe someday, but that's far in the future." Paula took over driving after they stopped for lunch.

Cassie soon dozed off, and Paula turned off the radio and enjoyed the silence. As they approached the Dempsey city limits, she peeked over at Cassie, still sleeping. Paula turned down the country road leading to the cemetery. *I can't believe it was just a week ago that I told Melvin I wasn't much for visiting gravesites yet look at me here now.* She parked the car under the shade of a bur oak and left it running. Easing out so as not to wake Cassie, Paula stood beside Cal's grave where the flowers that hadn't yet been blown away by the prairie winds lay wilting atop the newly mounded earth. She stood silently, her head bowed as if in prayer, as the setting sun cast an orange hue over the horizon.

She took a deep breath and said, "Cal, I'm sorry I doubted you, but I wish you'd trusted me enough to tell me about Melinda. About your past with her and about buying the resort. But, I'm not angry. Just sad. Sad about so many things now that you're gone. I'm sad that I'll never get to kiss you again, or hold you and be held by you. That we missed out on going to Happy Valley together because maybe this damned image you have of me as Goldilocks prevented you from being totally honest with me. So, maybe I am angry with you a little, but I'm angry with myself, too."

She wiped her tears with the back of her hand, barely aware of the beauty of the prairie sunset unfolding in front of her. "But I'm going to be okay. Not today, maybe, or even next week, or next month, but one day soon. This trip to Happy Valley made me realize that I have what it takes to make a life for myself, and you're the reason I made the trip, so thank you. I know this isn't how you intended for things to happen, but thank you anyway. I will always love you."

She turned to walk away then spun on her heel and faced the grave again with a twinkle in her eye. "Oh, by the way, I'm going to adopt a pet. Maybe a yappy little dog, and I'll eat in the living room sometimes. I might go back to college. Who knows? Maybe I'll even watch TV in bed."

Hearing her words out loud, Paula's heart soared. On the wind, she could've sworn she heard Cal chuckle, and that brought a smile to her lips. She nodded her head. *Yes, taking control feels just right.*

THE END

ABOUT THE AUTHOR

Leslie Noyes grew up in the panhandle of Texas many, many years ago. She married her high school sweetheart, and they now reside in the panhandle of Florida with their cat, Gracie. They have two terrific children and five wonderful grandchildren, and nothing else really matters. You can visit her on-line at **www.nananoyz5forme.com** or on Twitter at **@NoyesNananoyz**.

Leslie and her co-writer, Scout